Adam Gielgud

Memoirs of Prince Adam Czartorysk

And his Correspondence with Alexander I - Vol. II

Adam Gielgud

Memoirs of Prince Adam Czartorysk
And his Correspondence with Alexander I - Vol. II

ISBN/EAN: 9783337141387

Printed in Europe, USA, Canada, Australia, Japan

Cover: Foto ©Raphael Reischuk / pixelio.de

More available books at **www.hansebooks.com**

PRINCESS ELIZABETH CZARTORYSKA.

(Mother of Prince Adam.)

Copied from an old Miniature.

MEMOIRS

OF

PRINCE ADAM

CZARTORYSKI

AND HIS

Correspondence with Alexander I.

WITH

DOCUMENTS RELATIVE TO THE PRINCE'S NEGOTIATIONS WITH PITT,
FOX, AND BROUGHAM, AND AN ACCOUNT OF HIS CONVERSA-
TIONS WITH LORD PALMERSTON AND OTHER ENGLISH
STATESMEN IN LONDON IN 1832

EDITED BY

ADAM GIELGUD

TWO VOLUMES
WITH PORTRAITS

VOL. II

SECOND EDITION

London

REMINGTON & CO., PUBLISHERS
HENRIETTA STREET, COVENT GARDEN

1888

[*An Alphabetical Index to this work will be found at end of this Volume.*]

Contents

CHAPTER I

1804-5

CHAPTER II

CHAPTER III

1804-5

CHAPTER IV

1804

CHAPTER V

1804

CHAPTER VI

1804-5

CHAPTER VII

1805

CHAPTER VIII

1805

CHAPTER IX

1805

CHAPTER X

1805

CHAPTER XI

1806

CHAPTER XII

1806

CHAPTER XIII

1806

CHAPTER XIV

1806

CHAPTER V

1806

CHAPTER XVI

1806

CHAPTER XVII

1809-10

CHAPTER XVIII

1810

CHAPTER XIX

1810-12

CHAPTER XX

1813

CHAPTER XXI

1813-14

CHAPTER XXII

1814-15

CHAPTER XXIII

1815

CHAPTER XXIV

1815-22

CHAPTER XXV

1831-2

CHAPTER XXVI

1834

CHAPTER XXVII

1839

CHAPTER XXVIII

CHAPTER XXIX

1853-5

CHAPTER XXX

1855-61

CHAPTER I

1804-5

I NOW come to one of the most important epochs of my life. Taking advantage of the Chancellor's wish for temporary retirement, the Emperor took steps to make it virtually permanent, being desirous of giving over to me the complete direction of the department of Foreign Affairs. This was one of his hobbies, and he did not rest until he had satisfied it. The Chancellor had announced that his health obliged him to take some rest. It was necessary to replace him, and I asked him whom he would like to be his successor. 'You, of course,' he said; 'that would be in the regular order of things, and could not be otherwise.' I have already said that this was also the positive and pressing wish of the Emperor. What could I do? Was I to accept so difficult and dangerous a post? Should I

not rather give up everything and retire? But to
retire at such a moment would have been to prove
that I did not feel equal to the difficulties of the task
offered to me. By remaining assistant to the Minister
I had not gained anything, and if I became Minister
I should not be more exposed to suspicion and
calumny than before. But what most contributed to
tranquillise my conscience was the thought that I
might inaugurate a system of policy which, being
based on equitable principles, might ultimately have
a good influence on the destinies of Poland. I foresaw a rupture with France; the establishment of
intimate relations between that power and Russia,
which the Russians accused me of projecting, was far
from my thoughts, for it was evident to me that any
understanding between the two empires could only be
fatal to Polish interests. Moreover, I was pressed on
all sides to accept the Ministerial portfolio. The
Emperor would not listen to any objection, and the
young men who were my colleagues did not want our
relations to be broken off by my retreat. Even the
old Chancellor urged me to accept the post. He left
it firmly persuaded that he would come back, but
before the end of the year the state of his health, and
perhaps the charms of a quiet life, made him change
his views; he wrote to me that he had decided to
quit the active service, but that he would not yet ask
to be pensioned, as he feared to abandon me to the
intrigues to which his absence would expose me. On
leaving the capital he told me that when he came
back he would keep open house, as was fitting

for a Chancellor, although hitherto he had never
invited any of the members of the diplomatic body.
In leaving me in his place he was sure that he would
be heartily received on his return, and he supported
me with all the influence he possessed in the Government offices and in the Senate; he had none over the
general public. He promised me to write often and
give me his advice. We entered into a very volumin-
ous correspondence, which touched me much on
account of the friendship it showed, but which I soon
could not follow or even read with attention, as my
whole time was absorbed in public business.

I accepted the post of Foreign Minister, and the
Emperor was as glad as a child; but the young
Russian party did not conceal its anger and excitement. Even the Empress thought that I had some
malevolent intention, or at least that I was wanting
in delicacy towards the Emperor in accepting so confidential an appointment in the teeth of the general
opinion (so at least she thought) and in spite of the conviction that I would thereby deprive the Emperor of
the affection of his people. She now absolutely ignored
me; this lasted more than a year, and did not cease
until after Austerlitz. It will be seen that I had
powerful adversaries; but having made my decision,
I did not flinch, and only thought how to acquit
myself of my task in the best possible way.

It so happened that just at the time when I was
appointed Foreign Minister several important Russian
diplomatists were at St Petersburg. I have already
alluded to Count Markoff, who, when the Chancellor

retired, was more determined than ever to quit the diplomatic career. He went to the estate Catherine had given him, and worried his neighbours with interminable actions at law. I made it my duty, so long as he remained at St Petersburg, to consult him on current affairs and on the difficulties which were occurring between Russia and France; he gave his advice with an air of cold and disdainful superiority, and I think left with a conviction that the policy of the Empire would be thrown into confusion. He had a very small opinion of Alexander, but was always ready to obey his slightest wish.

Count Razumovsky, who had come on short leave from Vienna, said to me in a half-contemptuous tone: 'So it is you who are going to direct us?' 'So it seems,' I replied. When he returned to his post he only addressed despatches to me on current affairs, and reserved more secret and important subjects for the reports addressed by him direct to the Emperor. This manœuvre was not successful. Alexander was offended at the Minister whom he had selected being so treated; he held that no one should have less confidence in any public functionary than he had himself, and ordered that all communications should pass through me. Count Razumovsky then entered into a private correspondence with me in which he concealed nothing, and similar relations were established between me and Count Simon Vorontzoff, the Ambassador in London. Vorontzoff was frank and loyal, but his opinions on men and things were too absolute, not admitting those shades between good and evil which it is only just to recognise. He had unlimited confidence in the judgment of his brother the Chancellor, and adopted the favourable opinions he had formed of me. His correspondence shows the interest he took in defending me against slanderous accusations, and in maintaining me in the functions which I performed at the Emperor's wish and that of the Chancellor. I am paying a debt of gratitude in here recognising the numerous and persistent marks of affection he showed me, though I cannot approve his political views or conduct. His faults were a consequence of his simplicity of character, which prompted him to an unreserved admiration of England, the only country which at that time possessed liberal institutions. Count Simon was deeply attached to Mr Pitt and some of his colleagues, and had an almost unlimited admiration for them. This prevented him from impartially watching the march of events and perceiving the true interests either of Russia or even of Europe in the general scope of his policy. The same fault was to be found with the Russian Ambassadors at Vienna and Berlin, except that neither Count Razumovsky nor M. Alopeus redeemed their defects by the good qualities of Count Simon Vorontzoff. The intimate relations of Count Razumovsky with various prominent personages at Vienna, and the servility shown by Alopeus to the leading statesmen at Berlin, were the cause of many inaccuracies in the reports they used to send me. Their only desire was to be on good terms with the Governments to which they were accredited, and they often nullified the effect of our communications by attenuating them at their pleasure. To prevent such abuses in future, the Emperor sent M. de Wintzingerode to Berlin. He was not disposed to be very friendly to Prussia, and was determined not to conceal anything as to the military resources of that Power or the uncertain policy of its statesmen. His reports gave little hope of there being anything to be expected from the co-operation of Prussia in the event of a rupture with France.

Another special envoy, M. de Novosiltzoff, was sent to London, as it was impossible to rely entirely on the reports of Count Simon Vorontzoff. This appointment was approved by the Chancellor and was consequently satisfactory to his brother. When he was last in Russia, the Ambassador had entered into a closer acquaintance with Novosiltzoff, and highly appreciated his intelligence and his political principles. Novosiltzoff had, moreover, been ordered to pass through Berlin, in order to sound the feeling of that Court before proceeding with the same object to London; he was also, if circumstances should render it desirable, to go to Paris to propose the most favourable conditions for the maintenance of peace.

After Count Markoff's retirement, the principal personages of Russian diplomacy were Count Razumovsky and Count Simon Vorontzoff; and the Chancellor's favourable opinion of me contributed greatly to smooth down difficulties which might have been raised by Ambassadors who were more experienced than myself. My Ministry was in some degree a continuation of the preceding one, though it was difficult to maintain the passive system of peace and tranquillity that had been adopted by Kotchoubey and pursued with more self-assurance and dignity by the Chancellor. A country accustomed to the continual successes of Catherine or the escapades of Paul could not be satisfied with a subordinate and insignificant part, even if it was thereby assured uninterrupted internal prosperity. Moreover, the foreign policy of a great State should in my opinion not be passive or lethargic, without any interest for the general good; this narrow way of looking at politics, this imperturbable gaze which soon becomes spiritless because it is always fixed upon one's self, cannot be consistent with the feeling of power and the desire of achieving distinction by noble deeds. Such a system defeats its own object, for, by producing an incapacity to rise to larger and more generous considerations, it creates improvidence and timidity, and leaves free scope to the ambitions of others. This had certainly not been the spirit of Russian policy in former days. No State, except ancient Rome, ever had a vaster, a more active, or a more persevering policy, though we must admit that it always disregarded the principles of justice and right.

The Czars of Moscow had had the instinct of conquest since the reign of Ivan the Cruel; they employed artifice and violence by turns, and succeeded with rare ability in augmenting their territories at the expense of their neighbours. It was under Peter the Great, however, that Russian policy first assumed

that decided and stable character which it has maintained to this day. All the objects which Russia
unceasingly pursues with indefatigable perseverance—
amounting to nothing less than the subjugation of the
greater part of Europe and Asia—were clearly conceived and designated to his successors by Peter the
Great. He gave the first fatal blows to Sweden and
Poland ; he began the struggle with Persia and
Turkey ; he placed himself at the head of the Greeks
and Slavs, and created a European army and navy.
The impulse which his iron will gave to the nation
still continues, and by an extraordinary concourse of
circumstances, Russia has come alarmingly near to
the attainment of his objects without Europe having
succeeded in stopping her. Internal difficulties may
from time to time have retarded her advance, but the
spirit of Peter still hovers over his empire, and his
pitiless ambition lies at the bottom of every Russian
heart.

There was, however, a time when Peter's policy
was forgotten and suspended ; this was at the beginning of Alexander's reign. Young, candid, inoffensive,
thinking only of philanthropy and liberalism, passion-
ately desirous of doing good, but often incapable of
distinguishing it from evil, he had seen with equal
aversion the wars of Catherine and the despotic follies
of Paul, and when he ascended the throne he cast
aside all the ideas of avidity, astuteness, and grasping
ambition which were the soul of the old Russian
policy. Peter's vast projects were ignored for a time,
and Alexander devoted himself entirely to internal

reforms, with the serious intention of making his Russian and other subjects as happy as they could be in their present condition. Later on he was carried away, almost against his will, into the natural current of Russian policy ; but at first he held entirely aloof from it, and this is the reason why he was not really popular in Russia. His character differed both in its good and its bad qualities from that of his people, and he was far from happy when he was in the midst of them.

After being placed at the head of affairs, I felt like a soldier who, being thrown by chance and friendship into the ranks of a foreign army, fights zealously from a feeling of honour and in order not to abandon his master and friend. Alexander's unbounded confidence made me feel it my duty to do my best to serve him, and to add lustre to his policy so long as I had the direction of it. Moreover, I firmly believed that it might be possible for me to reconcile the tendencies of the Russian nation with the generous ideas of its ruler, and to make use of the Russian craving for glory and supremacy for the general benefit of mankind. The object was a great but a remote one, to be pursued consistently and with perseverance, and to be executed with patience and skill. I thought it was worthy of the national pride of the Russian people. I would have wished Alexander to become a sort of arbiter of peace for the civilised world, to be the protector of the weak and the oppressed, and that his reign should inaugurate a new era of justice and right in European politics.

This idea quite absorbed me, and I endeavoured to reduce it to a practical form. I drew up a scheme of policy which I sent in the form of a circular to all the Russian representatives at Foreign Courts. This circular, which was intended to inaugurate the new system, and was based on the principles which I afterwards developed in my ' Essay on Diplomacy,'* prescribed a line of conduct characterised by moderation, justice, loyalty, and impartial dignity. My efforts in this direction, however, were fruitless, owing to the innumerable difficulties I encountered and the rapid march of events which brought about my fall. But, so long as I remained in office, I did my utmost to direct the course of Russian policy in accordance with the above principles, although not so completely as I should have wished. One is often compelled by circumstances to modify one's ideas, and to make painful concessions which sometimes frustrate plans long elaborated and cherished.

My system was just the one to delight Alexander in the mood in which he then was. It gave free scope to the imagination and to all kinds of combinations without requiring immediate decision or action. He was the only man in his Empire capable of understanding my aims and adopting my principles through conviction, and even as a matter of conscience. At the same time, he only entered into my ideas superficially; being satisfied with the general principles and the phrases in which they were expressed, he did

* ' Essai sur la Diplomatie, Manuscrit d'un Philhellène, publié par M. Toulouzan.' Paris and Marseilles, 1830.

not think of going more deeply into them or appreciating either the duties which the system imposed upon him or the difficulties which would necessarily impede its realisation. My colleagues, who seemed to share my opinions on many points, listened with approval to the details of my system of policy, which comprised the emancipation of the Greeks and the Slavs. So long as the only matter in question was the supremacy of Russia in Europe and the increase of her power, those who listened to me were on my side; but when I passed to the objects and obligations which should be the consequence of such supremacy, to the rights of others, and the principles of justice which should check ambition, I observed that my audience grew cold and constrained.

My system, through its fundamental principle of repairing all acts of injustice, naturally led to the gradual restoration of Poland. But I did not pronounce the name of my country, not wishing to raise all at once the difficulties which a course so opposed to all preconceived ideas was sure to encounter. I spoke only of the progressive emancipation of the nations which had been unjustly deprived of their political existence, and I named the Greeks and Slavs as those whose restoration to independence would be most in conformity with the wishes and the opinions of the Russians. It was tacitly understood between the Emperor and myself that the principle was to be held equally applicable to Poland, but that for the present no mention should be made of that country. I felt the propriety and necessity of this. No Russian was ever on his own initiative or of his own will favourable to Poland; and I afterwards became convinced that there is no exception to this rule.

One day, when in an intimate conversation with my colleagues we spoke of the vicissitudes through which Poland had passed, Novosiltzoff told us that when he was travelling in that country at the time of the Kosciuszko Revolution, he was stopped by some peasants who asked for his passport. It was in German, and none of them could read it, so they sent to a German who lived in the neighbourhood. When the latter arrived, Novosiltzoff, who spoke German, begged him to interfere in his behalf, upon which the German assured the peasants that there would be no harm in letting Novosiltzoff pass, and he was then allowed to proceed to the army of the Prince of Nassau, who was besieging Warsaw. I strongly expressed my disapprobation of the German's conduct, which greatly astonished my colleagues, as they thought any step would have been justifiable to save Novosiltzoff. This showed how different were our respective points of view; and similar incidents often happened in the course of our relations. I had no reason to conceal my thoughts, and no one was better informed of them than the Emperor himself.

Although the new system of policy was often criticised on account of its vagueness and utopianism, it soon had serious and practical results. It was impossible to take a prominent part in European affairs, to come forward as a judicial and moderating influence, to prevent violence, injustice and aggression, without coming into contact with France at every step. She would have been a dangerous rival if she had wished to play the same beneficent part; but being led by the unlimited ambition of Napoleon, she sought to do the very contrary of what we wished. A collision sooner or later was inevitable.

Napoleon could not suffer any rivals in the career upon which he had entered. All the attempts which were made to act on an equal footing with him failed. His ally had either to carry out his plans or become his enemy. Scarcely had my system of policy been decided upon than by a sort of instinct our relations with the First Consul became colder, and the communications on both sides clearly showed by their tone that neither was disposed to make concessions to the other.

CHAPTER II

EXECUTION OF THE DUC D'ENGHIEN.—RUPTURE WITH FRANCE.—THE
ENGLISH AND AUSTRIAN AMBASSADORS.—UNIVERSAL OPPOSITION TO
NAPOLEON.

MATTERS had now arrived at such a point between
Russia and France that any incident might have
brought about a rupture between the two Governments ; and this could not long be deferred under the
system pursued by Napoleon. The origin of the
rupture was in this case of a special kind, as no
material interest was involved : it was simply a question of justice and right.

The seizure of the Duc d'Enghien,* by a French
detachment in an independent country with which
France was at peace, and his trial and execution which
immediately followed, produced a general feeling of
stupor and indignation which those who did not
witness it could not easily realise. The Emperor
Alexander and his family were most strongly impressed by it, and did not hesitate loudly to proclaim
their horror and detestation of the deed. The news
came on a Saturday ; on the following day the whole

---

* The Duke was seized by the orders of Napoleon on the 15th March 1804, a
Ettenheim, in Baden. He was taken to Vincennes, where he arrived on the 20th,
tried by a military commission, and executed the same night.

of the Court went into mourning, and the Emperor and Empresses, as they passed after mass through the room in which the diplomatic body were in attendance, took no notice whatever of the French Ambassador, though they spoke to various persons who were next to him. It was indeed impossible for a Power which proposed to carry out the policy adopted by the Russian sovereign to be indifferent to such a violation of justice and international law. I drew up a note on the subject which made some noise at the time ; it was sent to the French Ministry by M. d'Oubril, the Russian Chargé d'Affaires in Paris. In this note Russia loudly protested against a deed which seemed to show entire forgetfulness of the most sacred laws. She demanded a satisfactory explanation—which it was evidently impossible to give. The reply soon came : it was harsh and insulting. Talleyrand, at that time Minister of Foreign Affairs, reminded Russia that when Paul was assassinated, France did not consider herself justified in demanding an explanation. In handing me this despatch General Hédouville gave me a letter which was intended to soften the bitterness of its language. Talleyrand instructed the Ambassador to address himself to me especially. He said that Napoleon had confidence in my character and intelligence, and felt certain that I would use my influence to prevent the two countries from being exposed to break a harmony which was not only useful to themselves but necessary for the welfare of Europe. These coquetries did not of course produce any effect upon me ; I regarded them as almost offensive ; and I drily replied that all the papers would be laid before the Emperor, that I had nothing to say until I knew his wishes, but that it seemed to me evident that a very different reply would have had to be given if France had really wished to maintain the friendly relations between the two countries.

There could no longer be any doubt as to the course the Emperor should take ; indeed all was foreseen at the time the first note was sent to Paris. I was instructed to draw up a memorandum, stating the question and proposing the means of dealing with it. The matter was so urgent, in view of the conduct of the French Government, that I had to work all night at this document.

[The following is a translation of the memorandum here referred to :—

April 5, 1804.

The incursion which the French have ventured to make upon German territory in order to seize the Duc d'Enghien and take him into France for immediate execution, is an event which shows what is to be expected from a Government which does not recognise any check upon its acts of violence, and which treads under foot the most sacred principles. His Majesty, indignant at so flagrant a violation of the most binding principles of equity and international law, is reluctant to maintain any further relations with a Government which is not restrained by any sense of duty, and which, being stained by an atrocious crime, can only now be regarded as a band of brigands. This act on the part of Buonaparte should bring down upon France a cry of revenge and condemnation from all the European States and be the signal for a general opposition to him ; but if the other Powers, struck with terror and deprived of energy, keep a humiliating silence at such a moment, would it be right for Russia to follow their example ? Is it not for her, on the contrary, to lead the way in taking steps to save Europe from the ruin with which she is threatened ? His Imperial Majesty, being moved by these considerations and by a feeling of what is due to his dignity, thinks it necessary to order the Court to go into mourning for the death of the Duc d'Enghien, and proposes loudly to proclaim his indignation at Buonaparte's iniquitous proceedings. His Majesty is the less disposed to pursue any other line of conduct seeing that the outrage which has been committed upon the whole family of European States, and upon humanity itself, has taken place on the territory of a Prince nearly related to the Emperor, and thus affects him doubly. Our august master, considering that in future it will be not only useless, but dishonouring, to continue in relation with a Government which has so little respect either for justice or for common propriety, is inclined to send back the French embassy and at the same time to recall the Russian embassy from Paris.

The Emperor is firmly convinced that it would not be in accordance either with his personal dignity or with the honour of his Empire to remain passive after the event which has occurred ; but he does not conceal from himself the partial and temporary inconveniences which might result from the decision which he thinks it necessary to take. His Majesty wishes to have the benefit of the wisdom of others in so important a matter, and he has accordingly assembled the members of his Council and diplomatists of known experience and ability for this purpose. He has ordered me succinctly to lay before them the state of the question and the decision he is disposed to take, with the reasons which have led him to it, in order to show the advantages and disadvantages which might result to the welfare of the world in general and of Russia in particular.

Since the re-establishment of the relations between Russia and France it would be difficult to point to any real advantage which has resulted from it to Russia. The French Government has not kept the solemn engagements into which it had entered with us, and our representations on the subject in favour of princes in whom the Emperor is interested have had no effect. On the contrary, the First Consul seems lately to have made it his task to cause Russia incessant annoyance by unreasonable demands and proceedings, notwithstanding the firmness with which his Majesty has opposed them. This brief sketch of the conduct of France towards Russia shows that we would not lose much by suspending all relations with her for the present. Such a course, besides being in accordance with the Emperor's sense of dignity and his outraged feelings of justice, also presents some purely political advantages. It is to be expected that an energetic step of this kind on the part of Russia at the present moment would be likely more than anything else to stimulate a general combination among the European States, to limit Buonaparte's ambition and violence. One may hope that the Courts of Vienna and Berlin would then also be led to take decisive action. These two Governments, the latter especially, acting from different motives, but both chiefly influenced by the terror with which France inspires them, could not hitherto be persuaded to abandon their attitude of passive submission, notwithstanding the offers and the very strong representations his Imperial Majesty has addressed to them. The Emperor, in taking the initiative of declaring himself in a manner which would leave no doubt as to his views and system of policy, would be in a position to address these two Courts in even more pressing language than before—to which the presence of his armies on the frontier would add weight—and would be able to ask for categorical replies as to the conduct they would pursue. Judging by appearances and the information in our possession, the Cabinets in question, if they were thus obliged to come to a decision, would elect to join Russia ; and it would perhaps be impossible to induce them to do so in any other case. The same might almost be said of Turkey, which seems full of confidence and good-will towards us, and quite alive to the dangers she has to fear from France.

Assuming, however, that Russia, after having come to a rupture with the French Government, should remain alone without an ally on the Continent, what would she risk by such a course? To suspend diplomatic relations is not to make war, and France cannot directly attack us. To reach us she would have to invade other States which would then be forced to, defend themselves and give us an opportunity of coming to their assistance. This could only increase the influence of Russia; an illustration of which is furnished by the part she played during the French Revolution, when, without being precisely at war, the relations between the two Powers were suspended. We should thus be freed from the embarrassments caused by our connection with France, and also from the presence of the numerous French agents spread all over the country.

Further, his Imperial Majesty may be sure to find in England, if necessary, a safe ally, always ready to join him.

Thus the advantages of the course proposed by his Majesty appear evident. Its disadvantages have also not escaped his attention, and they will now be here indicated.

There can be no doubt that as soon as the French Government is informed that Russia has decided to break off her relations with France, its first step will be to avenge itself on all the States that are protected and maintained by his Majesty. The kingdom of Naples will be its first victim in the south. Once the French are masters of that country, our troops at Corfu would be in danger so long as the reinforcements ordered by his Majesty (which cannot arrive for some months to come) do not reach them. In the

north it is possible that the French would attack
Denmark, which, though inclined to make a vigorous
resistance and certain to be promptly relieved by his
Imperial Majesty, is not prepared for so sudden an
aggression.

If the seizure of the Duc d'Enghien had taken place
three months later, Russia would have been in a much
better position to act. The views of Austria and
Prussia would then have been clearer and more decisive,
Denmark would have been ready, and our troops in
the Ionian islands, having been reinforced, would have
been in a position to secure Greece and relieve Naples
by means of an understanding with England. Buonaparte's difficulties would also have been increased;
and we should perhaps have done him a service by
furnishing him with a pretext for giving up his plans
of a Continental war which his Imperial Majesty,
desirous of sparing the blood of his subjects, would
not have wished to break out except under the most
favourable circumstances and after having exhausted
the means which might have been furnished by a
negotiation at Paris of all the European Powers.

However well-founded the above considerations
may be, the event which has just occurred obliges us
to disregard them, or at least only to treat them as
accessory. His Majesty cannot pass unnoticed the
atrocious proceeding of the First Consul without a loss
of dignity, and without showing Europe, France, and
Buonaparte himself, that the latter may do anything
with the certainty that no one will oppose him.

It would seem at first sight that a means might

be devised of attaining the object in a different way.
Without concealing its just indignation, the Russian
Court might, instead of coming to an immediate
rupture with Buonaparte, confine itself to going into
mourning for the Duc d'Enghien, declaring in Paris
that the Emperor could not see with indifference the
violation of German territory—especially of the dominions of the Elector of Baden, from which the Duc
d'Enghien had been dragged to his death—and asking
to be informed whether the French Government did
not disavow a deed so iniquitous and so much opposed
to international law.   This would lead to explanations
which might take some two months longer, and give
Russia time to complete her preparations in the North
and South of Europe.   The French Government would
doubtless not submit to the humiliation of acknowledging its misdeed, which would be almost as
damaging to it as the misdeed itself, and a rupture
would be the necessary consequence; but we should
have gained time.   Against this plan it is to be remarked that directly it became known in Paris that
mourning for the Duc d'Enghien had been ordered at
St Petersburg, and especially that M. d'Oubril was
making a communication on the subject, the tenour of
which could not be otherwise than very disagreeable,
the First Consul would be the first to act by sending
back our embassy from Paris and recalling his from
St Petersburg.   He would thus show that he dares
to affront Russia and does not fear her power; in a
word, a considerable part of the advantages which
would result from the action of Russia on this occa-

sion would be lost if Buonaparte were given the opportunity of forestalling us by a decision similar to that proposed by his Majesty, and thereby setting us at defiance in the eyes of Russia and of Europe.

The original idea, therefore, seems preferable. The first step is to put the Court into mourning; then we should recall our embassy from Paris, retaining the French one here until the Russian Chargé d'Affaires leaves France. Above all, two couriers should be sent to Naples and Copenhagen to warn the Governments in those towns of the decision of his Majesty and its probable consequences so far as France was concerned. As to Corfu, orders should be sent to the troops to hold themselves in readiness against any sudden attack, and pending the arrival of the reinforcements, to raise a corps of Albanians so as to strengthen our forces as much as possible. The details of the measures to be ultimately taken cannot be entered into here, and must form the subject of a separate memorandum.

In the official despatch which our Chargé d'Affaires would present to the French Government on leaving Paris, its conduct relative to the German Empire and the Kings of Naples and Sardinia, in violation of the most formal engagements, should be forcibly commented upon. It might be thought that a last effort should on this occasion be made in favour of the princes who will immediately after be abandoned by Buonaparte, and as a proof of the interest his Majesty takes in them, that it should be proposed to him as the only acceptable satisfaction, and as an indispensable condition for the maintenance of the relations between Russia and France, that the compensation promised to the King of Sardinia should be at once paid him, and that the kingdom of Naples and all the countries forming part of the Empire of Germany should be immediately evacuated, with a solemn engagement not to send French troops to them again. Such a proposal, however, would be useless, and would perhaps only embitter the hostility of the First Consul towards the princes in question. A refusal would be certain, and should be avoided. Moreover, such a proposal would not be in accordance with the idea of his Majesty to break off relations with a Government which no longer deserves to be called one, and with whom any further connection would be dishonouring. The more the Emperor's moderation and his generous and disinterested principles are known, the greater will be the impression made by his decision on the French nation and the whole of Europe. If, however, the French Government should really so much wish to maintain its relations with Russia as to be disposed to accept the above conditions, it would propose them itself, and his Majesty could then, if he thought proper, consider the proposal.

Having thus endeavoured briefly to state both the beneficial and the injurious consequences which might flow from the decision his Majesty believes it to be his duty to take, and to show the difficulties which would arise in executing it, I have to add that the Emperor wishes those whom he has to-day assembled to state their opinion, according to the data

I have set forth (which I am prepared to complete if they do not appear sufficient), on the best means of action under present circumstances, and especially as to whether reasons of State or of prudence would render it necessary to suspend a decision rendered imperative by the Emperor's sentiments and his feeling of dignity. Their opinion is also desired on the following points :—

(1) Whether it will be right, after the announcement of the Court mourning, at once to take final steps for a rupture, or to endeavour to gain time by negotiation.

(2) If the latter, in what sense the negotiations should be opened.

(3) How far consideration is due to the princes whose only hope is in the Emperor's protection.

(4) What steps should in any case be taken to provide as much as possible for the safety of these princes, and especially of the King of Naples, who is in the greatest danger.

(5) What steps should be taken generally in order not to lose any of the advantages which should be obtained from the Emperor's decision in a manner both honourable and glorious to himself, and to remedy the inconveniences which might be connected with it.

Having thus carried out his Majesty's orders, it only remains to me to point out the importance of keeping absolute secrecy as to the object of the discussion which is about to take place, as both the Russian Embassy and the princes, whom we wish to expose to the least possible risk, would be in great danger if the matter should transpire. His Imperial Majesty feels perfectly safe on this point, knowing thoroughly the high character and the zeal for the service of those whom he has assembled.]

The somewhat crude language of this memorandum was owing to the haste with which it was drawn up, there being no time to moderate the violence of some of the expressions in it. After reading it, the Emperor called a Council and invited each of its members freely to state his opinion, as he wished the question to be thoroughly considered. The discussion, however, was not a very animated one. The majority of the Ministers took no interest in foreign politics, and thinking they knew what was the Emperor's wish, they had neither the capacity nor the inclination to oppose it. Kotchoubey was the only member of the Council who gave a reason for his vote. He said, and every one felt the truth of his statement, that to break off relations with France was not in any way dangerous to Russia, as France could not reach her, while such a step would spare Russia many embarrassments which are inevitable when one deals with a government which claims to be the sole dominating power in Europe. Count Romantzoff, then Minister of Commerce, and afterwards Foreign Minister and Chancellor, raised some objections, as he had a leaning for Napoleon and an aversion to England. He was a diplomatist of the school of Catherine, and his absolutist theories converted Alexander some years later to the doctrines and tendencies of the old

Russian policy. He admitted that after what had occurred it would be difficult to abstain from taking some steps to prove to the world that Russia would not submit to an affront on the part of France, or allow her to have the last word; but he thought it would have been better not to place one's self in such a position. While recognising that considerations of honour and respect for international law should have due weight, he thought that material interests should also be considered, and that in announcing an irrevocable decision it was necessary to be certain of the advantages and support on which one could rely. Russia was free at any moment to cast her power on either side; her decision should, however, be based not on abstract principles, but on considerations of advantage and security. He asked whether the consequences of the step Russia was about to take had been duly weighed, whether we were clear as to the results we wished to achieve, and whether we had any security for the advantages which were expected to accrue or against the dangers which might arise.

I answered that the proposed course did not involve any danger to the Empire; that its object was to satisfy a sentiment of honour and equity, without any idea of obtaining advantages which we did not want; that the Emperor was satisfied to fulfil with dignity and honour a duty to the rest of Europe, and that his position left him ample time to consider what more should be done if the interests and the security of his Empire should require it. This ended the discussion; the Emperor approved the memorandum, and ordered its proposals to be carried into effect.

I then sent for M. de Rayneval, the French Chargé d'Affaires (the Ambassador having gone on leave), and handed him a note explaining the motives of the Emperor's decision, together with passports for his immediate departure. He received my communications very calmly, without making any remark, which indeed would in the circumstances have been superfluous. It was only right, at a moment when he was about to leave St Petersburg with the whole embassy, to remove as much as possible any difficulties or disagreeables attending so sudden a departure, and I accordingly helped him as much as I could in this respect. Both General Hédouville and M. de Rayneval afterwards thanked me for the services I had rendered them. The facts of the case were not correctly described by contemporary historians. The nature of the relations then established between France and Russia was unprecedented. The motive of the rupture was quite a novel one in the annals of diplomacy, for it was not a Russian prince that had been executed, and the Cabinet of St Petersburg had no direct grievance of its own. The sole cause of the rupture was the violation of international law. The result produced a state of things which was not war, and the subjects of the two States were not threatened by the dangers produced by war; it was simply an announcement that we could not remain in relation with a Power which had no respect for the most elementary principles of justice. The case was like that of a man whose society we drop because his conduct is opposed to our principles, though not such as to justify our sending him a challenge.

None of the other Powers followed the example of Russia; but it must be admitted that she was at that time in an exceptionally favourable position. She alone of the Continental Powers had managed to preserve her dignity and her independence. Unassailable by Napoleon now he had no navy, she threatened him by her disdainful calm, like the stationary cloud which is believed to be loaded with storm and thunder. Russia should have maintained this imposing attitude as long as possible; applications for support and expressions of esteem and deference came to her from all sides. She should not have abandoned this unique position unless it were proved that her interest and those of the other powers required her to enter into action; but things turned out otherwise.

[The following communications on this subject were addressed by Prince Adam Czartoryski to the Chancellor :—

To Count Vorontzoff.

St Petersburg, *May* 7, 1804.

I see with real pain from your last letters, Monsieur le Comte, that you were not quite satisfied with what has been done in the matter of the Duc d'Enghien, but I am none the less grateful to you for the frankness with which you have expressed your views. You do not say anything as to the two notes presented at Paris and at Ratisbon;* yet in them we only lay stress on the violation of neutral territory, which is in accordance with your views. If your Excellency had seen the way in which the matter is considered here, and the sensation it has produced, you would have been convinced that even if I had thought the sort of pressure which had been put upon the Cabinet should have been resisted, I should not have been strong enough to do so, and that only a man of your weight and consideration could have had any chance of succeeding. No one could have wished for your opinion more than myself, but I assure you that the matter did not brook delay ; if anything was to be done, it had to be done at once.

I now come to the negotiations with Austria. The Emperor received your letter with gratitude, together with your observations which I communicated to him. The decisions which have been arrived at are, in principle, in conformity with your Excellency's opinion, and I flatter myself that the modifications I have introduced will meet with your approval. To make things safer I had a conference here with Count Stadion to discuss with him the draft of the autograph letter which was to be sent to Vienna. He raised difficulties on every word that was at all precise in its meaning, and I accordingly had to limit myself to vague and general expressions in which he concurred. Judging by the Ambassador's talk and the policy of his Court, the Emperor thought, as it

* This was the note addressed by Russia on the 7th May 1804 to the German Diet at Ratisbon, protesting against Napoleon's conduct.

seems to me with reason, that it would be better not to settle anything for the present as to the renewal of the Russo-Austrian Alliance, but to make it depend on Austria's conduct, and the way in which she may enter into the execution of more precise stipulations should such be found necessary. .   .   .

The Emperor will leave shortly for Revel; he will only be away ten days, as he does not wish to be absent from St Petersburg until he knows what turn things are taking. I am going with him, and M. de Tatischeff has kindly undertaken to look after the letters and receive the Ministers as he did when I was away last year. Hédouville complains bitterly of the way in which he is being treated in Russian society. This is very wrong, and I wish I could prevent it. He has just asked in the name of his Government for a private audience of the Emperor, but it will be refused."

To Count Vorontzoff.

St Petersburg, *May* 29, 1804.

I write to-day, Monsieur le Comte, not to answer your letters, for which I am infinitely grateful, nor to render you an account of my correspondence since my last letter and his Majesty's return, but only to send you the replies we have received from Paris and d'Oubril's reports as to what passed there. These despatches are being copied, and in order not to delay the departure of the messenger I have only time to

---

* He left St Petersburg and ceased to be French Ambassador there on the 7th of June 1804.

tell your Excellency that the Emperor's personal opinion is that at this moment he cannot with propriety continue his relations with France, unless she consents to fulfil her engagements with us relative to Naples, the King of Sardinia, and Germany; and that after the insulting note* which had been received from Paris, he can only sacrifice his just resentment in so far as not to cause injury to his allies. If we succeeded in bringing about the evacuation of the kingdom of Naples, in obtaining an indemnity for the King of Sardinia, and in liberating Hanover, the Emperor's dignity will be intact, and he will have done much good to his friends and to Europe; if France does not yield on these points, d'Oubril should I think leave Paris, and Russia should decline to recognise the newly proclaimed Emperor on any other terms. Meanwhile we will do our utmost also to persuade Vienna, Berlin, and even Constantinople to refuse the recognition without obtaining some return.

Such, in brief, are our ideas here. But his Majesty desires above all to have your Excellency's opinion on the subject. There are some difficulties which might impede the execution of the plan. Supposing, which is most probable, that all our demands are not refused, and that France consents to evacuate Naples, it will be necessary to negotiate as to the indemnity to the King of Sardinia and even the evacuation of Hanover, besides guaranteeing the neutrality of those countries. For this a Chargé d'Affaires would not be

* See page 15.

sufficient; and M. de Tatischeff has had the good idea of sending in that case M. Stackelberg to Paris with full powers to treat, but without any diplomatic office.

Another question is the way in which we are to deal with various points of the French reply. A very delicate one is the allusion to the death of Paul, while in our despatches we spoke, not of the Duc d'Enghien's execution, but only of his seizure on neutral territory. This is characteristic of Buonaparte's maliciousness. Are we to take up this point? And if so, how? Can we pass it over in silence, seeing that our Court has never admitted that Paul died a violent death, as is shown by the manifesto of the present Emperor? Moreover, Talleyrand's argument is as false as it is insulting, and they wish to reproduce it in the note which they will send to the Diet. On all these points the Emperor wishes for your ideas and advice. Tchourakoff will be with you again in three days, and I beg your Excellency to send him to me as soon after as possible, with your remarks on the principal points and in general as to the line of conduct you think should be adopted; we will do our best as to the details. The interruption of all relations seems to me inevitable, and cannot do us any harm; war will perhaps follow, but that depends upon the turn things will take. Meanwhile I can announce to you that the King of Prussia has signed a declaration* almost similar to ours; it is in our hands, and it secures the rest of Northern Europe. He has at the same time, however, promised the French not to allow Russian

* Dated May 24, 1804.

troops to pass through his territory to attack them. All that relates to this matter will at once be sent you.

Hédouville has asked for leave on account of his health, and will leave Rayneval as Chargé d' Affaires. D'Oubril's messenger had not arrived, but after waiting a few days we could not keep Hédouville any longer, as he himself came several times to get his passport. He had no message to deliver when he went, and maintained an absolute silence as to the affairs of the day. I send you the note I gave him with his passports.

Vernègues has been given up and Cassini has left Rome. The Pope's Ambassador will be sent back; this decision seems to me indispensable, but I do not quite know what is the form in which it should be notified to him.

I should like to do everything for the best, but often I confess that I fear I do not acquit myself of my task as well as I should. The details you have kindly given me of your return here have given me great pleasure, and I feel very strongly this proof of your confidence. It is with real joy I shall see you here again; and I am always grateful for the advice your frankness and your friendship dictate to me. Pray excuse my bad writing and believe in my respect and sincere attachment.

P.S.—The news from Georgia are good. The Czar of Imeritia has submitted, and has taken the oath of allegiance.]

CHAPTER III

1804-5

AFTER the diplomatic rupture consequent upon the execution of the Duc d'Enghien, it became indispensable to come to an understanding with the only Power except Russia which thought herself strong enough to contend with France—to ascertain as thoroughly as possible what were her inclinations and designs, the principles of her policy, and those which she could be led to adopt in certain contingencies. It would have been a great advantage to obtain the concurrence in our views of so powerful and influential a State as England and to strive with her for the same objects ; but for this it was necessary not only to make sure of her present inclinations, but to weigh well the possibilities of the future after the death of George III and the fall of the Pitt Ministry. We had to make England understand that the wish to fight Napoleon was not in itself sufficient to establish an indissoluble bond between her Government and that of St Petersburg, and that such a bond, to be permanent, must be based not on a common feeling of revenge, but on the most elevated principles of justice and philanthropy.*

This was a delicate and difficult mission. It was confided to Novosiltzoff, who, as a member of the Ministry and of the Secret Council, was fully acquainted with all our opinions and plans. As has been already stated, he made numerous acquaintances during his stay in England, and he had not only obtained a perfect knowledge of the language, but had studied the social organisation and the resources of the country. He was also on intimate terms with the Ambassador, whose personal feelings had to be considered ; and he thus seemed in every respect fitted for the task entrusted to him. On leaving he was furnished with two sets of instructions, one official and the other secret ; in the latter I endeavoured to explain to him all the points we wished to gain, or as to which it would be proper to sound the views of the British Government. I also gave him a letter to Mr Fox, who at that time had the entire confidence of the Prince of Wales and the men of his party. Novosiltzoff found Mr Pitt not disposed to accept all our proposals, and the Ambassador, Count Simon Vorontzoff, in his admiration of the narrow policy of the British Cabinet, constantly opposed the modifications we wished to introduce. Owing to the difficulties thus raised, or to other reasons, Novosiltzoff did not exe-

---

* This was the first time that any Power proposed a settlement of European differences by international arbitration. The idea was originated by Prince Adam Czartoryski, and worked out by him with the assistance of the Abbé Piattoli (see pages 92 to 94.).

cute the mission to our satisfaction. It required much prudence and reserve, but also great firmness in following instructions; while he only hinted at the conditions to which we attached the greatest importance, did not mention the name of Poland, and did not allude to the precarious state of Europe as a result of iniquities which demanded redress. There were also some points as to which he was instructed not to make any compromise without first referring to his Government. One of these was the demand that England should evacuate Malta, as she had bound herself to do. This question had been the subject of a debate in Parliament, during which Lord Nelson held that by evacuating Malta England would not expose herself to any serious inconvenience. Be this as it may, the haughty refusal of England gave us the right to withdraw from the negotiation at the beginning; our dignified attitude would have been a proof of our sincere desire for justice and the prosperity of Europe, and must have made a great impression on England herself, by showing her that our just reclamations should not be disregarded. Moreover, it would have given Novosiltzoff facilities for negotiating in Paris. Instead of doing this he hurried back to St Petersburg, leaving matters to be directed by England at her pleasure.

[A preliminary Treaty between Russia and England was, however, concluded on the 11th of April 1805. It stipulated that the contracting parties should endeavour to form a general league of the European Powers against Napoleon, and to collect a force of 500,000 men for the liberation of Europe from his yoke. The objects of the league were to be the evacuation by the French troops of Hanover and other parts of Northern Germany and of Italy; the independence of Holland and Switzerland; the restoration of the King of Sardinia in Piedmont; and in general the establishment of a state of things in Europe calculated to prevent future aggressions. The secret instructions to M. de Novosiltzoff, and other diplomatic papers relative to the Anglo-Russian negotiations of this period, will be found in the following chapters. As to the question of the possession of Malta by England, it is not referred to in the Treaty, and was not raised by Russia until after it was signed. Some curious information on this subject will be found in the letters from Count Vorontzoff in Chapter VIII (pp. 69 to 77), in Lord Stanhope's Life of Pitt, Vol. III, p. 333, and in an interesting collection of despatches edited by Mr Oscar Browning under the title of 'England and Napoleon in 1803,' which has been published by the Royal Historical Society.

Lord Nelson's remarks on the article of the Treaty of Amiens, which bound England to evacuate Malta, were made during a debate in the House of Lords on the Preliminaries of Peace with France on the 3rd of November 1801. They were as follows (Parliam. Hist. 1801):—'To speak next of Malta: when the noble earl (Earl St Vincent, First Lord of the Admiralty) sent him down, the Mediterranean was in the hands of the French, and on his return from the battle of Aboukir, he thought it his first object to blockade it; because he deemed it an invaluable piece of service to rescue it from the hands of the French. In any other point of view, Malta was of no sort of consequence to this country. It was true it contained a most extensive and commodious harbour, with a strong fortification, which would at least require 7000 soldiers to man the works. By the preliminaries, Malta was to be put into the possession of a third Power, and he repeated that in any hands but those of the French it became immaterial to us.'

The Russian emissary in the Anglo-Russian negotiations of 1804-5, M. de Novosiltzoff, afterwards became notorious in Poland as the persecutor of the Polish children in the University and the Schools of Lithuania. Prince Adam Czartoryski, in a letter addressed to his friend, Mr Fox Strangways, Under Secretary of State for Foreign Affairs, on the 18th of July 1836, thus speaks of him: 'The papers here announce the approaching arrival at Brussels of M. de Novosiltzoff, President of the Council of the Empire. Do you know him personally? You are aware that he played an odious part in the history of the misfortunes of Poland, and that he is regarded by my countrymen as the most implacable and despicable enemy our country has ever had. I should not be surprised if some Poles gave him a bad reception should they meet him; the sight of him would make them furious by recalling all the evil he has done. It is said that he is going to the Hague, and thence to London. This unexpected journey of a personage who has become eminent in Russia is probably not without a political object.   Perhaps he is instructed to study the policy of England on the spot, and find out what you have decided to do in the East—to endeavour to calm you and delude you.   He will speak to you of the old friendship between the two countries. Perhaps he will hold out to you a proposal of arrangement and an amnesty for the Poles.   His language will be most conciliatory; he will profess the most liberal opinions, and his mission, if he has a formal one, will be a mission of peace, of concord, of forgetfulness of all offence, and of the harmony and reciprocal confidence of past times.   Be on your guard. There will not be a word of truth in all this.   He is a man without faith or principles, but very clever and astute, and with much knowledge.   He has been several times in England, both as a traveller and on a mission to Mr Pitt.']

[*The secret instructions given by the Emperor Alexander to M. de Novosiltzoff, and other documents relating to the negotiations with England in* 1804-5, *are in Chapters IV to IX.   The concluding portion of the Memoirs forms Chapter X.*]

CHAPTER IV

1804

COMPLETE as is the confidence which I place in the zeal and experience of my Ambassador at the Court of London, the nature and importance of the circumstances of the moment, which may become decisive for the tranquillity of Russia and the fate of Europe, require the presence in England at this juncture of a man who, while having long enjoyed my unlimited confidence, has been in a position to become thoroughly acquainted with my opinions and views, and would be thereby enabled both to inform me clearly and precisely how far the Court of London is inclined to share them, and to direct in accordance with my wishes any negotiations which might have to be undertaken.

I could not make a better selection for so grave and delicate a mission than by entrusting it to you, as you fulfil all the conditions necessary for carrying it out. I accordingly furnish you with these secret instructions, which are to serve as a complement and a commentary to those received by my Ambassador, and will guide you in preventing any arrangement between Russia and England not based on principles, or likely to lead to results, contrary to my just wishes.

A combination of the resources and forces of Russia and Great Britain would no doubt constitute a vast mass of power, and might promise the most satisfactory results. But I would not wish to contribute to it unless I have the assurance that it will be employed for a really useful and beneficent object. I have already explained myself on the subject in my rescript to Count Vorontzoff of which you are the bearer. But several essential points could only be alluded to in general terms in that document; and it will be for you to take to England further explanations and developments in regard to them.

The most powerful weapon hitherto used by the French, and still threatening the other European States, is the general opinion which France has managed to promulgate, that her cause is the cause of national liberty and prosperity. It would be shameful to humanity that so noble a cause should be regarded as the monopoly of a Government which does not in any respect deserve to be the defender of it; it would be dangerous for all the Powers any longer to leave to France the great advantage of seeming to occupy such a position. The good of humanity, the true interest of the lawful authorities, and the success of the enterprise contemplated by the two Powers, demand that they should deprive France of this formidable weapon.

Such is the first object as to which I desire to come to an understanding, if possible, with the British Government, and you will point out that it must be an absolute condition of an intimate and cordial union between Russia and England. Being repugnant to any reaction, I would wish the two Governments to agree that far from attempting to re-establish old abuses in the countries which will have to be emancipated from the yoke of Buonaparte, they should, on the contrary, be assured of liberties founded on a solid basis. This is the principle which, in my idea, should guide the conduct of the two Powers, and their proclamations should always be in accordance with it.

As, before thinking of the liberation of France, we should have to deliver the countries which she oppresses, the first thing to be considered would be how to regulate their future position. The King of Sardinia, with regard to whom Russia and England have contracted engagements, could not be omitted in the arrangement of the affairs of Italy, and he would be perhaps the first to give us a useful example. The safety of Europe requires not only that he should be restored to the throne, but that his share of the territories to be recovered from France should be as large as possible. At the same time the two Powers, while restoring him to the throne and increasing his dominions, would be fully justified in jointly urging him to give his people a free and wise constitution.

He will no doubt himself perceive that his own interest will require him to proclaim a promise to this effect and keep it. It is only by so doing that this prince would be able personally to be useful to the common cause.

The political existence of Switzerland is also of essential interest to the safety of Europe. It is necessary as much as possible to give that country a defensible frontier and strengthen it in its position with regard to other Powers. I think it should be given a Government, based on local requirements and the wishes of the people, which, without falling into the errors of the old system, should be strong enough to take advantage of the resources of the country and make its neutrality respected.

The same principle should guide our policy with regard to Holland, where the national character and wishes should be impartially considered in deciding upon the form of government which should be supported. If the restoration of a hereditary Stadtholder, with a suitably limited amount of power, should be found necessary, Russia and England might come to an understanding as to the selection of the family on which this dignity is to be conferred—either some German Prince who would have a right to our advocacy and on whom we could rely, or some member of the reigning family of Prussia or Denmark, so as to gain a claim to the alliance of one of these Powers; or it might be made a compensation for concessions made by other States. . . . As regards Germany, its present position is certainly not compatible either with the welfare of the German nation or of Europe generally. Should we allow part of Germany to be absorbed by the two Powers which have long coveted it, and at most form a third great State in the midst of Germany? Such a measure would involve so much injustice towards the princes of the Empire who would have to be dispossessed that it can hardly be thought of. Could one succeed in establishing a more intimate union, a sort of more concentrated Federal Government among the various States which compose the German Empire, and if so would it not be desirable to exclude from it the Prussian and Austrian monarchies, whose too unequal forces destroy all balance and patriotism? This will have to be maturely considered if the future organisation of Germany should have to be dealt with.*

I now come to the line of conduct which I am convinced it would be indispensable to pursue with regard to France. After having by our successes abroad, and by the just and liberal principles professed by us, inspired general respect and confidence, we should declare to the French nation that our efforts are directed not against her, but only against her Government, which is as tyrannical for France as for the rest of Europe; that our only object is to deliver from its yoke the countries which it oppresses, and that we now address ourselves to the French nation not to preach revolt and disobedience to law, but to urge all parties in France to trust the allied

* The same views as to Germany are expressed, almost in the same language, in some notes made by Mr Pitt in 1803 (see Lord Stanhope's Life of Pitt, Vol. III, p. 269).

Powers, whose only desire is to emancipate France from the despotism under which she is suffering and to make her free to chose any government she may herself prefer.

Assuming that, for the good of Europe and of France, it is necessary that the constitution there should be monarchical, any proposal to that effect would have to be made by the nation itself: one might endeavour to suggest it, but any intention to that effect should not be declared too soon.

The Cabinets of St Petersburg and St James's will have to come to an understanding on all these points, and also as to the individual and family who might be called upon to reign in France—if the Bourbons, which of them, and what conditions he should be called upon to subscribe to, the most essential of which would be that he should submit to the constitution which would be adopted by the nation. I look upon the choice of a king as a secondary matter, and I will not for my part attach any importance to it except in so far as it might impede or facilitate our operations.

This is not the place or the moment to trace the different forms of government which should be established in these various countries. I leave you entire freedom to treat with the English Minister on this important subject. The principles should undoubtedly everywhere be the same, and it will be above all things necessary to agree as to that point. Everywhere public institutions should be founded on the sacred rights of humanity, and so as to produce the order which is their necessary consequence; everywhere they should be based on the same spirit of wisdom and benevolence. But the application of the same principles may vary according to locality, and the two Powers, in order to come to an understanding on this subject, will take steps to obtain on the spot just, impartial, and detailed information on which they can rely. It is in strictly following such a line of conduct, in tearing off the masks worn by governments which for their private objects alternately have recourse to despotism and to anarchy, carefully separating their interests from those of the people over whom they tyrannise, that we may hope for the sincere assistance of the latter, and produce a general enthusiasm for the good cause whose results would be incalculable.

The adoption of the course above indicated in intimate concert with England would not only be the true and perhaps the only means of restricting French power within its just limits, but would also contribute to fix the future peace of Europe on a solid and permanent basis. The object would be, first, to attach nations to their Governments, by making it only possible for the latter to act for the benefit of their subjects; and secondly, to fix the relations of the various States towards each other on more precise rules, which would be so drawn up as to make it the interest of each State to respect them. . . . When peace is made, a new treaty should be drawn up as a basis for the reciprocal relations of the European States. Such a treaty might secure the privileges of neutrality, bind the Powers who take part in it never to begin a war until after exhausting every means of mediation by a third Power, and lay down a sort of new code of international law which, being sanctioned by the greater part of the European States, would, if violated by any one of them, bind the others to turn against the offender and make good the evil he has committed. . . Should the two Governments agree in the line of policy thus sketched out, they will easily come to an understanding as to the conduct they should pursue with regard to the other Powers who would be made to join in the struggle. The fear of losing the support of Russia and the subsidies of England will decide Austria to follow our impulse in the war which she is already inclined to begin as our ally. As to Prussia, it will be difficult to induce her willingly to enter a combination against France. Her engagements towards Russia are known to you, and it will be for consideration whether it would not be better to force her to take a side either with or against us than that she should remain neutral. Russia especially can put great pressure upon her, and the Berlin Cabinet, by the double engagement it has taken not to allow either Russian or French troops to pass through its territory, might find itself in the difficult position it wished to avoid. But whoever may be our allies, the English Ministry, if it adopts our ideas, will feel the necessity of not allowing any other power completely to penetrate our views, and of only directing our allies towards the proposed object by such means as we may possess of acting upon them.

The Ottoman Empire is another country whose fate will have an influence on that of the rest of Europe. The most intimate concert is necessary between Russia and England with regard to the line of conduct which should be adopted towards Turkey. It cannot be disputed that her weakness, the anarchy of her administration, and the growing discontent of her Christian subjects, are all elements which stimulate speculative ambitions and are diametrically opposed to the principles which we hold are the only ones that can bring about a stable condition of tranquillity in Europe. It will doubtless be desirable to arrive at some arrangement with regard to Turkey which shall be in conformity with the good of humanity and the precepts of sound policy; but it cannot at present be foreseen how far this could be done. The two Powers will not be wanting in loyalty even to an essentially tyrannical government; and this would be the chief obstacle. But if the Porte joined France (for one can never be quite sure of the sincerity of its professions)—if a war and its results rendered the further existence of the Turkish Empire in Europe impossible—the two Powers would regulate among themselves the future fate of the parties concerned. So long as the Turkish Government can be preserved in Europe, it will be necessary not to lose its confidence; but in any case the considerations hereinafter stated should not be lost sight of in our relations with it, and should be maturely weighed, especially before deciding as to the renewal of the treaty of alliance which the Porte proposes to Russia and England. In consenting to the proposal, it will be necessary at least to secure, if possible, a more happy existence to the Christian populations which are suffering under the domination of the Porte, and by that very means to render such domination less precarious; and since we should do so much to preserve the Turkish Empire, it would be desirable also to foresee the advantage we could derive from its government, weak as it is, to paralyse the opposition of France, to which Power a rupture with the Porte might be injurious in several respects. My ambassador in London, following the instructions in this sense which he has received, has doubtless already entered upon a discussion on this important matter with the British Ministry. It will necessarily form part of the general arrangement here sketched out, and you will take care that it shall be suitably combined with the rest of the plan to be adopted.

A further point to be considered is the obligation which would fall upon the two Powers after so costly a struggle to obtain some advantages for themselves to compensate them for their expenditure and to show to the people that their own national interests have not been forgotten. Russia especially will have the right to demand that if her neighbours, such as Austria, Prussia, and Sweden, obtain advantages which it will be necessary to promise them in order to induce them to act, she should have equivalent ones. The peace of Europe could only be preserved by means of a league, formed under the auspices of Russia and England, which would be joined by all the

second class States and by all those who really wish
to remain at peace. In order that such a league
should effectually resist the disturbers of peace and
be firmly established, it is necessary that the two protecting Powers should maintain a certain degree of
preponderance in the affairs of Europe, for they are
the only ones which by their position are always interested in order and justice being maintained, and
which, by their union, would be able to maintain it.

Among the important points of which you will
have to treat with the English Government the most
difficult will be that of making it feel the propriety
and necessity, at a moment when it would re-establish
order and justice in Europe in concert with Russia,
also to consent to make some change in its maritime
code—the only matter as to which the British Cabinet
is not free from reproach, and which enables its
enemies to injure it by exasperating the neutral
Powers. Some concessions on this point, not of a
character to do any real damage to the commerce of
England or to her preponderance on the sea, would
destroy the fears and the mistrust of the neutral
States and sincerely attach them to Great Britain. . . .

St Petersburg,
September 11, 1804.

Signed :—Alexander.

Countersigned :—Prince A. Czartoryski.

CHAPTER V

1804

MEMORANDUM DRAWN UP BY PRINCE ADAM CZARTORYSKI IN 1804, SHOWING
THE RUSSIAN PLAN FOR THE RE-ARRANGEMENT OF EUROPE IN THE
EVENT OF THE COMBINATION WHICH WAS THEN BEING PROJECTED
AGAINST NAPOLEON PROVING SUCCESSFUL.

AUSTRIA will obtain Bavaria and such frontier in Swabia and Franconia as may suit her : also the Tyrol and a new frontier on the side of Venetia and Dalmatia.

The Archduke Charles and the late Grand-Duke of Tuscany will obtain principalities in Germany and Italy. Venetia would suit one of them.

Piedmont will be returned to the King of Sardinia with Genoa and part of Lombardy. This will form an intermediary and respectable Power which it is the interest of Russia to consolidate as much as possible ; the same interest exists as regards the kingdom of the two Sicilies, which will be returned to its legitimate sovereign.

Prussia will obtain in North Germany the States of the Grand-Duchy of Berg, the Duchy of Mecklenburg, Fulda, Anspach, etc. Sweden will obtain a new principality in Germany, according to her wish and convenience.

France will retain as a frontier the Alps and the Rhine up to a point to be specified.

Holland will again become a Republic, with a hereditary Stadtholder, and with part of the Austrian Netherlands returned to her. The independence of Switzerland will be guaranteed.

All the German States which will not be absorbed by Austria and Prussia will form the German Empire, a country intermediary between France, Austria, and Prussia, to be federated with Switzerland and Holland.

The Emperor of Russia, taking the title of King of Poland, will have all the territories that belonged to Poland before the first partition, together with the country called the Kingdom of Prussia, so that his new frontier would extend from Dantzig to the sources of the Vistula, and thence along the Carpathians as far as the source of the Dniester.

Note by Prince Adam Czartoryski

The compensations above granted to Austria and Prussia are sufficient to compensate those Powers for the cessions they would make to Russia. Nearly the whole of Germany can at this moment be made the subject of negotiations, in view of the conduct of her princes, which does not give them any claim to consideration. Italy also will, if necessary, serve to satisfy Austria ; but it would better suit the Court of Vienna to seek compensation in Germany, the southern territories of which interest us less than any other part of Europe, and where, moreover, a sort of balance would always be kept up by the jealousy of France and Prussia.

As to Prussia, she might, if such a course should be absolutely necessary and England consented to it, be also offered the Kingdom of Holland.

It is desirable, however, for the general good that the proposals made above should if possible be adhered to.   If they were adopted, we should have after the peace five great Powers in Europe : Russia, England, France, Austria, and Prussia. Of these, Russia and England, having the same interests and views, would probably remain united ; the three others could hardly make an alliance to disturb the equilibrium that would thus be established, but their policy would have to be watched and controlled.

Further, there would be three considerable masses of intermediary counterpoises, each of which would have its own particular federation, namely, Spain and Portugal, Italy, and Germany proper. These three masses would have the greatest interest in attaching themselves to Russia and England, and sustaining their influence, as it would also be the interest of those two Powers to defend and strengthen them. In such a European arrangement Russia would thus have a marked preponderance, which would be the more assured as France and England would then be rivals for her friendship.

I have not mentioned Turkey, which it would perhaps be best, after re-establishing her rights under old treaties, to leave for the moment in her present condition, except as regards the proposed change in Servia, the reunion of Cattaro to Montenegro, and the Ionian Republic. If the question should ever arise of definitively settling the fate of the Ottoman Empire in Europe, the Powers which it would be necessary to satisfy should only obtain stations and rectifications of territory that might be suitable to them, but the mass of the Turkish territories in Europe should be divided into separate States, governed locally, and bound to each other by a federation, upon which Russia would be able to secure to herself a decisive and lawful influence by means of the title of Emperor or Protector of the Slavs of the East which would be accorded to his Imperial Majesty. In any case this influence would be established by the part the Russians will have taken in the liberation of these territories, by identity of religion and origin, and by a wise policy and a skilful selection of posts to be occupied by our troops.

If the consent of Austria should be necessary, she might be given Croatia, part of Bosnia and Wallachia, Belgrade, Ragusa, etc. Russia would have Moldavia, Cattaro, Corfu, and above all Constantinople and the Dardanelles, together with the neighbouring ports which would make us masters of the Straits. France and England could be offered some islands in the Archipelago or establishments in Asia or Africa.

CHAPTER VI

1804-5

LETTERS RELATIVE TO THE RUSSIAN NEGOTIATIONS WITH ENGLAND AND
AUSTRIA.

FROM PRINCE ADAM CZARTORYSKI TO THE CHANCELLOR
COUNT VORONTZOFF.

8th November, 1804.

I HASTEN to inform your Excellency that the concert* with the Court of Vienna was signed two days ago, and that the Russian and Austrian couriers bearing this news left yesterday evening. The drift of this instrument is already known to you ; the eventuality of an attack on the kingdom of Naples is provided for in it. The Austrian Ambassador insisted that a clause should be added to the effect that such an attack shall not be provoked by his Sicilian Majesty, and, in order to avoid any misunderstanding, we have endeavoured to state as precisely as possible in a separate article what is to be meant by the word 'provocation.' The point relative to the Court of Berlin is inserted in a separate and secret article, and

* This was a secret Convention pledging the two Empires to united action against France, with a view to preventing any encroachments by that power on Germany, Turkey, or Naples.

the Convention concludes by Austria promising reciprocity to Russia in the event of her being attacked by Prussia. The Austrian Ambassador had no instructions as to this, but he signed the article *sub spe rati.*

The article on the subsidies is the one that gave us most trouble. Austria asks two millions for the preliminary preparations and four millions a year. We had to promise our good offices with England in this respect, although we felt that the demand was exorbitant ; but we did so only on the understanding that if the Court of London should not supply the whole of that sum, the stipulations of the concert were to remain none the less valid. This indispensable condition was not signed by the Austrian Ambassador, as his instructions did not justify him in doing so. The matter was arranged subject to further declarations. Notwithstanding this, we thought it best to sign, as we thought it would be difficult for the Court of Vienna to refuse its ratification, which we must wait for before we can regard the matter as definitively settled. I forgot to say, with regard to the number of troops, that Austria is to give 235,000 men and we 115,000, which makes 350,000 in all.

The worthy Admiral Warren* has just left, full of gratitude for the friendship which has been shown him here and the kindness of the Emperor. The new Ambassador, Lord G. L. Gower, whom as yet I have only twice seen in my house, seems to me thoroughly

* Sir John Warren, British Ambassador at the Russian Court.

conversant with the matters with which he will have
to deal. The Court of London is not quite satisfied
with us, but I hope it will gradually become so, and I
do not despair of matters taking a good turn. They
complain in London of the mystery in which we
shroud our negotiations with Austria. At Vienna
they are very glad of it, and if the matter had not
been kept an impenetrable secret, the pusillanimous
Austrian Cabinet would not have gone so far with us
as it has done. . . .

2nd December, 1804.

The Court of Vienna wishes to make advances to
Berlin to try to draw Prussia into a concert with us,
but I have little hope of success in this direction.
Prussia wishes to preserve her neutrality with regard
to France as well as with regard to ourselves ; that is
I think her system, which at the moment of rupture
might become very embarrassing. Altogether the
problem of how to deal with Prussia is not an easy
one.

We are now drawing up instructions for Italinsky
relative to a new treaty of alliance with the Porte
which will I think appease the alarms of Mr Pitt.
So long ago as 1790 his system was based on the
greatest jealousy of any new acquisition on the part
of Russia.

CHAPTER VII

1805

REPORT FROM M. DE NOVOSILTZOFF, GIVING AN ACCOUNT OF THE
RESULT OF HIS NEGOTIATIONS WITH MR PITT.

I HAVE had preliminary conversations, first with Lord Harrowby, and afterwards, on two different occasions, with Mr Pitt, on the principles which, in the present state of Europe, any coalition which it might be possible to form would have to follow in order to have any reasonable prospect of establishing the balance of power, bringing back France into her old limits, and placing the general tranquillity of Europe on a solid and stable basis. These conversations have shown me that the opinions of the British Ministry entirely coincide with the intentions of his Majesty the Emperor, as regards the points which I had the opportunity of touching upon. Thus Mr Pitt, in a rapid statement of his point of view, said he was firmly persuaded that it was necessary to tear away from the French Government the mask with which it was always seeking to hide its offences against humanity in general and the independence of nations in particular, and that for this purpose no means should be neglected of undeceiving those sovereigns (if any) who, notwithstanding the experience of so many public misfortunes, still persist in not seeing that the great extension and enormous power which France has acquired, coupled with the unbridled ambition of Buonaparte, threaten Europe with total ruin.

Having seen how much the ideas of the British Ministry with regard to public affairs approximate to those of his Majesty the Emperor, I thought it my duty, in my conference with Mr Pitt, to enter into the greatest detail, and take up the various matters in their proper order. I began by saying that it gave me very great pleasure to see from all that Mr Pitt had said that the benevolent views of his Imperial Majesty were so much in accordance with those of the British Cabinet ; and that all the remaining subjects which I had to bring forward were, properly speaking, only a development of the same principles. Nevertheless, as the matter of which we were treating was in itself of such great importance that it cannot be dealt with too precisely, I requested him to permit me to resume my statement of it from the beginning, and to take up in their natural order all the various points which relate to it, so as the more easily to distinguish the principles as to which we are agreed from the subordinate matters which will have to be discussed and regulated afterwards.

Mr Pitt found that what I had said was perfectly just, and I accordingly entered upon my statement. I began by pointing out that what we had to agree about turned naturally on two principal points : one comprised the objects which the two nations would propose to attain by the convention which they would draw up; the other the means best calculated to ensure as complete a success as possible. There can be no doubt, I said, that the objects in question, taken collectively, should be reduced to a single one only— that of restoring the equilibrium of Europe and establishing its safety and tranquillity on more solid bases ; but as this object involves a great number of ideas, I thought it best, for the sake of order and precision, to divide it into three distinct parts, which might be regarded as so many periods through which a coalition formed between Russia and Great Britain would have successively to pass in order to arrive at the ultimate object proposed.

The first object, in the opinion of his Imperial Majesty, is to bring back France into its ancient limits, or such other ones as might appear most suitable to the general tranquillity of Europe. The second is to place natural barriers to the ambition of Buonaparte, so as to prevent France from further aggressions in future ; and the third is to consolidate the order of things which would be established by an intimate and perpetual alliance between Russia and Great Britain, and by a compact between those Powers, the countries which they would liberate from the yoke of France, and any other States which might be disposed to join them for the maintenance of a condition of affairs indispensable for the balance of power.

Mr Pitt said that this view was entirely in conformity with his own ; and then I proceeded to the means which his Imperial Majesty thought would be best calculated to attain the three objects above stated.

With regard to the first, I remarked that the means for attaining it might be stated as follows :—

1. The employment of as large a force as possible against the common enemy.

2. The employment of it in the most advantageous manner.

3. The reduction of the enemy's strength to the utmost possible extent.

His Majesty the Emperor of Russia being practically unable to make effectual war upon France without the assistance of some of the great Continental Powers, it is evident that in order to bring against the enemy a force in proportion to the greatness of the enterprise, the two Powers, once they agree by a convention as to the principles on which they are to act, would turn all their attention to the task of binding Austria and Prussia, or, if it should be impossible to do this as regards both, at least one of these Powers, to form a coalition (which the Ottoman Porte, Sweden, and perhaps Denmark, would probably join) with Russia and Great Britain against the extension of France and the barbarous conduct of Buonaparte.

The *conditio sine quâ non* of this coalition would be that none of the members of it should in any case be able to make a separate peace on its own account. Great Britain would on her side engage to grant to these Powers such subsidies as the urgency of the case might render indispensable, to furnish transport ships, and to employ her own land forces in as great numbers as possible on every occasion where such assistance on her part might be useful to the common cause.

In this way there can be no doubt that the forces which might be used against France would be more than sufficient; the only question would be how to employ them in the most efficacious manner. In order to do this, I said, it is necessary that the two Cabinets should agree as to the points of attack, the best plan of military operations to be adopted, and the means to be employed for preserving among the combined armies a unity of aim and the greatest possible harmony in all the operations they might undertake. I added, in order to avoid any digression from my principal subject, that I would not fail afterwards to communicate to Mr Pitt all I knew of his Imperial Majesty's ideas on this matter.

I next passed to the means of reducing the enemy's strength. These, I said, would chiefly consist in the liberation of Holland, Switzerland, and Italy from their enslavement to France, and in the endeavour to employ them for their own defence as part of the coalition. I remarked at the same time that no means should be neglected which might prepare them for this purpose as soon as the coalition should begin to be formed. It was above all things necessary to gain their confidence by not leaving them any doubt that the two Powers which would be at the head of the coalition would not be actuated by personal views, and would only strive to recover and consolidate their political independence; that all the fortresses which would surrender to the armies of the coalition would be taken in the name of the nation to which they belong, and would be restored to it when it obtains a settled government after joining the coalition.

If the language and conduct of Russia and England are always in accord with these principles, they would not only produce the desired effect, but in all probability would prepare France herself for salutary changes in her government and render the task of the coalition much less difficult in other respects.

Mr Pitt answered that he entirely agreed to all I had said, and that he only wished to point out that no means should be neglected of bringing Prussia into the coalition. He suggested various inducements which might be held out to her with this object, and he also spoke of indemnities which might be promised to Austria. It seemed to me, however, that there were several other matters to be settled first, and I merely said that the principle which his Imperial Majesty thought should be followed in any overtures that might be made was to offer only what could not be refused; by so doing we should avoid the mistake which had been made recently, when all the efforts that were made were attributed solely to a wish of profiting by a general dismemberment. I added, however, that it was not very likely that we should be able entirely to avoid making some offers; his

Majesty had some ideas on the subject which would be communicated to him hereafter by our Ambassador.

As to the subsidies, Mr Pitt said that England would go as far as would be within the limits of possibility. 'We will give £5,000,000, perhaps a little more ; and this is all we can do, for if we wished to go further, besides the want of means, there would be the additional objection that our trade with the countries which would be subsidised would not admit of our sending them a larger sum. We will, however, fix the 1st of January as the date on which the subsidies will begin ; this would be three or four months before the troops can be sent into the field. The sum thus obtained would be pretty considerable, and might serve to cover part of the expense of preparations.'

I next represented to Mr Pitt that with regard to the second object—the imposition of natural barriers to the ambition of Buonaparte which would both keep France within her boundaries and prevent her future aggrandisement—his Majesty thinks the most trustworthy means, and the only one on which we could rely, would be to surround France with States which would be strong enough at least not to fear the first blows of an invasion, and which would thus be capable to a certain degree of making their independence respected. Starting from this principle, it is most necessary that at the close of a successful war the condition of Holland, Switzerland and Italy should be considerably improved, and their strength increased by suitable augmentations of territory. The old Germanic Confederation, divided into so many little States which have almost ceased to have any connection with each other, is in striking contrast to the object with which it was formed, and should also engage the serious attention of the two Courts. His Imperial Majesty's ideas on this subject would, I added, be stated to Mr Pitt by our Ambassador, to whom I had been charged to communicate them; and having no personal predilections, he would gladly receive any proposals that might be made to him by the British Cabinet. Being firmly persuaded that nothing can give more energy to a nation, and render it more respected abroad, than a good Government founded on just and equitable principles which attach people to their country and to its lawful authorities, his Majesty would wish to come to an understanding with the British Cabinet as to the form of Government to be introduced and encouraged in the countries which would recover their independence. . . .

Finally, in order to attain the third object—that of consolidating the new state of things by the beneficial influence which would be exercised through a permanent alliance between Russia and England, an alliance which nothing could dissolve but a total change of system and principles on either side—his Majesty thinks that the means of achieving this object would spontaneously present themselves as soon as an agreement is arrived at on the question of principle. The arrangements above indicated would be based on the interests and the security of the nations which would be liberated; and nothing would then remain but to fix on clear and precise principles the

prescriptions of international law and ascertain how
far they can be made predominant over the special
laws of each State.

Mr Pitt listened to my statement with much
attention, and when I had ended, he said : 'The principles on which his Imperial Majesty wishes to make
a convention with Great Britain and to act against
the usurpations of France are in all respects as an-
alogous to the sentiments of his Britannic Majesty
and of his Ministry as it is possible to desire, and they
are at the same time so well adapted to the tendencies
of the nation, and so much in conformity with the
character and opinions of the individuals who compose
it, that the Government could only maintain its popularity by literally following them.   Moreover, the
interests of England—the Sinking Fund, the National
Debt, our trade, and the progress of our industry—all
demand that in the policy we are to follow we should
not neglect any measures which might bring about
and solidly establish a general peace.   The British
Cabinet has always been so intimately penetrated with
these sentiments that it has never ceased, either during war or peace, loudly to profess them and to give
proofs of its disinterestedness by every sacrifice it has
been capable of making.

*Supplementary Memorandum handed to Mr Pitt as
a development of the ideas expressed by him.*

The Cabinets of St Petersburg and St James's will
agree as to the above points and come to an understanding as to the individual and the family which

should be called upon to reign in France. If the Bourbons, which of them, and at what moment he should be informed of his selection; what line of action he is to be required to adopt, and to what conditions he is to subscribe, the most essential one being that of submission to the constitution that might be adopted.

This selection is regarded by his Majesty the Emperor as a secondary matter, and he would not, so far as he is concerned, attach any importance to it except in so far as it might impede or facilitate operations.

Mr Pitt is of opinion that these points can only be determined upon as events occur.

(A confidential note in accordance with the above agreement was presented by Mr Pitt to the Russian Ambassador on the 19th of January, 1805. The text of this note will be found in Alison's History of Europe, vol. vi, p. 667).

CHAPTER VIII

1805

EXTRACTS FROM LETTERS ADDRESSED TO PRINCE ADAM CZARTORYSKI BY COUNT VORONTZOFF, THE RUSSIAN AMBASSADOR IN LONDON, RELATIVE TO THE FURTHER PHASES OF THE NEGOTIATIONS FOR AN ALLIANCE WITH RUSSIA.—REFUSAL OF ENGLAND TO EVACUATE MALTA OR ALTER THE MARITIME CODE.

LONDON, $\frac{7}{10}$th *January* (1805).

I SAW Mr Pitt this morning with M. de Novo-siltzoff. He told us that Buonaparte's letter,* and the answer here given to it, oblige him somewhat to change the plan which had been as good as agreed upon between us. It is necessary, he said, both in England and abroad to prove that what we desire is a sure and stable peace for the future independence and security of Europe. This being the case, pro-

---

* Proposing peace with England. This proposal was thus referred to in George III's speech from the throne on the 15th of January, 1805 :

'I have received pacific overtures from the chief of the French Government, and have in consequence expressed my earnest desire to embrace the first opportunity of restoring the blessings of peace, on such grounds as may be consistent with the permanent interest and safety of my dominions ; but these objects are closely connected with the general peace of Europe. I have, therefore, not thought it right to enter into any more particular explanation without previous communication with those Powers on the Continent with whom I am engaged in confidential intercourse and connection with a view to that important object, and especially the Emperor of Russia, who has given the strongest proofs of the wise and dignified sentiments with which he is animated, and of the warm interest which he takes in the safety and independence of Europe.'

posals must be made to Buonaparte that he should give up part of his possessions and abandon his interference in the affairs of the neighbouring Governments. No one, Mr Pitt added, is better qualified to make such proposals than the Emperor of Russia, who is neither a neighbour nor an enemy of France, and who only desires to obtain a permanent peace for Europe; the proposals should be clear, precise, and categorical, and made so as to exclude all negotiation, and to be either accepted or rejected. If Buonaparte accepts them, he should be required to evacuate, within a brief specified period, the territories he has no right to possess; if he rejects them, hostilities should be begun at once. We should, he concluded, in order to be prepared for the latter contingency, work without intermission, and have everything ready for crossing the frontier.

LONDON, 2ⁿᵈ *January* 1805.

After many delays I am at length able to send this by courier. The weight of business which falls upon Mr Pitt from all sides, and the quite recent entrance of Lord Mulgrave into the Cabinet,* are the chief cause of these delays. Buonaparte's proposal of peace has also partly contributed to them. It is not possible for an English Ministry to reject an offer of peace without a motive; the country would not allow it to continue the war at its pleasure. The Government must therefore show that it desires an honourable peace and one that would ensure the

* As Foreign Secretary.

safety of Europe. If Buonaparte rejects their conditions, the nation will support the Ministry in a
continuance of the war.

You will see from my official letter, and especially
from the draft Treaty which accompanies it, that
there is a talk of from four to five hundred thousand
men for acting against France. This arises from the
usual practice in time of war; the enemy exaggerates
the number of his troops, and one's allies even surpass
this exaggeration; and as some surprise is felt at the
little result which has been attained, it is thought
that the number of troops must be increased. It is a
known fact that during the terrible campaign at the
beginning of the last war, when Prussia received
subsidies from England for a great army which was to
take the offensive, she never had half of the effective
troops for which she was paid. Instead of having
80,000 men, she had less than 40,000, and she wasted
them during the whole campaign in besieging
Mayence, which could have been taken by 30,000
men in less than six weeks if the King of Prussia had
acted honestly. Austria, too, during the first two
campaigns, never had more than 40,000 men in Italy,
and during the last campaign 60,000, while the Vienna
Cabinet alleged that 60,000 were engaged in the first
campaigns and 100,000 in the subsequent ones. The
same happened in Swabia, in Switzerland, and on the
Upper Rhine. This is the reason of the obstinacy
with which the Government here insists on armies
being employed in such great numbers, though they
will find it difficult to obtain subsistence. . . .

I must here tell you that all you will find in the official despatches of the English Ministry as to arranging indemnities for Prussia and placing independent Powers between Holland and France and on the left bank of the Rhine are not really matters to which importance is attached here. Mr Pitt has often told me, and repeated to me yesterday, that these expedients are proposed because no better ones have been found, but that if any plan more likely to be effective for the purpose of keeping France in her ancient limits could be devised, the British Cabinet would gladly accept it, as it desired nothing more than the peace of Europe and the maintenance of a permanent friendship with Russia.

LONDON, 26 *January* (N.S.) 1805.

Russia and England should, and can, save Europe. England ardently wishes it, and will do her utmost to co-operate with Russia in this holy work; it only depends therefore upon the latter to employ the means with which England has decided to furnish her. The King, Mr Pitt, all that is great and enlightened in the country, and, which is more important, the whole nation (for this is the only country in the world where the people are not treated like a flock of sheep) desire a permanent alliance with Russia. . . .

Lord G. L. Gower, in a cipher despatch dated the 12th or 13th October (O.S.) says that Count Stadion,* after having received despatches from his Court, had stated to him that the Emperor, his master, had so

* The Austrian Ambassador at St Petersburg.

long hesitated as to the course he should adopt in present circumstances, because for two years he had seen an intimate alliance between Russia, Prussia, and France, the result of which was that these three Powers disposed of everything in Germany in a manner prejudicial to the power and even the security of Russia ; but that now Russia prefers to follow another system more in conformity with the welfare of Europe, being calculated to restore to it the independence of which France has deprived it, the Emperor, his master, no longer doubted the good-will of the Emperor of Russia, and was resolved to second his views, provided he be supported by Russian troops and English money.* This despatch, which Lord Mulgrave showed me, and which Mr Pitt afterwards showed our friend,† has given us all great pleasure. Here they are ready to do everything.

LONDON, ¹⁹⁄₂₂ *April* 1805.

I am sending by to-day's courier a despatch to M. de Novosiltzoff announcing that the Court here acquiesces in the proposals he is to make to the Corsican, whom he will find in Italy. . . . I take this opportunity of repeating that I intend to leave this country next spring. Matters are tending towards a coalition or a peace, and this should be settled before the winter, after which my stay here will almost cease to be necessary. If they send in my place a man of frank and straightforward character, not given to

---

* The preliminary Convention for an alliance between Austria and Russia against France was signed on the 25th October 1804.

† M. de Novosiltzoff.

compliments, he will gain the confidence of the King, of the Ministry, and of English society in general. An intriguer and a flatterer would only inspire contempt.

LONDON, 10th May 1805.

(Written in sympathetic ink).

I am sorry to see our people do not understand the constitution of this country, which is very different from its theory, as stated in the works of Blackstone and his abbreviator Delolme.   It rests with the nation to decide as to any point which it may deem absolutely necessary, and no administration, however strong, would dare to go against that decision : if it did, it would be overthrown, prosecuted, and punished, and what it had arranged against the public wish would be disavowed and annulled.   Such a question is that of the restoration of Malta, the possession of which entails much expense on England, but which she feels it indispensable to keep at any cost, in order that the Mediterranean should not become a lake belonging to France, who would be mistress of all its shores, and thus be placed in a position to attack Sicily, the Ionian Islands, the Morea, Crete, and above all Egypt, whose possession by the French troops would induce them before long to attack the British possessions in India.   If Lord G. L. Gower had agreed to the evacuation of Malta and the new maritime code which is again brought forward by our Government, his action would certainly not have been ratified here.   He would have been recalled with disgrace, perhaps prosecuted,

and would have lost all his reputation. . . . You tell
me that if England will not yield Russia will not
ratify the Convention.   That being so, I can only
regard the negotiations as broken off.   The Continent
will be enslaved, and this country will either make
peace before Christmas and keep Malta, or will continue a defensive war which will cost it little money
and which will preserve the rock which is the cause of
all the existing difficulties.

LONDON, ₁⁸ₛ *May* 1805.

. . . The English nation is quite decided not to
give up Malta.   I have been here twenty years ; I
have done my best to make myself acquainted with
the country, the Government, and the national character, and when I say it is not in the power of the
Government to make this cession, I express not only
the feeling of the Ministry and the most respectable
members of the opposition, such as Earl Spencer and
Lord Granville, but also the unanimous sentiment of
all the most estimable and independent persons that
influence public opinion. . . .   I may be blamed for
not having in my official reports stated that England
would never consent to the evacuation of Malta, but I
could not anticipate that such a demand would be
made by our Government, as the matter was never
mentioned to me, and in the conferences which M. de
Novosiltzoff had with Mr Pitt, both alone and in my
presence, there was no question of England abandoning Malta. . . .   The proposed new code of maritime
law is equally out of the question, and Lord Harrowby

assured me that if Lord G. L. Gower had yielded on these two points he would have been recalled, and never again employed in the diplomatic service. The Government here would have preferred that he should have altogether refused to accept the note you addressed to him on the subject of the maritime code, and that he should have replied to you verbally that Great Britain simply adheres to her practice during the last two centuries in this matter, which is in accordance with her treaties with Russia, Sweden, Denmark, and Holland. The result of accepting the Russian proposal, added Lord Harrowby, would be to give France facilities for maintaining and augmenting her naval forces to the detriment of England ; and this is a further reason why England will never accept it at any cost. France may obtain supplies for her navy from other countries in time of peace, but England will never allow her to obtain them in time of war.

I have done all that was humanly possible to mitigate the bad impression produced by my communication on the King, Mr Pitt, and Lord Harrowby, who, though still too unwell to take an active post in the administration, assists at the Cabinet Councils, where he possesses the influence given him by his great talents and the extreme deference paid to his advice by Mr Pitt. I begin to hope that some means may be found of avoiding a rupture of the negotiations, which during the first four days was almost decided upon. I endeavoured to gain time by persuading them not to send an unfavourable answer at once, and

meanwhile I have had several conferences with Lord
Mulgrave and Lord Harrowby. The latter seemed
somewhat shaken on my pointing out that if the proposed alliance between Russia and England should
fail by the absolute rejection of the Emperor's
demands, the result would be the enslavement of the
Continent. He said he would think about the
matter further, but added that he had never seen his
friend Mr Pitt, with whom he has been on intimate
terms for more than twenty years, so deeply grieved
as he was at the difference between the two Courts;
but he was unshakeable, and he never shrank from
any danger when he saw it was necessary to incur it
for the maintenance of the honour and the interests
of his country. As to the King, I have employed
the services of Count Münster, in whom his Majesty
has the greatest confidence. He undertook the task
with zeal, and spoke to the King some days ago in
order to prevent a rupture between the two countries,
and with some success, but as I knew the Ministry
would have to be at the fêtes at Windsor, and the
King, who is incessantly occupied with public business,
would be sure to have private conferences with Mr
Pitt and Lord Harrowby at which the question of the
provisional treaty made at St Petersburg would
probably be finally settled, I begged Count Münster
to let me know how things are going on. Last
night I received a note from him by express which
gives me some hope. I shall probably see Lord
Mulgrave to-morrow or the day after, when I will
have the reply of the Government. . . .

P.S. — 1/2 *May.*   The gleam of hope that some compromise might be arrived at here to satisfy our Government has disappeared.   I learn that Mr Pitt has looked for one in vain, and that in order not to be disavowed and blamed by the nation he will be obliged to give up the co-operation of the Continental Powers, as our Court has peremptorily declared that it will not ratify the Treaty unless this country will abandon Malta.   They have begun to prepare a long reply, which will be in great detail.   I do not think it will be handed to me before five or six days hence.

[The Treaty of the 11th of April, 1805, was not ratified, owing to the difference between Russia and England as to Malta and the maritime code, until the month of July following, and the Russian Government only consented to ratify it after placing on record its opinion that the restoration of Malta and the alteration of the maritime code would be in conformity with 'the principles of equity and justice,' and would be 'the most efficacious means of securing the success of the cause.'   (Despatch from Lord G. L. Gower to Lord Mulgrave of the 21st July 1805, and note from Prince Adam Czartoryski of the same date, both in the Record Office.)].

CHAPTER IX

INTERVIEW BETWEEN THE RUSSIAN ENVOYS AND MR PITT (SEPTEMBER 1805) AS TO THE QUESTION OF GIVING UP HANOVER TO PRUSSIA.

THE negotiations for bringing to a practical issue the convention of the 11th of April having been procrastinated through the refusal of England to give up Malta and alter the maritime code, Alexander, who had meanwhile begun to disregard the advice of his Ministers, and to take the government of Russia into his own hands, entered with Austria into a campaign against France, and made overtures to Prussia with a view to drawing her into the alliance. Prussia asked as the price of her co-operation that England should give up Hanover to her and provide her and her German allies with subsidies to enable them to carry on the war. Another special envoy, M. d'Oubril, was then sent by the Russian Government to London. The following extracts from a letter from Count Vorontzoff describe the interview which took place with Mr Pitt on this occasion :—

LONDON, $\frac{14}{26}$ *September* 1805.

I am very grateful to you for having sent M. d'Oubril to me. He has given me explanations as to the papers of which he is the bearer, and which have caused me inexpressible astonishment. But the thing is done, and nothing remains but to bow to the decrees of Providence, which seems still to protect the Corsican. I feared the Berlin interview, and my presentiment is verified. All the weapons of intrigue and sycophancy must have been employed against weakness and irresolution. I know too well your judgment and your elevation of mind to doubt for an instant that you have used all your efforts to prevent the evil that has been done, and I pity you very sincerely at not having been able to prevent it. As your private letter did not contain anything that I could not communicate to Mr Pitt, and it referred me for further explanations to M. d'Oubril, I sent it to Mr Pitt with a request that he should return it to me, and that he should defer his opinion on the papers I would communicate to him the same morning until after hearing the explanations which M. d'Oubril and myself would give him on all the points which might seem new to him. He returned me your letter with thanks, assuring me that it had not been communicated to anybody, and that he would be very glad to see M. d'Oubril. Though prepared to receive a disagreeable communication, and accustomed to master his countenance, one could see his emotion on reading the documents I gave him, which he handed to Lord Mulgrave after he had finished them. The proposal that the King should exchange a patrimony which his ancestors had enjoyed for more than a thousand years struck him deeply. He told me that, knowing his

Majesty's attachment for his German subjects and his
inflexible character, he would break off everything if
such a proposal were made to him; and what is
worse, being old, infirm, and extremely sensitive, it
might even place his life in danger. M. d'Oubril and
myself then pointed out that matters had arrived at
such a point that everything must be done to avoid
so perilous a contingency as Prussia remaining in-
active, or even turning to the side of France, after
the disasters suffered by the Austrian army through
the folly or the treason of Mack;* that it was therefore
necessary to bring her over to our side at any cost
during the period of four weeks given to Buonaparte
to arrive at a decision; and that the demands on
which Prussia insists should not be flatly rejected.
Mr Pitt replied that though England would also have
reason to complain of the other articles of the proposed Convention, she will not object to them. 'All
the subsidies that Prussia asks for herself, for Saxony,
for Hesse, and for the Duke of Brunswick will be
given; we shall be delighted to agree to any other
indemnity that Prussia may wish to have, but as for
the exchange of Hanover, no Minister would be
imprudent enough to make such a proposal to the
King, and great care will be taken always to conceal
it from him.' He added that in all these proposals of
peace that are being made to Buonaparte there is a sort
of affectation not to speak of England, as if the Powers

---

* The Austrians under Mack, after occupying the line of the Iller from Ulm to
Memmingen, were outmanœuvred by Napoleon, who gained a position on the Danube
in the Austrian rear, upon which Mack surrendered at Ulm and the Austrian army
was broken up.

wanted to make him believe that they did not trouble
themselves about her. This did not produce much effect
upon the Ministry, as England does not fear France,
but wishes to liberate the Continent; but it will produce a bad effect in the country if Buonaparte publishes
the proposals which have been made to him at the very
time when Parliament has to be asked for enormous
subsidies for Powers which ostentatiously affect complete indifference as regards England. I endeavoured
to account for this omission by the urgent need of
bringing over Prussia to the alliance, and d'Oubril
justly remarked that if there had been any question
of inserting a provision as to the interests of England,
the limit of four weeks would not have been sufficient,
as it would have been necessary to write to London
and wait for an answer, which would depend on
favourable winds, and might not come for months.
This would have been playing into the hands of
Prussia, who wishes to gain time and put off as long
as possible her final decision. Mr Pitt afterwards
admitted to me that this explanation was a valid one,
but he added that it could not be produced in Parliament. He further objected to the passage in our
official despatch in which occurs the following phrase:
'Moreover, the extraordinary defeats suffered by the
Austrian armies might have given them a right to
regard themselves as freed from this obligation,' *i.e.*,
that of not making peace except in concert with an
ally. He remarked that if, instead of gaining a
signal victory and depriving the enemy of nineteen
ships of the line, the English fleet had been beaten

at the battle of Trafalgar, and England had then
negotiated a separate peace, thinking herself freed
from all engagements to the allies with whom she has
treaties stipulating that peace should not be made
except by common agreement, would such a course
have been thought right at St Petersburg and
Vienna? As to this point we fell back on the
necessity of pleasing Prussia, in order to draw her
into the war, as we were persuaded that Buonaparte
would reject the conditions of peace, and the Court of
Berlin would then be forced to show its hand. We
added that the crudity of the expressions to which he
objected was to be excused by the extraordinary
urgency of the case, as the Emperor was only a few
days at Berlin and Potsdam, during which there was
a constant struggle with the Prussian Minister, so
that there was really no time to weigh words. After
we had left Mr Pitt, M. d'Oubril suggested to me
that I should soften some of the expressions in
our official despatch which had shocked Mr Pitt, and
I accordingly went back to him to ask whether he
would agree to this being done. He replied that this
would make his task much easier with his colleagues
in the Cabinet. At length everything was pretty
well accepted here, though with evident repugnance,
except the exchange of the electorate, as to which Mr
Pitt spoke to me very strongly on various occasions
in several conversations which I had with him. He
repeated to me that such a proposal might either kill
the King or drive him mad, and that after losing a
sovereign so much esteemed and cherished, the country

would no longer consent to bear the enormous sacrifices of money it was making for continental wars. To provoke so fatal a crisis as the death or insanity of the King would therefore be most ruinous to the interests of Europe.

I conjure you to weigh well the considerations above stated, and I hope I shall be spared the pain of presenting the memorandum which is being prepared at Berlin and which will be rejected here. The weakness with which the Emperor has, in order to please Prussia, lent himself to a communication so offensive to the King of Great Britain, and so contrary even to the true interests of Russia, will be even more felt here when his Ambassador presents a detailed memorandum on the subject.

(Subsequently a despatch, dated $\frac{\text{23rd October}}{\text{4th November}}$ 1805, a copy of which is in the Record Office, was addressed to Count Vorontzoff by Prince Adam Czartoryski, urging that the cession of Hanover to Prussia was a *conditio sine quâ non* of obtaining the Prussian alliance; but England persisted in her refusal to consent to the cession. The result was that Prussia remained neutral during the war, and afterwards obtained Hanover from Napoleon as a bribe for her alliance.)

CHAPTER X

1805

IN order to understand the political movements of
that time and the animosity with which all Europe
wished to fight Napoleon, notwithstanding the defeats
he had inflicted upon her, it is necessary to recollect
what was the state of public opinion in Europe.
Those who had become enthusiastic at the outbreak
of the French Revolution had looked upon Buonaparte as the hero of liberalism; he seemed to them
destined by Providence to make the cause of justice
triumph and to remove by great actions and immense
successes the innumerable obstacles presented by facts
to the wishes of oppressed nations. When they saw
that Napoleon did not fulfil their expectations their
enthusiasm diminished. The French Republic and
the Directory had no doubt acted culpably and fool-
ishly, but though they were deceived as to the means,
they remained faithful to the end; they had done the
greatest harm to the cause of freedom, but had not

deserted it. They might in course of time have learnt the right means of doing justice and emancipating nations; but no such illusions were possible when Napoleon became the ruler of France. Each of his words and actions showed that he would act only by the force of bayonets and of numbers. By ceasing to be the champion of justice and the hope of oppressed peoples, he lost one of the strongest elements of the power of the French Republic, and descended to the class of ambitious tyrants, with immense talents it is true, but with motives as mean as theirs. This made other Powers attack him without scruple, as a scourge of humanity; and the general opinion of Europe on this subject spread to Russia, thereby drawing the Cabinet of St Petersburg into a course of policy in which it lost sight of the part Russia was really called upon to play.

The peace of Amiens, which had been hailed with equal enthusiasm on both sides of the channel, had been broken by an act which Napoleon resisted with his usual violence, but in which he had right on his side. He demanded the immediate evacuation of Malta, which England had only occupied on the express condition that she should withdraw from it when peace was concluded. It had been agreed on all sides that the future destiny of this island was to be regulated by the Powers in concert. England haughtily refused to execute this clause of the treaty, and the war was at once resumed. At this time Lord G. L. Gower,* the British Ambassador appointed

* Father of the present Lord Granville.

by the new Ministry, arrived at St Petersburg. He was
then a young man, but he had much natural prudence,
and an instinct of propriety which manifested itself in
every word he uttered, and in the manner in which he
did business. He showed me entire confidence, and
even sincere friendship. He was accompanied by Sir
Charles Stewart, who had already had an opportunity
of acquiring diplomatic skill in various embassies
where he occupied the post of secretary. These two
personages were afterwards well known in Paris,
where they repeatedly succeeded each other. Lord
G. L. Gower, who afterwards became Earl Granville,
allied himself with the Whigs, while Sir Charles
Stewart, who became Lord Stewart,* remained with
the Tory party. Lord G. L. Gower arrived in
Russia with important despatches intended to draw
the Emperor into an alliance and active military co-
operation against France. The Austrian Government, whose leading Minister was at that time M. de
Cobentzel, at the same time sent another ambassador,
Count Stadion, to sound the real intentions of Russia.
The English representative spoke with as much decision as the Austrian one did with timidity and reti-
cence. The latter was in constant alarm lest he
should compromise himself by his proceedings being
known too soon in London, and we had for some time
to conceal them from the English Government,
thereby incurring its reproaches, of which Count
Simon Vorontzoff made himself perhaps too devoted
an organ.

* Afterwards Marquis of Londonderry.

In descending into the arena Napoleon had cast aside everything that could have led people to believe that he had a high and generous mission. He was a Hercules abandoning his task of succouring the oppressed and thinking only how to employ his strength in order to subjugate the world for his own advantage. His sole idea was to re-establish absolute power everywhere, with its old forms and the greater part of its inconveniences. So long as he governed, his ambition and injustice eclipsed those of all other enemies of mankind; he seemed like a sinister and devouring flame rising above all Europe. In every country men who valued their national dignity, who were brave and high-principled, were unanimous in their opposition to him. He had no supporters anywhere except among those in whom fear was the strongest motive. As soon as this feeling began to subside, there was but one voice of opposition to the man who, after having made himself an ordinary despot, had everywhere wished to impose his yoke on the other European sovereigns.

The policy of Russia from the beginning of the reign of Alexander could, after what I have said of his opinions, only be one of conciliation between parties and Powers whose policy bore the character of mutual exasperation. It was with this object that the Emperor had allowed himself to be drawn by Prussia into taking part in the complicated question of indemnities in Germany. The parties interested in this matter showed a partiality and a disposition to give and accept bribes which did them little honour, and were not at all in accordance with the Emperor's pure intentions. While supporting the claims of princes who were related to him, and somewhat too partial to Prussia, his sole object was to rescue Germany with as little injustice as possible from the confusion into which she had been thrown by the Revolution and the French wars.

The spirit which at that time animated the Russian Cabinet rendered it eminently suited to speak to inflamed Europe in terms of peace and conciliation. The character of the sovereign and of his Ministers, which always has an influence on policy, must have added weight to the conduct which was then adopted by the Cabinet of St Petersburg, and its words would doubtless have been received with general readiness and confidence.

After the retirement of Count Panin, whose principles and manner might have inspired foreigners with distrust, Count Kotchoubey, who succeeded him, and especially the Chancellor Count Vorontzoff, possessed in a high degree the qualities necessary for ensuring their acceptance as mediators by the parties most hostile to each other. The Chancellor sincerely wished to remove difficulties, to tranquillise animosities, and to do justice while hearing both sides. His language was always calm, conciliatory, and dignified, never showing irritation at the obstacles he met with.

On each of the occasions which divided Europe and constantly fomented war, Russia had repeated the offer of her mediation; it was never, however, sin-

cerely considered and was always rejected, especially
by France.

The history of the Consulate and the Empire is
the history of Europe up to the end of the reign of
Napoleon. This work, which may be called immense,
inspires an interest which is always sustained by the
ability of the narrative; it is full of details calculated
to interest and instruct the reader, who is lost in admiration before so much practical and profound information
in the various branches of administration and policy.
M. Thiers, in beginning his magnificent work, is
enamoured of his hero, but this does not prevent him
from being afterwards impartial and even severe
towards him. He strives to be always unbiassed, and
generally is so; but I may be permitted to point
out that in some cases he has not done all that is demanded by a quality so important in a historian.

The somewhat disdainful way in which he speaks
of the young men by whom the Emperor of Russia
was surrounded does not seem to me quite just; these
men were not all so very young. Count Kotchoubey,
M. de Novosiltzoff, and the new Ministers, were of an
age sufficient to protect them against such an epithet.
In any case the assemblage of these men round the
Emperor had the great merit of withdrawing Russia
from a fatal groove. Disorder and corruption were
succeeded by a regular and orderly régime, and the
Empire could place itself on an equal footing with the
other disciplined countries of Europe. As for foreign
policy, the idea of making Russian ambition serve an
honourable and just object does not seem to me to

deserve the somewhat severe criticism which M. Thiers has applied to it. Napoleon was, I think, greatest during his consulate; a great administrator, great by the means he employed for the restoration of finance in France, great by his victories and his policy, which tended towards peace. But even then he allowed himself to be led into committing acts of useless severity and cruelty. He seems to me less great when I see him seduced by Imperial dignity, occupied with ceremonials, titles, and ancient etiquette, and with a crown on his head. All that looks like vanity diminishes true greatness. But the author of the 'History of the Consulate,' by the complaisant eloquence of his descriptions, proves that this did not lessen his admiration. Yet he perceives that Napoleon, once started on this course, will no longer deviate from it, and will be fatally drawn to the last goal of an unlimited vanity and ambition.

I ask which of these two policies was the more conscientious, the more moral, the wiser? Was it the one which was inspired by the mad longing for universal empire, or the one which took its origin in the dream—if it should be so thought—of peace and justice?

By dint of victories, Napoleon had raised up a new order of things; but its short duration and its total destruction have proved that its first idea was not more practical than other projects of his which M. Thiers calls chimerical dreams. The latter had at least the excuse of noble and ardent aspirations, while the plans of the conqueror were only a result of passion and personal interest carried to the highest point.

M. Thiers was acquainted with the part played by the Abbé Piattoli in the negotiations which were opened at this period. He acknowledges that the Abbé was a man of some merit, but he does not seem to me to have rendered him complete justice.

The Abbé Piattoli was invited to come to Poland by the Princess Lubomirska, my aunt; she charged him with the education of Prince Henry Lubomirski, whom she had adopted. During my first visit to Paris in 1776 and 1777, having entered into relations with Prince Henry, I naturally found myself under the influence of the Abbé Piattoli—an influence which could only produce a very salutary effect. The Abbé, like so many others who bear this title, was a layman. He was a very learned man, had successively devoted himself to various branches of science, and wrote with great facility. He also had a warm heart, and was capable of self-devotion. M. Thiers does not seem quite to understand that people may devote themselves to an idea which has taken possession of their souls, only from a feeling of generosity. This is what happened to the Abbé Piattoli. No sooner was he in a position to understand the condition of Poland and her mode of government, than he conceived the idea of working at her deliverance, and persisted in doing so as long as he could hope that the idea might be realised.

The state of my country, before all the convulsions through which it has passed since, was very different

from what it is now. It was a dead calm after the
storm. The recollections of the Confederation of Bar*
no doubt existed in the nation ; there was an anti-
Russian party, but it was weak, and its efforts were
powerless to produce any resistance to the arbitrary
acts of the Russian Embassy. The most famous
names in the country, those which were pronounced
with the greatest respect, had distinguished themselves during the Confederation of Bar. I wrote a
memorandum on this subject from the dictation of the
Abbé Piattoli. It was sent by a safe hand to my
parents, whose opinions were known to me, to Marshal
Ignatius Potocki, and to General Rzewuski, both of
whom were sons-in-law of the Princess Lubomirska.
It was hoped that this document would exercise a
salutary influence and bring about some practical
results. I recollect having passed a whole night in
copying it, and it was very well received. Piattoli
now became a steadfast adherent of the Poles and
their cause. He continued to occupy himself with
the education of Prince Henry, and accompanied the
Princess Lubomirska to England, Vienna, and Galicia.
When he came to Warsaw during the Great Diet he
was appointed Secretary to King Stanislas, after
the latter, having thrown off the Russian yoke, had
joined the national party. He contributed by his
influence and his councils to maintain the King in the
new course which he had sincerely adopted. Later
on, when this unfortunate sovereign, yielding to the
advice of the Chancellor Chreptowicz, his Foreign

* See note to page 31, vol. I.

Minister, submitted to the fatal decisions of the Confederation of Targowitza, the Abbé Piattoli resigned a post in which he no longer had any hope of doing good.

Piattoli had much imagination, and this afforded him the means of getting out of difficulties, but he always showed remarkable disinterestedness and good sense. After the fall of Poland, he found a refuge in the house of the Duchess of Courland, who had known him at Warsaw. This was at the time when she had returned to claim from the Great Diet her rights over Courland. Her patriotic Polish sentiments were very strong, and she never abandoned them. The affairs of Courland took her to St Petersburg, and Piattoli accompanied her there. We met again with mutual pleasure ; he did not forget our former relations, and sought to renew them, while I was delighted to have the opportunity of using so trustworthy and able an instrument. A mere indication of the chief points of a negotiation or of a political system was sufficient to enable him to develop all its consequences. He generally did this in too much detail, but he readily abridged or modified his statements in accordance with the remarks that were made to him.

M. Thiers had seen the first draft of a statement of this kind made after some conversations we had had together as to our plans and the best means of executing them. To form a judgment on so incomplete a piece of work, written on the spur of the moment, would be more than severe ; it would be unjust, and this no doubt was far from M. Thiers' intention. I certainly was not under any illusion as to the numerous difficulties which would arise, some of which were insurmountable. The possession of Gibraltar by the English was not based on any principle of justice; on the contrary, it was a violation of international law. By giving it up England would have been able to detach Spain from France and bring her over to the general interests of Europe. Count Strogonoff, in proceeding to his post at Madrid, was to pass through London and to touch on this question with all possible reserve and with the consideration due to British susceptibilities. This was, so to say, an endeavour to begin a reform in the policy of the English Cabinet— an endeavour which did not produce any satisfactory results.

The plan was rejected as a whole, but it contained the points which reproduced themselves on every occasion when there was a question of reconstituting the map of Europe. They were repeatedly brought forward either by Germany, the Netherlands, or Italy, and they had occupied Carnot when he was a member of the Directory. It was, in fact, in the nature of things that they should come to the front on various occasions.

The proposals of Russia were of a nature to satisfy France; but the cold reception which they encountered in England, and especially the peremptory refusal to evacuate Malta, gave Russia sufficient reason for withdrawing from the coalition. If this resolution had been firmly adhered to, it would have given the negotiations a different character, and would have produced different results.

The tendency of public opinion in Europe also manifested itself in Russia, and carried along with it the Emperor and his Privy Council. To oppose it would have been regarded as showing an inclination to yield to French promptings. Austria was already arming; she insisted on the adoption of a general plan of military operations with the object of guaranteeing her against the danger of foreign invasion. It was necessary to think of preparing such a plan in case hostilities should become inevitable. This was done at St Petersburg with Austria on one side and England on the other; the latter was to furnish the necessary funds for arming Europe. The negotiations lasted for some time, and presented great difficulties; the exigencies of Austria seemed excessive to the English negotiators. At length, however, by means of reciprocal concessions, an agreement was arrived at. Part of the subsidies was received for Prussia, whom we incessantly spurred on and kept informed of our movements by more and more urgent despatches. I must admit that the improbability of Prussia entering into the concert of the Powers was not what I most regretted. I did not neglect any argument calculated to persuade her, but I foresaw with satisfaction the necessity of disregarding her interests in the event of a refusal, for in that case Poland would have been proclaimed a kingdom under the sceptre of Alexander. He would have been received with enthusiasm, for at that time this was the only possible way of resuscitating Poland, which even France had forgotten. Meanwhile Napoleon, as if he wished to remove all possibility of a peaceful solution, had had himself crowned King of Italy,* without any reserve as to the rights of succession. By seizing the Genoese Republic, threatening Naples, and not leaving any prospect to the House of Savoy, he increased the general reprobation and also deprived Russia of all hope of obtaining the conditions which she had made it a point of honour not to abandon.

The only course now open was to prepare the means for a struggle which seemed inevitable. The great difficulty consisted in arriving at an arrangement by which England should agree to furnish subsidies of the amount demanded by Austria. This was not an easy matter; yet, thanks to our intervention, an agreement was arrived at. £3,000,000 were granted to the Court of Vienna, and a like sum was appropriated for overcoming the hesitations of Prussia. The military part of the arrangement was executed without delay. An army composed of Russian and Swedish troops assembled in the island of Rügen and at Stralsund; the Russian troops were commanded by General Tolstoï. Another Russian army corps, assembled at Corfu, was to set sail for Naples. An army under the orders of General Kutusoff moved towards the Austrian frontier in order to be available to assist General Mack, who was concentrating his forces at Ulm. Finally, General Michelsen advanced towards the Prussian frontier in order to put an end to the uncertainties of the Berlin Cabinet. All these various movements took place in

* On the 26th May, 1805.

accordance with a plan proposed by Austria and discussed between the two Powers. It seemed to meet the exigencies of the situation ; if it failed, it would be through the fault of the Austrians. Should Prussia not consent to join us, we were to go on without her.

The time had come for the Emperor Alexander to approach the theatre of events. But as the hour of action drew near I perceived that his resolutions grew weaker. We started, however, and during our journey M. Alopeus' couriers brought us reports of the anxiety produced in Berlin, both upon the King and his generals, by the Russian advance. Alexander decided to stop at Pulawy, at the house of my parents, to whom he wished to pay a visit.

The plan of forcing a passage through Prussia was not yet abandoned, and the Emperor also persisted in his idea of declaring himself King of Poland. I wrote to Count Razumovsky to prepare the Court of Vienna for this idea. Austria did not show any opposition to it, but she laid down as a condition that the old frontier of Galicia should be maintained.

Lord G. L. Gower, on his return from a trip to England, met us on our journey and informed us that if we had to force a passage through Prussia, England would pay Russia the subsidy originally intended for the King of Prussia. He also said that if Poland were to be restored, England would give her consent.

I left Brzesc so as to arrive at Pulawy four and twenty hours after the Emperor. I found every one in agitation, and making preparations for the Emperor's reception. Major Orlowski was specially charged with the preparations, and entered into communication with the Austrian authorities in the neighbourhood of Pulawy. Besides the Emperor and his suite, we were expecting the arrival of two army corps, those of General Michelson and General Buxhoewden. Prince Poniatowski was warned of the Emperor's plan relative to the restoration of Poland ; he was to place himself at the head of the movement and give it a national character. Immediately after my arrival at Pulawy, Polish agents went to Warsaw to announce the arrival of the Emperor, who was received by my parents on the following day. He spoke to them kind and friendly words, by which they were deeply touched. He seemed glad to find himself in a softer climate, and among people who were sincerely devoted to him. My mother, my sister, and my brother, tried to make the fortnight he passed at Pulawy as agreeable to him as possible.

Meanwhile the Emperor's resolution to force a passage through Prussia had been greatly shaken, and he sent Prince Dolgorouky,* who was glad to undertake a mission which seemed to be fatal to my hopes, to the King of Prussia to ask for an interview. It was just at this time that the Emperor Napoleon, who had not as much consideration as Alexander for circumstances which he regarded as of little importance, forced a passage through a Prussian province which was an obstacle to the execution of his plans.

* ' A young officer, full of presumption and ambition, an enemy of the coterie of clever young men who were governing the Empire. He sought to persuade the Emperor that these young men were betraying Russia in the interest of Poland. (Thiers' History of the Consulate and the Empire, Book xxii.) See also Vol. I of the present work, p. 331.

The King of Prussia, offended at this conduct, gave a free passage to the Russian troops, and Prince Dolgorouky, triumphant, came to ask the Emperor to go to Berlin to come to an arrangement with the King as to the ulterior measures. This resolution for the moment dissipated the hope of a restoration of Poland; but although the project was foiled, it proved to Napoleon that Poland had not ceased to exist, and that it was necessary to occupy himself with her future destiny—a necessity which he seemed to have forgotten since the Treaty of Lunéville and since the Imperial dignity had absorbed all his attention. The Emperor left Pulawy promising to return. We passed through Warsaw without stopping except at Vilanov, whose proprietor offered us a breakfast. Prince Poniatowski was there, with various other persons, who accompanied the Emperor on horseback up to a few leagues from Warsaw. They went back saddened at the disappearance of the first gleam of hope for the country.

In passing through Posen we met my eldest sister, who was returning to Pulawy with her two wards. The Emperor paid her a visit, and was amiable as usual. She afterwards told me that she was struck by the beauty of his features. He was indeed very attractive, and his charm of manner at once won the attachment of all with whom he came in contact.

Alexander was evidently much relieved on learning that the King of Prussia had given his consent to the passage of the Russian army. We arrived at Berlin,*

---

* On the 25th of October.

and our reception was most brilliant. The Queen
used all her fascinations to make the Emperor's stay
at Berlin agreeable to him and to remove the difficulties raised by M. de Haugwitz. Another Minister,
M. de Hardenberg, whose influence increased as
matters began to take their present turn, and who was
moreover supported by the Queen, succeeded in bringing the negotiations to a successful result. The
Treaty of Potsdam was signed on the 3rd of
November 1805. The union of the two princes was
confirmed by an oath of eternal friendship taken on
the tomb of Frederick the Great. A month was
allowed to Prussia for her war preparations, and the
day, even the hour, of the commencement of hostilities
was fixed in case the proposals to be presented by
Haugwitz should not be accepted. Meanwhile, the
Archduke Anthony came with the most disastrous
news as to the progress of Napoleon. The Emperor
and his suite hastily left Berlin to meet the Emperor
Francis, who was proceeding to the army corps commanded by General Kutusoff. The latter, in accordance with the plan sent him from Vienna, had
entered Austrian Silesia through Galicia.

It would be superfluous to recapitulate here the
events which are so admirably described by the author
of the ' History of the Consulate and the Empire.' I
will only cite some facts which could not have come to
M. Thiers' knowledge, and I will add an opinion which
does not in all respects coincide with his. I will not
do this without a certain feeling of regret. M. Thiers
has treated me with an indulgence, I might almost say

with a preference, which has deeply touched me, and I wish here to express my gratitude to him.

From Berlin the Emperor proceeded to Weimar, where he wished to pay his sister a visit. The old Grand-Duke still lived; though of advanced age, he was full of life and strength. He was an excellent horseman, and in former years had ridden the whole distance between Carlsbad and Weimar. He seemed desirous of reviving the memory of his ancestor, who had distinguished himself in the Thirty Years' War.

We were received with marks of true affection, and after making the acquaintance of several illustrious writers who were assembled at the Court of Weimar—such as Goethe, Schelling, Herder, and Wieland—we continued our journey. Alexander was anxious to arrive at Olmütz, where the Emperor Francis was waiting for him. This much tried and threatened prince strove to console his allies by telling them that it was not the first time that such disasters had befallen him.

The few days we passed at Olmütz were employed in coming to an understanding as to the operations we were to undertake. Colonel Weirother, who was to act as chief of the general staff, had already passed some time at Pulawy, and had obtained much influence over Alexander's mind. He was an officer of great bravery and military knowledge, but, like General Mack, he trusted too much in his combinations, which were often complicated, and did not admit that they might be foiled by the skill of the enemy. His presence at Olmütz and that of Dolgorouky, whose

impetuous ardour acted on the Emperor's mind, contributed not a little to reassure and animate him.   Just
at this moment arrived the Count de Cobentzel.*
He spoke some imprudent words as to its being
necessary for sovereigns to place themselves at the
head of armies in times of difficulty.   The Emperor
thought these words were meant as advice, perhaps as
a reproach.   He did not pay any attention to our
remonstrances, and would not believe what we continually repeated to him—that his presence would
prevent General Kutusoff from exercising any real
authority over the movements of the army.   This was
especially to be feared in view of the General's
timorous character and courtier-like habits.

The Emperor accordingly proceeded to the field,
while I was retained a few hours at Olmütz on
business.   When I had got through my work I
started also.   A few leagues from Olmütz I found
the Emperor Francis and his suite breakfasting on
the grass.   He invited me to join them, but I
refused, as I was anxious to see Alexander.   After
proceeding four leagues further, I arrived at Wischau,
which was occupied by Russian troops ; they had just
obtained a slight advantage over a French detachment
which left some prisoners behind in its retreat.   The
Emperor had gone to the front, and there was much
rejoicing at head-quarters.   The question now was
what steps to take in face of the French army.
Napoleon had advanced as far as Brünn, and his outposts were extended on a line parallel to ours.   I

* At that time Vice-Chancellor of the Austrian Empire.

found the Emperor Alexander almost at the outposts, very satisfied at the success obtained at Wischau, and surrounded by young officers.

They were discussing whether a movement should be made to the left so as to bring the army in touch with that of the Archdukes Charles and John, who had repulsed Prince Eugene in Italy, or whether it would be more advantageous to move to the right so as to join the Prussians who were, at a moment previously determined upon, to advance and take part in the operations of the combined armies. The former alternative was adopted, thanks mainly to the influence of Weirother and other Austrian officers.

The best course would have been to abstain from any offensive movement, as such a movement would be likely to expose the army to danger. Time should have been given to the Archdukes to arrive, and it was above all necessary to wait till Prussia should declare herself and move her army, which was eager to fight.

It was not probable that Napoleon would leave Brünn and place himself at a distance from his reserves and his supplies; but even if he had made such a mistake, the Russian army should have declined to accept battle, and should have retired to meet the supports which were coming up. It was here that the Emperor Alexander and his advisers were in fault. They imagined that Napoleon was in a dangerous position, and that he was on the point of retreating. The French outposts had an appearance of hesitation and timidity which nourished these illusions, and reports came at every moment from our outposts announcing an imminent movement of the French army to the rear. Alexander forgot the extreme importance of the moment, and thought only of not allowing so good an opportunity to escape of destroying the French army, and dealing Napoleon a decisive and fatal blow.

During our flank movement we perceived, on the heights which concealed from us the French position, officers who came up one after the other to observe our march. Our movements were carried out in an orderly manner and placed the army in the position it was wished to take up. We were now so situated that we should have had no difficulty in approaching the Archdukes, in case—which did not seem probable—Napoleon should wish to follow us.

On the 1st of December, the day when Count Haugwitz arrived in Napoleon's camp with the ultimatum which, in the event of its rejection, was immediately to be followed by the co-operation of Prussia, the Emperor of Russia had since the morning received letters from Prince Dolgorouky, loading him with praises for having, as the Prince said, increased by his presence and his brilliant valour the courage of his troops.

Everything in the French army seemed to announce a resolution to attempt a retreat. It was therefore decided to advance, in order to take advantage of this disposition of the enemy. Although it was not expected that they would resist, the precaution was taken to fix the line of march of each army corps.

Colonel Weirother was entrusted with this task ; he thoroughly knew the ground, which he had several times gone over and even measured. I did not take part in the military council assembled to carry out this decision, as it was entirely opposed to my opinions. I do not know whether General Kutusoff was admitted to it ; but his advice was certainly not listened to.

The instructions which were to direct the movements of each General did not, I think, reach them till the morning of the 2nd of December. On the evening of the 1st it was cold and foggy, and the Emperor, surrounded by those who were more especially attached to his person, proceeded at a foot pace in the direction where the movements were to begin on the following morning. We met a detachment of Croatian Grenzers ;* they struck up one of their sad national songs. This song, combined with the temperature and the fog, produced a melancholy impression, and some one remarked that the following day was a Monday, a day regarded as unlucky in Russia. As the Emperor was passing over a grassy mound his horse slipped and fell, and he was thrown out of the saddle. Although the accident was not serious, it was regarded by some people as a bad omen.

At daybreak on the following day, about seven o'clock, the Emperor, surrounded by his friends, proceeded to the place which had in the general plan been fixed as the centre of operations. The united armies were composed of the corps of Buxhoewden,

* Soldiers raised in the Croatian province known as 'the Military Frontier.'

the vanguard commanded by Prince Bagration, the Guards corps under Miloradovitch, a reserve force which should have remained under the direct orders of General Kutusoff, and an Austrian corps under the command of Prince John of Liechtenstein, which was to take part in the battle should it come to fighting.

When we had arrived at this point, I looked round in every direction and saw a vast plain. A column of Austrian infantry which seemed to me rather loose in formation came to arrange itself in order of battle. Anxiety was impressed on the faces of the Austrian General, the officers, and even the soldiers. The artillery officers alone did not give way to the general depression, and expressed absolute confidence in the effect of their guns. Our wings did not seem to be in any way secured ; on the right were to be seen the Guards, who, following the plan traced out to them, were to move off to a greater distance, which would render it difficult to render any assistance on that side, while on our left it was impossible.

The outposts had from the early morning attacked the French at various points without gaining any advantage. Suddenly we perceived some French columns advancing rapidly and pushing back the corps opposed to them. When I saw the promptitude' of the French troops, it seemed to me to augur ill for the result of the day; the Emperor also was struck by the rapidity of this movement, which caused a real panic in the Austrian ranks. It is to be observed that there was no cavalry at this important point, which should have been the centre of operations.

A moment later there was an outcry for the Emperor's safety ; everyone turned his horse and galloped off. I did the same as the others, and reached a height from which I could see what was passing on the side of the Russian Guards corps, to which was attached nearly the whole of the cavalry. I saw very distinctly several charges executed in succession by the two lines of the enemy's cavalry, each of which took the offensive in turn, and was then withdrawn, passing some enclosures which seemed to embarrass their movements. These charges, which were frequently repeated, kept me for some time on the hill. A moment later, as I was advancing towards the scene of action on the right, between the Guards corps and the French, I met Prince Schwarzenberg. I urged him to restore order in the detachments near him, and to stop their retrograde movement. He seemed at first inclined to yield to my representations, but directly afterwards he told me he feared to interfere with plans which were already in full execution. Having met almost at the same moment a large battery of Russian artillery, which its commander, utterly disconcerted, was leading in an opposite direction to that of the battle field, 'I forced him to turn back and help the columns which were fighting in front. By a fortunate accident I constantly met the Emperor at the different points which he visited in succession : he often sent me forward to see what was passing, and sometimes I was left completely alone.

It was necessary to prepare for retreat, and the

Emperor proceeded to a point opposite Austerlitz, which was still occupied by the corps of Bagration, now the rear guard of the army. He was met there by his aides-de-camp—General Lieven, General Miloradovitch, and Prince Michael Dolgorouky, the younger brother of Prince Peter and much wiser than he. He had been shot in the thigh, which did not prevent him from remaining on the field. I also saw the unfortunate Weirother, who had wandered from point to point and by bravely exposing his life strove to remedy the evil of which he had been one of the chief causes. He was tired out and in despair, and hastened away without making any attempt to excuse himself. Those of the officers who had been fortunate enough to make some prisoners presented them to the Emperor with many protestations of devotion, constantly repeating that they were ready to shed their blood for the glory and the safety of the Empire.

I do not know what had become of our friends, but none of them were present at this meeting. Being separated by the confusion which was everywhere prevalent, they did not succeed in finding the Emperor, and I think they lost all their baggage. While we were standing round the Emperor, General Miloradovitch apostrophised me in somewhat singular fashion, saying, 'How is it you are so calm?' At the same time he indicated to me by a look the aide-de-camp General Lieven, whose countenance showed great anxiety and profound depression.

It was necessary at once to take measures for

sending orders to Bagration, who was quite alone in face of the victorious columns of Napoleon; for it was to be feared that disorder might also spread into his army corps. General Wintzingerode was directed to take orders to Bagration to retire into Austerlitz and maintain himself there as long as he could without exposing himself to a disaster.

Soon after we heard the cheers of the French soldiers; they announced the arrival of Napoleon in the midst of his troops. It was growing dark; the generals left us to return to their respective posts, and the Emperor, to ensure his safety, was obliged to take the road to Holitsch. Having advanced to see what was passing on our left, I met General Buxhoewden and his columns completely routed. The poor General had lost his hat, and his clothes were in disorder; when he perceived me at a distance he cried, 'They have abandoned me! They have sacrificed me!' He continued his retreat, and I hastened to join the Emperor.

Night came on, and we proceeded at a foot pace on the road that leads to Holitsch. The Emperor was extremely depressed; the violent emotion he had experienced affected his health, and I was the only one to bring him some relief. We thus passed two days and three nights before arriving at Holitsch. As we went through the villages we heard nothing but the confused exclamations of people who seek forgetfulness of their reverses in drink. The inhabitants suffered, and scenes of disorder were everywhere around us. After some hours we arrived at a village somewhat larger than the others, and found a bed-room for the Emperor. We had a little rest, but our horses were kept ready in case of pursuit. Indeed if some French squadrons had been sent after us to complete our defeat, I do not know what would have happened. There were no regiments nor army corps left in the combined armies; there were only disorderly bands of marauders increasing the general desolation of the scene.

I should have liked to bring the two Emperors together so as to ensure the safety of both, but I did not succeed. The Emperor Francis went off in a different direction, but he charged me from time to time to communicate to Alexander some words of consolation. These were always the same, assuring us that he had already experienced similar disasters, and that although the blow fell mainly upon himself, he was far from losing hope. . . .

   *   *   *   *   *   *   *

[The Memoirs of Prince Adam Czartoryski here come to an end. He was dictating them during his last illness, and death interrupted his work; but he left behind him a mass of letters, diaries, and other documents relating to subsequent periods of his career, a selection from which will be found in the following chapters.]

CHAPTER XI

RUSSIA AND PRUSSIA AFTER THE BATTLE OF AUSTERLITZ.

THE battle of Austerlitz was fought on the 2nd of December 1805. On the 26th of that month, Napoleon signed a treaty of peace with Austria at Presburg, and meanwhile Alexander and his Ministers were consulting as to the best means of retrieving the humiliation that had been inflicted on the Russian Court. On the 17th of January, 1806, the following memorandum on the situation was presented by Prince Adam Czartoryski to the Czar :—

'The fate of the European Continent is for the present in the hands of three Powers—Russia, France, and Prussia. The relations which will be established between them—the system of policy which each will follow—the moderation, avidity, energy, or weakness, which will inspire its views and measures—will either bring about the enslavement of the smaller States, or secure to Europe at least a period of calm and tranquillity, if not of permanent independence and happiness.

'As I propose more especially to treat in this memorandum of the political relations of Russia with Prussia, I shall only speak of France in so far as she has an influence on those relations. I will first examine the principal features of the policy of each of the three Powers.

'Russia does not wish to acquire anything for herself, but she is not willing, and she ought not, to lose the place and character which a century of glorious achievements has assigned her. Satisfied with her advantages, her only ambition has been to preserve the weak against the attacks of the strong; her weapons have been appeals to right and justice, and she has only used force when those weapons have proved ineffectual. When the employment of force has also not been successful, the general confidence of mankind has been her reward, or has at least made her forget her temporary reverses.

'Between France and Russia, which, when Europe was in its normal condition, could hardly come in contact with each other, is Prussia: timid by system and by the necessity of economising her resources, she can do nothing alone either against Russia or against France. If these two Powers were equal in influence and in activity, Prussia would be entirely justified in keeping on good terms with both of them. But one is constantly encroaching on its neighbours, while the other seeks only to protect them against such encroachment; and it is therefore both the duty and the interest of Prussia to join Russia in forming a barrier against France. This task devolves upon Prussia as

a first-class State.   Russia, on the other hand, should
not neglect anything that could enable Prussia to play
such a part with success, unless it were evident that
either from necessity or under the influence of
private interests, Prussia would refuse to undertake
the task, in which case Russia would have to seek
other combinations to protect the weaker Powers and
herself against attack. . . .

'It is to be remembered that during the recent
war Russia in vain exhausted all her means of per-
suasion to induce Prussia to take part in it. The
latter Power drew a line of demarcation which im-
peded the operations of the belligerents, and while
affecting to be neutral, was really the ally of France,
receiving as her reward the great advantages she has
derived from the partition of Germany.

' When, after the treaties of Lunéville and Amiens,
Buonaparte began to make in the midst of peace
conquests more important than those which he had
achieved during the war—when by his arbitrary
conduct he violated the rights of nations and the
integrity of neutral States—Prussia was the first to
guarantee him in the possession of the territories he
had seized, to pardon, excuse, and justify his aggressions. . . . When the danger became greater,
and Russia strove to bring about a combination of
the Powers to oppose Buonaparte's rapid progress,
Prussia was invited to take part in it, but she always
declined, at the same time making great professions
of impartiality and of attachment to the Emperor's
person. Our wishes, she said, are for the success of

Russia's plans, but we have adopted a system of rigid neutrality, and moreover we are without resources, and to make preparations would place us in the greatest danger. So determined was the King of Prussia to reject Russia's proposals, that he punished General Zastrow for having communicated them to him. To put further pressure upon Prussia, Russian troops were sent to her frontier; but the only result was that Prussia protested against being thus threatened, and placed her army on a war footing. The Russian troops then withdrew; and this condescension was only followed by new disasters. While the negotiations were going on, the French defeated the Austrians and entered Prussian territory, arriving as far as Olmütz before the Russians could come to the assistance of their allies. This violation of Prussian territory on the part of France seemed at first to change Prussia's attitude towards that Power, but she never became an effective member of the coalition. She imposed the most onerous conditions on her acceptance of the Russian proposals, and although Russia was ready to accept them, the King was evidently unwilling to come to an understanding with us as to a plan of campaign, and his Government conducted the negotiations in such a dilatory manner that no practical result was arrived at.

'Prussia might in this have been influenced by her jealousy of Austria, her rival; but after Austria was beaten by Buonaparte and forced to sue for peace, the conduct of the Berlin Cabinet towards Russia was the same, though the Emperor offered it all the forces at his disposal if it would join him against France.

'The King of Prussia could at that time have brought an army of 299,000 men into the field, as will be seen from the following table :

Prussian troops, not including reserve battalions,			193,000 men
Saxon	„	„	15,000 „
Hessian	„	„	16,000 „
Hesse-Darmstadt troops		„	8,000 „
Brunswick	„	„	3,000 „
English and Hanoverian troops,		„	24,000 „
Russian	„	„	40,000 „

Total of troops under the immediate orders
      of the King of Prussia,   299,000 men

'This enumeration was made by Baron Hardenberg after the battle of Austerlitz.

'Russia acted entirely in the spirit indicated at the beginning of this memorandum. She had a right to hope for a close union and perfect confidence and concert in the resolutions which were to be arrived at by mutual agreement, and expected no other reward for her cordiality.

'But from that moment there was an end of all frank intercourse, and only the appearances of friendship were retained. Prussia made an arrangement with France, not only without consulting Russia, but even without communicating to her the engagements into which she had entered. The Cabinet of Berlin received from Buonaparte the price of its complaisance. Whether through weakness or through fear, the King appears to have agreed to all that his counsellors wished; the only point he bore in mind was that the retreat of the Russians was the probable condition of the acquisition by Prussia of a country belonging to the Emperor of Russia's ally.* Thus Prussia, while reserving to herself up to the last moment the power of employing the forces of the allies, only took advantage of their being in the field to make an arrangement with France for her own benefit and to their detriment. Such conduct, pursued with such uniformity and perseverance, could only be the result of unavowed motives, which often constitute the secret springs of the policy of States and are to be inferred from their geographical position and the nature and degree of their resources.

'The power of Prussia is factitious; created by genius, it can only be sustained by a policy of greed and deception. In constantly adding to her territories she has absorbed into herself heterogeneous elements, and she keeps up an army quite out of proportion to her revenue and her population. To consolidate and extend her resources is the principal object of her policy; every other consideration, except that of fear, is subordinate to it. She consequently seeks her advantage everywhere, and interferes for this purpose in every European question; but knowing her weakness, she always avoids proceeding to extremes. She withdraws directly a question has to be dealt with by the sword, because she has not sufficient means in

* Hanover, then belonging to England, was ceded to Prussia by France by the Treaty of December 15, 1805.

herself to carry on a war. This want of power, combined with the wish to play a part and the necessity of keeping it up, leads Prussian policy into combinations which are essentially opposed to the interests of Europe and to any great or generous views with regard to Russia. The latter Power seeks to protect and strengthen the smaller States, while France successfully pursues her system of aggression and destruction ; and so long as this is the case Prussian policy will take the side of France against Russia. Though Buonaparte's ambition and greed are insatiable, Prussia will firmly believe, perhaps not without reason, that by assisting France she can only gain, while by opposing her she will be destroyed like her neighbours.

' In striving to strengthen her dominions, Prussia takes care to extend her influence as much as possible. She wishes not only to be paramount in the north of Germany, but also to remove all foreign influence from it, especially that of Russia ; and with this object she seeks every means of preventing and paralysing all developments of Russian influence in that quarter. Moreover, she is and always will be the rival of Austria in German affairs, while our policy is to support Austria in Germany in order that she should not interfere with us in Turkey. France, on the other hand, will always be the natural ally of Prussia against Austria. Nor has Prussia so much to fear from France as from Russia. We wish to be masters of the Niemen and the Vistula ; these rivers are so necessary to our trade, and so close at hand, that our attention has frequently been directed to them, and they must become ours sooner or later.   Prussia knows and fears this ; she will always endeavour to diminish our weight and our resources in Europe, in whatever direction we may attempt to extend them, but especially if we turn our eyes to Austrian Galicia, for if we possessed that country we could at any moment send troops into the very centre of the Prussian Monarchy.   Prussia is the open rival of Austria, and does not conceal her jealousy and distrust of her ; but in secret she dislikes us perhaps even more, now that crippled Austria inspires her with less fear. . . .   All these reflections lead to the conclusion that not only will Prussia never be the sincere ally of Russia, but that she will rather secretly incline to France, and ultimately perhaps revive the old coalition between France, Prussia, and Turkey.

'But though there is so little hope of sincerely attaching Prussia to Russia, it is none the less true that the union of these Powers can alone at this moment save Europe, and that nothing could be more injurious than an intimate *rapprochement* between Buonaparte and Prussia.   The more the inclination of the latter to join France becomes manifest, the more should we strive to prevent such a tendency from becoming too predominant at Berlin, and take advantage, with the support of a powerful party in the Ministry and at Court, of every circumstance favourable to our interests in order to diminish its influence. . . . At the same time we should be most careful not to be led into taking mistaken steps.   It would be most useful to bind Prussia by some precise engagement, and every means should be taken to attain this object. Berlin should become one of the chief pivots of Russian policy; our agents there should make themselves acquainted with every detail of the views and relations of the Prussian Court, so as to be capable of deciding on every proposal that might be made to them. In no case should they be authorised to confirm or guarantee the advantages Prussia might gain from her complaisance to France; on the contrary, they should be instructed to show Prussia that Russia cannot tolerate a system entirely opposed to her views, and inspire her with a fear of Russia almost, if not quite, as great as that of Buonaparte. . . . They should endeavour to point out to the King of Prussia that his interests coincide with those of Europe generally, and withdraw him from the influence of the members of his Cabinet, who are devoted to France either by principle or through corruption.

'The chief object of our negotiations at Berlin should be to make Prussia enter into defensive engagements, which would not be limited to the north of Germany, and which would especially include the preservation of the Ottoman Empire. These should, if possible, be accompanied by a guarantee of the order of things which would be established by a treaty of peace between France and Russia, and also between France and England, specifying among the territories to be guaranteed those of Turkey. A plan of military action should also be drawn up between

Russia and Prussia, for the eventuality of France attacking one of the guaranteed territories. . .

'It is possible that Napoleon's violent character may produce a renewal of the war in North Germany; in that case we should support Prussia with all the forces at our command, and we should at once give her an assurance to that effect. If the King sincerely wishes to join Russia and act as a buffer to Europe, facts will soon prove his sincerity. . . . But I must repeat to your Majesty that it is necessary to guard against too many concessions to the Berlin Court. The past has proved that Russia has nothing to gain from them. . . By trusting Prussia and blindly following her suggestions, Russia will run a great risk of disaster. Such suggestions can only be in the Prussian interest, which is nearly always opposed to that of Russia and of Europe; and by yielding to them we can only be led into taking steps which would deprive us of the respect of the world, and of the attachment and confidence of our true allies. Meanwhile Prussia would continue to enlarge her territory, and become a formidable Power, even to Russia herself. . . A war with Prussia is an event which circumstances must bring about sooner or later, and we should at once make our preparations for waging it with success.'

CHAPTER XII

1806

DISAGREEMENT BETWEEN THE CZAR AND PRINCE CZARTORYSKI AS TO
THE POLICY OF RUSSIA BEFORE THE BATTLE OF AUSTERLITZ.—
NEGOTIATIONS WITH ENGLAND.—THE LATTER PROPOSES TO GIVE
HOLLAND TO PRUSSIA AS AN EQUIVALENT FOR HANOVER.

It will have been seen from the last part of Prince Czartoryski's Memoirs (chapter x) that the Emperor Alexander, who since the Memel interview* had always been strongly inclined to an alliance with Prussia, notwithstanding her treacherous policy, was on this and other points at issue with his Foreign Minister during the momentous year which closed with the battle of Austerlitz. Prince Czartoryski, in a private letter and memorandum addressed by him to the Emperor in April 1806, gives the following details on this subject and on the negotiations with England during that period :—

' Your Imperial Majesty will appreciate my motives in attaching to the enclosed memorandum on the policy of your Cabinet. . . . some remarks

See Vol. I, pages 281 and 282.

addressed solely to yourself, and stating the whole truth without concealment or palliation. Sovereigns are so inseparable from the States which they govern that in speaking of their vicissitudes it is impossible to avoid dwelling on their personal conduct; which indeed often determines the success or the decline of Empires.

'Few reproaches have been made to the Russian Cabinet with so little justice as that of having allowed itself to be carried away by exaggerated ideas of self-sacrifice to the general good of Europe. Those who made such a reproach forgot that not only the reputation but the safety of Russia depended on the general good; and they were not aware of all the conversations with your Majesty during the past two years, in which ideas were repeatedly brought forward as to the combinations which might be advantageous to Russia—such as the possession of Moldavia and Wallachia, the Vistula as a frontier, the reunion of the Slavonic and Greek populations, etc.—as acquisitions of territory and securities for her trade. These ideas were always rejected by your Majesty, and it would consequently have been difficult to entertain the plan of a partition of Europe with Napoleon.

'But events were showing that the need of extending our influence and our territory might become more and more urgent either in order to maintain Russia in the place she ought to occupy or to establish a real and durable peace. It seemed, therefore, that the only course to be followed was one based on the purest and most disinterested sentiments. But I perceived, perhaps too late and with great pain, that your Majesty had no deep or decided conviction as to the subjects which engaged the attention of our Cabinet. The consequence was that after a plan of action of which you had approved had been partly carried out, you continually changed your mind, and we were obliged to reconsider the whole question as if no agreement had been arrived at.

' When the news of the death of the Duc d'Enghien came to St Petersburg, your Majesty will remember that though the despatches I prepared on the subject were very strongly worded, they were not intended to be made public, and that it was your Majesty alone that gave the impulse for further action. This energy gave me hope, for it seemed likely to develop in your Majesty that decided conviction which until then had not sufficiently shown itself in your actions.* War now seemed to me inevitable, but you thought otherwise. You thought up to the last moment that Austria would not dare to fight, and that this would serve as an excuse to Russia also to hold aloof. The consequence was that though the steps taken by the Cabinet by the express orders of your Majesty pointed directly to war, no preparations for war could be made in the interior of the Empire. . . . Your Majesty did

---

* ' Prince Czartoryski was the principal author of the system of European arbitration which had led Russia to take up arms against France. This system, which was used by Russian statesmen as a mask for their national ambition, was in Prince Czartoryski prompted by a sincere and frankly conceived idea. . . . He addressed to the young Emperor, formerly his friend, and now again becoming his master, noble and respectful remonstrances which would do honour to a Minister in a free country, and are far more creditable in a country where resistance to the sovereign is an act of rare devotion and remains unknown to the public.' (Thiers' History of the Consulate and the Empire, Book xxiv.)

not think proper to order a sufficient levy of recruits, though the necessity of such a measure was repeatedly pointed out to you. This indecision was most injurious and dangerous, as was strikingly shown in our conduct towards Prussia. The proposal to send Russian troops to act for Austria and against Prussia had been entirely approved by the most eminent personages in Europe. It was this that decided the Archduke Charles to declare himself for war, as he considered it a proof that Russia wished to make war in earnest. Pitt and Fox also agreed. " If hostilities take place with Prussia," said the latter, " they should be pushed on vigorously and without regard to other considerations."

'It is true that your Majesty afterwards told us that you had all along intended to regulate your conduct by the great probability that the King of Prussia would finally decide to join us. But who could answer for this? The disastrous result of our operations is to be attributed to the Memel interview, which I look upon as one of the most unfortunate events that have ever happened for the interests of Russia, both through its immediate consequences and those which have followed upon it since and will in the future. The intimate friendship established at that interview, after a few days' acquaintance, between your Majesty and the King caused you to look upon Prussia not as a political State, but as an individual dear to you. This personal connection with the sovereign of a State whose interests are mostly opposed to those of Russia continually hampered the action of our Cabinet, and finally prevented the adoption of vigorous and decisive measures at the beginning of the campaign. In my opinion the suspension of the order to march the Russian troops into Prussia, and your Majesty's departure for the army, were the chief causes of all the misfortunes that have happened to us. I strove in vain to represent to you all the inconveniences which would result from your presence with the army, and my forebodings have unfortunately all been realised. Your presence transferred the responsibility of the generals to yourself, and you had neither the experience nor the knowledge necessary for taking the command. Meanwhile the order to send the troops into Prussia still remained suspended; yet each day of delay was a day lost for Russia and Europe, and gained for Buonaparte. He advanced and we remained stationary.

'Moreover, since your Majesty's departure from Pulawy your opinions and sentiments underwent a notorious change which necessarily exercised great influence on our operations. You sent away those in whom you had previously trusted, and although I accompanied you in your journey to Berlin, you rejected all my proposals and showed by your statements that your views and system of action had entirely changed. . . . The inference which was drawn from all this at Berlin was that your Majesty's policy was different from that of your Cabinet; this naturally encouraged the duplicity of the Prussian Government, and influenced the stipulations of the

unfortunate Treaty of Potsdam,* at the foot of which
I shall always regret that circumstances compelled me
to place my name.

' If you had listened to the advice we were constantly giving you, at first not to go to the army,
and afterwards not to remain with it, but to ask the
King of Prussia for an interview in order to move
him to decisive action, the battle of Austerlitz would
not have been fought and lost, or, if lost, would not
have had the results which followed upon it.† General
Kutusoff, left to himself, would have avoided a battle
until the Prussians should have joined his army. This
would have obviously been the right course. Buonaparte's interest was not to lose time ; ours was to gain
it. He had every reason to risk a decisive battle and
we to avoid one. Your Majesty will recollect that I
repeatedly spoke to you in this sense, advising that
the enemy should be harassed by partial combats and
that the bulk of our army should march into Hungary
to effect a junction with the Archduke. And if your
Majesty had not been on the battlefield, you would have
been able to issue your orders calmly and without
precipitation. How could you do this in the midst of
the confusion at Holitsch, where you were surrounded
by people who loudly accused the Austrians of treachery and declared that the Russian army was absolutely
incapable of fighting any longer ?

* Signed on the 3rd of November 1805.

† 'The young Emperor refused to listen to any more advice, as he thought
himself more clever than his advisers. Prince Adam Czartoryski—honest, grave,
ardent under a cold exterior, who had become the inconvenient censor of the weakness and instability of his master—maintained an opinion which must have
completely alienated him. He thought the Emperor's place was not with the army.'
Thiers' History of the Consulate and the Empire, Book xxxiii.

'In the midst of this agitation and clamour it was impossible to say anything in favour of Austria or of the interests of Europe. People declared that your Majesty had done enough for others and that you must now think of yourself—as if your glory and your safety had nothing in common with the fall of Austria and your other allies. You thought fit to reply to me in this sense when I ventured to speak in favour of the King of Naples; and you told the Emperor Francis that he could not reckon any longer upon your army. I was so deeply penetrated, however, with the great evil of such a complete abandonment of the cause which we had embraced that I took it upon myself to write to Berlin in another sense without being authorised to do so by your Majesty. But this step could have no result, since your Majesty thought it necessary to say to the Prussian Minister here that you would leave Prussia at liberty to come to an arrangement with France. . . .'

In the memorandum which accompanied Prince Czartoryski's letter he remarks, referring to the preliminaries of the battle of Austerlitz :—

'Prussia was a chief element in the plan that was about to be executed. It had been decided that she was to be brought into the coalition at any cost, and it was in every respect the interest of Russia especially to do so, as in sending a considerable force beyond her frontiers she could not leave behind her so suspicious a neighbour as Prussia. If the Court of Berlin had yielded, the success of the plan as a whole could not have been doubtful. If it had resisted, and our armies had been sent forward on the day agreed upon, they would have found the Prussians on a peace footing, and in no way prepared to receive us. . . . Our true policy was to make war upon Prussia : that would have been the safest, perhaps the only, means of success in our great undertaking. . . . The operation against Prussia was put off till the 16th of September, by which date it was calculated that Kutusoff's army would cover Bohemia and threaten Silesia, while the other armies entered southern and ducal Prussia ; and by that date the Prussians had had time to make preparations. But even then the Court of Berlin admitted that its troops would evacuate the districts up to the Vistula. We might at least have taken possession of those districts, and if we had gone further, our success would not have been doubtful. The Prussians may be good soldiers, but they are easier for the Russians to beat than the French. Moreover, we should have fought them in a country entirely devoted to our interests. The enthusiasm among the Poles was general ; all Poland was ready to rise *en masse,* and asked that the sovereign of Russia should add to his titles that of King of Poland. None of our allies could have objected to such a course, as they had all sanctioned the plan of marching into Prussia. England, who until then had, in accordance with her old principles of policy, been jealous of our exercising a preponderant influence over Prussia, now declared war upon her, destroying her trade in the North Sea while we

did the same in the Baltic; she even went so far as
to give us, for the purpose of acting against Prussia,
all the subsidies she had offered to that Power for
action against France. . . .

We lost all these advantages by our vacillation;
our armies stopped on the Prussian frontier, and the
violation of Prussian territory by the French * made
Prussia more disposed to join the coalition. The
original plan of invading her territory was now abandoned, and your Majesty's Ministry did their best to
bring her over by conciliation, as she was no longer to
be made to yield by terror. . . Russia has been re-
proached for using her good offices in London to
negotiate the cession of Hanover to Prussia.† But
as to this point, we may appeal to people who were
then at Berlin and were aware of the negotiations, as
difficult as they were disagreeable, which led to the
Treaty of Potsdam. . . . Anyhow, we succeeded in
making England understand the urgent motives which
had led us to yield to the wishes of the Berlin Cabinet.
She agreed not to break off the negotiations, to sign
the treaty for the subsidies, and to assist in obtaining
some other acquisition for Prussia—even to assure
her the possession of Holland. Russia reserved to
herself equivalent acquisitions. . . .

Nothing was yet lost; General Mack's defeat had
even established the preponderance of Russia over
Austria to such a degree that people looked upon
your Majesty as the future saviour of the Austrian

* See page 99.
† See Chapter IX.

Monarchy. . . But the next four weeks were wasted in mutual complaints, and ended in the battle of Austerlitz, in a feeling of extreme exasperation between Russia and Austria, in the retreat of the Russian army from Moravia, and in the abandonment of Europe to her fate.

CHAPTER XIII

1806

SHORTLY after the appointment of Mr Fox as Foreign Minister in the administration of 'all the talents,' formed by Lord Grenville after the death of Pitt, the following correspondence took place between Mr Fox and Prince Czartoryski :—

From Mr Fox

DOWNING STREET,
17th March 1806.

Relying on the confidence with which your Excellency was so good as to honour me last year as a private individual, I think I have almost a right to ask for a continuance of your kindness in the situation in which I am now placed. I would not, however, have done this, notwithstanding all the value I attach to the honour of your friendship, if I did not entirely adhere to the opinion I expressed to M. de Novosiltzoff that a full and reciprocal confidence between the two Courts is absolutely necessary both for

the good of them both and for that of the whole of
Europe. I was unfortunately not able to approve the
plan of last year, and I did not conceal my opinion on
the subject. Would to God that the last words I said
to M. de Novosiltzoff in the presence of the Prince of
Wales—whatever you do, take your time, piano, piano
—had made more impression! I beg you not to
think, Monsieur le Prince, that I remind your Excellency of all this in order to boast of my foresight. If
I look back on the past, it is only to obtain more
instruction as to the future. A proposal of peace
such as I wished to be made when I had the honour
of writing to your Excellency a year ago* would perhaps be out of place in present circumstances. Russia
has taken too prominent a part in the war now to
assume the office of a mediator. But since Buonaparte's last speech to his legislative assembly there are
many people who think he will send us some proposal
at least tending to a negotiation.† Might I venture
to ask your Excellency what would be your opinion as
to the course to be adopted in such a case? The first
answer would necessarily depend on the nature of the
overtures to be made to us. They might be made in
such a way that it would be necessary to reject them
without discussion; but let us suppose they will be too
plausible for us to do this. In that case it seems to
me that it would be well in the first instance to accept
the overtures, at the same time declaring that it will

---

* This letter cannot be traced in the Czartoryski Archives.

† The letters which passed between Talleyrand and Fox on this subject were laid
before Parliament in 1806. They are published in Lord Russell's *Memorials and Correspondence of Charles James Fox.*

be necessary that his Majesty the Emperor of Russia should take part both in the treaty and in the negotiations which may lead to it. I have not at this moment any reason to believe that any overtures whatever will be made to us: I speak only in accordance with the ideas of those who attach more weight to Buonaparte's language than it seems to me to deserve. Your Excellency will see that I speak to you frankly. If you will equally show confidence in me I will not misuse it.

Let us now consider the contingency—unfortunately the most probable one—that the war will continue even without matters coming to a negotiation. I must begin by saying to your Excellency plainly that I have in no way altered my old opinions, that offensive alliances are not at all to my taste, and that as they exist, our best course would now be to give them as far as possible a defensive character. A good opportunity now seems to present itself for attaining this object, and at the same time showing that we are resolved to oppose injustice and aggression. The King of Prussia has seized the electorate of Hanover ; his pretext is that he wishes to protect it by his troops, and under this pretext he deprives the King and the Regency even of the civil government of the country. He asserts that his occupation of the electorate is only to last until a peace shall settle its fate, but he has not distinctly stated that he will then restore it to the Elector. We have made representations to him on this subject, and Lord G. L. Gower has been instructed to communicate them to your Excellency. If the powerful support of your Court could induce Prussia to act nobly on this occasion, infinite good would be the result. In the first place, we would show Europe that the King of England still preserves his influence in Continental affairs, which is a great point, and further, that he employs this influence not to attack others, but to defend himself.

The King of Prussia has given up Anspach and Bayreuth; he should not be helped nor even encouraged to retake them, but he should be made to abandon the odious system of compensating himself with the property of others. In the event of Buonaparte retaliating on Prussia for such an honourable policy by making war upon her—which I do not think probable—she will have to be defended with all the forces at our disposal. Your Excellency has much more means than I have of conjecturing what the conduct of Austria would be under such circumstances. I am inclined to think that she would at least do no harm, if she is not able to do any good. It might perhaps be said that even with your support we would not be able to persuade his Prussian Majesty to abandon an object which it is reported that he has long coveted. But we would at least have shown him that he can never hope to have quiet and legitimate possession of it; and so far as our interests are concerned, we would remain in precisely the same situation as that which we now occupy. Moreover, I think one should in any case avoid the appearance of wishing to lay down the law to the King of

Prussia, or of provoking him to war against France. Let him temporise as much as he thinks proper; I would be the first to advise him to do so; but let him not attack any other State, whether strong or weak.

As to Austria, I am very glad to hear that public opinion thinks the friendship which has so long existed between her and Russia has not been altered as much as people thought some months ago. A friendly understanding, and if possible a perfect harmony, between all the countries which are not dependent upon France is to be desired more than ever. Even with regard to those which are more or less under her subjection it would I think be necessary to avoid every kind of offence and not to show any feeling of revenge. Opportunities might, for what we know, arise in the course of time which two Cabinets united as ours are, might by judicious conduct employ to advantage. The existing state of affairs, if we look to the present or the future, is truly disheartening. It cannot be remedied by a *coup de main*: a wise and consistent course of conduct can alone enable us to do so. If we cannot reduce the enormous power of France, it will always be something to stop its progress.

I have thus entirely opened my heart to you, mon Prince. Let us seek to work together for the good of our respective countries and for that of all Europe. The more the two Courts and their Ministers understand each other, the better for our common cause.

Your Excellency will of course understand that this letter, like the others which have passed between us,

is of a confidential nature, to be placed under the eyes
of the Emperor or not, as your Excellency may think
proper.   Neither Lord G. L. Gower, in whom I have
the greatest confidence, nor anyone else, knows the
contents of it.

Accept, Monsieur le Prince, etc.

(Signed)   C. J. Fox.

Answer from Prince Czartoryski.

Your Excellency has anticipated me by the letter
you were good enough to write to me on the 17th of
March, as I was about to address one to you to
express my joy and my congratulations on your
entrance into the Ministry, and to ask for a continuance of your confidence. I now hasten to convey to
you the expression of these feelings, and to add my
sincere thanks for the frank and friendly manner in
which your Excellency has expressed yourself in
your letter. Pray believe me when I say that
personally I attach very great value to the friendly
and confidential relations which you are good enough
to encourage me to maintain, and that no one can be
more convinced than myself of the reciprocal advantage, I may say the necessity, of an intimate union
and an invariable concert between our two Courts.   It
is to England and to Russia that the remains of
Europe will cling, and their only hope of salvation is
in the union of these Powers.

I know too well your Excellency's views not to
be certain that you have seen with much pain that

your forebodings as to the undertaking of the allied Courts should have been so completely realised.   But you are at the same time too just not to agree that there was not after all any positive reason for supposing that our efforts would have such disastrous results. It was not the plan that was in fault.   Its failure was due to circumstances which the Russian Cabinet had not the means either to foresee or to prevent.

But it is useless to look back upon the past except for drawing useful lessons from it ; what should occupy us is the present and the future.   I will respond to your Excellency's frankness by also opening to you my mind on the subject.   The communications which Count Vorontzoff lately made to you have partly done this already.   We have explained our views with the greatest confidence and detail, and the British Government must have been satisfied with the principles which we developed. Several of the matters referred to in the first despatch rather required to be discussed confidentially and in much detail than to be treated officially, and as to this the two Cabinets will have to come to an understanding hereafter.   The despatches which Count Strogonoff* will receive to-day will furnish him with new and very ample communications for your Excellency ; you will see that we do not wish to conceal from you any of our thoughts, and that our invariable principle is to do everything in common and in concert with England.

The aspect of affairs is indeed disheartening, and

* The special envoy sent to London to negotiate with Mr Fox.

I entirely agree with your Excellency that the defensive principle should preferably be adopted in the transactions and the conduct of the European States. It is the principle held by the Powers which are opposed to the subversion of Europe, and never was there a more offensive policy than that of Buonaparte. Yet although a union for purposes of defence is always in principle the most useful one, there can be no doubt that when the time for action arrives it is indispensable, or at least more advantageous, to take the offensive if possible.

It may be that the circumstances of the moment and the nature of the elements with which it would be necessary to act are such that although a different policy would be more suitable, one is forced for the present to maintain a passive attitude on the Continent, and to avoid provoking new difficulties which might give rise to new disasters. If such be the case —as your Excellency seems inclined to suppose— peace with France is only the more necessary, and it becomes the only course open to us. I confess that even if it were only a patched-up peace to last but a short time—if it were only a truce which would give us but a precarious and temporary security—it would still be better for the Continent than the present state of things, and it becomes clear that circumstances oblige us to see the danger increase and come nearer to us without our being able to prevent or meet it. On our side it may be said that peace is a necessity to us ; we can neither reach the enemy nor do him any serious harm ; it would therefore be better, as it seems to me, to bind him by some arrangement so as to arrest his advance if only for a short time, and make him believe and declare that he is also at peace with us.   I must here remark that an attack on the part of the Turks, if we leave them the choice of the time when it is to be made, might also be inconvenient. It would begin on our frontiers, and at a time when the Turks would have completed their armaments, and the French been enabled to prepare all the means they could employ in favour of Turkey and against us.   These various considerations lead me strongly to desire that the overtures which have been made by Your Excellency to M. de Talleyrand should produce some satisfactory result.   Russia would certainly have awaited the consequence of these overtures, if the affair of Cattaro* and the dangers which threaten Austria had not obliged us to hasten a direct discussion with Buonaparte, as the only means of escape from the embarrassing position in which we find ourselves, between the necessity of giving up to the French an important post—the stepping-stone, so to say, from which they could easily proceed to the execution of their designs on Turkey—and the fear of exposing unhappy Austria to the resentment of Buonaparte and to complete ruin.

The explanations which I am giving here to Lord G. L. Gower on this subject, and those which Count Strogonoff is instructed to develop to your Excellency, will, I trust, be of a kind to satisfy you,

---

* After the battle of Austerlitz the Russian troops occupied Cattaro, in order to prevent its being taken by the French, to whom it had been ceded by the Treaty of Presburg.

and will prove to you that the fundamental maxim of our policy continues to be not to separate ourselves from England and to pay the greatest attention to her wishes and her advice.

It is not impossible that Buonaparte, after convincing himself that he cannot succeed in bringing either of us to an isolated negotiation, will at length agree to treat with the two Powers in concert. This would be a great point gained. Moreover, whatever might be the necessity and urgency for Europe of peace with France, it would not I think be inopportune to come to an early understanding as to the measures to be taken, if the continuation of the war should become inevitable; for it must be anticipated that the more Buonaparte will perceive the great need of peace on the Continent, the less inclined will he be to accept reasonable conditions. Any overtures you may eventually make in this respect would be eagerly received here, and would be treated with the greatest possible consideration.

As regards Prussia, I do not lose the hope that the just and energetic conduct * of the British Cabinet with regard to her, will have a salutary influence on her policy. The more considerable the losses of Prussian trade will be, the more the general outcry of the Prussian people, who already lift up their voices against the action of their Government, will become threatening, the less will Prussia be in a position to

* *i.e.*, the blockade of the Prussian seaports, and the capture by the British fleet of Prussian merchant ships, after Prussia had seized Hanover and closed the Elbe and the Weser to British trade.

continue her present policy. She will have to abandon it in some way or other. Our measures with regard to her are fundamentally in accordance with your wishes; but our relations with her, and our situation generally, are not the same. We flatter ourselves that we may yet be able to withdraw Prussia from the shameful dependence to which she has submitted herself; the present moment of crisis, and the extreme embarrassment in which she is plunged, are perhaps even propitious for such an endeavour. This is the sole reason why we do not think we ought entirely to reject the explanations and protests which she is incessantly sending us, and we wish meanwhile to stop her at least in the design which she might have formed—if she had had nothing to care for or to expect from us—of abandoning herself more and more entirely to the will of Buonaparte and the execution of the plans he is meditating.

I do not know if your Excellency will agree to all the opinions I have expressed, but I flatter myself that you will at any rate be satisfied with my extreme frankness and unreserved confidence.

I have thought it right to show the Emperor the letter you have done me the honour of writing to me. His Imperial Majesty has expressly charged me to express to you, sir, how charmed he is at the wisdom and thoughtfulness of your views. He desires that his Cabinet should remain in intimate harmony with that of his Britannic Majesty, and your entrance into the Ministry has caused him much satisfaction. This disposition on his Majesty's part can only add to all the motives of State which sincerely bind the Court of St Petersburg to that of London.

Count Strogonoff will have the honour of handing this letter to your Excellency, and I take the opportunity of particularly recommending him to you. I beg you to show him entire confidence (which you may do without the slightest fear); he will deserve it by the frankness and cordiality with which he will make his communications to you, and I flatter myself that at my request your Excellency will not on your part fail to encourage him in this conduct by acting towards him in a similar manner.

Your Excellency will not take it ill that I have shown your letter to Lord G. L. Gower. I did not think any harm could result from my doing so, and as he handed me your letter himself I could hardly have done otherwise in view of the intimate friendship which exists between us. It is with pain that we hear he wished to leave his post; I should infinitely regret it, and I will confess to your Excellency that I would much desire that Lord G. L. Gower should remain with us for some time longer, especially during the difficult circumstances of the present juncture. Your Excellency will pardon me if in this wholly private and confidential letter I have thought I might be permitted not to conceal this wish from you.

If M. d'Oubril should go so far as Paris, it is very possible that circumstances may cause him to go on to London, perhaps with some mission from the French Government. Should this be the case, I recommend him beforehand to your Excellency's kindness Lord G. L. Gower will have given you good accounts of the selection of M. d'Oubril ; he is a safe man, on whose prudence and principles the two allied Courts may wholly rely.* This leads me to request your Excellency to speak of him in the same terms to the English Plenipotentiary who may proceed to France, and to instruct him to have confidence in him.

P.S. of the 13*th of May* 1806. My letter to your Excellency was written long ago, but the despatch of the courier who was to take it was put off from day to day. In the meantime we have received despatches from London which inform us of the issue of your *pourparlers* with France. I open my letter to add this postscript, as I cannot avoid expressing to your Excellency how satisfied and enchanted we are here at the wisdom, the loyalty, and the energy which your Government has shown on this occasion. The good faith and the constant interest of which it gives proof to Russia demand entire reciprocity on her part. I will not here multiply assurances and protestations on this subject, for between us they seem to me entirely superfluous. Moreover, the communications which you will receive, several of which are much in arrear, can only refer to the state of affairs anterior to the present moment. I am glad to look upon the present relations between the two countries (and surely your Excellency will agree with me on this point) as those of two parts of the same body. There is no difference

---

* This estimate of M. d'Oubril's character was unfortunately not borne out by his subsequent conduct in Paris (see Count Vorontzoff's letter of the 7 19 October, 1806, page 163).

in our objects, in our principles, in our intentions ; and
our discussions can only turn on the most proper mode
and the most suitable means of realising our common
wishes according to circumstances.—Receive, etc.

(Signed)   A. CZARTORYSKI.

Count Strogonoff, the Russian special envoy,
arrived in London in March 1806, and Count Vorontzoff, the Russian Ambassador, in a letter to Prince
Adam Czartoryski dated the $\frac{10}{31}$ March, thus describes
his impressions of the interview which took place
between the two Russian diplomatists and Mr Fox :—

'I will add to my official reports, for your personal
information alone, that Fox wishes for peace at any
price, and that he would abandon all his allies to obtain it, but that he will not succeed, as the nation is
too strongly opposed to a shameful peace, and Buonaparte, flushed with victory, will not offer him any
other, especially as he knows Fox's immoderate desire
to end the war. Lord Grenville and the British
nation will oppose him, for they wish for a peace that
shall be honourable and arranged in concert with us.
Moreover, the great majority of people here are convinced that England will run less risk in continuing a
purely naval war than in making peace with the
Corsican, in whose good faith nobody trusts. The
Cabinet would not, however, be overthrown if it made
peace together with us.

You will see from my official despatches that Fox
has the strange idea of our troops quitting Sicily in
order to leave the English alone to defend it. He

could not support this proposal by any valid reason, and this confirmed my belief that with all his intellectual vivacity, which in his parliamentary speeches even rises to genius, he is not a man of judgment, and still less a statesman; that he is merely a party leader of great astuteness and a master of intrigue, and that he will never shine in the Ministry as he did in the Opposition.'

Prince Adam Czartoryski gives further particulars as to Mr Fox's Foreign Policy at this period in the following extracts from a memorandum presented by him to the Emperor in his capacity of Minister of Foreign Affairs :—

Memorandum of the 30th May 1806.

In the communications made to us by the Cabinet of St James's we are urged to bring the important questions pending between us to a definitive issue.

The British Ministry at one time thought there might be a means of opening negotiations with France. It took part in a correspondence started by Buonaparte himself; but the only preliminary point on which the Cabinet of London was bound to insist —that of not arriving at any definite conclusion except in concert with Russia—has just been rejected by the French Government. England now considers the negotiation broken off; she has arrived at the conclusion that Buonaparte evidently does not wish for peace, and that therefore she must make up her mind to war. At the same time England has been grievously insulted by the inexcusable conduct of

Prussia towards her, who has violated on this occasion all the obligations that were imposed upon her by the dictates of ordinary morality and by international law. The British Government has been obliged to take the most energetic measures against Prussia, and it must be admitted that it neither could nor should have done otherwise in reply to so direct an attack upon the interests and dignity of the King of England and so manifest a violation of international law.*

Strong in her rights against France and Prussia, and in her consciousness of the frank and loyal policy she has pursued towards Russia, England thinks herself entitled to regard us as an ally on whose co-operation she can reckon with perfect security. She rightly thinks that very energetic measures can alone bring about such a peace as is to be desired; her Government shows the necessity of striking a great blow on the Continent in order to restore the balance of Europe, and proposes that, as a matter both of convenience and of justice, this blow should be directed against Prussia.

To secure the success of such an undertaking, the British Government thinks it will be necessary to follow Buonaparte's plan, namely, the assemblage of considerable forces on a single point, so as to obtain a decisive result.

England recognises the inconveniences of our position between Turkey and Prussia, and asks what is the probability of our not being at war with those two Powers directly she attacks one of them.   The

* The annexation by Prussia of Hanover.

British Cabinet thinks we might direct our efforts against either, and, in the event of our doing so, hopes we will push our conquests as far as possible, and offers us assistance and subsidies. But it would prefer that we should attack Prussia, so that she might suffer exemplary punishment for the duplicity she has shown during recent events. The example of a sovereign increasing his power and territory by a policy of servility towards France would encourage the other Powers and dissipate the hope of any States besides Russia and England uniting against Buonaparte.

At the same time the British Government still sincerely desires peace, and it would prefer a policy of conciliation to one of war, if by such means the desired object could be attained. Mr Fox even suggests a separate negotiation with France, Russia and England, each negotiating on its own account, but first coming to an understanding as to the essential conditions which are to be sought or rejected. Foreseeing that Russia, before stating any opinion on this suggestion, would desire to reconcile Prussia with England, Mr Fox states the conditions on which such a reconciliation might be brought about, namely, a raising of the blockade and a satisfactory arrangement as to Hanover.

Let us now consider our present position and the probable consequences of Russia deciding to maintain the passive position, midway between peace and war, in which she now stands.

The humiliation of Austria, the blind submission

of Prussia to Buonaparte's will, the occupation of the greater part of Germany by French troops, and the invasion of the whole of Italy, are not the only results of importance to us which have followed from the last campaign. Turkey, over whom our safety requires us to maintain exclusive influence, not only strives to withdraw herself from it, but already begins to defy us. M. d'Italinsky* reports that the Porte has requested that the Dardanelles should be closed to Russian war vessels and transports, that Turkey permits flagrant outrages upon persons under our protection, and that she will not refuse a passage to a French army through the Herzegovina and Montenegro if Buonaparte should desire it.

Russia is thus in a critical position ; but it will become even more so if she persists in maintaining a system of inaction. If England finds that we absolutely decline to join her either in a war or in arrangements for peace, she will find our alliance rather a burthen than an advantage, and will seek other means of attaining the objects of her policy. Turkey would then entirely emancipate herself from our influence ; Sweden would become indifferent, if not hostile ; and the rest of Europe, not seeing any hope of Russian support, would have no alternative but to attach herself to Buonaparte's chariot. In that case the latter will certainly not be idle. The Polish provinces have long attracted his craving for glory and activity, and already he is spreading a report that the Princess of Saxony is to marry some member of the Buonaparte

* The Russian Ambassador at Constantinople.

family who will become King of Poland.   Another of his objects is the regeneration of the Ottoman Empire ; and it is not to be denied that notwithstanding her present decrepitude, Turkey could cause us great difficulties if Buonaparte should make himself master of all her resources and direct them against Russia.

It would appear from the above considerations that the principal and essential thing for the safety of Russia is to maintain, and even to draw tighter, the bonds which unite her to England.   Russia is perhaps more interested even than England in not abandoning an intimate alliance which is now more necessary than ever to save the remains of independence in Europe. What would tend above all to make such an alliance desirable to your Majesty is the composition of the present English Ministry and the principles by which it is actuated.   It shows in its policy as much moderation and wisdom as energy and loyalty.   The conduct of England with regard to neutral commerce displays both the prudence and the liberality of her Government; and the loyalty it showed to Russia when France offered England an advantageous peace demands entire reciprocity on our part.

Being deeply convinced of the truth of these remarks, and considering the fatal results which would follow from the ties which unite us to Great Britain being loosened or broken, I do not hesitate to express the opinion that the honour of Russia, her dearest interests, and her safety, imperiously require her not to separate her cause from that of England.

[Although, in consequence of the annexation by Prussia of Hanover and the closing of the Elbe and Weser to British trade, Mr Fox retaliated by blockading her harbours and seizing her merchant ships, neither England nor Russia sent any troops against her. Meanwhile the aggressive policy of Napoleon and the excesses of his soldiers caused an explosion of patriotic indignation in Prussia which her King found it impossible to resist. The Prussian Government demanded that the French troops should be recalled, and after some angry discussion Napoleon attacked the Prussian army and completely destroyed it at Jena (14th October 1806).]

CHAPTER XIV

1806

RESIGNATION BY PRINCE ADAM CZARTORYSKI OF THE POSITION OF
MINISTER OF FOREIGN AFFAIRS IN RUSSIA.—RETROSPECT OF HIS
POLICY IN THIS CAPACITY.—HIS OPPOSITION TO AN ALLIANCE WITH
FRANCE AT THE EXPENSE OF ENGLAND.

ON the 17th of June, 1806, Prince Adam Czartoryski,
after repeatedly requesting the Emperor Alexander
to relieve him of the duties of Foreign Minister,
finally retired from that post. He had, as will be
seen from the following letter, ample reason to justify
him in taking this step, but the chief cause of his
having done so was one that he could hardly state in
precise terms to the Emperor. He had only accepted
his position in the Ministry because he believed that
by so doing he might be of service to Poland. Alexander's persistence in seeking the alliance of Prussia
convinced him that this belief was a delusive one, and
his sole motive for remaining in the Russian Ministry
thus ceased to exist. Moreover, the hopes of the
Poles had been raised by the approach of Napoleon ;
if France were to make war again upon Russia, which
seemed more than probable, Napoleon would doubtless

strive to secure the support of the Poles by promising to restore their independence, and in that case it would be impossible for Prince Adam to continue to direct the foreign policy of a State with which his country-men might be at war.

Prince Adam Czartoryski to the Emperor.

22nd of March 1806.

It is not with the object of exaggerating to your Imperial Majesty the dangers which threaten your Empire, or of uselessly alarming you as to its position, that I have prepared the memorandum which I now submit to your consideration. It has been dictated by sincere zeal, and after mature reflection. I have thought it indispensable to point out to your Majesty some of the dangers by which you are surrounded and which you do not seem to perceive. Russia is really in a very critical position. Her difficulties and yours, Sire, may increase in a degree which I cannot contemplate without fear. I therefore think there is not a moment to be lost in proposing to your Majesty the only measure which can render possible all the others which must be necessitated by circumstances—a measure not sufficient to secure the safety of the State, but without which it would become too precarious, if not quite unattainable.

Until the late war began there was a certain degree of uniformity in the action of the Government, for your Majesty showed some confidence in the persons with whom you consulted, and usually discussed affairs before deciding upon them. Even then, however, the necessity of introducing more unity among the various departments of Government constantly made itself felt. The disasters we have experienced must be partly attributed to the fact that such unity was not sufficiently established, and that afterwards it was totally destroyed at the moment when it became more necessary than ever to preserve it. . . .

Your Majesty will permit me here to observe that I have been greatly surprised to see that you assume the sole responsibility not only of every measure, but of every detail in its execution; while the object of the establishment of your Ministry was to guarantee you against such responsibility. You possessed the means of calling any of your Ministers to account for any failure of Government policy; but the fault of such failure must now fall upon you, as you wish to do everything alone, both in military and in civil matters. . . . If the passive policy of your Government should bring war into your frontiers—a by no means impossible case—I could not answer for the conduct of the Poles; I would even fear the effect that such an example might produce on the Russians. Already the latter see with pain that the glory of the State is diminished and its pride humiliated. If our frontiers are crossed by the enemy, the fault will be thrown on your Imperial Majesty, and the talk on this subject in the two capitals is not reassuring. . . . But if you do not attach any belief or value to the opinions which I have taken the liberty of expressing, nothing will remain to me but to retire with the satisfaction of having done my duty. In that case your

Imperial Majesty will recognize the justice of my request that I should be allowed to quit my post at once. I will not remind you of all that has passed since my return here,* how little attention you have paid to my proposals ; . . . and you are too considerate to wish to impose upon me any longer the painful obligation—I may say the martyrdom—of participating in an order of things and executing measures which in my opinion are directly opposed to the good of the Empire and your own.

Your Majesty thinks the system into which you have been led by your Cabinet is the source of all the disasters we have experienced. I could not conceal from you, on the other hand, that I am convinced that the true reason of our disasters is that you have not followed that system with frankness and decision ; that you have departed from the plan that was agreed upon ; and that you have withheld your confidence during its execution from those with whom it was formed, so that there was neither unity nor sequence in what has been done since. My opinion is that the principles which until then had regulated the conduct of the Russian Cabinet, should continue to direct it ; that they are the only ones which it can properly adopt ; and that the greatest energy and activity can alone rescue Russia from the difficult position in which she is placed. Your Imperial Majesty appears to be of quite a different opinion : you look upon the principles which have guided our action as noxious and dangerous, and you

* After the battle of Austerlitz.

seem especially to avoid any measure which would be consequent upon them. Whichever view may be correct, it is equally necessary either that you should require me to retire, or that I should ask permission to do so.

Such are my reasons for begging of your Imperial Majesty to allow me to retire. They are strengthened by the peculiar circumstances in which I am placed. . . Your Majesty will recollect that I was far from desiring my present post, and that I even long declined to accept it, foreseeing the unpleasantnesses I should have to suffer as a Pole. Since then, almost from the time when I took up the duties of my office, I have not ceased to look forward to the moment when you would permit me to resign it into your hands. . . .—I am, etc.   (Signed)   A. CZARTORYSKI.

In a memorandum addressed to the Emperor on his retirement from office, Prince Adam thus describes the policy of Russia towards England and the other Powers during the time that he was Minister of Foreign Affairs :—

'. . . The new English Ministry* not having made any statement to us of its policy, this silence inspired us with some anxiety, notwithstanding the confidence we felt in the British Government. We had learnt that Mr Fox had made some overtures to M. de Talleyrand through the Prussian Minister Jacoby, and that negotiations had consequently taken place between England and France, which the British

---

* The Grenville Ministry, formed in January, 1806, after the death of Mr Pitt.

Cabinet had not communicated to us. This afforded
us a reason for also entering into *pourparlers* with
the Cabinet of the Tuileries in order not to remain
isolated, or at least to place us in a position to do
everything that the interests of the State might
require.

'Meanwhile the British Cabinet informed us that
Mr Fox had proposed to M. de Talleyrand a provisional arrangement between England and France,
subject to the consent of Russia, such arrangement
to be null and void in the event of Russia refusing to
acquiesce in it. Mr Fox at the same time invited us
to take part in the negotiations, and we had reason
to believe that he wished to make peace at any price.

'Although it is certain that a war would be the
only means of breaking the yoke which was oppressing
a great part of Europe, yet, if through the weakness
of some Powers, the ill-will of others, and the pusil-
lanimity of all, there was no means of making a
vigorous resistance to France, it was desirable that a
state of hostilities which was only of advantage to
Napoleon should cease.

'Such was the view we expressed in London; and
Austria and Prussia equally desired peace. But it
had yet to be ascertained whether peace was possible;
if not, we should at least acquire the conviction that
the only cause to be adopted was to enter on a vigorous
and combined war. M. d'Oubril was accordingly sent
to Vienna and Paris to sound the views of the French
Government, and Lord G. L. Gower was fully informed as to this mission. . . .

'Shortly after M. d'Oubril's departure, an essential change occurred in the situation. From the moment that the British Cabinet became certain of the treachery of Prussia, a new turn was given to the opinions and views of the English Ministry, which now showed us the greatest confidence. France having repeatedly refused to treat with England and Russia together, the Cabinet of St James's at once broke off the negotiations, and declared that it would not resume them except in concert with its ally. It showed throughout equal loyalty and moderation.

'Having declared war against Prussia, England represented that it was necessary for the allies to strike a decisive blow on the Continent, so as to produce a strong impression of their energy and power, and thereby encourage the States under Buonaparte's influence, and at the same time to render him more moderate in his pretensions. In laying this plan before us, the British Ministry declared itself ready to enter into any other projects we might form either in the west or the south, and to support them with all the means at England's disposal.

'Though for various reasons your Majesty did not think fit to accept the English proposals,* you were deeply touched by this noble and loyal conduct, and you gave strict orders that no arrangement should be concluded with France except in concert with the British Cabinet. . . .

'Having now arrived at the period when the

---

* An allusion to one of the causes of Prince Czartoryski's resignation.

Ministry of Foreign Affairs has passed into other hands, I may be permitted, Sire, to submit to your Majesty a rapid survey of the system which has been followed under my direction, of its results, and of the state of affairs in Europe at the moment of my retirement.

'Since the rupture of the Peace of Amiens, Russia has had constantly to protest against the violation of treaties by the ruler of France, notwithstanding the most precise stipulations. She has constantly been threatened by the gigantic increase of a new Empire, which, by destroying and subjecting its neighbours, necessarily tended to fall with all its weight upon Russia, as the only Power capable of struggling with France for the Empire of the world. . . . There was but one mode of resisting Napoleon with any chance of success, namely, the creation of a system of general alliances. No European Power was capable of facing Napoleon alone ; it was therefore necessary that all the greater Powers should unite to defend the existence of each of them. Russia especially was bound to support her neighbours in order to prevent their falling a prey to the conqueror, and affording him additional resources which he could use against her. This system, worthy of a great Empire, and conformable not only with its own interests and those of its allies, but with the good of humanity, was created by Russia.

'During the last two years Russia and her allies have four times made overtures of peace to Napoleon, and on each occasion the shameful conditions which he imposed and the outrageous pretensions which he put forward rendered peace impossible.

'Events which could hardly have been expected* have profoundly shaken the system, but have not destroyed it. Mutual confidence and the wish to bring together the threads of an indispensable union of which your Imperial Majesty would be the soul and the centre remained; the allies who were neither restrained by fear nor debased by discouragement continued their intimate relations with us.

'At the moment when your Imperial Majesty deigned to permit me to transfer to other hands the Ministry of Foreign Affairs, the situation was as follows:

'The successes of France over your Majesty's allies, however alarming their consequences may appear, only added new ruins to those of other States without adding any solidity to the fabric of the French Empire. A greater number of dismembered countries and humiliated nations increased the general confusion; Napoleon's power was increased, but not made any more secure.

'Austria was silently reorganising her forces, and was still turning her eyes to Russia. She gave us marks of confidence which we hastened to accept and cultivated with the object of renewing our old relations and securing her aid in case of need.

'Prussia, notwithstanding her disgraceful concessions to France, had not entirely bound herself to her, and sought by very secret and confidential negotiations with us to repair the faults of her policy.

* A further allusion to the disagreement between Alexander and Prince Czartoryski.

'Sweden, always faithful to her elevated and generous sentiments, defied the threats of the Berlin Cabinet and remained steadfast to her alliance with Russia and England. . . .

'The Porte, though led astray by the fatal suggestions of French agents, disguised its malevolent designs, and did not dare entirely to break the bonds which united it to Russia.

'Finally, England—the only Power which by her dominion over the seas can in combination with us still justify the hope of a possible equilibrium in Europe—always faithful to our alliance, always frank in her transactions with us and strict in fulfilling them, showed herself ready to second us everywhere, and was actually doing so most effectually in the Mediterranean and on the Adriatic.'

Sir A. Alison (Hist. of Europe, vol. vii. p. 155) suggests that Prince Czartoryski's retirement was caused by the Prince having been in favour of making an alliance with France at the expense of England, while his successor 'supported the English in opposition to the French alliance.' There is no foundation whatever for this suggestion. As will be seen from the papers here published, Prince Czartoryski was throughout a devoted adherent of the alliance with England and an uncompromising adversary of Napoleon. Moreover, when M. d'Oubril signed the treaty of alliance with France (July 20), Prince Czartoryski had already ceased to be Foreign Minister; and that he and his political friends strongly disapproved of M. d'Oubril's conduct is shown by the following extracts from letters addressed to the Prince by Count Vorontzoff, the Russian Ambassador in London :—

'SOUTHAMPTON, $\frac{14}{26}$ *July,* 1806.

'What I feared, and yet hoped would not happen, has come to pass. I have just learnt, to my great grief, that you have resigned your post, my dear Prince. I pity the Emperor and my country, and I cannot conceive how he could have been induced to accept your resignation.

I congratulate our mutual friends M. de Novosiltzoff and Count Kotchoubey on not having wished to separate from you. It is easy for those who know you as I do to understand that your resignation has been the consequence of a complete change in our political system, and that this change was opposed to your principles and views and to your high spirit. Your resignation does you honour ; I am proud to have such a friend. . . .'

'SOUTHAMPTON, *5th August* (N.S.) 1806.

'I cannot blame you ; on the contrary, I can only approve your noble conduct on this occasion. Your counsels, which tended only to the glory and the good of the State, were not followed. The Government had fallen into the hands of intriguers, and you refused to soil your honourable name by lending it to their shameful transactions. It is only through d'Oubril's knowledge that your resignation was imminent and inevitable that he was able to cast eternal shame on Russia.

'WALCOT, 7/19 *October* 1806.

'Mr Battye has sent me here your letter of the 25th of August, which you gave him for me. The reasons you give for your resignation had been already anticipated by me, as I felt certain that a man of your judgment and character could not consent to carry out a policy contrary to his opinions and based on cowardly principles which could only bring danger and dishonour to the State and the sovereign who dictated them. . . .

'I am now staying at Lord Powis's estate in Shropshire, and Count Strogonoff came the day before yesterday to bid me good-bye. I showed him your letter, and he handed me the one he had received from you. The contents of these two letters prove to me that I had rightly guessed the motives of d'Oubril's infamous conduct. He knew that you were no longer in office; that Baron Budberg, like all Livonians, was attached to Prussia, whose interest is to keep Hanover and obtain other advantages from France, to promote dissensions between Russia and England, and to reconcile Russia with the Corsican, and that the Emperor is weak, pusillanimous, and also attached to Prussia. If he succeeded, he would be decorated and rewarded both by Alexander and Napoleon; if he failed, Budberg would see that he escaped punishment. I did not however guess that the Emperor had given instructions to a subordinate behind the back of the Minister who was his chief, and that the subordinate, though selected and protected by the Minister, concealed from him the instructions he had received. This passes belief, and would in itself have been a sufficient justification for your resignation. .   .   .

I can assure you positively that the King of England and his Ministry know and appreciate you, and that Fox alone is doubtless very glad to see your withdrawal from the Ministry of Foreign Affairs. Lord G. L. Gower speaks of you with the greatest respect, esteem and attachment.'

[See also Thiers' History of the Consulate and the Empire, Book xxiv: 'M. d'Oubril was strengthened in his idea of signing a treaty of peace with France by the fact that there had been a change in the Russian Ministry while he was on his way to Paris. Prince Czartoryski and his friends having wished to enter into more intimate engagements with England, not necessarily in order to continue the war, but to be in a more advantageous position to treat with France, Alexander, fatigued by their remonstrances, and fearing to be too closely bound to the British Cabinet, had at length accepted their resignations, which had been frequently submitted to him, and had replaced Prince Czartoryski by Baron Budberg. The Baron was formerly the Emperor's tutor and a friend of the Empress Dowager, and had neither strength nor inclination to resist his master.'*]

* The above views are further confirmed by a letter in the Record Office addressed by Mr Stuart, then Chargé d'Affaires at St Petersburg, to Lord Grenville on the 20th of August 1806, in which Mr Stuart says that he assured Prince Czartoryski 'that the high opinion his upright and honourable frankness had inspired in England would remain unsullied, and that although the real state of the case could not hitherto be perfectly known, his character was not implicated by the slightest suspicion to his disadvantage on the part of his Majesty's Ministers.'

CHAPTER XV

1806

THOUGH Prince Adam Czartoryski had ceased to be
Minister of Foreign Affairs, he remained for many
years after one of the most esteemed and valued of the
Emperor Alexander's counsellors, and there are
numerous memoranda on both internal and external
Russian policy in the Czartoryski archives which were
prepared for the Emperor by the Prince after his
resignation. Among these is the following paper,
dated the 5th of December 1806, 'On the necessity of
restoring Poland to forestall Buonaparte : '

'In the struggle which is to decide* on the fate of
Russia and of Europe, Poland has at this juncture of
affairs become a principal object of consideration with
the two Empires which are about to come into
immediate collision with each other ; but she is looked
upon by each of them in an entirely different manner.
For the French she is a source of safety, an object

* It will be observed that this memorandum was written after Napoleon's
victory at Jena.

which animates their courage and strengthens their perseverance; it is in Poland that Buonaparte sees his standpoint for fighting Russia and penetrating within her old frontiers. Though moving away from his centre of operations, Poland would furnish to his fertile genius and indefatigable activity the same resources as France—a population easily exercised in the profession of arms, brave and experienced officers, money, provisions, and an attachment to the existence, the honour, and the liberties of their country so deep that it will move them to the highest efforts. For Russia, on the other hand, the Poles are a motive of continual anxieties and suspicions; they have frequently been used by Buonaparte as a bugbear to the partitioning Powers. Though Poland affords all the resources capable of supporting the war and powerfully contributing to the defence of the throne, the Russian Government fears to make use of the Poles lest they should turn against it. . . . Under these circumstances Poland diminishes the power of Russia in the same proportion as she augments that of France.

'It is obviously desirable, in the Russian interest, to reverse this state of things; and to obtain such a result there is only one way: to proclaim Poland as a kingdom, the Emperor declaring himself King on behalf of himself and his successors for ever.

'The advantages of such a step—equally magnanimous and politic—would be incalculable. The general enthusiasm it would excite in all the Poles, the gratitude which would rally all Polish hearts and arms round the throne, would entirely change Russia's situation and that of her enemies. Instead of seeing her provinces exposed to Buonaparte's seductions, she would be able to raise their inhabitants against him; and Russia, instead of having an immense frontier exposed to the colossal Empire of France, would, by re-establishing Poland, create an outpost behind which she would remain intact with all her forces at her command. Moreover, every cause of anxiety for Russia as to the conduct of the Poles, and every motive for speculating on such conduct on the part of her enemies, would be for ever removed—an inappreciable advantage for the internal happiness, tranquillity, and power of the Empire.

' If Poland is declared a separate State, with the Emperor as King, Buonaparte's difficulties in invading Russia will be immeasurably increased; . . . . and should he succeed in overcoming them, he will have to pursue our armies into the interior of Russia, as they have very wisely been ordered to retire until they are sure of victory. He would then find himself cut off by the hostile Poles in his rear, and his defeat under such circumstances would mean nothing short of the absolute surrender of himself and his army. . . .

' It may be objected that to declare Poland a Kingdom would be to separate from the Empire one of its integral parts; but this separation would only be apparent. The crown of Poland would be irrevocably attached to the throne of Russia; and the Empire would at the same time gain the remainder of Poland. Imperious circumstances have forced Russia

to commit the great political fault of allowing Poland
to be partitioned instead of entirely possessing it.
This fault has, to a great extent, been the cause
of the misfortunes which have since overwhelmed
Europe ; should it not now be made good ?

'No doubt, in order to produce the desired effect of
inflaming the enthusiasm of the Poles, it would be
necessary to give them a government in conformity
with their wishes and their ancient laws. . . . But
these benefits would render the bond between the
Empire and the Polish nation stronger and more
indissoluble.   The more a nation is governed in
accordance with its wishes, its character, and its
habits, the more devoted it is to its rulers.   The
kingdom of Hungary, notwithstanding its special
liberties and prerogatives, has for centuries been an
example of fidelity and one of the firmest supports of
Austria.   Maria Theresa was saved by the Hungarians.
The King of France was all-powerful in the provinces
which had preserved their estates and privileges, and
it was Brittany, Poitou, and Anjou which have up to
the last moment been the defenders of the throne, of
religion, and of the nobility.

'A further objection might be raised on the score
that by reuniting Poland under her sceptre Russia
would be despoiling her ally the King of Prussia.
But the master of the Prussian monarchy is now
Buonaparte ; he exercises all the rights of a conqueror
there, and is advancing towards Prussia's frontier provinces, which he proposes to disturb by a revolution
that will threaten ours. The question at issue, there-

fore, is not the seizure of the property of an ally, but the forestalling of an active, inexorable, and aggressive enemy; the depriving him of a booty which if he obtains would cause a terrible conflagration in the Empire. This would indeed be the only means of saving Russia's ally; for otherwise she will perhaps not be able to continue the struggle and obtain some compensation for the House of Brandenburg in forcing the enemy to agree to an equitable peace.

'As to Austria, such an arrangement could not, of course, be made without frank and loyal negotiations with the Court of Vienna. But the basis of the arrangement is too just, and the House of Austria would be too sensible of the dangers it incurs, not to promise a speedy and successful result of these negotiations. . . .

'The only question which remains to be solved is whether, supposing the proclamation of Poland as a separate State is decided upon, Russia should act at once or wait until Napoleon makes overtures to the Poles. The first course would appear the preferable one. As soon as Russia enters into the fitting explanations with the Court of Vienna and the preliminary steps are taken in Poland to secure that the project shall be fully carried into effect, nothing should delay its immediate execution. On the contrary, the matter is urgent, and the slightest delay might weaken or destroy the results of this important operation. All the advantages of taking the initiative would be on Russia's side, and she would not have to combat the pride of a violent and self-willed man who

has not hitherto known what it is to withdraw from
a course of action after publicly proclaiming that he
has decided to adopt it.

'The preliminary steps to be taken would be the
issue of proclamations by the Russian generals, circular letters to influential personages in the country,
and instructions to governors and commanding officers,
to show a friendly attitude to the Poles, to ensure
discipline in the troops, and to levy recruits; and the
despatch of intelligent and zealous agents to the
Polish provinces.   The King of Prussia would be
informed in the most considerate manner of the
reasons and the necessity for the proposed measure,
and would be given the hope of compensation as soon
as the events of the war should permit, and preparations would be made immediately for the reorganisa-
tion of the new kingdom and for reconciling the
inalienable rights of the sovereign with the institutions
and customs most congenial to the Polish nation, a
considerable part of which they have retained under
the paternal Government of his Majesty the Emperor.'

The following was the Emperor's reply to the
above memorandum and other similar proposals which
were made to him by Prince Adam in conversation :—

The Emperor to Prince Adam Czartoryski
(Written in pencil and without date).

I have received the paper you have thought fit to
address to me.   You wish for a discussion, and I am
ready to grant it; but I cannot help telling you that

I think it will be useless, as our fundamental principles are so diametrically opposed to each other. After pointing out the critical position in which Russia is placed and the evils she has to fear, the only means you propose for meeting the danger may be reduced to two :

1. That I should declare myself King of Poland.

2. That my Ministers of War and of Foreign Affairs should be changed.

The discussion of the first of these points would be too long, but I am ready to state my views and the reasons which guide my conduct. As to the second point, I am satisfied with the services which the Ministers in question render me. Who is this perfect Minister of whom everyone would approve ? Is it General Suchtelen ? I tell you plainly that I do not look upon him as possessing the qualities required of a War Minister, and that of the two I do not hesitate for a moment to give the preference to General Viasnitinoff. Nor do I see anyone for the Foreign Department. Would it be a Panin or a Markoff? I must esteem those with whom I work; it is only on this condition that I can give them my confidence. Clamour troubles me but little ; it is generally nothing more than the effect of party spirit. Are not you yourself an example of this? Have you not been exposed to the criticism and animosity of the whole nation ? I must also remark that it would have been better if the Committee * had not employed a stranger

* The 'Secret Council,' to which Prince Czartoryski still belonged. See Vol I., p. 257.

to copy such a paper as the one I am answering. In order to bring us together again it will first be necessary for us to agree that, whatever may be said in the Committee, our individual and mutual relations shall remain intact, and that we should follow the example of English Members of Parliament, who, after saying the most bitter things to each other in the House in the heat of debate, are excellent friends when the debate is over.—Ever yours,

ALEXANDER.

The Emperor to Prince Czartoryski.
(Without date).

I was far from intending to give you pain. As I was speaking of such important matters, I was obliged to do so in accordance with my conviction, and I expressed myself accordingly. In the concluding part of your memorandum you offer to hand me a detailed and general plan of the measures to be taken in succession to those which you propose. If you like, we can meet in committee to-morrow, after dinner at six o'clock. We will make the plan together, and then discuss it.—Ever yours,

ALEXANDER.

[Prince Czartoryski's proposal was not accepted, and the result was that when Napoleon entered Warsaw (at that time belonging to Prussia), on the 18th of December, 1806, he was received by the

Poles with enthusiasm. Deputations came to him from all parts of Poland, a provisional Government was established, and volunteers presented themselves in great numbers to be enrolled in the French army.]

CHAPTER XVI

1806

PROPOSED PEACE BETWEEN RUSSIA AND NAPOLEON.

On the 21st December 1806, Prince Czartoryski, who was still a member of the Imperial Council, addressed the following Letter and Memorandum to the Emperor Alexander proposing that he should treat for peace with Napoleon:

'Novosiltzoff and myself have of late several times had the opportunity of expressing to your Majesty our conviction that it is necessary to endeavour without delay to treat for peace with Buonaparte before our army can be attacked. I think we cannot at this moment give your Majesty a more real proof of our attachment, than to continue to press this advice upon you.

'Having heard that Lesseps was about to leave, I can no longer hesitate to lay before your Majesty the annexed memorandum which had been prepared on the subject.

'You will consider, Sire, the bad effect which would be produced by overtures of peace made only after a defeat, while at this moment, even if we gained some victories, such overtures could in no way be prejudicial to us. I would suggest that your Imperial Majesty should have the memorandum, which we take the liberty of presenting to you, discussed in your Cabinet Council. It would be only right that you should not take the sole responsibility for a step which might have decisive consequences.'

MEMORANDUM ON THE NECESSITY OF OPENING NEGOTIATIONS OF PEACE WITH NAPOLEON.

Present State of Affairs.

Hardly a month has passed, and the disasters of Prussia, following each other with unexampled rapidity, have completely destroyed her. A considerable portion of Prussian Poland has been invaded, Warsaw is occupied by the French troops, large levies have been organised, and the inhabitants of the Polish provinces are fired with the hope of recovering their independence as a nation—a hope stimulated by Napoleon's numerous proclamations.

The Hanseatic towns, Mecklenburg, and Holstein, have been involved in the ruin of the German Empire; Stralsund has been invested.

It is with all the forces and united resources of the French Empire, of Germany, and of Prussia, that Napoleon is approaching our frontiers.

While our enemy, as active as he is fortunate, is

making such terrible progress, we have only managed to reunite the various corps which compose our great western army, and are only beginning the preparations for the arming of the militia which have been ordered by your Imperial Majesty.

Notwithstanding the immense resources of this Empire, we must not lose sight of the fact that for the present we have only one army to oppose to the victorious armies of Buonaparte; that our recruits cannot be ready to fight till next spring; that our militia levies will come in slowly, and that time will be necessary to enable them to furnish corps capable of coming into line with the regular army and supplying our losses; further, that useful as they may be in combining the operations of a partisan war with those of a powerful regular army, they might be equally injurious, should that army be routed, by increasing the confusion and danger.

Under these circumstances every faithful subject of your Imperial Majesty—every good Russian— must be struck by the sad truth that the Russian Empire is nearly in the same situation as Prussia was last October.* All the regular troops we can dispose of are on the frontier. If these are beaten, an immense extent of country will be at the mercy of the French conqueror, and the elements of insurrection which he has doubtless spread in our western provinces lead one to fear that a lost battle would have incalculable consequences.

* Before the battle of Jena.

Necessity of Peace.

In presence of this alarming picture of the situation the want of peace becomes a universal sentiment, and should unite all hopes, wishes, and parties.

The enlightened politician and the determined soldier will both agree to ask themselves why pacific overtures should not be attempted rather than to persist in a struggle whose danger is imminent and directly menaces this Empire.

Objection.

How can we forget the maxims of energy, perseverance, and loyalty, which are the foundations of true greatness and a sure policy, and which have always guided the Russian Cabinet? Did we not on this principle refuse to ratify the Treaty of the $\frac{8}{20}$ July?* Would not an offer of peace compromise the national glory and show that we feel our weakness?

Reply.

Energy and perseverance have their limits, beyond which they become obstinacy or rashness. They should aim only at objects which are attainable, and whose pursuit is not accompanied by dangers out of all proportion to the advantages to be secured. These great qualities do not only manifest themselves in military operations; the latter have to be skilfully combined with political measures.

---

* The Treaty of Peace signed by M. d'Oubril at Paris. See page 161.

Difference of Circumstances.

The circumstances which have drawn Russia into this war, and which have made its prolongation indispensable, were essentially different from the present state of things.

Former Circumstances.

It will be remembered that in 1801 Russia was at peace with the French Government, whose friendship she cultivated.

The insults and provocations of all kinds, and violations of the most solemn treaties, which were perpetrated by the Cabinet of the Tuileries, forced your Imperial Majesty at first to complain, and then to make alliances to support common rights and share common dangers. The war which followed, becoming every day more fatal, also became every day more necessary.

Yet the enemy was far from having attained the point to which his astonishing successes have since brought him. Europe still afforded considerable means of opposing the overflow of his ambition.

Sacred engagements and those political considerations which constitute so essential a portion of the power of a State, did not permit Russia to abandon her allies or to sacrifice their hopes to her particular advantage.

The Cabinet of your Imperial Majesty was then obliged to develop all its forces to prevent or avert the fall of the neighbouring States, which served her as a barrier against the colossal Empire of Buonaparte, or through which it still had means of making a diversion.

So long as these motives and views existed, it was impossible to advise a peace which, owing to the complication of interests and the sacrifices that would be demanded by an enemy intoxicated with success, could only be a shameful one and could in no case reassure us as to the future.

Present Circumstances.

Now that by a succession of reverses, to which there is no parallel in history, all the countries that Russia has endeavoured to save are reduced to timid inaction, or have altogether disappeared from the ranks of the European States, there is no longer any question of protecting States on our borders ; our borders themselves require to be protected. Our Empire is about to engage in a direct conflict with the French Empire, for the defence, not only of our integrity, but, if we may venture to say so, of our existence.

The war, so far as we are concerned, has changed its nature. The supreme interest of the State—-the salvation of the Empire—must become the sole object of our policy at this new epoch of a struggle equally memorable and unfortunate for so many beaten nations.

Without ceasing to watch over the general good of Europe—without losing sight of the feeble hopes of our crushed allies—the indefeasible law of our own preservation is the only one that should guide us; all other duties and interests must give way to it.

Our policy thereby becomes independent, and if a tolerable peace, affording some elements of safety, could be concluded, there is nothing to prevent our entering into negotiations; on the contrary, every consideration should induce us to do so.

Even the safety of our allies makes such a course imperative; for if by a sentiment of false delicacy, by false principles of loyalty, or by personal feelings, we exposed ourselves to perish in order to save them, our fall would not alleviate their misfortune, but aggravate it by depriving them of the most distant hope of preserving what remains to them, or of some day repairing their disasters.

It is therefore evident that the changes which have occurred in our political relations, and in the situation of Europe, call upon us to seek peace as urgently as the position of affairs before the ruin of the Germanic Empire and the destruction of Prussia deterred us from doing so.

We should treat for peace without losing time.

If the necessity of this measure is agreed upon, it must equally be admitted that the negotiations should be opened as soon as possible, and that there is not a moment to be lost.

It is an incontestable principle in politics that peace should be offered at a time when one is in a position to insist upon it, or at least to accept it with dignity.

Our armies are intact; the enemy is no doubt aware of the formation of our reserves and the numerous levy of our militia. Soon he will hear of the patriotic offers which will be brought to the foot of the throne by all parts of the Empire; he will also be informed of our successes against the Persians, and the advantageous positions we have just occupied on the Dniester and the Danube. He is certainly not ignorant of the obstacles to his advance—the distance, the climate, the season of the year—in a war which would be equally long and dangerous. His first interest, therefore, will be again to astonish Europe by the rapidity of his combined movements, and to strike a decisive blow. He will hasten, therefore, directly he is able to do so, to fall on our great army with all the weight of his troops in order to force a battle; and our wise intention of evading one might perhaps yield to the vivacity of his pursuit, or to the thought of the pain it would give our generals to abandon the field to the enemy.

Such a situation cannot last long. Now or never is the time to talk of peace, if we do not want to wait till we are forced to beg for it after a reverse. And what peace could we hope for from a conqueror, whose pride would be swelled by his victory over the best troops in the world, and who would increase his claims and his demand for revenge according to the greatness of the vanquished?

Let us suppose—for it is prudent to anticipate the worst in our calculations—that our great army is dispersed, and our Western provinces are agitated

by the hope of recovering their independence, or by
the grant of liberty to the peasants. Shall we allow
the conflagration to spread in these rich territories?
Can we foresee where it would stop? Would we consent to the humiliation of offering territorial cessions
to the conqueror? And if so, within what limits; or
would we be entirely at his mercy?

These considerations, improbable as the supposi-
tion on which they are based may be, show that we
ought to attempt to prevent such terrible extremities
by concluding peace. The occasion naturally presents
itself now that the war is assuming a new character.
Before it begins between these two great nations,
whose collision would shake the Continent, is it not
natural that an effort should be made, even if only in
the interests of humanity, to stop it?

Moreover, Buonaparte himself, in his address to
the Senate, has declared that he is ready to make
peace with Russia and England, and even with
Prussia. Even more; he declares that the system of
making separate peaces, hitherto followed by the
French Cabinet, has only produced delusive truces
and given rise to new coalitions, and that he will now
only consent to a general peace with all the Powers
concerned. He has thus, so to say, taken the first
step, and it is for us to take the second, if we do not
wish to leave him the advantage he is always claim-
ing, of having professed peaceful sentiments in the
midst of his success and yet never having been
listened to.

This new phase in the policy of France, however

insidious may be its motive, offers Russia a plausible
pretext for proposing to open the negotiations, and
our Cabinet may take it the more frankly, as the
other belligerents are equally concerned in it.

On what basis can we treat?

The point here to be considered is on what basis
we can expect to get peace.

We must not forget that peace is, as has been
shown above, absolutely necessary to us; that in
present circumstances the sole object of the negotiations should be the safety of the Empire, isolated as
it is at present from all that it had to preserve abroad;
that all interests not affecting that object, or only
indirectly affecting it, have become subordinate to it;
and that we must be satisfied even with a tolerable
peace, provided it offers elements of security to
Russia.

All else that we could hope for as regards ourselves and our allies—whether in augmenting our
preparations and our efforts, or in gaining some
advantages, or through the support of other Powers,
or the skill of diplomatists, will always be an object
of our wishes and even of our action, but we should
not consider it essential to realise such hopes, or
regard their non-fulfilment as an insurmountable
obstacle to peace. We need be the less obstinate on
this point,' that as our enemy is ready to accept
negotiation in common for a general pacification, our
allies, especially England and Prussia, will each look

after their own interests, and we shall relatively have greater latitude in working for ours.

The Treaty of $\frac{8}{20}$ July last not to be revived.*

Acting on the principle above indicated, it is unnecessary to observe that the Treaty of $\frac{8}{20}$ July last cannot be revived either by Russia or by France ; for, on the one hand, the evacuation of Germany by the French, as stipulated in that Treaty, can no longer be hoped for after the late immense conquests and aggressions of Buonaparte, and on the other, we now have what we did not have then—compensations to demand for the district which our safety compelled us to occupy in Turkey.

Bases of the Negotiation.

1. The greatest facilities would be given as to the arrangements Napoleon might be disposed to make either with England or Prussia or with any other Power as to the countries he has occupied since the renewal of the war.

The true and permanent interests of Russia are in no way opposed to the creation of new States of a moderate size near our frontiers, even if the enemy were to retain them under his protection.

2. We should, however, demand as a *conditio sine quâ non* that the French armies evacuate within a brief period the countries in question, and retire beyond the Weser, or at least behind the Elbe, so that

---

* This is the Treaty signed by M. d'Oubril, in Paris, but not ratified by his Government. See page 161.

their passing beyond those limits without our concurrence should be regarded as equivalent to a declaration of war.

3. Russia would restore all the fortresses and the
territory she may occupy at the date of the treaty;
she would consent not to keep Cattaro and even, if
absolutely necessary, to evacuate the Seven Islands, on
the express condition, however, that

4. France shall not keep that portion of Dalmatia
which formerly belonged to Venice, and Cattaro at
least shall not in any case be placed under her
rule.

As the integrity and independence of the
Ottoman Empire are of as great interest to Russia as
to France, and the two Powers equally wish to
guarantee it, it will only be just that there should be
perfect reciprocity in this respect. Whatever guarantee the Cabinet of the Tuileries may require from
Russia on the north, the Cabinet of St Petersburg
will have a right to demand a similar guarantee in
the south. The Porte has itself every interest in
seconding us in this demand, and Austria and England will be called upon to take part in the arrangement.

5. The crown of Sicily would be retained in the
possession of King Ferdinand. If Buonaparte were
to demand that the title of King of the two Sicilies
should be recognized in favour of Joseph his brother,
one might grant it without any territorial or sovereign
rights. Although this matter might seem of indirect
importance to Russia, it affects her safety and pros-

perity too greatly not to form an essential object of the negotiations.

6. The kingdom of Sardinia will be maintained and guaranteed by all the Powers which have treaties with the King.

7. If England can make peace on the basis indicated by Buonaparte in his address to the Senate, *i.e.*, the retention of Malta, the island of Ceylon, the Cape of Good Hope, and her conquests in Mysore, Russia will accede to such an arrangement, without, however, interfering with regard to any difficulties which might ultimately be raised with regard to the negotiations between France and England.

8. If Sweden should accede to this peace, the two contracting Powers will guarantee her present possessions.

9. Indemnities could be afforded for the King of Sicily or Sardinia by the bay of Cattaro, the Seven Islands, or the part of Dalmatia which formerly belonged to Venice, should it be given up. Dalmatia might also be used for making useful exchanges of territory with Austria.

10. The happy idea of destroying the Barbary States having been formerly suggested by Buonaparte, would probably be now accepted by him, and these States would also afford a means of making arrangements whose results would be of general interest.

Similar negotiations will at once be opened in Austria, at Constantinople, in England, and at the other Courts, with a view to obtaining their concurrence or intervention as regards the objects of the proposed treaty.

[After the so-called 'Polish Campaign,' during the winter of 1806-7, Napoleon made peace with Russia at Tilsit (July 7, 1807). Although Prince Czartoryski had ceased to be Minister of Foreign Affairs at St Petersburg, he was present at the negotiations, and still exercised considerable influence over Alexander's mind, as will be seen from the following letter from the British Ambassador, Lord Granville Leveson Gower, urging him to use his good offices with the Emperor to prevent his concluding a one-sided peace with Napoleon:—

Mon Prince,

La confiance que vous m'avez toujours témoignée, et la conversation confidentielle que nous avons eue à Tilsitt, m'a fait espérer que vous ne le trouverez pas indiscret de ma part de m'addresser à Votre Excellence sur les bruits qui courent dans ce moment au sujet de l'armistice, et les négociations de paix qui la suivront. Les raisonnements sur la nécessité d'arrêter par la voie des négociations les armées Françaises sont trop bien fondés pour que je puisse en disputer la validité, mais il me semble que de consentir à une paix séparée après toutes les déclarations qu'a fait l'Empereur à cet égard, sera en effet avouer que la Russie se trouve au bout de ses moyens, et les ites fâcheuses qui en résulteront sont incalculables. Ce n'est pas l'Angleterre qui en souffrira le plus ; pour obtenir une paix générale solide et équitable je suis persuadé que la cour de Londres fera de grands sacrifices—et c'est bien l'intérêt de toutes les puissances qu'on ne fasse pas la paix sans son consentement. Tout ce qui tend à relâcher les liens qui unissent la Russie et l'Angleterre doit être nuisible aux deux Empires, et si jamais la France trouve le moyen de séparer ces deux cours, c'en est fait de l'indépendance de l'Europe. Je suis persuadé que votre influence, quoique le portefeuille ne se trouve plus dans vos mains, peut beaucoup faire dans ce moment si critique ; usez-en pour le bien général, je vous conjure. Pardonnez, mon Prince, la franchise avec laquelle je vous ai écrit, et sera-ce trop abuser de votre bonté de vous prier de me répondre avec confiance ? J'y ai des droits, parceque personne ne vous est plus attaché.

Avec tous les sentiments que je vous ai voués, je suis votre dévoué serviteur,   G. L. GOWER.

A MEMEL, ce 23 *Juin* 1807.

One of the chief articles of the Treaty of Tilsit was the creation of the Duchy of Warsaw, under the rule of the King of Saxony, out of the Polish provinces annexed by Prussia in the various partitions. This event produced some characteristic manifestations of Polish patriotism. Several persons gave up the whole of their property for the maintenance of the Polish army ; others raised and equipped entire regiments at their own expense. Six regiments —one of artillery, two of cavalry, and three of infantry—were raised and placed on a war footing entirely by four individuals in a few weeks. Those who were less rich supplied battalions, companies or smaller bodies of men. As the country was nearly ruined by the stagnation of trade and the constant passage of troops, those who thus came forward to increase the national forces had to sell their family plate, jewels, and even wedding-rings.]

CHAPTER XVII

1809-10

THE creation of the Duchy of Warsaw by Napoleon, and the augmentation of its territory by part of Galicia after the war between France and Austria in 1809, in which the Polish troops greatly distinguished themselves, had gradually restored in some degree to the Polish provinces south of the Vistula the powers of an independent State, though its sovereign, the King of Saxony, was practically the vassal of Napoleon. Under these circumstances Prince Adam Czartoryski gradually withdrew from the Imperial Council* at St Petersburg, and retained only the post of Curator of the University of Wilna, which had been conferred upon him by the Emperor Alexander together with the portfolio of Foreign Affairs. This post gave him extensive powers over the educational establishments in Lithuania, which he completely

---

* The date of his last communication to the Council (on Russian Finance) is the 29th of January, 1810.

reorganised and developed in a national sense. He did not, however, lose sight of his favourite idea of reconstructing Poland as a separate kingdom under the sceptre of the Emperor of Russia ; and the following are notes, written by himself at the time, of his conversations with Alexander on this subject in 1809-10 :

12th November, 1809.

. . . Referring to Napoleon's letter to the Emperor and M. de Champagny's despatch on Poland, I said that I could only be pained at the knowledge that the Emperor is now made the chief enemy and persecutor of the Polish nation and name ; that it was only to please him that Poland had been abandoned and deprived of all hope ; and that he carried his animosity so far as even to wish the name of Poland to be effaced from history.

The Emperor at first defended himself against this charge. He said that his personal sentiments had not changed, that they had long been known to me, that he was bound by the duties of his position, and that every Russian Emperor would have done the same. I answered that I could not on this point separate the Emperor's personal inclinations from his political opinions ; that he had himself recognised that the restoration of Poland could be accomplished not only without injuring the interests of Russia, but on the contrary, to her great advantage, by uniting the two crowns on his Majesty's head. The Emperor replied that all this might be true, but that the thing was not practicable, and that it was therefore necessary to adopt another line of conduct. I at once rejoined that I could not understand this reasoning. If a certain policy was desirable in itself, it should not be adopted at one moment and dropped the next: if opportunities had been neglected or had not presented themselves, the proper course was to wait for new ones and in the meantime to prepare the ground, instead of alienating the nation by measures of undeserved rigour. Upon this the Emperor cast down his eyes and said : ' If at least one could expect some return on the part of the Poles ! '

I replied that I could not see what he had done to gain the affection of the Poles : ' Could anything be more revolting than the conduct of the three Powers with regard to Poland ? And is it surprising that the idea of seeing their country restored should fill the Poles with enthusiasm and bring them together ? It is thought that the peace will diminish this enthusiasm. I think otherwise, and the airs of triumph with which the papers here proclaim that the Poles have been deprived of all hope seem to me rather of a nature to serve Napoleon than to do him harm, as they will cast all the odium of his conduct on your Majesty. No one will now doubt that it was at the instance of your Majesty, and in order not to have war with Russia, that Napoleon yielded on a point which he would otherwise never have abandoned, and this can only embitter the Poles against you. . . .'

The Emperor replied that I knew his sentiments as to the partition of Poland, and that he still thought that all the evils from which Europe is now suffering date from that event. It could not, however, now be remedied. He did not see any means of executing the plan he had formerly contemplated with regard to Poland; all that was possible was to grant a separate organisation to the provinces now under his rule, but even that would require much consideration, and would meet with much opposition in Russia. I said that knowing his liberal sentiments, which had been the origin of the connection with which he had honoured me, the only difficulty I could perceive would be the possibility of Napoleon opposing the scheme; and that this made me anxious to know whether in the numerous conversations he had had with Napoleon he (the Emperor Alexander) had ever touched upon the subject. The Emperor replied rather vaguely that the matter had recently been in question during the Austrian war. Here he stopped short, and added that Napoleon would never consent to such a thing, as his sole idea was always to influence the Poles and use them as his tools.

I then remarked that the grant of a separate constitution to the Polish provinces now belonging to Russia would probably meet with more opposition in the Empire than the idea of uniting the whole of Poland to it. This I felt convinced was necessary for the security of Russia; but I feared that when Russia would recognise that such is the case, it would be too late. The Emperor said that if he went to war with France it would certainly be advisable that he should declare himself King of Poland in order to gain over the Poles to his side. I answered that it would then be too late; and seeing that the conversation had lasted too long, I did not wish to carry it any further.

December 26, 1809.

I had written to the Emperor to ask him for a short interview, and in doing so I specially mentioned my wish to speak to him about the continuation of my leave, which was about to expire. Some days later, after a dinner at my mother's, the Emperor came to me and asked me to go to him on the following day, as he wished to speak to me. I inferred from this that he wished to speak about the contemplated changes in the organisation of the Council which were just then the talk of the town. Not knowing what the Emperor's plan was or what he might propose to me, I was a little anxious, for it is always disagreeable to listen to a sovereign's proposals when one has every reason to decline them.

Next day I went to the palace, and after waiting for some time, I was admitted to the Emperor's presence. He first asked me what I wanted. I mentioned various private matters to him, and then begged him to allow my leave to be prolonged. He said he thought I had intended to stop longer at St Petersburg, and that he had consequently believed it might have suited me to have more active employment. He then informed me that the Council was to assume a new shape, with more extensive functions and an organisation for the formation of which that of similar institutions in France and England had been taken as an example ; that he had divided the Council into four sections—War, Home Affairs, Finance, Justice and Law—and that a place had been assigned to me in the fourth section. There was also to be a further discussion by the general body of the Council of the matters that had been dealt with in the sections ; but it was for the latter that good workers would be most required. I replied that I was extremely honoured by the confidence his Majesty was good enough to place in me, but that my reasons for soliciting a prolongation of my leave were already known to him—the advanced age of my parents, from whom I had been long separated ; the care of my health, with which the climate of St Petersburg did not at all agree ; and the habits and tastes which I had contracted during my prolonged absence from active service. The Emperor said he had no idea of disturbing my arrangements, adding that he had expected I should leave him, but had thought I would postpone my departure till the summer. I replied that I intended before the summer to pass some time at Wilna, where my presence was necessary in order to arrange the affairs of the university. . . .

The Emperor then told me that all the severe measures which had been taken with regard to the Poles would be revoked, that a decision to this effect had been arrived at, but that it would not be published for some weeks to come. He added that the motives which had impelled him to take these measures had ceased to exist, and that now he had reason to be tranquil as regards Poland. I thanked him, and asked what were the reasons for his tranquillity; was it only the passage in M. de Montalivet's speech,* or was there any other reason, such as an engagement no longer to contemplate the restoration of Poland? I knew from the conversations which I had had with the Chancellor, that there was some question of this between the two Cabinets, and I remarked to the Emperor that in that case he would himself be obliged to enter into a similar engagement, and would thus tie his hands. The Emperor made an evasive reply, merely saying that there was no question of what I was thinking about.

He then asked me as to the public feeling in Poland. 'Events,' I said, 'have revived the sentiments of fifteen years ago. The hope of the restoration of Poland seemed for a while to the Poles less possible; but now it is as if a half-cicatrised wound were accidentally reopened. It is thought that their hopes might have been diminished in consequence of the last peace with Austria, and certain letters and despatches from Napoleon which have been made public. Be this as it may, public feeling is nevertheless at the same stage as it was fifteen years ago. Moreover, there is the Duchy of Warsaw, which has

---

* The following was the passage here referred to. It occurs in the 'statement of the situation of the Empire,' presented by M. de Montalivet to the French legislative body on the 1st of December, 1809:

'The Duchy of Warsaw has been augmented by part of Galicia. It would have been easy for the Emperor to join the whole of Galicia to this State; but he did not wish to do anything which might have caused anxiety to his ally, the Emperor of Russia. Nearly the whole of the Galicia of the old partition has remained in the power of Austria. His Majesty has never had in view the restoration of Poland. What he has done for the new Galicia was prompted less by policy than by honour; he could not abandon to the vengeance of an implacable prince a population which had displayed so much ardour in the cause of France.'

been considerably augmented by the late war and which helps to strengthen and maintain the patriotic sentiment. It is a sort of phantom of ancient Poland which produces an infallible effect on all who regard that country as their real fatherland. It is as if, after you had lost a dear friend, his shade should come to assure you that he will soon be restored to you in person.

'Your Majesty must not be astonished at sentiments which I hold in common with all Poles. I do not speak to you as a sovereign: I beg you to lay aside that character and only to keep that which was the first cause of my attachment to you. . . . Your Majesty will remember that when I returned from Italy I had not the least idea of entering your service. When you wished to employ me, I repeatedly declined, and my chief reason was that being a Pole, my position might become delicate and difficult. I foresaw that circumstances might arise in which the interests of my country might be opposed to the duties of my office. Your Majesty replied that there was at that time no reason to anticipate such a thing, but that if there should be at some future period I would be at liberty to act as I thought proper. I must now say that the general impression produced on all my countrymen by circumstances, and by the existence of the Duchy of Warsaw, has also produced its effect upon me. I cannot help taking the strongest interest in my country.

'In my opinion a man who is not attached to his country is despicable. To disown one's religion, ones'

parents, one's country, is in my eyes equally odious.
These are feelings with which I was born, which education has strengthened, and which in me will never
change. Moreover, my brother, my sisters, and all my
family are in Poland, and I will confess to your Majesty
that this is one of the reasons which make me wish not
to mix myself up with any affairs here. It is not enough
for me to be clear, straightforward, and sincere in my
actions; I also wish to be so in my sentiments and my
thoughts. I am therefore glad to have been able to
open my mind completely to your Majesty, and to
explain myself to you without any reserve. My first
object is to preserve my own esteem ; my second is to
preserve that of people whom I am accustomed to love
and respect. Should at any time your Majesty think
fit to confiscate my property and order me to be shot,
I will bear my fate with equanimity if you will do me
the justice to think that I was an honest man who
always spoke the truth and never deceived you.'

The Emperor seemed satisfied, and said that he
had never misunderstood me, and that the way I had
explained myself to him did me credit. For a moment
he was absorbed in thought ; then, as if suddenly
rousing himself, he said : ' There is no other means of
arranging all this than our old plan of giving a constitution and a separate existence to the kingdom of
Poland by attaching the title to the Russian crown.'
' We must wait,' he continued, ' until Austria commits
some blunder (fasse une bêtise) and provokes a new
rupture with France ; then we may find means to
come to an understanding with Napoleon, and give

compensation to the King of Saxony.' He added that in the meantime it would have been well to proceed in this sense with the provinces now belonging to the Empire, and to take the title of Grand-Duke of Lithuania; but that in presence of so skilful an antagonist as Napoleon, he had feared to awaken his suspicions and lead him to anticipate Russia by proclaiming the independence of Poland himself.

. . . As to this matter having ever been discussed in the Emperor's frequent conversations with Napoleon—a subject regarding which he had hitherto always avoided to give me any precise answer—Alexander stated positively that no mention had been made of it between the two Emperors. At Tilsit Napoleon had spoken with much levity about Poland and the Poles, and at Erfurth there was too much to do for them to touch upon that subject. I expressed my regret that his Majesty had not taken an opportunity of sounding Napoleon on the matter, and I added that notwithstanding the despatches and speeches of his Ministers, Napoleon had succeeded in spreading among the Poles a conviction that he not only had the interests of Poland at heart, but that he had a feeling of special affection for her. . .

His Majesty replied that Napoleon was a man who would not scruple to use any means whatever so long as he attained his object. As I had for some time heard various rumours in the society of St Petersburg as to Napoleon's fits of epilepsy and his being threatened with mental derangement, I asked the Emperor whether there was any truth in these

reports. ' Napoleon will never go mad,' he answered ;
' the thing is impossible, and those who believe it do
not know him. He is a man who in the midst of the
greatest troubles keeps his head cool ; all his fits of
passion are only meant to intimidate, and are often
the fruit of calculation. He does nothing without
thoroughly considering and foreseeing the consequences of his acts. . . One of his favourite sayings
is that nothing should be undertaken without a plan.
In his opinion there is no difficulty that cannot be
overcome if you find the right mode of proceeding.
Once that is found, the rest is easy ; while if the
simplest matter possible is undertaken without finding the method of doing it, all is spoilt and no result
is obtained. His health is excellent ; no one can
bear fatigue and hard work better than he does ; but
he requires eight hours' sleep a day, though he does
not keep regular hours. He is not eloquent either in
speech or in writing ; I have heard him dictate letters
in an abrupt and unconnected style.' . . .

I remarked in the course of this conversation that
the Emperor still retained a sort of partiality for me,
but that he had no very strong desire to keep me. . . .
As for Napoleon, it is clear that Alexander under-
stands him thoroughly ; that Napoleon has preserved
a marked influence over his mind ; and that he greatly
fears him.

5th April 1810.

About three weeks ago the Emperor, whom I had
not seen for some time, suddenly sent for me. After

talking about private matters and the grant of an amnesty to those inhabitants of the Polish provinces of Russia who had joined their countrymen of the Grand-Duchy of Warsaw in the war against Austria, the Emperor mentioned that he had a plan of uniting the eight Polish provinces under a separate administration, and asked my opinion on the subject. I requested to be given time for reflection. The problem was a difficult one. How could I give the Emperor any hope that the means to be adopted for producing a reconciliation between him and the Poles would be efficacious? And as regards my country, might not the result be a civil war? Yet I thought it best to reply, partly as a matter of courtesy, partly because the future was so uncertain that I considered it undesirable entirely to break a thread which under different circumstances might become valuable.

After a few weeks I came back to the Emperor and read to him a memorandum in which I stated my views. . . . The Emperor interrupted me at the beginning with the remark that it was not only for the eventuality of a war, but to gain the affection of the Poles in any case, that he thought of doing something for them. He then listened without saying a word, but with much attention. It was only when I stated that the most suitable time for doing something in favour of Poland was past, that he again interrupted me. 'In writing that,' he said, ' you were no doubt thinking of the year 1805 and my stay at Pulawy.* I now see myself that that was a

* See page 99.

favourable moment—perhaps a unique one. We could then have done easily what can only be done now with great trouble ; but it must not be forgotten that we would have had the whole of the Prussian army against us.'

I answered that another very favourable opportunity occurred at the time of the last war with Austria, during which Russia could easily have demanded the restoration of Poland. 'That would have brought about the total ruin of Austria,' was the Emperor's reply. 'Any how,' I rejoined, 'the course which was followed was the worst, for it did not save Austria, whom it threw into the arms of France ; it annoyed Napoleon ; and it was of no material advantage to Russia.'

When I had finished reading, I apologised for not having arrived at any definite conclusion ; I could not say more, as I was imperfectly informed of what was going on, and I did not know what was the predominant feeling in the Polish provinces. 'Bah !' said the Emperor, 'it is not difficult to know what people think in the provinces and in the Grand-Duchy. The Poles would follow the devil himself if he would lead them to the restoration of their country. But I am satisfied at what you have written ; it will help me to reflect on a subject which has so long occupied my attention. I have sought all kinds of means of realising my wishes, but have not arrived at any satisfactory solution. The greatest difficulty is to find an indemnification for the King of Saxony ; this could only be done by still further dismembering that unfortunate King of Prussia.'

I remarked that the greatest difficulty was to obtain the consent of France, and that if this were obtained the rest would be easy. The Emperor agreed, saying that Napoleon's interest was not to change the present state of things, as he cared much less for the good of Poland than to use her as a tool in the event of his making war upon Russia. He at the same time admitted that it was natural that the inhabitants of the Grand-Duchy of Warsaw, in view of the respective forces of the two Powers, the talent and experience of the Polish generals and armies, and Napoleon's great chances of victory in any war, should not be inclined to throw themselves into the arms of Russia at the risk of losing the fruits of the efforts they had made for so many years. This was entirely my view of the case; and the Emperor then told me some of his ideas for bringing about a restoration of Poland.

One of these was to enter on a sham war with the Grand-Duchy, so that by a preconcerted arrangement the Russian troops might occupy positions in which they would be joined by the Polish troops, and then fight the French together. Such a plan was obviously chimerical; its difficulties were palpable, and it involved a war against Napoleon with very uncertain chances of success.

Another plan was to form a kingdom of Poland out of the Duchy and Galicia, and to allow the inhabitants of the Polish provinces of Russia to serve in the new kingdom as if it were their own country. This idea surprised me; but the Emperor explained that the

Poles, being thus satisfied, would have no reason to oppose Russia ; that there would then be no longer any cause of dissension between Russia and France ; and that the evil would thus be got rid of by amputation instead of by cure. The Emperor's tone in saying this led me to believe that the idea might have been suggested to him by the French Ambassador, that it had been discussed between them, and that he might be disposed to adopt it as a convenient method of avoiding war with France.

The Emperor concluded by saying that he would consider all these ideas, and that he wished me also to seek a clue to the object he had in view. I replied that I was far from desiring to damp his Majesty's good intentions, but that so far as I could see there was nothing to be done immediately beyond taking the measures I proposed in my memorandum. I added that I thought the present year would not come to an end without producing events more serious and decisive than any that we had yet seen. The Emperor, interrupting me, said in an impressive tone that he thought it would not be this year, as Napoleon was entirely occupied with his marriage ; but that he expected there would be a crisis next year. ' We are now in April,' he continued ; ' it will be nine months hence.' *   While saying these words, and indeed throughout the conversation, the Emperor had a severe and fixed look, which reminded me of his haggard gaze after Austerlitz.

* Napoleon's Campaign in Russia did not begin till more than two years afterwards (June 22, 1812).

CHAPTER XVIII

1810

ALEXANDER, notwithstanding his promises, did nothing for Poland, and Prince Czartoryski then determined to take no further part in Russian affairs, and to devote himself exclusively to his own country. This decision was only arrived at after a hard mental struggle, which he thus describes in a paper dated the 20th of June 1810 :—

In the difficult circumstances in which I am placed, and which are exposed on all sides to misunderstanding and misjudgment, I owe a sincere account of my actions to those who take an interest in me, in order to spare them as much as I can the pain of finding themselves deceived in their opinion of me. Seeing me as I am, their judgment may console me for the injustice of the majority, from which I shall perhaps not escape.

I seem continually to hear two voices which ring with equal force in my ears. One speaks as follows :—

‘ Your position is, no doubt, extremely difficult,

but your difficulties themselves trace out for you the course you should follow. . . You have played a part in Russia which for a time made you a prominent figure on the theatre of European politics. In doing so you acquired general esteem, and when you resigned office your withdrawal was regretted by the Governments and nations which were suffering under the devastating system of Napoleon. After your resignation, you maintained the opinions you had advocated when in office, and Cabinets and patriots still looked up to you as one of those by whom Europe could be saved.

' Will you now discard the principles you have proclaimed, attach yourself to the chariot of the tyrant, and become the tool of his projects, which in your opinion are fatal to the happiness both of present and future generations ?

' You owe nothing to Russia or to the Emperor whom you have served well as long as you could. But do you owe nothing to yourself and to Europe ? And to what would you sacrifice such grave considerations and precious advantages ? Not to the evident good of your country, but to vague hopes and dreams. . . . Can you believe that Buonaparte sincerely wishes for the good of any country ? All he wants is to make your countrymen his tools, and he will be ready to abandon them directly his interest requires him to do so.

' Would it be right for you to participate in such projects ? Your country has nothing to reproach you with ; you have been useful to your countrymen while you were in office; you have done your utmost to restore Poland. Under present circumstances it is difficult, if not impossible, for you to take an active part in Russian affairs; but on the other hand you should at least not mix yourself up with what is going on in your country. You should hold aloof, and remain neutral and passive as long as the present storm lasts.'

While I listen to these reasons and feel their force, the other voice says to me :—

'It is true that your position is different from that of the other Poles. They feel it, and they give you full credit for the conduct you have pursued hitherto.

'But your duties are changed. You passed under the rule of Russia together with the rest of your country. Circumstances placed you in the service of Russia, not as a Russian, but because you were a Pole. You belonged to Russia because Poland was destroyed; the cause having ceased, the effect as regards yourself should cease also. . . . It was solely your personal relations with the Emperor that led you to enter his service, notwithstanding the strong reasons to the contrary which you repeatedly urged to him. When he insisted upon your compliance, though still a Pole at heart, you honestly and zealously laboured in the interest of Russia. . . . There was an interval when all hope of restoring Poland had disappeared. Directly it revived, you strove to make the possibility of the restoration of Poland serve to glorify the Emperor, and to unite by the bonds of a common advantage the

two interests which were most dear to you. But your
counsels were not heard; your plans were not followed.
The interests you wished to unite again parted from
each other, and you retired in time to avoid a situation
where you must have been guilty either on one side
or the other. These interests have grown more and
more divergent and will become entirely opposed to
each other. You should leave a service and a State
essentially hostile to your country, and bent on crushing out its existence and that of your countrymen.
Nor is this all. A moment will come when you will
have to take an active part—when Poland is declared
independent and will be in arms to maintain her
existence. This will probably be when France is
at war with Russia, and every Pole who then holds
aloof will be looked upon by his countrymen with
contempt. . . .

‘When people say Buonaparte should not be supported by the Poles because of his unjust and
oppressive conduct towards other nations, they forget
that there is not a single act of iniquity committed
by Napoleon of which the Powers which partitioned
Poland did not themselves set the example. It is
not for them to become the champions of principles
which they have trodden under foot. . . . A characteristic trait of the Polish nation is to love one’s
country above everything, and to be ready to
sacrifice everything to recover it. Will you be
more sensitive to what happens on the Tagus and
the Adige than on the Vistula—be indignant at
the acts of injustice committed with regard to other

nations, and indifferent to those inflicted on your own ? . . .

'Buonaparte has never done any harm to Poland; he alone has held out his hand to her and has done all he could for her. The Poles condemn his policy as other nations do; they pity the Spaniards, and are ashamed to be obliged to fight against them; but no nation can be expected to commit suicide in order that other nations may be benefited. The Poles regret the necessity of their being attached to Napoleon's fortunes, but they cannot refuse benefits at his hands which are not offered them by any one else. They have done everything to prove their ardent wish to owe their national existence to the Emperor Alexander; but he has rejected all their overtures. On one side they find interest, support, and hope; on the other, animosity, persecution, and discouragement. The dearest interests of Poland, supported solely by France, have by the present conduct of the Cabinet of St Petersburg become diametrically opposed to those of Russia. Poland is ready to do the will of any Power that will help her. Buonaparte alone has hitherto done so, and she hopes through his assistance to recover her name and her existence as a nation. If she is wise, circumstances may perhaps enable her to come successfully out of the general cataclysm which is approaching, and she may by her efforts prove to the Russian Government and nation that it would be useful to bring her over to their side, and to unite the two nations by bonds of mutual advantage and interest.

'As to your position in the matter, it is quite clear. You have loyally served the Emperor, and you have always told him the truth : he knows better than anyone your sentiments with regard to Poland. You owe him a certain amount of consideration, which cannot, however, outweigh your duties to your country. The policy you proclaimed as a Russian Minister was in accordance with your duty and the state of Europe at the time. There was then a hope that resistance to Napoleon would be efficacious, and it was certainly right that Russia should attempt it. Circumstances are now entirely different, and as a Pole you can no longer advocate the same policy as when you were Minister of Russia, and Russia had not made a treaty of peace with France. Your principles, however, have always been the same; your period of office in Russia was merely an episode in your career.

'In Poland you cannot play a passive part. No family has more distinguished itself by its attachment to the country than yours, and though still young, you have already fought for Poland,* and your words as well as your deeds have been those of a patriot. Your countrymen have full confidence in you, and you cannot refuse them your assistance without dishonour.

'There is no question of your becoming a satellite of Buonaparte; no one wishes you to do so. Nor is it necessary for you to decide too soon or without sufficient reflection. But you will have to come forward at the moment when the fate of Poland will

* At the battle of Granno, in 1792 (see Vol. I. page 53).

hang in the balance, when there will be no doubt as to the motives of those who declare themselves, or excuse for those who will withdraw at a time when your country will make decisive efforts to recover its existence.

' Will your relations of friendship with the Emperor excuse you?   Those relations have almost ceased; and your duty to your country is superior to any claims of friendship.   Moreover, if you have sacrificed that friendship for the interests of a country which has been the cause of the ruin of Poland, how could you do less for your own country ?'

Such are the two voices that speak to me one after the other, and the same arguments have been expressed to me with even more force by persons who are dear to me and whom I respect.   Being thus placed between two such opposite opinions, I ought to decide for myself which I should follow: but I confess that I cannot yet clearly see any way of escape from the labyrinth in which I am enclosed.

My reason does not lead me to any result, for the arguments on both sides seem to me to have equal weight.   But at the bottom of my heart the feelings and motives which speak for my country are paramount, and I would be happy were I able to follow them without constraint.   I was born with these feelings; my education developed them; they are deeply graven in my heart.   I think no one loves his country with more passion than I do.   To keep the esteem of my countrymen and to do good to my country is the only glory that would give me pleasure ; and if her misfortunes continue and my reputation perishes with her existence, I shall at least have the consolation of knowing that I have never acted from any motive that is not just and honourable.

CHAPTER XIX

1810-12

AFTER Prince Czartoryski had returned to Poland he devoted himself entirely to his educational work as Curator of the University of Wilna; but finding that a Commission under a Russian Governor had been appointed to report on one of the colleges in his district and decide as to the future organisation of the college, he sent his resignation to the Emperor in a letter dated the 1½ November, 1810. The following correspondence then took place between Alexander and the Prince :—

THE EMPEROR ALEXANDER TO PRINCE CZARTORYSKI.

ST PETERSBURG,
25th December, 1810.

MY DEAR FRIEND,—I have received your letter, and

I will not conceal from you that it has given me much pain. You wish to break the only public connection which exists between us, and after an intimate friendship of more than fifteen years, which nothing has been able to alter, we are to become strangers to each other, if not by our sentiments, at least in our public relations. This is a thought which it is painful to me to dwell upon, the more so as I believed the moment had arrived when our intimate relations might be developed to their fullest extent. . . . As to that unfortunate affair of the college, I had not the slightest wish to cause you pain, and I did not intend to do anything after receiving the report of the Commission without first consulting you. . . .

But there is a more important subject which requires immediate consideration. It seems to me that the time has arrived to prove to the Poles that Russia is not their enemy, but their true and natural friend; that although Russia is represented to them as the sole obstacle to the restoration of Poland, it is not improbable that Russia will be the Power to bring about that event. . . . This has always been my favourite idea; circumstances have twice compelled me to postpone its realisation, but it has none the less remained in my mind. There has never been a more propitious moment for realising it than the present; but before going any further I should like you to answer categorically and in the greatest detail the questions I must put to you before proceeding to the execution of my plan.

1. Have you sufficient *data* as to the feeling of

the inhabitants of the Duchy of Warsaw; and if so—

2. Have you a well-founded belief that they would seize with avidity any offer giving them the *certainty* (not probability, but *certainty*) of their regeneration?

3. Would they accept it from whatever quarter it might come, and would they join any Power, without distinction, that would espouse their interests sincerely and with attachment? It is self-evident that the proclamation of their restoration would have to precede any decision on their part, and would have to be such as to prove the sincerity of the conduct which would be adopted with regard to them.

4. Have you, on the other hand, reason to suppose that various parties exist in the country, and that consequently—

5. One cannot reckon on a unanimous resolution eagerly to take the opportunity of the first offer made for the regeneration of Poland?

6. What are these parties? Are they equal in importance, and who are the individuals that may be regarded as their leaders?

7. Do these parties also exist in the army, or should it be regarded as more united in opinion and feeling?

8. Who is the officer that has the greatest influence upon opinion in the army?

These are the most important questions I have to put to you at present. Directly I get your answers, I will give you further information as to my plans. . .

I must beg you to keep the contents of this letter

absolutely secret. I rely on your prudence, and I feel certain you will take care not to mar a work to which your country would owe its regeneration, Europe its deliverance, and you personally the glory and the pleasure of having co-operated in it, and having thereby proved that your conduct has throughout been consistent, and that those of your countrymen who relied upon you in the past have been justified in their expectations. If you second me, and lead me to hope that the Poles, and especially the Polish army, are practically unanimous in desiring the restoration of Poland from whatever quarter it may come, success, with the help of God, will not be doubtful, for it is based not on a hope of counterbalancing the genius of Napoleon, but solely on the diminution of his forces through the secession of the Duchy of Warsaw, and the general exasperation of the whole of Germany against him. I annex a short table of the auxiliary forces which would be at the disposal of each side.

This is what I had to say; consider it calmly. Such a moment presents itself only once; any other combination will only bring about a war to the death between Russia and France, with your country as the battlefield. The support on which the Poles can rely is limited to the person of Napoleon, who cannot live for ever. Should he disappear from the scene, the consequences to Poland would be disastrous; while if by joining Russia and the other Powers which would certainly follow her, the moral strength of France should be overthrown, and Europe delivered from her yoke, the existence of your country would be established with unshakeable solidity. . . .

I await your answer with the greatest impatience, and am always yours, heart and soul.

My best remembrances to your parents, your sisters, and your brother.

(Signed) ALEXANDER.

Note on the Forces which might be opposed to each other.

On one side—

      100,000 Russians
       50,000 Poles
       50,000 Prussians
       30,000 Danes
      ———————

Total 230,000 men, who might at once be reinforced by 100,000 more Russians.

On the other side—

       60,000 French (it is stated there are only 46,000 in Germany, but I add those who might be drawn from Holland and the interior of France).
       30,000 Saxons
       30,000 Bavarians
       20,000 Würtembergers
       15,000 Westphalians and other German troops
      ———————

Total 155,000 men.

It is more than probable, however, that the example set by the Poles will be followed by the Germans, and then there will only remain the 60,000 French. And if Austria, in return for the advantages we shall offer her, should also enter the field against France, this will add 200,000 men to our side against Napoleon.

PRINCE CZARTORYSKI TO THE EMPEROR ALEXANDER.

$\frac{15}{30}$ *January* 1811.

SIRE,—Your Imperial Majesty will easily imagine with what attention and extreme interest I have read your letter of the 25th of December. . . . Allow me to express to you my deep gratitude for your benevolent intentions regarding my country, the favourable recollection you have retained of her in your political combinations, and the special proof of confidence which you are good enough to give me on this occasion, and which I will endeavour to deserve by carrying out your instructions with all the zeal and prudence at my command. . . . I will at once reply to your questions; but my replies, as you will have foreseen, can only be of a preliminary kind.

So far as I have been able to observe the public feeling in this country, I see a unanimity of intentions and objects both in the army and among the inhabitants of the Duchy of Warsaw. Their sole wish and object is the restoration of Poland—the reunion of all its parts into a single national body, under a national and constitutional régime. The differences of opinion which are observable as to the amount of

confidence to be placed in generals and other prominent personages, and as to their talents and patriotism,
cannot properly come under the designation of party
feeling, and these differences would either disappear or
have a quite subordinate influence if the higher
interests of the country were at stake. Unanimity,
therefore exists ; but it would be necessary to convince
everybody that the salvation of the country and the
realisation of greater and more solid advantages
demand a total change of policy and the abandonment of the only supporter that the Duchy has as yet
possessed.

The certainty of the regeneration of Poland would,
as it seems to me, be received with gratitude and
eagerness from anyone that could offer it, provided
that the manner in which it should be offered and
brought about inspired more confidence and greater
guarantees of success than the inhabitants of the
Duchy believe themselves to possess through their
union with France. The great difficulty in the
execution of your Majesty's plan would be at once
to produce such a conviction in the minds of the
Government, the army, and the inhabitants of the
Duchy.

This, indeed, is the gist of the whole question.
However just the grievances of the Poles against
Napoleon may be, he has yet persuaded them that it
was not want of good-will, but absolute want of power,
which prevented him from carrying the work of their
regeneration any farther, . . . and that at the first
rupture with Russia, Poland would be restored. To

this feeling is added gratitude for what Napoleon has already done, and repugnance at the idea of turning against him, just at the moment when he most reckoned upon its co-operation, the new Polish State which he has created. To all these considerations must be added the fact that the French and the Poles are brothers in arms, and the idea that while the French are the friends of Poland, the Russians are her bitter enemies—an idea which has been considerably strengthened by the events of the late war.

A further difficulty is created by the fact that there are 20,000 Polish troops in Spain, whom their friends and relatives in Poland would fear to sacrifice to the vengeance of Napoleon. Moreover, in the expectation of a war with Russia, many Poles have sent their children to be educated in Paris, as being at present the safest place in Europe; and these would be so many hostages in Napoleon's hands. Finally, Napoleon has hitherto been so uniformly successful, even in the most dangerous undertakings, that people think he will always conquer in the end, however much appearances may be against him. . . .

In order to meet these objections it would be necessary to make the Poles some offer so distinctly advantageous to their country as to overcome all personal considerations. They must be treated with magnanimity, for with all their faults they have the qualities which appeal to the heart and the imagination. The three following points would for such a purpose be indispensable: (1) The restoration of the constitution of the 3rd of May 1791, which is graven in ineffaceable characters on all Polish hearts; (2) The reunion of the whole of Poland under one sceptre, thereby putting an end to a state of things which separates members of the same family from their relations and estates merely because they are under a different government; (3) The re-establishment of outlets for trade, the closing of which has impoverished the country; and (4) A reasonable prospect of success in a war with Napoleon. . . . As to this last point, I can hardly believe that Napoleon could not get more than 15,000 men in Holland and France to come to the support of the 16,000 he has in North Germany. What has become of the new levy of 150,000 recruits? . . . And are you quite sure that you would have 100,000 men at your disposal at the beginning of the war? I have so often seen in Russia 100,000 men on paper represented only by 65,000 effectives. It would also be well to state precisely whether by the Power which will offer to restore Poland you mean Russia.

I have answered as well as I can your principal questions. As to the most influential man in the army, he is undoubtedly Prince Poniatowski, the Commander-in-Chief and Minister of War, whose personal character secures him an influence over his subordinates greater than that of any other chief.

In a few days I will go to Warsaw and sound the opinions of the leading personages there. . . . I regret your Majesty has not stated more precisely what you propose to do, and what you expect of the Poles, so that there should be no misunderstanding on either side.   This alone could furnish sufficient arguments to influence the decision of those who will have to choose between the two alternatives.   I forgot to ask if when developing this plan you do not intend to make an effort to bring about a general peace and gain your ends without war.   I cannot tell you, Sire, with what hopes and fears I am continually agitated.   What happiness it would be to labour for the deliverance of so many suffering nations, for the restoration of my country, and for your Majesty's glory!   What happiness to see those different interests combined which fate seemed always to oppose to each other!   But often I fancy that this is too magnificent a dream ever to be realised, and that the genius of evil, which seems always to be on the watch to break up combinations too fortunate for mankind, will also succeed in destroying this one.   I am, with the profoundest respect, &c.

THE EMPEROR ALEXANDER TO PRINCE CZARTORYSKI.

St Petersburg,

31st January 1811.

MY DEAR FRIEND,—I received your interesting letter of the $\frac{13}{25}$ January on the evening of the day before yesterday, and I hasten at once to answer it.

The difficulties which it points out are very great, I admit; but as I had foreseen most of them, and the results are of such supreme importance, the worst course to follow would be to stop half-way. . . .

I will begin by replying to the chief points in your letter—

(1) The Power to which I referred as willing

to take in hand the regeneration of Poland is *Russia*.

(2) By such regeneration I mean the reunion of everything that formerly constituted Poland, including the Russian provinces (except White Russia), so as to make the rivers Dvina, Beresina, and Dnieper the frontiers.

(3) The government officials, the established authorities, and the army, should be entirely of the Polish nationality.

(4) As I do not well remember the constitution of the 3rd of May, I cannot decide anything until I see it, and I shall be obliged if you will send it me. In any case a liberal constitution will be offered, such as to satisfy the wishes of the inhabitants.

(5) In order to convince them of the sincerity of my offer, the proclamations of the restoration of Poland must precede everything else, and it is by them that the execution of the plan is to commence.

(6) But the conditions *sine quâ non* on which I offer this are—

1*st*. That the kingdom of Poland shall for ever be united to Russia, whose Emperor shall in future bear the title of Emperor of Russia and King of Poland.

2*nd*. That a formal and positive assurance shall be given of a unanimity of disposition and feeling in favour of such a result among the inhabitants of the Duchy, to be guaranteed by the signature of the most prominent persons among them.

I will now endeavour to diminish your fears

as to the insufficiency of the military means at my disposal.

The army which is to support and fight by the side of the Poles is completely organised, and is composed of eight divisions of infantry, each comprising 10,000 men, and of four divisions of cavalry, each of 4,000 horses. This makes a total of 96,000 men, to which should be added fifteen Cossack regiments of 7,500 horse—106,500 in all. Non-combatants are not included.

This army will be supported by another of eleven divisions of infantry, a division of grenadiers, the Guards' division, four divisions of cavalry, and seventeen Cossack regiments—total, 134,000 men.

Finally, a third army, composed of reserve squadrons and battalions, supplies 44,000 combatants, reinforced by 80,000 recruits, all clothed and trained for some months in the depôts.

The army of Moldavia might in case of necessity also detach some divisions, without on that account being unable to maintain its defensive position, and the armies of Finland and Georgia, together with the corps in the Crimea, would remain entirely intact.

Two initial difficulties present themselves:

1*st*. The reunion of Galicia would create a difficulty as regards Austria. It is most necessary to treat her with consideration and avoid offending her in any respect. I have therefore decided to offer her Wallachia and Moldavia as far as the Sereth in exchange for Galicia. But it would be indispensable to postpone the reunion of Galicia until Austria gives her consent, so as to prove that we have no views that might be prejudicial to her.

The Kingdom of Poland would, therefore, in the first instance be formed of the Duchy of Warsaw and the Russian provinces.

2*nd.* The compensation to be given to the King of Saxony* presents a second difficulty which I find it not so easy to overcome. But I do not consider that I shall be bound to do so unless he comes over to my side.

Having thus stated the facts, I will enter upon a discussion of the subject generally.

It is beyond doubt that Napoleon is striving to provoke Russia to a rupture with him, hoping that I will make the mistake of being the aggressor. This would be a great blunder in present circumstances, and I am determined not to make it. But if the Poles were willing to join me, that would put an entirely new face on the matter. Being reinforced by the 50,000 men who constitute their army, by the 50,000 Prussians who could then also join me without risk, and by the moral revolution which would be the infallible result in Europe, I could advance to the Oder without striking a blow.

I agree with you that a proposal of peace might in that case be properly made. If it is not accepted, and war becomes inevitable, let us consider impartially the alternatives which are open to the Poles and the probable results of each of them.

First alternative, that of the Poles remaining on the side of France and co-operating with her.

This may be subdivided into two cases:

----

* The King of Saxony was Grand-Duke of the Duchy of Warsaw.

1st. Russia having decided not to take the offensive, it is possible that Napoleon will not do so either, at least so long as the affairs of Spain occupy him and the great mass of his troops are engaged there. In that case matters will remain as they are, and the regeneration of Poland will consequently be postponed to a more distant and very uncertain period.

2nd. If, on the other hand, Napoleon should attack Russia, and at the same time proclaim the regeneration of Poland, his proclamation could only have effect in the Duchy of Warsaw, for it would be necessary to deprive Russia of her Polish provinces by force of arms. Meanwhile the Duchy of Warsaw and the Polish provinces would become the theatre of war and of all possible devastation. It may thus be asserted with certainty that after such a war, whatever might be its result, Poland would be only a vast desert, and its inhabitants the greatest sufferers by the war.

Such is the probable result of the restoration of Poland being proclaimed by France.

Second alternative, that of the Poles joining Russia and co-operating with her.

The infallible results of this would be—

1st. That the regeneration of Poland, instead of being postponed, would precede any other event.

2nd, That this regeneration would comprise the Duchy of Warsaw and the Russian provinces, with a tolerably certain hope of its being extended to Galicia.

3rd, That the theatre of war, instead of being in the heart of Poland, would be transferred to the Oder.

Such are the *infallible* results, while the *probable* ones might be :

1*st*, A complete revolution of opinion in Europe.

2*nd*, A very marked diminution in the forces of Napoleon, increasing the chances of success ; for Napoleon would find it very difficult to withdraw his forces from Spain, being engaged with a nation bitterly hostile to him, and having 300,000 combatants in the field, which would not be satisfied with his retreat, but would take advantage of the new war Napoleon would have on his hands to invade France.

3*rd*, The deliverance of Europe from the yoke which oppresses her.

4*th*, The employment for the defence of Poland, as a kingdom annexed to a strong Empire, of the forces of that Empire.

5*th*, The revival of trade and prosperity, a liberal constitution, and a public revenue based on the real wants of the country, and not, as now, applied solely for the maintenance of a too large army destined to serve the ambitious plans of Napoleon.

Even the fears that you express as to the fate of the 20,000 Poles in Napoleon's service do not seem to me well founded, for the worst that could happen to them would be that for a time they would be regarded as prisoners of war .   .   .   .

To resume : so long as I cannot be sure of the co-operation of the Poles I am decided not to begin a war with France. If such co-operation is to take place, I must receive *indubitable* assurances and proofs of it ; it is only then that I shall be able to act in the manner above stated. In that case you must send me all the necessary papers, such as proclamations, the constitution, and other indispensable documents. . . . . Our correspondence is an absolute secret, and even the Chancellor knows nothing of it, though I have often discussed the question with him. As to my military preparations, I have given them a defensive character, . . . and have sent a letter to Napoleon explaining that I am obliged to take precautionary measures, but that I am determined to adhere to my system of policy, and will certainly not take the offensive. I must confess, however, that as rumours are being spread at St Petersburg that I am about to assume the title of King of Poland, I endeavour to put an end to them by declaring that the thing is impossible and cannot occur. Such rumours are at present rather injurious than useful, though they prove that the plan would be highly approved by the Russians.

I must also warn you that I know from a good source that you are being watched by the French Minister of Police. You must therefore double your precautions. . . .

I shall expect your answer with impatience. Yours for life, heart and soul.

Pray remember me most kindly to your parents, your brother, and your sisters.

THE EMPEROR TO PRINCE CZARTORYSKI.

ST PETERSBURG, 1*st April*, 1812.

I do not know, dear friend, whether you have guessed the cause of my silence.

Your previous letters had left me too little hope of success to authorise me to act, and I could not reasonably do so without some probability of success. I have therefore been obliged to resign myself to waiting for events, and not provoking, by any step on my part, a struggle whose importance and danger I thoroughly appreciate, though I do not believe I shall be able to avoid it. I also had certain information that you were being watched : and in order not to expose you to the least danger, I thought it best to allow a considerable time to elapse before resuming our correspondence. . . Finally, our projects have acquired a publicity which could only be very prejudicial to them, so much so, that they were talked about at Dresden and in Paris. . . .

A rupture with France seems inevitable. The object of Napoleon is to destroy, or at least to humiliate, the last Power in Europe which remains independent of him, and in order to attain this object, he puts forward pretensions which are inadmissible and incompatible with the honour of Russia.

He wishes all our trade with neutrals to be stopped ; .but this is the only trade which is left to us.

He also asks that, while deprived of every means of exporting our own productions, we should not raise any obstacle to the importation of French articles of luxury, which we have prohibited, not being rich enough to pay for them.

As I shall never be able to consent to such proposals, it is probable that war will follow,* not-

* It did, in the month of June following.

withstanding all that Russia had done to avoid it. Blood will flow, and poor humanity will again be sacrificed to the insatiable ambition of a man who seems to have been created as its scourge. You are too enlightened not to see how any liberal ideas with regard to your country are in his eyes out of the question. Napoleon has had confidential conversations on this subject with the envoys of Austria and Prussia, and the tone in which he has spoken to them, shows in its true light both his character and his indifference towards your countrymen, whom he looks upon only as the instruments of his hatred of Russia.

This war, which seems inevitable, frees me from all obligation to consider the interests of France, and leaves me unshackled in working out my favourite idea of regenerating your country.

All that remains to be done, therefore, is to decide upon the most advantageous course to be followed for securing the success of our plans; and in order that you may be better able to form a judgment upon them I think it useful to give you some indications as to the military operations I propose to undertake.

Although it is not impossible that we may push on with our forces to the Vistula, and even cross it so as to enter Warsaw, it is more prudent not to reckon on the resources and the prestige we should acquire from the possession of that city. We must therefore make the provinces the centre of our action.

Several very important questions will have to be settled in this connection.

Which is the most suitable moment for declaring the regeneration of Poland? Is it directly the rupture takes place, or after our troops will have gained some marked advantages? If the latter, would it be useful for the success of our plans to organise the Grand-Duchy of Lithuania as a preliminary measure and give it one of the two constitutions of which I send you drafts, or should the grant of a constitution be postponed until the whole of Poland is restored?

It is on these vital questions that I invite your candid opinion, and I would also wish you to state which of the constitutions you think preferable.

I will not here discuss the chances of Russia in the coming struggle. I will only remind you of the immense extent of territory which the Russian armies have behind them and into which they can retire, while Napoleon's difficulties would increase the further he proceeds from his resources. Once the war begins we are resolved not to lay down our arms. Our military resources are very great, and the public feeling is excellent—altogether different from that boastful spirit which you witnessed during the two preceding wars. . . . People think reverses are quite possible, but for all that they are resolved to maintain the honour of the Empire at any cost.

If under these circumstances the Poles should join them, the effect would be immense, and the Germans, forced by Napoleon to fight on his side, would certainly follow the example of the Poles.

Sweden has concluded an offensive and defensive alliance with us. The Crown Prince has a burning desire to become the antagonist of Napoleon, against whom he has an old personal grudge, and following in the footsteps of Gustavus Adolphus, he only wishes to be useful to a cause which is that of oppressed Europe.

Your idea of Napoleon consenting to a restoration of Poland, by placing her under the rule of a King who is also Emperor of Russia, is a chimerical one. He will never agree to a measure so advantageous to Russia, especially at a moment when he thinks only of destroying her. He will never attribute to complaisance on the part of Russia her inaction when he invaded Prussia, for it was impossible for us to interfere, in view of the absolute want of energy on the part of the King of Prussia, who thought only of saving Berlin and his palace.

Adieu, my dear friend, Providence alone knows what will be the issue of the great events which are preparing. It would have been a great pleasure to me to see you again, if only for a short time, at so interesting a crisis, at Wilna, for which town I shall leave in three days; but I dare not propose this to you, knowing the danger to which it would expose you. Be guided in all this only by your prudence, and believe me, etc.

[The further development of the plans referred to in the above correspondence was interrupted by the Russian Campaign of 1812. On the 26th of June in that year, immediately after Napoleon had crossed the Niemen, the Polish diet assembled at Warsaw under the presidency of Prince Adam Casimir Czartoryski, Prince Adam's father, and proclaimed the restoration of the whole of ancient Poland as an independent State. All the Poles in the Russian service were called upon to leave it, and Prince Adam, who still held a post under the Russian government as Curator of the University of Wilna, repeatedly urged the Emperor to accept the resignation which the Prince had already tendered on several previous occasions. Alexander took no notice of these letters, and directly the campaign was over the correspondence between him and the Prince as to the plan of a reconstruction of Poland was resumed.]

LETTER FROM PRINCE ADAM CZARTORYSKI TO THE
EMPEROR ALEXANDER.

$\frac{1}{2}\frac{9}{1}$ *December* 1812.

. . . The events of the war having taken a turn which seems to be decisive, I fear no one will now plead to your Imperial Majesty for the interests of my country, and I have accordingly sent Mr K. with the accompanying papers, in the hope that they may convince you.

I have no hope in the Continental Powers; they will strive to divert you from an idea which will be offensive to them, and which is too noble for their Cabinets to understand. What reassures me is that England, in view of her clear interest, and of the opinions of the Prince Regent, cannot fail to appreciate the plan. . . .

If your Imperial Majesty, at the moment when the Polish nation is expecting the vengeance of a conqueror, will hold out your hand and offer it that which for her was the object of the war, the effect would be magical.

If you would adopt the idea relative to the Grand Duke Michael,* I would take it upon myself to get

* The Grand-Dukes Constantine and Michael were the Emperor's brothers.

everything signed without delay.   I think it my duty not to conceal from your Majesty that a cause of incessant anxiety and terror to the Poles is the Grand-Duke Constantine, who is your heir-apparent; and this is the reason why they would prefer another branch.   A King of Poland with 300,000 men under his orders would be able at any time to destroy what his predecessor may have established.   It is this which makes the Poles so desirous of obtaining a regular constitution, though even that could not guarantee them against acts of arbitrary violence.   But whatever arrangement you may prefer on the basis I have submitted to you, I do not think I am saying too much when I assure you that it would be settled to your entire satisfaction.

The Emperor Alexander to Prince Czartoryski

LEYPOUNY, 13*th January* 1813.

I received your interesting letter of the 15th of December 1812, with its enclosures, two days ago . . . and to-day I have also received a document signed 'The Minister of the Interior, Mostowski,' and addressed to me.   I do not lose a moment in answering you, and this letter will also serve as an answer to M. Mostowski.

The proposals in these papers, and the personal sentiments with regard to myself expressed in them, have touched me very deeply.   The successes by which Providence has wished to bless my efforts and my perseverance have in no way changed either my sentiments or my intentions with regard to Poland. Your countrymen may therefore abandon any fears they may feel: vengeance is a sentiment unknown to me, and my greatest pleasure is to return good for evil. The strictest orders have been given to my generals to treat the Poles as friends and brothers.

To speak candidly, in order to realise my favourite ideas as to Poland I shall have to overcome some difficulties, notwithstanding the brilliancy of my present position.

In the first place, opinion in Russia would be against them. The sacking by the Polish troops of Smolensk and Moscow, and the devastation of the whole country, has revived old hatreds.

Next, if I were at this moment to publish my intentions with regard to Poland, the result would be to throw Austria and Prussia entirely into the arms of France; while it is essential to prevent such a result, especially as those Powers already show themselves very disposed to join me.

These difficulties will be conquered with a little wisdom and prudence. But for this it is necessary that you should second me, by justifying in the eyes of the Russians the predilection which I am known to feel for the Poles and their ideas. Trust me, my character, and my principles, and your hopes will not be deceived. As military events develop themselves, you will see how dear the interests of your country are to me, and how faithful I am to my old ideas. As to the form, you know I have always preferred liberal ones.

But I must plainly tell you that the idea of my brother Michael cannot be admitted. Do not forget that Lithuania, Podolia, and Volhynia are hitherto regarded as Russian provinces, and that no possible reasoning could persuade Russia to see them under the rule of another sovereign than the one that rules Russia. The name under which they would continue to form part of Russia is a difficulty that would be more easily overcome.

Pray communicate this letter to the persons whose co-operation you think necessary, and urge your countrymen to show good-will to Russia and the Russians, so as to wipe out the recollections of the campaign, and thereby facilitate my task. On my part, in order to give the Poles a proof of the sincerity of my intentions, I have given orders to my army not to occupy Warsaw; but for this it is necessary that no foreign troops should remain there, and Polish ones least of all, so as to deprive us of the anxiety of leaving a foreign garrison behind us. Pray urge the members of the confederation and the Government on my part, to remain quietly at Warsaw, and promise them that they will not regret their doing so.

As to the military operations, besides the armies now in the field, each regiment of the whole army has already in the rear a reserve of 1000 men per regiment of infantry and two squadrons per regiment of cavalry, completely equipped and mounted, and is also provided with reserve companies of artillery, to enter the ranks of the active army in the spring. Besides these reserves a levy of 180,000 men is at this moment taking place, which will serve to reconstitute the reserves of the regiments as soon as they are incorporated in the active army. Moreover, all the militia, foot, horse, and artillery, are on the march under Count Peter Tolstoï to form a corps of observation in Volhynia. The energy of the nation is beyond praise, and I am decided to push on the war not only during this winter, but until a general peace is established in a manner suitable to the security of Russia and of Europe. . . .

(Signed) ALEXANDER.

KRASNOPOL,
3rd January 1813.

P.S. It has taken me two days to write this letter, as my time was taken up with the affairs of the army and other business.

As my letter bears a certain official character, I cannot allow it to go, my dear friend, without adding a friendly word for you. Success has not changed me either in my ideas on your country or in my principles generally, and you will always find me such as you have known me. Say many things from me to your parents and your sisters.

If, as a result of all these events, I should be able to stay for a moment with your family this would give me immense pleasure. Yours heart and soul.

PRINCE CZARTORYSKI TO THE EMPEROR ALEXANDER.
WARSAW,
23rd April (4th May) 1813.

Sire,—. . . In returning from Kalisz, I met Prince Anthony Radziwill at Nieborow. He gave me some details which it is well for your Imperial Majesty to know. The King of Prussia is not at all opposed to the existence of Poland. He feels the necessity of satisfying the wishes of the Polish nation, and considers them just and reasonable. He was astonished at your Majesty not having as yet done anything definite for the Poles, and complained that whenever he wanted to touch upon the subject you seemed much embarrassed and talked about something else. He asked Prince Anthony to go to Warsaw to sound public opinion and confer with me. From all this it would seem that the King of Prussia would agree to any measure your Majesty might think fit to take in this sense. . . . There are, in fact, no difficulties in the way of your undertaking so far as the King of Prussia is concerned; on the contrary, he will himself contribute in a large degree to remove those presented by the Russian army, whose opinion will always be preponderant at St Petersburg. . . . I know that the Russian officers here mostly speak in this sense either by conviction or in order to flatter the inhabitants.

I hear with pain that an order has been given at head-quarters to confiscate the estates of all who serve in the Polish army. This order seems to me unjust and without an object; people should not be punished for serving their country and obeying the orders of their sovereign, recognised as such by your Majesty. . . I confess that it gives me much sorrow to see measures so inconsistent with the policy of generous equity which you have adopted—the noblest and the most useful, even if only looked upon as a matter of interest.

PRINCE CZARTORYSKI TO THE EMPEROR ALEXANDER.
WARSAW, 27*th April* 1813.

. . . Those who know your Imperial Majesty cannot admit the slightest suspicion of the loyalty of your sentiments or fear that you do not intend to fulfil the hopes you are holding out to the Poles ; . . . yet those who have to carry out your policy are doing their utmost to defeat it.

The five Governments of Lithuania, instead of enjoying the benefits you wish to grant them, are suffering under an administration more unjust and arbitrary than any of those that have preceded it. No one's property, life, or honour is safe. Any official prompted by a desire of revenge or greed of gain may ruin the most innocent citizen and the whole of his family—. . . in a word, the Government and the authorities, instead of protecting the inhabitants placed under their care, seem to think it their duty to persecute and plunder them. You have no idea, Sire, of the evil that is being done in your name, for if you had you would put a stop to it. . . The inhabitants are in despair, and though hitherto they have been quiet, they may be driven to insurrection, not by a hope of success, but because they think it better to perish than to remain in their present condition.

CHAPTER XX

1813

AMONG the English friends of Prince Czartoryski was General Sir Robert Wilson. This officer had fought under Wellington at Talavera, was afterwards Military Attaché to the allied armies in Poland, and was tried for conniving at the escape of Count Lavalette, who had been condemned to death as an accomplice of Napoleon. When Sir Robert Wilson was asked at whose instigation he had assisted Lavalette, he replied: 'I was born and educated in a country in which the social virtues are considered as public virtues, and I have not trained my memory to a breach of friendship and confidence.' *

The following are some of his more characteristic letters to Prince Czartoryski :

> ' Russopol,
> ' *January* $\frac{3}{13}$, 1813.

'My Dear Prince—I received your letter with a transport of pleasure. Your absence had always been

---

* Diary of Henry Crabb Robinson, vol. ii. p. 6. Sir Robert Wilson was Member of Parliament for Southwark from 1818 to 1831, and then re-entered the army, ending his career as Governor and Commander-in-Chief of Gibraltar.

a matter of deep regret to me, and your vacancy in
the circle could never be supplied. To hear from you,
to know that I was preserved in your esteem, was a
high gratification, but I became prouder when I found
that you still considered me as a champion true to that
most interesting cause, the re-establishment and
happiness of your brave nation. I participate in all
your feelings, and am in accord with all your sentiments. Your friend will tell you what I have done,
and I pledge myself to you that everything which can
be attempted to promote the object shall be put in
execution with a zeal as ardent as your own. It is a
matter in which, as an Englishman, I feel so much
interest that I would sustain the plea with every
personal sacrifice if it would tend to the desired
accomplishment.

'There are many potent reasons why delay will
prove detrimental to Russia (I cannot be more ex-
plicit on that subject, but you will discover my
allusion, having so well judged of the past and specu-
lated on the probable future), if fatal prejudices refuse
the only security that offers for advantages obtained.
The Emperor's firmness, the patriotism of the nation,
and the courage of the army, cannot be too highly
estimated or applauded, but Buonaparte's errors and
the climate have assuredly brought his misfortunes to
the degree that they have reached. If Buonaparte
had been opposed by a chief who had only common
military skill or energy he would indeed have perished
altogether ; but as that, or rather *those* opportunities
were lost, as the favours of the good genius of the
world were scorned at Maloslavitz, Krasnow, and the

Beresina, Russia must not trifle with her interests. Half measures—timid policy—will prove her ruin. It is for the Council of the Empire to repair in some degree the mischief which an inadequate direction of the military powers has occasioned, for I consider the escape of Buonaparte, even with his wreck, a serious mischief that may cost her dear, and which certainly entails great inconveniences. I use mild terms— milder perhaps than I should if we conversed together. I long to see you, and certainly I will. I have very much to say to you on a variety of subjects, but if it was only for the pleasure of seeing you half-an-hour. I would go several hundred versts. . .

'England has been a little uneasy, and I do not think the Government quite settled. Lord Wellesley and Lord Grey must in my opinion be brought into office. All will then be well, and *you* will have firm friends. *Pars pro toto.* We only want to see the operation performed by others than Buonaparte. That Corsican never will attain the object so as to receive our countenance, and I think the Poles themselves must be sensible that he takes no real interest in their welfare—that he considers Poland but as a stepping-stone to his ambition. His is such protection as vultures give to lambs, covering and devouring. . . .

'I am obliged for a few days to be at the Imperial head-quarters, but in general I rove about as usual, and I have not been behind at the most interesting turns of the chase. . . . I have escaped *sauf et sain*. My nose only has been in danger, but it was in very serious danger. For once in my life I shrank from

Glory's pursuit, or rather lamented I had been wooing
a phantom who seemed resolved to wring off the noses
of his votaries.   Mine were only fears; but how many
thousand poor wretches have suffered all the mutila-
ting horrors of the angry climate.   This campaign has
certainly cost both armies very near half a million of
men, and I calculate that more than 100,000 have
perished with misery more terrible than any one heard
except the Roman crucifixions of the Jews.   I have
seen sights of woe and could tales unfold—but, like
Hamlet, I am forbid.

'Adieu, my very dear Prince.   Keep me in your
kind remembrance and believe me your gratefully
attached friend, servant, and *colleague*,

'Rob^r. Wilson.'

'Kalisch,
'*February* 27, 1813.

'I have only this day, my ever dear Prince,
received your letter from Dubnow.   I am afraid your
messenger will depart before I can communicate the
result of some conversations that I expect on this
interesting subject, which should engage every statesman's, of every country's, serious attention, and every
honest man's affections.

'I have never been unfaithful to the *sacred
pledges*.   Co-operation in such a cause has ever been
considered by me as a self-approving act, teeming
with more joy and dignity of pride than all the
distinctions which were conferred on those who
originally resisted the appeals which your country
made to justice and to honour.

'Poland has proved that the maxim is not infallible which recommends division to assure conquest. The spirit of independence has been unconquerable, although its efforts have not been undeviating. . . .

'Head-quarters is not so cheerful as heretofore in our happy time. There are many good fellows in the army, but circumstances have been unfavourable to former good fellowship which prevailed anywhere and everywhere. The campaign has been one of great rudeness: toil and endurance with few social pleasures. The tone was *ab origine* discordant. Your return would, however, rally gaiety and concord. God grant it! Ever yours, with affectionate attachment,

'ROB'. WILSON.'

'*September* 8, 1813.

'MY DEAR FRIEND,—You must not suppose me forgetful of you or of my engagements. There is no Lethe so potent as to erase these duties and affections from my remembrance. There is no centrifugal force so strong as to withdraw me from our united base. The distraction of affairs, the difficulty of communication, and the desire of seeing a person long expected, but who has arrived, prevented me from writing since I left Prague.

'I have now to urge your seizure of the *earliest* opportunity to make a journey to this part of the world. Approach the Emperor of Austria, and as soon as possible see Lord Aberdeen, our Ambassador to him. All is arranged for your visit, and he eagerly expects you. You will find him all you wish. I lost no time in introducing the subject to his notice.

He saw the moral and political advantages as I
do, and on this and every other matter he will pursue
the *honestum* as the most useful course of proceeding.

'Lord A. comes so fully aware of your value that
he longs to make your acquaintance and converse on
various matters. His society will not be indifferent
to you. Come you must, and speedily, if you seek to
found your fame on the foundation of patriotism. I
have also procured high friends in other quarters. In
good truth, I have devoted all my best efforts to the
subject since we parted, and with very gratifying
success. Come, and we shall triumph. If you come
not, not only much but all may be lost. You will of
course make a suitable pretext for this journey, and
excite neither jealousy nor suspicion. As soon as I
hear you are within tangible reach, I will go to you,
as in all probability I shall be transferred to the
Austrian Embassy, [where] I can act more independ-
ently. . . .

'We have had short but severe service. The
worst spectacle which I beheld was the savage blow
by which destiny struck down Moreau and so many
national hopes. . .

'I do not enter into military or political details.
All I can say is comprised in the statement of my
belief that the events since the 17th of August* have
increased the desire of peace in pacificators, disposed
belligerents to negotiation, and that to the prejudice
of war's amateurs peace will be made before the
winter.

'Come, come, come, without loss of time. As an

---

* The date on which Austria joined the coalition against France.

inducement I will not be angry if you pass by Landeck
and remain there forty-eight hours.

'Your ever affectionate friend,

'R. Wilson.'

'We were on march to assist Blücher, but B^{te}'s
return to Dresden recalls us.'

CHAPTER XXI

1813-14

THE policy of Austria towards Poland did not realise
Sir Robert Wilson's sanguine anticipations, and the
hostility shown to the Poles by the Russian authorities, notwithstanding the friendly professions of their
Imperial master, made it improbable that Alexander
would be alone able to carry out the restoration of
Poland. As there was a talk of a Congress being
assembled at which the Polish and other questions
would be dealt with by the Powers collectively,
Prince Adam Czartoryski sent his secretary, Biernacki,
to London to sound the Government as to its intentions with regard to Poland and to bring the Polish
question generally before the British public. During
his stay in England M. Biernacki kept a diary which,
though unfortunately incomplete, gives some curious
details as to the leading men in the political and
literary circles of London at that period.

He left Pulawy on the 12th of September 1813,
and Warsaw on the 17th. Travelling was slow and

difficult, owing to the inundations and the crowds of Russian soldiers on both banks of the Vistula, who behaved as if they were the masters of the country. On the 20th he arrived at Königsberg, where he observed that the lower classes still spoke Polish, though the province had so long been in the hands of Prussia. He asked some educated Prussians the reason of this, and they answered, with some surprise at his putting such a question, that Polish is the national language of the people, and that 'you cannot make a whole nation speak a foreign language.'

On the 22nd he reached Pillau, and embarked on board the 'Commonwealth,' Captain Hesketh, for Carlscrona, in Sweden, where he arrived on the 28th after a very rough passage. From this place he drove for four days and five nights to Gothenburg, which he calls 'the newest, cleanest, and most regularly built city in Europe.' He remarked that 'the more wealthy merchants, chiefly Englishmen, had beautiful country houses in the vicinity of the town, with magnificent gardens and well-kept farm buildings.'

He left Gothenburg on the 6th of October in her Majesty's Packet 'Lark,' Captain Sherlock commander. Among his companions were an Irishman, 'elegant, *bon vivant*, and a little feather brained,' 'a romantic and polite Scotchman,' and 'a well-known character who is convinced that he is John of Gaunt, Duke of Lancaster. He amused us greatly, and reminded me of Swift's saying that out of every hundred of his countrymen five are mad.' The 'Lark' was a vessel of 16 guns; there was plenty of amusement on board, and the *cuisine* was excellent.

One day at noon M. Biernacki went down into the cabin to dress for dinner, when as he was shaving he heard cries of 'clear for action!' This, however, did not disturb him, as he thought they were merely rejoicing at having caught a turbot or some other fish ; but soon after the captain called out to him, ' D— your razors ! It's no time for shaving. The French are coming !' M. Biernacki then hurried on his clothes and went on deck, where he found everything ready for action and was ordered to take charge of a gun. The French ship, which was much larger than the 'Lark,' advanced straight upon her, but seeing her guns and crew, sheered off. ' I was very glad to see this,' he says, ' and especially so when I was told that the ' Lark,' being a packet-boat, was forbidden to pursue an enemy—which under the circumstances seemed to me a very sensible rule.'

M. Biernacki arrived at Harwich on the 16th of October. 'I have often heard and read,' he says, ' that directly you set foot on English soil you breathe more freely. My own impressions carried me even further : not only are one's physical movements more free, but the first few days of one's stay in England have an even greater influence on the mind. It is a feeling like that of gratified ambition ; you imagine yourself to be in a more dignified position than you were before you landed, and are prompted to regulate your conduct accordingly. . . . At St Petersburg, on the other hand, the visitor breathes with difficulty, neglects himself and his duties, and becomes less orderly and courteous than usual.'

In London, M. Biernacki put up at the 'Spread Eagle,' Gracechurch Street, and he thus describes his first impressions of the city : 'Thousands of people from all parts of the world, of various complexions and costumes ; thousands of carriages, carts, and cattle ; the horns blown on the coaches, of which 2000 leave and arrive in London daily ; the trumpets of the newsboys, the bells of the postmen ; the street bands, the constant fights between thieves and their victims, and the crowds of beggars, make one deaf and produce a confusion of mind which lasts for several days, until one gets accustomed to this incessant turmoil.' On the third day after his arrival, M. Biernacki obtained an appointment with Lord Castlereagh at six in the afternoon in Downing Street. The interview lasted till a quarter to eight. He found Lord Castlereagh cold but frank in manner, speaking with much deliberation, full of preconceived notions to which he obstinately adhered, and imperfectly informed as to Polish affairs. He did not express himself with facility either in English or in French.

After M. Biernacki had fully developed the plan of a reconstruction of Poland, Lord Castlereagh objected that if Poland were restored the old anarchy would probably be revived, upon which M. Biernacki reminded him of the Constitution of the 3rd of May and the sittings of the diet of 1788-92, in which, notwithstanding the excitement produced by the French revolution, the debates were conducted with as much order and regularity as in the English Parliament, which the Polish Deputies took for their example. To this Lord Castlereagh made no reply, but he said that it would be ungenerous on the part of his Government to encourage the Poles by empty promises to indulge in hopes or attempt enterprises whose object it is not in the power of England to promote. 'England,' he added with much emphasis, 'is, in fact, so placed that she must scrupulously avoid everything that could give rise to distrust either between her and her allies or between any two Powers on the Continent belonging to the alliance. It cannot be assumed that any of the partitioning Powers will consent to return the provinces they have taken from Poland, and I cannot think it possible to effect the restoration of Poland by mere negotiation ; the only means of doing so is by the sword. If the Poles rose in arms for this purpose, England might, under other circumstances than the present, effectually assist them. But recent experience does not incline me to wish for such an event, as the result would not be worth the bloodshed and material ruin which such a struggle would involve. In my opinion the Poles should now submit to Russia and endeavour to gain her favour. England is prevented by treaties with her allies, and by her duties to the English people—which must always be the first consideration —from mixing herself up in such a matter ; there might, however, be means of bringing the Polish question before the British public.' He then pledged M. Biernacki to secrecy, and the latter asked for a similar promise as to his mission, explaining that Prince Czartoryski had purposely sent to London so obscure an individual as himself in order to prevent inconvenient reports or disclosures.

M. Biernacki next called upon Mr Canning, though from what 'he had heard of his character and political position,' he felt convinced 'that not the slightest assistance was to be expected of him.' 'Mr Canning,' he says, 'has much wit, but does not possess the ability which in England is necessary for dealing successfully with public affairs. He writes stanzas, elegies, and epigrams, and this rather does him harm with the serious public. The general opinion is that though he is the most fluent and attractive speaker in the House, he wants staying power; that he has excellent ideas, but not sufficient industry or perseverance to carry them out. . . The affair which led to his duel with Lord Castlereagh, and in which Mr Canning played so shameful a part, has, though it took place eight years ago, not been forgotten by the British public, and has left an indelible stigma on his character. But what injures him most in public opinion as a politician, is his unscrupulous ambition; there is a general feeling that he would even plunge the country into war, if by so doing he could please the Court and re-enter the Cabinet.' The following letter addressed by him to M. Biernacki after their first interview, shows that Mr Canning's French, like Lord Castlereagh's, was far from perfect:

'Oserois-je vous prier, Monsieur, de vouloir bien prendre la peine de me venir voir ou demain, ou l'après demain entre midi et une heure.

'Je suis bien fâché de vous donner cette peine-là. Mais je suis au lit, et fort incommodé d'une grosse rhume. Néanmoins, si vous préféreriez de revenir ici aujourdhui même entre une et deux heures, je serois prêt de vous recevoir.

'Aies la bonté de m'indiquer le jour qui vous conviendra.'

The impression derived by M. Biernacki from his interviews with Mr Canning was that he was 'more polite than is the case with Englishmen generally. He was eager for an opportunity of attacking the Ministry, and seemed better informed than Lord Castlereagh as to the affairs of Poland. He told me that since 1791, when the Opposition loudly advocated the Polish cause, Polish affairs had ceased to occupy the attention of the British Government and public. He expressed interest in our cause, but this was evidently not so much on account of the thing itself as of his own political objects, and he asked me with much curiosity about the people with whom I had talked and the views they had expressed. . . . He warned me against asking the Opposition to take up the cause of Poland. The Opposition, he said, is not only quite insignificant, but is despised on account of its impotence, as the Ministry defeats by means of its majority everything that the Opposition proposes. He did not think the Ministry could take up the question in Parliament, as they wanted money for subsidies to Austria, Prussia, and Russia. It was true that there was a great deal of talk in Parliament on behalf of Poland in the time of Pitt ; but this was not prompted by any partiality to the Poles or any feeling that their independence was necessary for the good of Europe ; Poland was simply made a stalking-horse for attacks on the Ministry. It was unfortunate for the Poles that the Powers which partitioned them were England's allies against Napoleon ; this was the reason of her silence in presence of the iniquities committed by those Powers in Poland. Moreover, those who advocated the Polish cause were also supporters of the French Revolution ; and this had led to a general belief in England that the Poles are people of the same type as the French Jacobins. Under these circumstances the ground was not very favourable in England for a movement on behalf of Poland ; and he would advise that urgent representations should be made to the Ministry, which has its hands free with regard to the Duchy of Warsaw, and even if there should be any secret conventions on the matter, England might yet wish for and advise an alteration of them.'

The following is a copy of the last communication to M. Biernacki from Mr Canning, who on this occasion wrote in English :—

' HINCKLEY,
' December 3, 1813.

' SIR,—I have received the honour of your letter of the 27th, and have forwarded that which came in it to Lord Granville Leveson Gower.

' I am very much concerned to hear of your indisposition ; and particularly so, that it prevented me from having the pleasure of seeing you again before I left town.

' Any interest that I might take in the subject on which you addressed yourself to me would, I am afraid, be of little avail, if you find nothing but indifference in other quarters.

‘ I am not without apprehension that you may have misunderstood something which passed between us respecting Lord Grenville. I expressed, what I feel, the highest respect for his Lordship’s character and abilities; and gave it as my decided opinion that anything which *he* might say on behalf of your country would carry the greatest weight, and would be altogether free from any danger of misrepresentation. But I by no means intended to lead you to imagine that *I* could take the liberty of introducing you, or of stating the object of your mission to this country, to Lord Grenville. Although much acquainted with him some years ago, we are not now in those habits of intimacy either publick or private, which would at all warrant my taking such a step; and, I confess, I should also feel myself restrained not only with regard to Lord Grenville, but to anyone else, by certain expressions in Prince Czartoryski’s letter to me, recommending a perfect silence on the subject of its contents.

‘ If you think it right to address yourself to Lord Grenville, and should find it necessary to refer his Lordship to me, merely for the fact of your having brought me a letter from the Prince Czartoryski, strongly recommending you to my good offices, I can have no difficulty in giving a satisfactory answer to such a reference; but I should not think myself justified in originating such a communication, or in entering with any other person into a correspondence on the object of your mission. Prince Czartoryski does not, in his letter to me, make any exception whatever to his general recommendation of secrecy.

‘ I have not had the opportunity of learning

whether Prince Czartoryski mentions your business here to Lord Granville Leveson Gower—or whether the letter to him be merely, as you suppose, a letter of introduction. I shall probably see Lord Granville Leveson Gower in the course of a few weeks. In the meantime I have not said anything to him of the nature of your business; nor shall I, unless I should find him informed of it.

'If there is anything in which I can be of service to you, a letter addressed to me at Gloucester Lodge will always be duly forwarded to me. I am, with great truth, Sir, your most obedient and faithful servant,   GEO. CANNING.'

'To M. BIERNACKI, at Mr DODD's, No. 12
Aldersgate Street.'

M. Biernacki's next interview was with Brougham, whom he was instructed to sound as to the best means of bringing the Polish question before the British public through the press. 'How am I to describe,' he says, 'this noble mind—what am I to say of him whose character, talents, eloquence, and knowledge, are celebrated in the whole of England, whose house is full of testimonials from towns and countries, and from families which he has saved? . . . I have observed that in other countries, and especially in Germany, a legal training narrows the mind. Here it has an opposite effect. As was formerly to some extent the case in Rome, the teaching of law is in England necessarily connected with that of the theory and practice of legislation, and is illustrated by fre-

quent discussions both in Parliament and in the Law
Courts on the objects for which laws were enacted.
The learning and practice of the law evidently tends
to make English judges and barristers large-minded,
thoughtful, high-principled, and merciful. . . . Mr
Brougham is cold and grave in manner, but it is
impossible not to perceive that he has a fertile
imagination which he has thoroughly under control,
and with the help of which he gains some of his
greatest successes.   He is fond of pictures and music,
is an accomplished *connaisseur*, and speaks French
better than is generally the case with Englishmen.

'Directly I broached the subject of Poland he
assured me that he had long taken an interest in that
country, that he had the best opinion of it, that when
a young man he had often thought of plans for its
reconstruction, and that he was ready to do everything in his power to bring about such a result.

'I then mentioned to him the idea of appealing to
public opinion on behalf of Poland through the
English press.   He promised me all possible assistance, asked for maps and books about Poland, and
wrote down a series of questions as to religion in
Poland, the national desire for independence, the
results of the partition, the state of parties, etc.,
which I took home to answer in full. . . . He
read my answers carefully, and we then agreed that
the first thing to be done was to write a short appeal*
to the English nation fully stating all the facts as to

* This pamphlet, the manuscript of which, in Brougham's handwriting, is in
the Czartoryski Archives, was published in 1814, under the title of *An Appeal to the
Allies and the English Nation on behalf of Poland.*   London, J. Harding, St James's
Street, 8vo. pp. 66.

Poland, of which they are at present profoundly
ignorant. He promised to do this as speedily as
possible. The next step would be to enlist the
interest and sympathy of prominent journalists, poets,
and other writers on behalf of Poland, so as to induce
them to write in her favour; also to interest the
Quakers, and the Irish Catholic party under the leader-
ship of Mr Grattan—a very powerful party which is
increasing in strength, has great influence, and will
readily assist us. Another party which it would be
very useful to enlist in the cause is that of Mr
Wilberforce, which comprises many eminent politicians,
such as Mr Vansittart, Chancellor of the Exchequer.

'As it would be impossible at present to obtain
anything from the Ministry, which has its hands tied
by the allies of England and matters of internal
policy, and it would not be expedient to help the
opposition to make Poland the occasion for a party
attack on the Government, we decided to try the
Burke party, which is not connected either with the
Government or the Opposition, and has some of the
ablest and most honest men in the House among its
members, who are generally esteemed both in Parliament and in the country. At their head is the Right
Hon. W. Elliot, formerly Secretary of State,* to
whom Burke dedicated his works.

'As public discussion is most in fashion here, and
it is very difficult to keep things secret, even in the
Cabinet, we arranged that Mr Brougham should
conduct the negotiations, I remaining in the back-
ground until it should become absolutely necessary

* Mr Elliot was not a Secretary of State, but Chief Secretary for Ireland in 1806.

for me to treat with such members of the party as might be most relied upon. Among these are Sir Samuel Romilly, a great favourite with the public, known as " the champion of British freedom and law ; " Sir Alexander Baring, a merchant prince who has made himself very popular by his patriotism, his talents, and his philanthropy ; and the young Marquis of Lansdowne, a man of great ability and weight in the House, with such a reputation for prudence that people say of him that " he was born in 1780, in the thirtieth year of his age." '

The following is a copy of the Right Hon. W. Elliot's reply to the letter written to him by Mr Brougham after the conversation described above :

'WELLS, 26*th December* 1813.

'MY DEAR SIR,—Owing to an accident, I did not receive your letter of the 18th inst. so soon as it ought to have reached me, which circumstance is the occasion of the lateness of my acknowledgment of it.

'No one, I assure you, can contemplate with more abhorrence than I do the various spoliations which Poland has undergone, and there is no one who could derive more joy and satisfaction from beholding her resume her due station amongst the nations of Europe. At the same time it is impossible for me to disguise from myself the many difficulties which stand in the way of the accomplishment of such a restoration. It obviously cannot be obtained without the concurrence of Austria and Russia (I may add Prussia), and it is but fair towards our Government to say, that even if they were to take up the cause with all the zeal and authority by which they could support it, their interposition could go little beyond exhortation, and means very inadequate, I fear, to bring about an object that must be attended with considerable sacrifices on the part of these Powers.

'With regard to the course suggested by the gentleman who has made to you the communication you mention, I confess it appears to me perfectly hopeless. If I understand it right, it is that the affairs of Poland should in some form or other be brought under the view of Parliament without his having made any previous disclosure to the Government on the subject of his mission. Now I feel the clearest conviction that this mode of agitating the matter could produce no beneficial results whatever ; and that on the contrary much censure would be cast (I think not wholly without reason) on the introduction of a topic which had been withheld from the knowledge of the Ministers of the Crown, although materially affecting the interests of his Majesty's allies, and of peculiar delicacy at the present conjuncture because hazarding the harmony and cordiality amongst them necessary to the continuance of that success which has of late accompanied their arms. In truth, too, almost under any circumstances, I should place little reliance on the efficacy of the exertions of a few individuals in Parliament in a cause which, to ensure it any chance of success, would require all the weight that the combined efforts of all the political parties in the country could afford it. Such a plan of proceeding would, at least as it strikes me, be attended with no solid utility,

and it might (and this is an idea at which I shudder)
by exciting delusive expectations and even premature
movements in Poland, involve that unfortunate country in still more grievous calamities than those which
she has already incurred.   These considerations will, I
acknowledge, render me very reluctant to share in the
management of the case ; and though I am unapprized
of the details of the extent of the views entertained, I
am anxious to give you immediately these my first and
hasty impressions (for I am writing under the fear of
losing the post) in order that the person who is
charged with the mission may not be prevented from
availing himself of any other means that may present
themselves to him for the furtherance of the business
committed to his care.

' Of course I shall strictly observe your injunction
of secrecy.   On my way to London it is probable I
may call at Milton, in which event (I conclude from
the tenor of your letter) I may show it to Lord Fitz-
william and Lord Milton, unless I have an intimation
from you of your wish to the contrary.

' It was my intention to have been by this time on
my road, but I have been detained by the illness of
my servant, who is not yet able to travel, and I therefore propose to remain here for about a fortnight
longer.

' I have only a moment left to add, that I am
always—most faithfully yours,

' W. Elliot.

' H. Brougham, Esq.
' King's Bench Walk, Temple, London.'

Describing a visit to Madame de Staël, M. Biernacki says:

'Madame de Staël is immensely popular at the British Court and among the public. Her sentimentalism, her enthusiasm, her singular opinions as to morals and politics, have in no way prevented her from gaining the highest consideration among all classes; it was enough that as an enemy of Napoleon she had been banished from the Continent and had taken refuge in England. Her extraordinary eloquence and readiness in debate inspire universal admiration, and the highest personages in the country seek her acquaintance. Her influence is, in fact, so great that, in spite of her many indiscretions and her advocacy of Russia, I decided to seek her assistance. . . . She spoke, at a *soirée* given by her, with the greatest enthusiasm about Poland and loudly praised the Poles, and her remarks were most strongly supported by Sir Samuel Romilly and Mr Dumont, the editor of *Bentham.* We shall see if she will write in the same sense; but her *soirées* are so largely attended that even in conversation she might help us.' M. Biernacki wrote her a long letter, urging her to advocate the cause of Poland, to which he received the following reply:

'Je n'ai jamais cessé de m'intéresser à la Pologne, et la noble pérséverance de ses malheureux citoyens est respectable et touchante—mais qu'espérer pour elle en ce moment! Si la personne qui m'a fait l'honneur de m'écrire une si belle lettre veut me voir, je la recevrai dans le secret le plus absolu, mais ce sera seulement pour lui exprimer l'admiration que m'inspire un sentiment national si courageusement conservé, si courageusement exprimé par les actions et les paroles.

'A. L. G. DE STAËL-HOLSTEIN, née NECKER.'

Brougham* was very indignant at this smoothly worded refusal, and drafted the following characteristic rejoinder, which, however, M. Biernacki did not send to Madame de Staël, as he thought it was too polemical to be addressed to a woman; upon which Brougham drily observed: ' Perhaps you are right; it would be best simply to tell her she knows nothing about the matter '—

' Je dois vous avouer très-franchement que votre réponse (signée pour comble d'inconséquence du nom de Necker), m'a donné une affliction sensible. Est-il possible que, toute clairvoyante que vous êtes, vous puissiez ne pas sentir que c'est précisément *dans ce moment* qu'il y aye quelque chose à espérer pour la Pologne? Y a-t-il la moindre probabilité que dans l'avenir elle verra un moment plus favorable? Dites-le donc, avec la franchise que je vous crois propre, proclamez que notre état est pour jamais désespéré. Mais je vous supplie de ne pas voiler l'insouciance pour tout ce qui n'est pas Suédois, ou Russe, ou Allemand—-l'indifférence pour tous les maux qui ne

* He thus states his opinion of Madame de Staël in a letter to Earl Grey, dated December 16, 1813, and published in Brougham's autobiography (Vol. II., p. 98): ' This brings me to the said gentlewoman, Madame de Staël, whom I really think you all overrate. Her book seems terribly vague and general and inaccurate. She certainly follows old Lord Lansdowne's advice in avoiding details " as the more dignified line." Besides, her presumption is intolerable, and on all subjects, on many of which she can know nothing—as, for instance, the German metaphysics, except so far as she may have rubbed some of them off Schlegel. I never have seen her, and shun her as I would an evil of some kind, having heard her talked of as a grand bore, and being sickened by the concurring accounts of her fulsome flattery of the Prince, Ministers, etc., etc., and her profligate changes of principle. In women such things signify little ; but she must (as Talleyrand said) be considered a man.'

viennent pas de Bonaparte—sous le prétexte (prétexte qui ne manquera jamais quand vous auriez vécu, et l'admiration de l'Europe, encore une * demi-siècle) que ce n'est pas encore "*le moment.*"

'Je ne vous cacherai point que j'attribue ce que vous m'avez dit bien plus à la légèreté d'un grand génie, qu'à la froideur d'un courtisan. Les lignes dont il est question ne vous seroient pas échappées si vous eussiez un peu réfléchi sur les intérêts graves et touchants que vous êtes dans le cas si puissament de servir. Si vous auriez senti aussi vivement que je le sache combien vous pourriez influer sur le bonheur de quelques millions en adoucissant leur sort, même quand il ne serait plus question de l'indépendance, j'ose vous croire incapable de vous refuser *à vous-même* un plaisir si vraiment inexprimable, pour toutes les tentations soit de l'espoir soit de la crainte que les cours dans leurs alternations de faiblesse et de cruauté puissent offrir. Encore réfléchissez—vous le devez à vous-même, au nom que vous avez tant illustré, à celui que vous héritez du meilleur des hommes.'

As will be seen from the following letters,† Brougham assisted M. Biernacki to enter into communication with some of the London newspapers:—

(Postmark of January 27, 1814).

'Jeudi.

'Monsieur,—Je crois que vous ferez bien de faire passer une note à

'Mons. Scott (l'éditeur du Champion) Catherine

---

* *Sic in orig.*

† These are exact copies from the originals in the Czartoryski Archives. It will be seen that Brougham's French, though fluent, was far from correct or elegant.

Street, Strand, Champion Office, pour le prier de faire attention au sujet de la Pologne dans son numéro de Dimanche.

'Vous pouvez l'envoyer *tout de suite* par la petite poste, en anonyme, mais comme Polonois.—Je suis toujours Votre fidèle ami, H. B.

'M. BIERNACKI, Mr DODD's, 22 Aldersgate Street.'

'VENDREDI.

'MONSIEUR,—Ayez la bonté de faire parvenir une note à Mr Perry,* le renvoyant très-respectueusement à la brochure pour les principes et les faits qui doivent servir de bases pour la discussion. Vous pouvez lui envoyer une exemplaire en même temps, et lui marquer que rien de plus vrai que les détails qu'elle renferme, mais que par menagement (à ce qu'il paroit) pour les alliés, surtout la Russie, ces détails sont bien au-dessous de la vérité! Aussi vous direz que les horreurs pratiquées depuis la dernière invasion excèdent même celles des anciens partages, et qu'après qu'il aura entamé la discussion vous lui indiquerez des autres anecdotes. En attendant vous pouvez marquer que probablement on va voir quelqu'unes des prédictions remplies que la brochure a données, et notamment sur la Russie, en le renvoyant aux pages où l'on fait mention de la Suède et la Norvège. Vous ferez bien de lui indiquer aussi les pages qui renferment les détails des confiscations et des malheureux résultats des partages à cause des changements de frontière, en lui témoignant que tous ces détails sont de toute vérité.

* Editor of the *Morning Chronicle*.

'Si vous envoyez une lettre dressée sur ce plan de bonne heure, rien ne l'empêchera de discuter le sujet demain matin. Je suis toujours, etc.,   H. B.

'Je serai chez moi entre 3 et 4 heures, mais vous devez envoyer votre lettre tout de suite.'

Among the journalists of the day with whom M. Biernacki corresponded was Leigh Hunt, who was at the time still confined in Horsemonger Lane gaol on account of his libel on the Prince Regent. M. Biernacki describes him as 'a young man full of talent and learning, romantic and ardent. His paper is one of the most popular in England ; it has a sale of 8000 copies a day, which, according to the usual calculation in such cases, would mean that it is read by 40,000 people.' The following is a copy of Leigh Hunt's article on Poland in the *Examiner* of January 30, 1814, which also contains some remarkable extracts from Brougham's pamphlet :—

'The allies are now supposed, and with great appearance of probability, to be advancing to a point at which they will not only be able to secure present peace for Europe, but to act upon an improved scale the part which has hitherto been performed by the enemy, and settle the destinies of nations in their turn.

For this change in their prospects and power they are eminently indebted, as they themselves acknowledge, to the popular opinion that has gone with them ; and it is desirable, on every account, that they should preserve this best of friends and strongest of coadjutors by fulfilling in their prosperity what they undertook to perform when the strife was doubtful. Their enemy has found to his cost, that opinion in these times is not what it was even fifty years back, and that it cannot be put on and off at pleasure, without risking something worse than a chill.

'People's eyes, therefore, are fixed with no small anxiety on the diplomatic proceedings of the allies, and the more so, from some

appearances of contradiction that have lately been witnessed in
their military declarations. For our part, though we are among
the most anxious, we confess we think little of these appearances.
If the allies crossed the Rhine after their professions of moderation,
and after their hint about not interfering with the natural boundaries of France, Buonaparte, by his own statement, seems to have
attempted trifling with them on the subject of peace, and it would
have been mere weakness on their part to lose more of their time.

'The proceeding does not compromise the sincerity of their professions;—it is at a peace the latter will be brought to the test.
Again, there may be a difference of temper in the proclamations of
the Austrian and Prussian Generals, without gainsaying the general
spirit of the confederacy. If the Prussian has something of a
vindictive tone, and taunts the French Emperor with some of his
former boastings, he may be supposed to construe the natural feelings of his master, and to speak the language of his irritated countrymen, without involving the cooler feelings of ultimate negotiation.
The Austrian Emperor has suffered less than the King of Prussia,
and is besides connected with Buonaparte, so that his servant speaks
in a more considerate manner. As to the Cossacks, of whom such a
ridiculous noise has been made, it is well known that they enjoy a
sort of mongrel independence, and that whatever antics they play
are to be traced to themselves and not to the Russian Commanders :
—their flags, therefore, with Paris on the one side and Moscow on
the other, have as little to do with the temper of the allied sovereigns,
as their beards and their brutality. If Napoleon had not played
the part of a brother barbarian, he ought to have taken shame to
himself for enabling such a tribe to come down and play the raw-
head-and-bloody-bones among the people of Europe.

'It is not the sort of tone then that may be adopted here and
there which is to settle our opinion of the allies and their principles ;
but the sincerity they shall exhibit, when they come to conclude
matters with Buonaparte, in acting up to their professions of
universal justice, and in securing us all for the future, as far as
they possibly can, against the irregular impulse of this or that man's
ambition.

'To this end, it will not be enough that they shall compel
sacrifices from Buonaparte ; they must make sacrifices themselves ;
they must take away from him one of the most pernicious arms of
his power against them,—the power of recrimination ; and prove to
all the world that they have not been trifling with that awful force,
those myriads of human beings, who have been fighting in their
cause.

'These sacrifices are luckily not many, or of great moment, especially after the more humiliating ones which the allies have borne in their adversity. They only consist in doing that justice to their neighbours, for which they have been calling upon Buonaparte on their own account. Austria has said, for instance, "Do not attempt to force Germans to be Frenchmen :—it is a vain as well as inhuman effort :" Russia has said, "Do not insult all my native feelings :—do not come where you are not wanted, and lord it over my territory :" Prussia has said, "Do not take from me my strength and my spirit, do not garrison my fortresses, plunder my villages, and leave me only the shadow of an existence." Now there is a voice which says all this and more to these very Powers,—to Austria, to Russia, and to Prussia :—it is the voice of Poland—a voice crying from the ground, —the voice of a country declared no longer in existence !—Here let the proof of sincerity be given ; here let a proof be given, that the allied Princes have been taught lasting as well as momentary success, and that the men of the old school are prepared to give up these vices in themselves, which they have justly united to put down in the man of the new.

'This is a most important subject, and involves, with regard to the allies, or at least to their principles, the very same question that is now agitating against Buonaparte. We have never lost sight of it ; but we confess that we should have waited a little before we urged it again, had it not been for a publication that has lately appeared entitled,—" An Appeal to the Allies and the English Nation in behalf of Poland." It may be thought invidious by some persons to interrupt the allies at present by any representations, calculated to fall in with French misrepresentation ; and such a pamphlet may appear to them a little like casting a stone into the mouth of our advancing friends ; but a direct charge to this effect would only prove to us that such persons were afraid to meet their subject, and considered the allies as afraid also ; and it is perhaps better upon the whole to make the representation, however unpalatable for the moment, while the gratitude of the allies to popular feeling is yet warm, the policy of doing right yet fresh in their eyes, and their temptations to do wrong not yet excited by the final grasp of success.

'The author of the pamphlet is evidently a true observer, who sees things in the gross as well as detail,—in their universal as well as their particular application. For a writer who can take so large a view as he does of the subject and its *principle*, we might be inclined to think that he takes rather too much pains to answer petty, Cabinet objections, and questions of interest ; but as politics go, and as questions of interest, by a proper reasoning, amount at last to the same thing as questions of principle, it may have been as well to show himself prepared at all points. What we like less, is an insidious way of occasionally putting his own apprehensions of the allies into the mouth of their enemies,— a kind of deprecating by proxy, and of imagining what other people might say of them, only to express his conviction that no such terrible want of principle can take place. It would have been better, we think, in a pamphlet on such a subject, to state at once what his own opinion of the allies would be, should they turn traitors to their profession,—and to state it too in the very broadest terms. If in the end they deserve it, he saves himself the pretence of a conviction to the contrary ; and if not, they can be the less offended with the plain speaking. But even the opportunities of humour which this underhand mode gives a writer, (and the one before us handles a pleasantry very easily), cannot compensate, we think, for the opportunities it gives to meaner understandings of doubting his good intention in general. Of this there cannot be the remotest suspicion. The writer may have his apprehensions with regard to the ultimate conduct of the allies, and we know some very excellent men who more than agree with him on that point ; but whoever he is, he is one that sees as clearly as any man the union of sound principle with policy, and who, notwithstanding his legal mode of occasionally putting his apprehensions, succeeds in convincing his reader that he feels as well as sees. The apostrophe to the "ill-fated Poniatowski" (p. 46) evinces cordiality of heart as well as justness of thinking.—But we are detaining the reader from a few extracts which it is our intention to give him, and which we shall give without any of these comments which the rest of the publication itself will abundantly supply.

'After stating that the subject of Poland need not be so painful to the allied Princes as some people may insinuate, since it was their immediate predecessors, not themselves, that made the partition, the author proceeds in a very successful manner to vindicate the Poles for having sided of late with the French, by putting a very strong and striking case, in which he supposes England to be lorded over by the latter, and suddenly visited by a Russian army, of which she takes advantage to try and shake off her yoke. He then enters into the subject historically, showing that " the great relaxation of public principles may be distinctly ascribed to the partition," and the Poles themselves, at the moment of their national annihilation, were removing the last flimsy pretext for the outrage by forming a new and free constitution. His next step is to prove, that the partition is not a thing gone by,—the discussion of which is no longer a matter of connection with present events; and as this may appear to some persons important to settle, and is settled by him very completely, we shall make a good long extract on the subject.

'"I question if the time be even yet come, when the miserable catastrophe can be adequately deplored that paralysed all those noble efforts, and blighted the fair prospect unfolded by them to the eyes of every friend of liberty. But one part of the calamity, that which pressed the most sorely upon the interests of the European community, will perhaps never be more deeply felt than at the present hour. I speak of the peculiar moment chosen by the confederate courts. The new constitution was enveloped in a cloud of foreign soldiery—the patriots were scattered abroad—the rudiments of the national army were dissipated—the country was overwhelmed, parcelled out, confiscated, jobbed, turned into money—blackened with garrisons, prisons, gibbets, cemeteries, and the desolate abodes of men who had perished for freedom—its separate existence finally destroyed—its name blotted out from the map, and forbidden to be any more uttered, as if it had been guilty of all the crimes whereof it had been the scene and the victim—but why enumerate particulars? Do they not all fall short of the deed itself?—The partition of Poland was completed AFTER the French Revolution had awakened slumbering royalty; had taught the force of France to burst through its ancient bounds; and had made national independence tremble in every corner of Europe.

'"This is the fact upon which, at the present moment, it imports us well to meditate. There is no getting over it. If Poland had been left as she was when those great changes began which the allies are now occupied in undoing, she would still have been one of the greatest Powers on the Continent. She was seized when even the pretences of 1772 no longer existed—when she was a safe, orderly, and peaceable neighbour. But above all she was seized in 1793 and 1794, at the very time when France was seizing Savoy, Belgium, and Holland. This is the matter which now presses itself upon our attention. We are recurring to sound and ancient principles. We are treading back our steps in order to get out of the slough in which we have been since the French Revolution, and to regain the eminence of a pure morality. We are endeavouring to undo as much as possible the recent changes of dominion, and to place the affairs of Europe on their former ground, with all the benefits of past experience. With what pretensions of consistency —by what powers of face, marvellous even in this unblushing age, can we meet either the enemy or the Polander, if the only change on which we are obstinately silent is one of the most momentous and least justifiable, and which our conscience tells us was effected in the very same month with the conquest of the Netherlands, admitted on every hand to be the fittest subject of restoration?

' " A pernicious but very flimsy heresy has been propagated on this question by some foreign politicians, the soundness of whose principles in other respects renders their mistakes the more dangerous. It has been said that the partition of Poland is now a mere matter of history, and that while the lapse of time exempts it from being again brought into discussion, the sanction of various treaties stops the parties to them from questioning it. This doctrine is so full of manifest absurdity, and so easily refuted by the whole system of those who adopt it, that one can scarcely imagine it to proceed from anything but a misplaced delicacy towards the partitioning Powers, and a determination to scare the enemy with big words and terms of law, from flinging at us a very favourite sarcasm in return for the many attacks of this kind to which we expose him. I would fain remind the very respectable persons to whom I am alluding, of the period at which they first treated this topic ; it was immediately after the Treaty of Lunéville, in 1801, not seven years after the final partition, the greatest in extent and the worst in all respects, except that it was not the earliest. Yet the advocates of this motley doctrine of a seven years' limitation of anti-Jacobin crimes, were the loudest against offences committed by France eight and nine years before the date of their invectives. Happily for Europe the same enlightened persons retain their influence over the popular opinions at the present day, and to it perhaps, next to the headlong rashness of the enemy and the temperate firmness of the allied chiefs, we owe the late successes. I hope their voice will be heard in the negotiations, and in the further prosecution of the war, should just terms be refused by France—I am sure they will spurn at the idea of considering the French conquests in the Revolution war as sacred ; and yet nearly twice seven years have elapsed since a treaty confirmed them ; so that both their doctrine of limitation and of *estoppel* by treaties, is much more applicable to these than to the last Polish partition. England too and France, I should think, may be reckoned something in a question of this sort, and they never by any treaty recognised directly or indirectly the dismemberment. Yet England as well as the allies themselves, by solemn treaties, recognised those French usurpations and new states created in the Revolution war, which all good men now hope to see restored to their ancient possessors. Even the Spanish usurpation was recognised by all the allies in succession, except England." pp. 22-25.

'The author then proceeds to exhibit the miserable state of
Poland after its partition, to calculate the little advantages the
partitioners have derived from their respective acquisitions of
territory, and to enumerate the frequent and striking disadvantages
they have experienced from the natural hatred of the Poles, in a
military point of view. The rest of the pamphlet is chiefly occupied
in answering objections on the score of Russian ascendency. We
shall make our other extract on the use which Bonaparte has made
of the Poles, as it brings the matter down to the time before us, and
refer our readers for the rest of the question to what will amply
repay their attention in the publication itself :—

'"The exact number of men drawn by the enemy from this quarter
it is neither very easy, nor very material to ascertain. Since 1806,
when he first held out hopes of restoring Poland, those numbers
have greatly increased ; and in the campaign of 1812, they did not
fall short of 100,000. The insecurity of the tenure by which the
country is held, may be seen from the events of the two Polish
campaigns. Immediately after the battle of Jena, the Prussian
troops were compelled to withdraw from Poland, as precipitately as
the French have lately done from Holland. No exertion was too
great for the country during that winter, notwithstanding the very
imperfect degree in which its wishes were met. Bonaparte, in
flattering them with the hopes of independence, had imposed one
very harsh condition, that the code Napoléon should be established.
Even on such terms, as if only anxious for existence, and careless of
the kind of being they should have, they accepted the offer. Let
us recollect that Emperors and Kings have in like manner received
their crowns, fettered by conditions that almost enslaved them to
their subjects or electors. So the Poles capitulated for national
existence, upon terms which could hardly be said to leave them a
separate people. But they amply performed their part of the con-
tract. The enthusiasm excited by the mere semblance of restoration
was universal. Many persons sacrificed nearly their whole fortunes
to the State. Entire regiments of between two and three thousand
men each, were raised and fully equipped by individuals in a few
weeks. Others furnished single battalions, or companies, or only a
few men, according to their means ; and all this—not from the
superabundance of their wealth, not by the sale of their plate and
jewels only ; but by selling or pledging their estates, and part-
ing with everything that could raise a farthing, down to the marriage rings of village dames, or the single silver spoon of a poor
country curate. The peace of Tilsit closed the campaign which had
been so materially influenced by the exertions of Poland ; and upon

the first breaking out of the war two years afterwards, she evinced
her sense of the benefits, unsubstantial as they were, which that
treaty had conferred. The same extraordinary efforts were renewed,
and the army of the Duchy rapidly over-ran the Polish provinces of
Austria, where they met with allies in every corner. Indeed similar
exertions were made in those districts themselves, and they were
rewarded by the incorporation of their better half with the Duchy,
at the peace of Vienna.—In 1812, a new attempt was made to soothe
the Poles with the hope of real independence, although the alliance
of France with Austria rendered it extremely difficult. The charm
was again found all powerful ; the people flocked from every quarter
to join the invading army, and expended their utmost means to supply
it. I question if an equal amount of contribution was ever raised
upon the same extent of a country merely agricultural ; and when
we reflect that it had been exhausted by half a century of misfortune,
the exertion seems scarcely credible. Besides the fixed war revenue
of about five millions sterling, it furnished as much more in provisions and stores to the army on its passage, with a further sum of one
million and a half in money. Such efforts, and the subsequent
exhaustion of the country in 1813, may have drained it of wealth ;
but the people remain ; iron is their gold ; and if the allies prefer
the neighbourhood of an unconquerable and friendly nation, to an
uneasy rule over hostile subjects, they have only to speak the word.
Let but the sound be heard which can really awaken Polish independence,—name to them the Constitution of the third of May, and
every plain will be alive with horse—every thicket of their forests
gleam with spears. All that Napoleon could do by offers, insignificant had they been sincere, will be forgotten in the exertions which
a substantial restoration would call forth. So impregnable a
bulwark never was raised against invasion, as Russia would present
to all the rest of Europe, while Prussia and Austria would no longer
touch upon that too powerful neighbour, and in a quarter where
their security has been the most precarious." pp. 47-50.*

'We shall take a hasty farewell of this work by going somewhat
farther than its author in our anticipations of what will be the
consequences, should the allied monarchs not perform what is

* 'The eulogium of Mr Burke on the Polish Constitution of the third of May,
is unbounded. It concludes with this passage :—" Happy people, if they know how
to proceed as they have begun ! Happy Prince, worthy to begin with splendour or
to close with glory a race of patriots and of Kings. . . . To finish all—this great good,
as in the instant it is, contains in it the seeds of all future improvement, and may
be considered as in a regular progress, because founded on similar principles, towards
the stable excellence of a British Constitution."—*Appeal from the new to the old
Whigs*.—The passage in the former part of these reflections was printed, before I
recollected the testimony of this great authority.' (*Note by Leigh Hunt*).

expected of them. In our opinion, they will not only be insecure
from future attacks of the enemy, and from the intrigues which
harass monarchs in general, but all that has happened in Europe for
the last thirty years will not save them and their subjects from the
danger of fresh revolutions; for if the times at present differ in any
one feature from what they were eighty or a hundred years back, it
is in the direct rank that understanding has taken in society, in the
universal circulation of intelligence and good sense, and in the
consequent and most formidable addition which has been made to
the power, and conscious power too, of public opinion. The people
have looked at their sovereigns, and the sovereigns, it is hoped, have
now looked at their people, with eyes of mutual understanding. It
is the interest of both to let this understanding be a good one.'

After seeing this article M. Biernacki wrote
Leigh Hunt a letter of thanks, which the latter thus
acknowledged in the *Examiner* of February 6,
1814:

'The letter written in French has been received,
and has given the editor one of those enjoyments
which he prizes almost above every other, and which
will always be a sufficient reward to him for what
little he may be able to do in a good cause.'

The Polish cause was also warmly taken up by
Mr Perry in the *Morning Chronicle* and Dr Stoddart
in the *Times*, which, according to M. Biernacki, was
'the only paper the Prince Regent allowed his
daughter to read;' but Brougham did not succeed in
getting any leading politicians except Earl Grey to
advocate it in Parliament, though Sir Samuel Romilly,
Wilberforce, Lord Lansdowne, Lord Holland, and
Cobbett, 'le franc, le sauvage, le farouche,' expressed
the greatest sympathy for it.

M. Biernacki, who, like most educated Poles of
that time, was fond of quoting Latin, sent to some of

his correspondents the following passage from Livy as a prophetic description of England's political mission :—Esse gentem in terris quæ suâ impensâ ac periculo bella gerat pro libertate aliorum, maria trajiciat, ne quod toto orbe terrarum injustum imperium sit, ubique jus, fas, lex potentissima sint ;—they did not, however, accept the suggestion.

'Englishmen,' says M. Biernacki, 'only do one thing at a time. Just now they think only of the war with France. . .. It is impossible to see the Ministers : they fear the fate of Percival (his successor especially), and are overwhelmed with work ; two messengers go to the Continent every day. Moreover, there is a split in the Cabinet. One party wishes to make peace at once on the French terms ; the other wishes to carry on the war in order to obtain further compensation for the sacrifices England has made. The Prince Regent favours the latter party, as he has made up his mind to bring back the Bourbons.' The only Englishman, in fact, who thoroughly identified himself with the Polish cause at that period was Brougham ; and he threw himself into the work heart and soul.

As stated at the beginning of this Chapter, M. Biernacki's diary is incomplete ; but it is accompanied by a collection of letters (besides those printed above), of which the following may be worth reproducing here :

From Tom Moore.

Mayfield Cottage, Ashbourne,
Thursday, Feby. 3rd.

Sir,—I believe I have to thank you for a very

able pamphlet, ' An Appeal to the Allies,' which I
have just received under a blank cover. It had already
been sent to me by a friend from town, but I am glad
you have given me an opportunity of expressing my
opinion of the book through a channel by which it
has a chance of reaching the author himself; as I
know that honest, sincere praise, even from so humble
an individual as myself, is one of the rewards that
such interesting labours look for. I have seldom seen
anything better meant or better executed.

Your very obliged st.

THOMAS MOORE.

To Mr HARDING,
Bookseller, St James's.

*From Brougham to Mr Vansittart, Chancellor of the
Exchequer.*

TEMPLE, *Feby.* 21, 1814.

DEAR SIR,—I am infinitely unwilling to give you
the interruption of reading a letter in the midst of
your manifold occupations at this singular juncture.
Yet I cannot refrain from expressing my obligations
to you for the patience with which you listened to my
Polish friend. His situation is one of extreme
delicacy—but as he is one of the most sincere and
devoted patriots, so is he likewise a person of excellent
sense and discretion in conduct. I am intimately
acquainted with everything relating to him and his
connections, and I can give you a most positive
assurance of his being trustworthy.

He is very anxious lest he should have failed to
convey his meaning with distinctness, and has begged

me to repeat several things for him; but I am quite sure his fears are groundless, and I shall confine myself to a single remark—viz., on the extreme importance of any, *even the smallest*, interest being shown with respect to the unfortunate country in question. Its possessors (especially Alexander) look to England a vast deal more than they will always acknowledge when they are treating with you. They regard the publick opinion here almost as much as our own Government does, and it is a matter of fact that they are influenced by it in the same way, though certainly they are not very mindful of the publick opinion among their own subjects. How much more, then, do they consider any expression of opinion or feeling on the part of our Government! It is very certain that the mere exhibition of some little interest (however little and however privately) in favour of the Poles, could it be made at the present time, would have great, immediate, and very practical effects on the happiness of many millions of people. I suspect the Emperor Alexander at least desires nothing more in that quarter than the authority of our Government to back him with his allies on the one hand, and his nobles on the other, to adopt a more paternal system.

But all these things (as well as the larger view of the subject) are undoubtedly familiar to you. I would therefore only further suggest that there are one or two topics on which you will derive some most curious and interesting particulars from the Polish gentleman. The commercial resources, yet unexplained, of his country I pass over as an obvious point. But he is possessed of some extremely singular circumstances respecting Buonaparte and his proceedings both in Poland and elsewhere, and if you remember to put him on the subject (especially of Buonaparte's conferences after his return from Moscow) and he should not be afraid of indicating the sources of his information, his account of it will greatly interest you.

I again beg your excuse for the interruption, and wishing you all manner of success in your present undertakings (which a person retired from politicks may very conscientiously do at this time), I remain, yours faithfully and sincerely,   H. B.

A single word addressed to me containing the time you desire to see him, and without giving you the trouble of writing a note, will at any moment bring him to you.

Brougham to M. Biernacki.

LANCASTER, *ce* 7me *Mars* 1814.

MONSIEUR,—Je n'ai fini mon voyage que ce matin et vous voyez que je profite de la première occasion qui se m'est présentée pour écrire la lettre au P.— Je l'ai envoyée ouverte afin que vous puissiez la lire avant de la cacheter.

Le jour même de mon départ j'ai addressé une lettre au Marquis de Lansdowne, en le renvoyant à M. Baring et MM. Romilly et Elliot pour les détails. Je l'ai remis entre les mains de M. Baring, qui ne tardera pas (à) vous présenter au Marquis. Ce que je lui ai dit doit l'intéresser autant qu'il est possible dans la bonne cause. Après l'avoir vu (si ça vous convient à vous et à M. B.) vous devez croire que la

semence est semée, et que l'on a fait tout ce qu'il
vous a été permis de faire dans les circonstances
actuelles. Je suis intimement persuadé que nous ne
ferons que du mal en entamant des autres communications dans ce moment.

J'espère que votre santé est rétablie, et que vous
êtes content de M. Tegart. Je me suis accusé bien de
fois de votre maladie. Je crains que je ne vous ai fait
trop travailler. Le repos et la maladie me sont presqu'
inconnus, et j'avois dû menager votre santé un peu
plus que je ne soigne la mienne. Faites moi le plaisir
de m'écrire, et de me marquer votre rétablissement.

J'avais oublié de vous prier de m'écrire de la
Hollande tout ce que vous aurez à remarquer, et de
me faire venir de vos nouvelles régulierement. Après
avoir quitté la Hollande, vous pouvez addresser vos
lettres à Mons. Van H. à la Haye, en le priant de me
les faire passer. Encore une chose—n'oubliez pas les
moyens d'entretenir les liaisons entre les deux pays, par
les voyages dont nous avons causé—et les avantages
que procurera à vos grands une éducation Anglaise.

Adieu. Portez-vous bien, et croyez que je suis
toujours, etc. H. B.

York, *ce* 24 *Mars* 1814.

Monsieur,—Je viens de recevoir votre dernière
lettre, ayant il y a deux jours reçu celle qui m'avoit
suivi de Brougham où (par contretems) on l'avoit
envoyée.

Je vous remets la conclusion de la lettre de M.
von H. qui regarde la Pologne, selon votre désire,*

* *Sic in orig.*

aussi ai-je ajouté un extrait de celle que je viens de
recevoir de M. Van Grendown sur ce même sujet.   Je
me confie entièrement à votre discrétion (qui m'est si
bien connue) que ces extraits ne parviennent à personne
excepter * le P., et que vous me le fassiez parvenir
quand vous en aurez l'occasion.

J'avais oublié de vous marquer une circonstance
touchant la discussion des affaires Polonoises à Liverpool.   Les essais qui y paraissent dans les journaux
de mon parti viennent (à ce qu'on me dit) des personnes
tout à fait inconnues des chefs du dit parti.   Ça
prouve au moins que la discussion commence à prendre.
J'en ai vu des autres preuves.

J'ai engagé M. Jeffrey à écrire quelque chose
pour vous dans son numéro qui doit paraître à la fin
d'Avril.†   La publication du dernier numéro a eu lieu
ici, et à Edinbourg depuis la quinzaine.

Je crois que vous faites bien de partir le plutôt
possible.   Tout est préparé ici.   La semence est
semée, et je serai toujours sur le qui vive pour en
recueillir les fruits.   Avant la discussion des négotia-
tions il n'y aura rien d'intéressant dans le parle-
ment.

N'oubliez pas de me donner de vos nouvelles, avec
tous les renseignements que vous pourrez de tems en
tems.   H. B.

LONDRES, *ce* 27 *Avril* 1814.

MONSIEUR.—Ne sachant pas exactement si vous
vous trouvez encore à la Haye, je n'entrerai pas dans
les détails de notre sujet.

* *Sic in orig.*
† The articles appeared in the *Edinburgh Review* of September 1814.

Mais je crois que vous serez bien aise d'apprendre que Lord Grey (sans la moindre communication avec moi) a entamé la discussion sur la Pologne dans la Chambre Haute il y a dix jours. La mention qu'il en a faite a été très-bien reçue et applaudie de tout côté. Il l'a fait d'une manière très-imposante et avec beaucoup d'adresse et de ménagement pour l'Empereur de Russie. Comme je vis dans la société de Lord G. presque journellement, et que je jouis de son amitié et de sa confiance dans toutes les affaires publiques, je suis persuadé qu'il me soupçonne d'avoir commencé la discussion du sujet, et que j'ai quelque raison pour ne pas l'avoir entamé avec lui, car il ne m'a jamais dit un mot là-dessus.

Dans la société je vois assez clairement que l'intérêt va toujours en accroissant, et que nous pourrons espérer quelque bon résultat. Je ne vais presque jamais dans les cercles sans entendre prononcer le nom de la Pologne, et toujours dans le meilleur sens.

Écrivez-moi, et croyez que je suis toujours, etc.,

H. BROUGHAM.

Par une bêtise impardonnable quelques-uns des journaux, en publiant le discours de Lord G., ont mis ' Courland ' au lieu de ' Poland.' Ils l'ont corrigé après.

Les Quakers etc., dans leur journal (*The Philanthropist*) ont bien rempli leur devoir vis à vis de notre cause.

FROM SIR SAMUEL ROMILLY TO M. BIERNACKI.

RUSSELL SQUARE,
Mar. 22, 1814.

SIR,—I return you many thanks for a sight of the

enclosed papers, which I have read with very great interest. No person can be more sensible than I am of the wrongs which Poland has suffered, or more convinced of the bad policy as well as the injustice of the conduct of all the States of Europe towards her.—I remain, Sir, with great respect, Your most obedient and faithful servant,

Saml. Romilly.

CHAPTER XXII

1814-15

WHILE Prince Adam Czartoryski was endeavouring through his secretary to obtain the support for his country of public opinion in England, the allies pursued their campaign against Napoleon with undiminished success. The crushing defeat of Leipzig (October 18, 1813) was rapidly followed by the invasion of France, the occupation of Paris by the allied troops (March 31, 1814) and the abdication of Napoleon at Fontainebleau (April 4, 1814). The Emperor Alexander, who had granted an amnesty to all the Poles who had fought against him under Napoleon in the campaign of 1812, now reverted to his former plan of reconstructing Poland as a separate State under his sceptre, and invited his old friend and counsellor to assist him in executing it. Alexander was accompanied by Prince Adam in his visit to London before the Vienna Congress, and in a despatch preserved in the Record Office, dated 'Paris, May 23, 1814,' General Cathcart, then British Ambassador to the Russian Court, informs Lord Castlereagh that 'the Emperor has been pleased this day to add the name of Prince Adam Czartorisky (*sic*) to the list of persons who are to attend him to London.'

When the Congress met at Vienna in October 1814, Poland was the first object of its deliberations, and Prince Adam played so prominent a part in them that Lord Castlereagh wrote to Lord Liverpool that the Prince, 'although not in any official situation, appears now the actual Russian Minister, at least on Polish and Saxon questions.'* The chief objections to the Emperor's proposal to restore Poland were, strange to say, not made by Austria and Prussia, whose Polish possessions would under that proposal have been united to the new Polish kingdom, but by Lord Castlereagh, on the plea that the creation of such a kingdom under the sceptre of the Emperor of Russia would make Russia too strong. He would readily consent to the restoration of Poland as an independent State with a sovereign of her own ; but knowing that this was too great a sacrifice to be expected of Russia, he insisted on the maintenance of the partition.†

* Despatch of the 24th December, 1814 (in the Record Office). In another despatch, dated the 5th November, 1814, Lord Castlereagh says : 'The day but one after the return of the sovereigns from Buda, the enclosed communication was delivered to me by an aide-de-camp of the Emperor of Russia. It was prepared during his Imperial Majesty's absence by Prince Czartoryski, the memorandum being written in concert with him by M. Anstetem, a Conseiller d'Etat in the bureau. I have reason to believe that Count Nesselrode was not consulted. The Emperor has latterly, on the question of Poland, ceased to act through his regular servants. It is unfortunately his habit to be his own Minister, and to select as the instrument of his immediate purpose, the person who may happen to fall in most with his views. This has been particularly the case on the present question, all the Russians, I believe without an exception, being adverse to his projects, considering them both as dangerous to himself and injurious to his allies.'

† 'Up to the period of the Congress of Vienna, no British statesman had ever set his hand to an instrument acknowledging, as valid acts, the two partitions of Poland. Had the British Plenipotentiary founded his objections upon this principle —had he positively refused to commit his Government to any such acknowledgment, and had he insisted on the erection of an independent Polish State, he would, to use his own words, have been applauded by the whole of Europe, whilst Austria and

An angry correspondence followed between the British Plenipotentiary and the Emperor, and at length the attitude of the latter and his Prussian ally (who hoped to get Saxony as a compensation for the loss of his Polish possessions) became so threatening that England, France, and Austria, by a secret treaty signed on the 3rd of January 1815, entered into a defensive alliance binding themselves each to bring, if necessary, 150,000 men into the field.

Prussia would not only not have opposed it, but, on the contrary, would have acquiesced in it with pleasure.

'Backed by such powerful support, as well as by the voice of public opinion throughout Europe, it is more than probable that he might have been successful: but the moment he gave up this principle, and told the Emperor that he was not indisposed to witness, even with satisfaction, that his Imperial Majesty should receive a liberal and important aggrandizement on his Polish frontier, and that it was to the *degree* and the *mode* to which he alone objected, he threw away the only weapon which he could successfully wield. The greater point was attainable, but the abandonment of the greater was fatal to the attainment of the less. There was —there could be—no answer to the following argument of the Emperor as to the share of the spoil, considered as a matter of spoil, to which he was entitled : "Mais lorsque l'Autriche et la Prusse ont contribué, comme alliées de la France, à dépouiller la Russie de la plus grande partie des provinces Polonaises ; quand la Russie a été obligée de les réconquerir ; lorsque la conquête du Duché de Varsovie devient aujourd'hui une compensation pour d'énormes sacrifices : il s'agit effectivement d'un nouveau partage, et dans ce cas, les stipulations qui ont accompagné celui de 1797 n'existent plus."

'Had Lord Castlereagh denounced the original, as well as the proposed, *partage*, instead of making appeals ad misericordiam, his remonstrances might have been effectual. But it was of no avail to tell the Emperor that he was exacting from his neighbours and allies an arrangement incompatible with their political independence, and that the demand by Russia to retain so large a share of Poland as that to which the Emperor laid claim, was a source of consternation and alarm to Austria and Prussia and of general terror throughout all the States of Europe.

'His Imperial Majesty's Austrian and Prussian allies had no claim upon his forbearance, and it was impossible to defeat the Emperor's claims when, on the principle on which they were made, no one could deny their justice.

'The partition being admitted, the degree and the mode could only be decided by the will of that party whose claims were the strongest, and whose power was adequate to support the claims. The result was, that Great Britain accepted the partition as a fait accompli, and that Russia obtained almost all that she asked for.

'Mr Cook, a man of considerable ability and firmness, who was Under-Secretary in the Foreign Office, and who accompanied Lord Castlereagh to Vienna, endeavoured in vain to rouse his chief to an uncompromising condemnation of the two partitions. He urged him to fling the treaties on the table of Congress, and to declare that nothing should induce Great Britain to acknowledge the validity of those acts. He urged in vain ; but he set the seal on the sincerity of his own opinions, by resigning at once his post of Under-Secretary of State. He was succeeded in Vienna by Mr Planta.' ("George Canning and his Times," by Augustus Granville Stapleton, p. 354.)

Ultimately, however, concessions were made on both sides, and the result was that by the Treaty of Vienna (signed on the 25th of February 1815) Posen was given to Prussia, and Galicia (except Cracow, which was to be a free town) to Austria, and the remainder of the Duchy of Warsaw was made a kingdom 'irrevocably attached by its Constitution' to the Russian Empire, and with the Czar as its King. It was also stipulated that 'all parts of ancient Poland, as it existed before the year 1772,' should enjoy the right of free navigation and trade, and that all its inhabitants, whether subjects of Russia, Austria, or Prussia, shall obtain 'a representation' and 'institutions which shall ensure the preservation of their nationality.' Thus did Europe, while stipulating for the preservation of the Polish nationality over the whole of ancient Poland, give the sanction of public law to a partition which Prince Talleyrand described as 'the prelude, in part perhaps the cause, and even to a certain extent the excuse, of the disorders to which Europe had been a prey.'[*]

Lord Castlereagh's despatches on the subject will be found in the 'Correspondence relating to the negotiations of the years 1814 and 1815 respecting Poland' which was presented to Parliament in 1863. The following extracts from memoranda drawn up at

* 'De toutes les questions qui devaient être traitées au Congrès, le Roi aurait considéré comme la première, la plus grande, la plus éminemment Européenne, comme hors de comparaison avec toute autre, celle de Pologne, s'il lui eût été possible d'espérer autant qu'il le désirait, qu'un peuple si digne de l'intérêt de tous les autres par son ancienneté, sa valeur, les services qu'il rendit autrefois à l'Europe, et par son infortune, pût être rendu à son antique et complète indépendance. Le partage qui la raya du nombre des nations fut le prélude, en partie la cause, et peut-être jusqu'à un certain point l'excuse, des bouleversements auxquels l'Europe a été en proie.' (Note to Prince Metternich, dated 19th December 1814).

the time by Prince Czartoryski show some of the
arguments on the Russian side of the question :—

'Hitherto experience has always proved that
people who are unhappy and dissatisfied are usually
restless, and that the surest way of keeping people
quiet is to make them contented. There is no reason
to believe that such a universal and infallible means of
pacification would not succeed with the Poles, who
have certainly shown themselves very active and
stirring ; but all their energy has been directed to a
single object, that of recovering their name, their
Government, and their nationality. It is difficult to
understand why people should when speaking of the
Poles call that " levity " which in speaking of other
nations they call " patriotism and perseverance." Such
a misuse of words may lead to false conclusions, and
there is not the slightest probability that the Poles,
after obtaining the essence of their demands, should
only become the more turbulent and disorderly. His
Imperial Majesty is convinced, after many years'
experience, that all classes in Poland have the same
wish, and he has had a new proof of this in the
addresses which have been sent him from all parts of
the Duchy of Warsaw. . . .

'His Majesty, after much consideration, has
arrived at the conclusion that the plan he proposes
would be the best in the interest of Europe generally.
By it he would keep acquisitions which he cannot give
up, but he would so organise his possessions as to
secure peace to his neighbours and to Europe.

'Suppose the name of the kingdom of Poland is restored, and part of the Duchy of Warsaw is reunited to

Russia.   This could not in any sense be dangerous to
Austria or Prussia, for the Emperor would guarantee
to them the possession of their parts of Poland, and
the slightest attempt to recover them would be
opposed by Austria, Prussia, France, and England,
leaving Russia entirely isolated. . .   It is not a little
more or less territory or fortresses that constitutes
the balance of power ; it is the parity of interests
which produces combinations in the hour of danger
that are far more formidable and effective than mere
arrangements of frontier.'

CHAPTER XXIII

SIR JOHN BOWRING, in his Memoirs of Jeremy Bentham (vol x, page 478, of the collected works) says that 'Bentham's hopes of being allowed to prepare a code for Russia were at this time (1815) strongly excited. His name and writings were very popular in that country. He had himself some—his brother, who had been so long in the Russian service, many—influential friends at the Court of the Czar. Dumont had lived long at St Petersburg, and his reputation and his labours were so associated with those of his master, that strong expectations were indulged that authority to prepare a Code would be communicated to him. The Emperor Alexander, who was fond of being considered the patron and protector of literary and learned men, sent to Bentham a diamond ring, which Bentham returned to the Imperial donor, with the seal of the box that contained it unbroken. His conduct has been deemed ungracious, but without reason. He cared nothing about diamond rings ; but he desired to legislate for the good of the Russian people. The Emperor would have had him communicate his observations—or rather reply to the questionings of a commission appointed to revise the Russian Codes. But Bentham knew that commission to be wholly incompetent to the work ; and its President, upon whom everything depended, was peculiarly unfitted for his task, so that Bentham refused to take any share in a drama of feebleness and insincerity.'

The following letters were addressed by Bentham to the Czar and Prince Czartoryski on this subject :—

To the Emperor of all the Russias.

SIRE,—The object of this address is to submit to your Imperial Majesty an offer relative to the department of legislation.

My years are sixty-six. Without commission from any government, not much fewer than fifty of them have been occupied in that field. My ambition is to employ the remainder of them, as far as can be done in this country, in labouring towards the improvement of the state of that branch of government in your Majesty's vast Empire.

In the year 1802, a work extracted, as therein mentioned, from my papers, was by Mr Dumont of Geneva, published at Paris in nine vols. 8vo., under the title of ' Traité de Législation Civile et Pénale,' etc.

In the year 1805 a translation of it into the Russian language was published at St Petersburg, (by order, if I am rightly informed, of your Majesty's Government).

Since the publication of that work Europe has seen two extensive bodies of law promulgated within its limits : one by the French Emperor, the other by the King of Bavaria. These two are the only bodies of law of any such considerable extent that have made their appearance within the last half-century. Of the one promulgated by the French Emperor, a complete penal code formed a part. In the preface to that authoritative work, my unauthoritative one is mentioned with honour : among the *dead* Montesquieu, Beccaria, and Blackstone; among *living* names (unless it be for some matter of fact) none but *mine*. In the Bavarian code drawn up by Mr Bexon, much more *particular* as well as copious *mention* is made of that work of mine, much more *eulogy* bestowed upon it.

In France under the immediate rod of Napoleon, in Bavaria under the influence of Napoleon, the generosity displayed by the notice thus taken of the work of a living Englishman could not but call forth my admiration.

Approbation is one thing; *adoption* is another. With mine before them, both these modern works took for their basis the jurisprudence of ancient Rome. Russia at any rate needs not any such incumbrance.

In the texture of the human frame, some fibres there are which are the same in all *places* and at all *times*, others which vary with the *place* and with the *time*. For those last it has been among my constant and pointedly manifested cares to look out and provide.

Of the particularities of Russia I am not altogether without experience. Two of the most observant years of my life were passed within her limits.

Codes upon the French pattern are already in full view. Speak the word, Sire,—Russia shall produce a pattern of her own, and then let Europe judge.

To Russia, it is true, I am a foreigner, yet to this purpose scarcely more so than a Courlander, a Livonian, or a Finlander. In point of local knowledge to place me on a level with a native of Russia—to *me* as to *them*—information in various shapes could not but be necessary. Any such assistance no person could ever be more ready to supply than I should be solicitous to receive and profit by it.

In my above mentioned work a sample of a *penal code* is exhibited. In the first place what I should humbly propose is, to do what remains to be done for the completion of it. For this purpose not many months would, I hope, be necessary.

Sovereign and father—in this double character it is on all occasions your Majesty's wish and delight to show yourself to your people. In this same character, even on the rough and thorny ground of penal law—in this same happily compounded character, addressing them through my pen, your Majesty would still show yourself the sovereign by his *commands*, the father by his instructions; the sovereign not more intent on establishing the necessary obligations, than the father on rendering the necessity manifest, manifest to all men, and at every step he takes thus justifying himself in their sight.

Reasons.—Yet it is by reasons that a task at once so salutary and so arduous can be accomplished :— reasons connected and that by an indiscontinued chain of references, on the one hand with the *general principles* from which they have been deduced, on the other hand, with the several *clauses* and *words* in the text of the law, for the *justification,* and at the same time for the *elucidation* of which they have been respectively framed. An accompaniment of this kind would form one of the peculiarities of my *Code*: a sample is given in my above mentioned treatise.

This sample was a challenge to legislators: the well-intentioned but strictly shackled Frenchmen shrunk from it. How acutely sensible they were of the usefulness of such an accompaniment, how they wished and how they feared to expose their works to so searching a *test*—how they tasked themselves to produce a sort of substitute test—(I mean a mass of vague generalities left floating in the air, and destitute of all application to particulars)—how sadly inadequate is that substitute—what excuse is given for the deficiency, and how lame is that excuse—all this may be seen in their respective works.

All *comprehensiveness, conciseness, uniformity,* and *simplicity*—qualities the union of which is at once so desirable and so difficult—such, as far as concerns the choice of words, are the qualities for which the nature of the work seems to present a demand. To infuse them into it, each in the highest degree which the necessary regard to the rest admits of, would, on this as on all similar occasions it has been, be to my mind an object of unremitting solicitude. With what promise of success, let the above mentioned sample speak. Whoever sees that *one part*, sees to all such purposes the *whole*.

In the midst of war, and without interruption to the successes or to the evils of war, a line or two from your Majesty's hand would suffice to give commencement to the work, to this the greatest of all the works of peace.

As to *remuneration*, the honour of the proposed employ, joined to such satisfaction as would be inseparable from that honour, compose the only reward which my situation renders necessary—the only one which my way of thinking would allow me to accept.

With all the respect of which the nature of this address conveys so much fuller an assurance than can be conveyed by any customary form of words, my endeavour would be to approve myself, Sire, your Imperial Majesty's ever faithful servant,

(Signed) JEREMY BENTHAM.

To Prince Czartoryski.
Q reen quare Place, Westminster,
21st *June* 1815.

DEAR SIR,—For one thing I must begin with casting myself upon the Emperor's forgiveness as well as yours ; that is the enormous length of time (upwards of a month), that has intervened between my receiving of the two letters, and the despatching of these my answers. Another thing for which, likewise, I must beg your indulgence, is—the rough state in which I am reduced to send a copy of mine to the Emperor, for your use.

Both trespasses have their source in an engagement under which the letter found me : viz. that of drawing up for this country, for the use of a voluntary association, a plan of National Education, in relation to which I may perhaps take the liberty of troubling you with a few words before the close of the present letter; or at any rate by the next messenger: the whole business was in danger of being put a stop to for an indefinite length of time had I not devoted myself exclusively to it. As to your copy (I mean of my letter to the Emperor) I hope you will find it legible, as consistently with my engagements, time could not be found for the copying and revisal of another fair one.

As to the original, you, as well as he, will (I fear) be sadly annoyed by it, were it only for the length of it. It was, however, absolutely necessary I should speak out, and I saw no hope of being able so to do, to any purpose, in any lesser compass. I hear it said everywhere that he is a good-natured man: by what you will find me saying to him, that quality will be put to the *test*. From me, if he has patience enough, he may thus *read*, what from a man in any other situation, it is not in the nature of things that he should either *read* or *hear*.

A bandage on his eyes—leading strings on his shoulders—on this part of the field of Government, such has hitherto been his costume. My aim is to rid him of those appendages: is it possible he should forgive me? Forgive me or not, that is not the point: that he should suffer himself to be rid of them, *that* is the one thing needful.

I hope this will not draw *you* into a scrape; a scrape on your part so perfectly undeserved: for no such thing as a *tale out of school* have I ever had from *you*.

If, by any thing I have said, an end should be put, not only to *that* correspondence, but to another which is so truly flattering to me, I shall be truly sorry; but it was necessary to run the risk, for I think you will agree with me that whether *with* it anything be done or no, without it nothing was at any rate to be done.

The letter addressed to his Majesty, I put into a separate packet. I avoid purposely any such attempt as that of making it pass through *your* hands. In relation to an official person there so frequently alluded to, it was absolutely necessary I should speak without reserve : and there seemed neither use nor necessity for *your* being involved in such business.

Even if it should be in the *constitutional* part of the field of law that my labours, such as they are, should be desired by you (though for reasons already given, *that* is the part in relation to which my hopes of being of use are least sanguine) I repeat my promise to put them under your command :

I. Because I do not absolutely despair of being able to do some good—here a little and there a little—even in relation to that branch.

II. Because (as I say to the Emperor) that is the branch which I imagine *you* had more particularly in view. But my expectations are much more *extensive*, as well as sanguine, in relation to the *Penal* and *Civil* branches : including, in both cases (though so far as concerns the organisation of the *Judicial Establishment* it belongs to the *constitutional* branch) the *system of Procedure.*—Why ?—Because in the *Civil* branch there will be a good deal of matter, and in the *Penal* a good deal *more* applicable, with little or no difference, under *any form of Government.* So far, therefore, I could myself *propose* matter, with a tolerable expectation of its being received, and thence with a proportionable degree of facility and alacrity : whereas in regard to *constitutional* law, in which is included the *form of Government*, it would be folly for me to pretend to originate anything considerable.— What is the monarch willing to *leave* or to *concede* to you nobles and the great body of the people, taken together?   What are the monarch and you nobles, taken together, willing to *leave* or to *concede* to the great body of the people?   What are the people at present in a condition to *receive*, if the powers, on which it depends, were willing to concede it to them?   What more, within a moderate space of time, may they be *expected* to come of themselves to be *in*, or to be capable of being put *into* a condition to receive,— and by what means?   All this, if known to anybody, is known to you:—not a particle of it to me.

When, near the close of the reign of poor King Stanislaus, a constitutional code for Poland was drawn up, *Bukati* * (I think it was he that was then resident here) sent me a copy of it.   What is become of it I do not exactly know.   But what I remember is—that people in general were here much pleased with it: myself among the rest, as far as I had looked at it ; which was very slightly ; for being deeply embarked in other pursuits at the time, nothing called upon me to suspend them for any such purpose as the study of it.

On the present occasion, *that* paper, is it intended to form the *basis*?   Here would be a field for experimenting in: and to a monarch with the whole Russian Empire under such entire command, what possible danger can there be from any such experiment?

<hr>

* See Vol. I., p. 160.

Under the Great Turk was not Ragusa even a Republic?   In such a case more real efficiency than what he would lose in the shape of *coercive power*, the Autocrat of Russia would gain in the shape of gentle *influence* : loss, were there any, would be all of it to the successor,—who, not having been the author of the *boon*, would not be a sharer in the gratitude :—But, even by him, he being used to the comparatively new state of things, the loss, if there were any, would not be felt.

It is now about forty years since I began to lift up my prayers for Poland.   The most intimate friend I had was John Lind, privy counsellor to the King, and under his Majesty, original institutor, as well as director, of a school for 400 cadets at Warsaw, and Governor of Prince Stanislaus, nephew to the poor king, whose business at our Court he did for a number of years, writing a letter from London every other post day ; Bukati being all the while the resident kept for show, because our King would not see in that character one of his own subjects.

Lind's first appearance at Warsaw was in that of reader of English to your father or your uncle, I forget which it was.   Oh, how he used to talk and talk of Poland !   And how he used to curse the Fredericks—great as they were—not to mention other persons.

Being of all countries and of no party, I have just sent off to Paris a large packet of printed copies of a part of the educational scheme to leading men there, Bourbonnites, Napoleonites, and Republicans promiscuously,—some of them old friends of mine.

If you follow the camp, perhaps you may make

prize of them: yet I should be sorry you should ; were
it only because while you are at Paris, you would
not be at *Warsaw;* and whether you are so or no, I
am of the number—and that I believe not a small
one—of those who are impatient for your being there.

Well, but about this education scheme: were it only
to account for the delay, a few words I find I must
trouble you with about it even here :—

An experiment of it is about to be made in a part
of that garden of mine which you saw.   It has for its
object the applying to the higher branches of learning,
and the higher as well as middling ranks of the community, that *new* system of instruction, of the success
of which you can not but be more or less apprized.

Brougham, Sir James Macintosh—and if I can
persuade him to lend his *name*—for that is all he can
have *time* to lend—*Romilly,* will be at the head of it.
For the *details* of the management there will be some
very efficient men, with whose names you can scarcely
be acquainted.   For reasons not worth troubling you
with, my fixed determination has been from the very
first, not to be of the number.   In the *Executive*
department of it, I accordingly bear no part : but of
the *Legislative* the *initiation* has fallen entirely to my
share.   My labours in that field had (I believe) already
commenced, when I had the honour of receiving you :
and, for want of their being completed, the business
was at a stand, and by a few days more of delay, the
season might have been lost—(I mean the time when
the expected *contributors* are in town)—and the execution of the plan deferred for a whole twelvemonth ;
and thereby perhaps finally defeated.

It is now in such advance, that everything which it is necessary to publish in the first instance, is either already in print or in the printers' hands. A copy or two will, I trust, be brought to you by the next messenger. On this field, at any rate, in doing what I have done, I consider myself as being at work not less for *Russia* and *Poland*, than for *London*. For the elementary branches, as taught upon the Bell and Lancaster system, *Paris* is already provided with a schoolmaster from hence. The son of a Protestant clergyman—Martin, I think, is his name—was in Louis XVIII's time sent from the south of France to a Lancasterian school for the express purpose of learning the method, and is now at Paris; and (I understand) much caressed there.

His business there is to *form* Instructors. The salary offered to him was £200 : for such a station, a very considerable salary at Paris. No, (says he) *that* would be too much. Success or failure depends upon the degree of economy. Such a sum (naming it, perhaps a quarter as much) is all that you need give. By this the price will be set to those who succeed me. If in my instance, in consideration of my being the first institutor, you see any claim to extraordinary remuneration, let *that* come by and by, when by experience you see what I have done. Just the same thing might the Emperor do for Petersburg and Warsaw. The expense—I mean the *necessary* expense—would be next to nothing ; and if this can not succeed with you, I am at a loss to think what else can.

For this purpose you will see how necessary it has

been for me to take a fresh peep into every nook and cranny of the whole field of art and science: my business having been to apply the new method of instruction to every part of that field that is deemed capable of receiving it. My endeavour has been to reduce the whole sketch into as narrow a compass as possible: and the narrower the compass the greater the quantity of time which it has cost me. Locke's Essay (so he tells us himself in his preface) is too long—Why? 'Because' (says he) 'I had not time to make it shorter.'

If upon the field of codification, it be in my power to throw any *light*, you see the terms upon which it is in the power of your Alexander to have it? Exactly those upon which God Almighty had *His*: a couple of words the whole of the expense.

I hope the Emperor will not be angry with me for returning his ring; if it had been a *brass* or a *glass* one, I would have kept it. If he will send the value of it, and no more, to my masters and employers, as above, for their *school*, I as well as they will be all gratitude. But of this in that ensuing letter with which this threatens you. Believe me ever, with the truest respect, dear sir, your most obedient servant,

JEREMY BENTHAM.

PRINCE ADAM CZARTORYSKI.

CHAPTER XXIV

THE POLISH CONSTITUTION.—PROMISE AND PERFORMANCE.—RUSSIAN
ATROCITIES.—REVOLUTION.

AFTER the negotiations at Vienna, the Emperor
Alexander issued a proclamation to the Poles, dated
$\frac{11}{23}$ May 1815, stating the chief points of the Constitution which was to be granted to the new kingdom of
Poland in conformity with the treaty. A provisional
government was formed at Warsaw, with Prince
Adam Czartoryski as its head, and the following letter
was addressed to him by Alexander on the same date
as that of the proclamation :—

VIENNA, $\frac{11}{23}$ *May* 1815.

During the time you have passed here with me,
you have had an opportunity of knowing my intentions as to the institutions which it is my will to
establish in Poland, and the improvements I desire to
introduce in that country. You will take care never
to lose sight of them in the deliberations of the
Council, and to draw the full attention of your
colleagues to them, in order that the action of the
Government and the reforms which it is bound to

carry out may be in accordance with my views. You
will not fail, if necessary, to take the initiative in this
respect, so as to hasten the progress of your task and
bring forward bills in conformity with the system
which has been adopted.

As you are equally acquainted with my ideas as
to the spirit in which I wish the selection of the
various officials to be made, you will not fail to
see that this is done in accordance with them. In a
country which has so long been tossed about by
disturbances and revolutions, it is of the highest
importance that a uniform and well combined course
should be pursued. This is what I wanted to recall
to your mind once more by this letter, which I allow
you even to show, so as to add confirmation to what
you will have to say in order to carry out my
intentions.   ALEXANDER.

The new Constitution, which was promulgated on
the $\frac{1}{27}$ November, 1815, established a Parliament of
two Houses, which was to meet every two years, a
responsible Ministry, and liberty of the press, and it
stipulated that all the officials should be Poles, and
that Polish should be the official language. It will
be seen, however, from the following letters addressed
to the Emperor by Prince Czartoryski, that, owing
mainly to the arbitrary proceedings of the Grand-
Duke Constantine, the military governor of the
country, this Constitution gradually became a dead
letter :

                                        ' 1815.

' As the bases of the Constitution provide for a

Ministry of War among the branches of the administration which, reunited under the same central control, make up the whole body of government, we think it our duty to seek the decision of your Imperial and Royal Majesty on the subject.

'The presence of the Grand-Duke Constantine in this country, and the special powers with which he is invested, have precluded all relations between the provisional government and the military administration, which is placed under a separate committee. This total separation between the civil and military administrations gives rise to the gravest difficulties. It has made it impossible for the Government to present to your Majesty a general report on the situation and the probable requirements of the State, as the army constitutes one of its principal elements. So long as the most considerable and expensive part of the administration remains entirely independent and isolated it cannot be subject to any control, and the expenditure of the country cannot be restricted in proportion to its resources.

'The Government, being constantly brought to a standstill in every measure which has any bearing whatever on military affairs, often finds itself obliged to give up useful reforms whose execution is only possible with the regular and zealous co-operation of the military administration.

'The savings we have endeavoured to introduce in the whole expenditure of the country, and especially in the civil administration, by reducing to the lowest possible point the number and salaries of the officials, will not produce any effect, and cannot be maintained, if the same spirit of rigid economy is not applied to the administration of the army, and if a certain proportion is not established between military and civil emoluments.

'Moreover, the administration of the army touches at so many points on the civil administration that they can neither be properly organised nor governed except on a uniform system.

'The above considerations, the certainty that the Polish army will immediately have to be paid out of the treasury of the Kingdom, and the fact that its revenues will not be sufficient for that purpose, have decided the provisional government to submit to your Imperial and Royal Majesty whether you will not think fit to order the creation of a Ministry of War to take the place of the military committee, and to be organised on the same principle as the two other Ministries. The first duty of this Ministry would be to present a plan for its internal organisation, and the Government, subject to your Majesty's approval, reserves to itself the duty of afterwards submitting to you its observations on the plan in question and the savings which might be introduced in the establishment of the army.'

'WARSAW, *June* 1815.

'. . . The general impression at the promulgation of the new Constitution has been as favourable as could be desired . . . . Its principles have attached the people to your Majesty, and after the long period of waiting, and the conduct of the Grand-Duke, the grant of the Constitution was necessary to produce such a result. The change in the Polish arms and the interference of the Russians with the Government have caused some pain, but the bases of the Constitution have made the people forget everything.'

'WARSAW, $\frac{17}{29}$ *July*, 1815.

'The organisation of the Ministries of the Interior and of Finance, and of the Courts of Justice, is about to be completed; the result will be a pretty considerable saving. Our first care was not to stop the course of government; the second is to introduce without delay all possible order and economy from the beginning. . . . I do not doubt that the result would be most satisfactory if it were not for the existence of an independent military authority with which the Government is not in a condition to struggle. I would not have ventured to touch on this delicate point if the urgency of the case did not oblige me to do so. . . .

'His Highness the Grand-Duke is not to be moved by any zeal or submission. He seems to have taken a dislike to the country which is increasing in alarming progression, and is the subject of his daily conversation. Neither the army, the nation, nor individuals find any favour in his eyes. The Constitution especially is made by him a subject of incessant sarcasm; everything that is matter of law or regulation he scorns and covers with ridicule, and unhappily his words have already been followed by deeds. He does not even adhere to the military laws which he has himself confirmed. He insists upon introducing flogging in the army, and he ordered some men to be flogged yesterday without paying any attention to the unanimous representations of the committee. Desertion is increasing, and will become general, and most of the officers are about to resign.

' It looks as if a plan had been formed for rendering your Majesty's benefits illusory and making your scheme fail from the beginning. In that case the Grand-Duke is, without knowing it, the blind tool of certain persons in his confidence who encourage his sombre and passionate temper. I fear the most lamentable results if he should remain here.'

' 31st July 1815.

' The position of the Government of your Imperial and Royal Majesty in this country has for some time become extremely painful and difficult, and I feel it my duty to bring to your knowledge details of which I would have wished never to be obliged to speak.

' His Highness the Grand-Duke has several times intimated to the Government that civil officials, magistrates, mayors, etc., should be brought before him, and the other day he placed the President of the town of Warsaw under arrest. Some days ago, too, his Highness issued a decree by means of which he will have the power of trying any citizen by court-martial.

' The provisional government cannot but recognise that such proceedings are contrary to the rules established in all countries for the public peace and security, and that they are especially in direct opposition to the Constitution which your Majesty has just granted to the country. . . Under these circumstances all the members of the Government are unanimously of opinion that the above facts should be laid before you with a view to your Majesty placing your Government in a position to carry out your will.'

'WARSAW, ⅒ *January* 1816.

'. . . Your Imperial Majesty are alone capable of maintaining the edifice you have raised. If you abandon it from the beginning to the attacks of those who are hostile to it, it must fall to pieces. What else can be the fate of a Constitution granted by you with so much solemnity and violated almost immediately after it was proclaimed? If we obtain the support which we have a right to ask of your Majesty, all will go well. I have observed with joy that so far as the Poles are concerned, more importance is attached to measures than to individuals. Our institutions, though as yet in the process of formation, are sufficient to work the Government machine, and since the establishment of Constitutional Government perfect harmony exists among all the Ministers. . . . Your Majesty's Lieutenant Governor,* however, though zealous, persevering, and enlightened, seems to consider that every wish expressed by the Grand-Duke Constantine must be regarded as that of your Majesty. He is ready to violate the Constitution at any moment if his Highness should require him to do so, and he has even plainly expressed himself to the Council in this sense. . . . Such a degree of submission in the highest official of the realm would make your Consti-

---

* General Zajonczek, a veteran who had lost both his legs in the Napoleonic wars.

tution a farce.   If you will inform him that you wish to respect your own work and cause it to be respected, and that his duties to his sovereign and his country may be combined with, but should never be subordinated to, his obligations to the Grand-Duke, he will no doubt carry out your will.   This, however, is an essential condition of preventing the ruin of the country. . .   You, Sire, are our destiny ; our only resources and hopes are bound up with your Majesty, and you alone can give permanent solidity to the institutions which you have created.'

'*17th April* 1816.

'Suicides have for some time been very frequent in the Polish army.   The annexed letter, the original of which is in the Grand-Duke's hands, shows the cause of most of these unhappy occurrences.   Its writer was a distinguished officer, aide-de-camp to General Krasinski, and a great favourite in Polish society. His example was followed by a sub-officer who killed himself because, as is stated, he could not survive the shame of the disgraceful punishments inflicted upon himself and his colleagues.   It is absolutely necessary that the army should be given a code of laws and regulations.   At present it is administered solely by caprice.   It suffers not from too much severity, but from constant humiliations and acts of arbitrary power.'

(*Enclosure.*)

'MY DEAR SISTER, . . . I can no longer bear what I see daily—my brothers-in-arms and my fellow-citizens dishonoured, the glory of our fathers trodden under foot, the laws of the best of sovereigns violated. I leave my poor country helplessly delivered up to the caprices of one man.

'How often have I nearly become an assassin! What a blow that would have been for you, dear sister ! I wished to sacrifice myself in order to free us from these shameful chains, but feeling that the result might not realise my hopes, I prefer to deprive myself of an existence which might become fatal to my country. . . . I know that I shall be accused of weakness ; I would have done this deed long ago if our holy religion and my attachment for you had not prevented me. But being now quite convinced that I can no longer be of use to my country, I and several of my friends have determined to leave this world. . .

'Give my sword to your son. Let him wear it, as I did, for his country and his friends.'

' SIENIAWA, 21*st August* 1821.

' I feel it my duty to submit to your Imperial and Royal Majesty some observations on the present condition of Poland. I do not often trouble you with letters, and I beg to be permitted on this occasion to write to you at greater length than usual. I have given a heading to each paragraph, so that your Majesty need only read those which may seem to you most worthy of attention.

' *State of Public Feeling.*—People's minds are in a state of extreme uncertainty and total discouragement. Everything seems unsettled ; every institution is in danger, and the most lamentable changes of system are expected. Nothing can be more pernicious than such a state of affairs, which stifles noble aspirations and leads weak people to look only after their own interests, in the belief that public considerations are disregarded by their Government.

'*Causes of Alarm.*—It is feared, from certain phrases which have been uttered by those who are supposed to be the confidential interpreters of your views, that you regard the Constitution as impracticable, useless, and involving too much expenditure, that the independence of Courts of Justice is to cease, that public education is to be restricted, that the diets are inconvenient obstacles which should be abolished, and that the Kingdom is to be governed like the other Polish dominions of the Empire. I do not know how much truth there may be in these discouraging rumours, but it is asserted that your opinions have of late undergone a complete change, and are totally opposed to those you held before. I can hardly believe this, and I appeal with confidence against those who wish to injure my country and its Constitution to principles and traits of character which should be above all passing circumstances.

'*Expense of the Army.*—It would be unjust to make a nation suffer for faults which it has not committed. You have been led, Sire, by motives whose force I am far from disputing, to decide that the expense of the Polish army shall not be diminished. But it is a fact that this expense is greater than the Kingdom of Poland within its present limits is capable of bearing, and that it is relatively greater than that borne for similar objects by various independent kingdoms, such

as Sweden, Saxony, Würtemberg, and Piedmont,
where, with greater resources, the military system is
less costly.

'*Limits of the Kingdom.*—When the fate of this
country was decided your Majesty will remember that
you magnanimously promised to reunite all the Polish
provinces under your sceptre and under a national
régime.   You yourself thought the regeneration of
Poland should be carried out on a more extended
scale ; the present Kingdom, smaller by a third than
the Duchy whose place it occupies, was in your eyes
to be a merely provisional creation.   Reasons of
prudence have led your Majesty to suspend the execution of this promise ; but would it not be obviously
unjust to punish the Kingdom for the restricted limits
imposed upon it, the extension of which the nation
would make the greatest sacrifices to procure?

'*The Constitution.*—The Constitution granted by
your Majesty has been subjected to much unjust
criticism.   It cannot be made responsible for the ill-
directed or superfluous expenditure of the administration, for this expenditure has occurred because the
Constitution was not sufficiently obeyed.   The army
is too large, the taxes are levied with extreme rigour,
justice would be impartial if it were not influenced by
persons above the law, and the system of police is sometimes inquisitorial and vexatious.   The Constitution
prevents nothing that is necessary ; unfortunately
it does not prevent that which is superfluous and
injurious to the state.   The introduction of measures
of the latter class depends entirely on your Majesty's
will, and the Diet should not be blamed for rendering

it difficult to introduce them. It is one of the
advantages of Constitutional Government that it
tends to stability ; the rejection of a bill simply leaves
things as they are.'

The above letter was, as will be seen from its date,
written shortly after the formation of the Holy
Alliance, the Congresses of Troppau and Laybach,
and the revolutionary movements at Naples, in Spain,
and in Piedmont. Alexander now gradually abandoned his liberal tendencies and gave up Poland
entirely to the cruel and arbitrary rule of his brother
Constantine. Prince Adam Czartoryski, seeing that
any further intervention with the Emperor on behalf
of Poland was hopeless, ceased all further correspondence with him on the subject, and in 1823 he gave up
his post of curator of the Wilna University, which he
had held for twenty years, the atrocious persecution
of the students by the Russian authorities rendering
it impossible for him any longer usefully to conduct
the affairs of the University, which had under his care
risen to the position of the first educational institution
in the Empire.

In 1825 Alexander I died and was succeeded by
Nicholas. Among the persons arrested in connection
with the outbreak at St Petersburg which preceded
Nicholas's accession were several Poles, who were
brought up for trial before the Senate at Warsaw.
Prince Adam, who was then in Italy, hurried to Warsaw
to take part in this trial as a member of the Senate.
After a careful inquiry, which lasted more than a year,
it was found that the accused had not taken any part

whatever in the rebellion, and had merely protested in a legal manner against the repeated violations of the Constitution. Prince Adam, as the father, so to say, of the Constitution and the chief adviser of the late Emperor in all matters relating to Poland, was naturally called upon to take a prominent part in the deliberations of the Senate on this matter, and his view of the innocence of the accused was accepted by the whole of the Senate with the exception of one member. The verdict was reversed by the Emperor, who ordered the Senators to be retained at Warsaw under the surveillance of the military authorities, and the accused to be taken to St Petersburg and imprisoned in the casemates of the fortress.

This outrageous measure was the beginning of the events which led to the Polish insurrection of 1830. The savage cruelties of the Grand-Duke Constantine, and the endless violations of the Constitution and deportations of distinguished citizens, are well known, and need not be recapitulated here. The Poles had for years been subjected to indignities which no high-spirited nation, with a patriotic and warlike army, could long tolerate. Revolutions were breaking out in France, Belgium, and Germany; Nicholas had ordered the Russian and Polish armies to march against the insurgents in those countries; and the Poles could no longer delay the outbreak which had for some time been in preparation. The whole nation—not only in the Kingdom of Poland, but in Lithuania, Volhynia, Podolia, and the Ukraine —rose against its oppressors. Constantine left the country with the Russian troops, the Polish throne was declared vacant, and Prince Adam Czartoryski was unanimously elected President of the National Government. A Russian army invaded Poland in February 1831, but it was repeatedly defeated by the Poles, though they were inferior in numbers. The Russians, reinforced by 20,000 grenadiers, were again beaten in the vicinity of Warsaw, and were forced to retire to Lublin for winter quarters. In April the Poles gained further victories, and the Russian army, dispersed in a marshy country, was almost annihilated, but new Russian troops constantly poured in from all parts of the Empire, while the forces at the disposal of the Poles were limited and they had great difficulty in procuring provisions and ammunition in consequence of Austria and Prussia having closed their frontiers to them. By degrees the Russian army retrieved its defeats; on the 7th of September, 1831, Warsaw was taken, after a sanguinary battle in which the Russians lost one-fourth of their troops, and the remains of the Polish army, including Prince Adam Czartoryski, who had fought in its ranks, were driven into Austria and Prussia.

CHAPTER XXV

1831-2

AFTER the collapse of the Polish Revolution of 1830-1
Prince Adam Czartoryski proceeded to London, where
he arrived on the 22nd of December 1831. The
revolution which had just taken place in France made
Paris an unsuitable starting-point for a European
intervention in Poland, as the other Powers on the
Continent looked upon the new French Government
with suspicion as representing the aggressive and
revolutionary tendencies of the year 1792, which it
was hoped had been finally crushed by the coalition of
1815. In London, however, a Liberal Cabinet had
come into power almost simultaneously with the outbreak of the Polish Revolution. This seemed a good
omen for the Polish cause, and the more sanguine of
the Poles already looked forward to an Anglo-French

coalition in their behalf and in that of the other oppressed nationalities. But as usual Ministers in office held very different language from that which they had used in opposition. The envoys in London of the Polish national Government, Marquis Wielopolski and Count Walewski (afterwards Minister under Napoleon III), reported that the Liberal Government, alarmed at the excitement in France and the cries of revenge for Waterloo, had come to the conclusion that the policy of England should be 'not to weaken Russia, as Europe might soon again require her services in the cause of order,' and to prevent Poland, whom it regarded as the natural ally of France, from becoming 'a French province on the Vistula.'* The Reform Bill and the Belgian Question, too, absorbed the attention of the Government and rendered it indisposed to take up so delicate and dangerous a question as that of Poland. Accordingly, although at the beginning of the Polish Revolution the British Cabinet had represented at St Petersburg that England, as a party to the Treaty of Vienna, could not consent to any violation of its provisions, it afterwards rejected the proposal of the French Government of July for a combined intervention with the object of stopping further bloodshed in Poland.

'London,' says M. de Gadon in his manuscript account of the Polish mission, 'was at that time the head-quarters of European diplomacy, as the Conference on the Belgian question, which presented many difficulties and dangers, was being held there. The

* Despatch of the 19th March 1831, from Marquis Wielopolski to the Polish mission in Paris, and of the 29th March and 8th April 1831, from Count Walewski to the Minister of Foreign Affairs in Warsaw (MSS. in the Polish Library in Paris).

chief men of mark in the political world were Earl
Grey and Lords Palmerston, Brougham, Holland,
Melbourne, Lansdowne, and Althorp, while among
the diplomatists at the Belgian Conference were
Talleyrand, Lieven, and Esterhazy. The feminine
influence in politics, which at that time was not
inconsiderable, was represented by Lady Holland, the
Princess Dino-Talleyrand, and the Princess Lieven.
The first of these, still bearing the traces of great
beauty—proud, witty, and imposing 'as a Czarina—'
assembled at her famous receptions at Holland House
all that was most brilliant by position, merit, or talent.
The Princess Dino, daughter of the last Duchess of
Courland and wife of the nephew * of Prince Talleyrand, had lived with the Prince for many years, and
was his constant companion. She had great influence
over him, and used to preside at the magnificent receptions in the French Embassy while Talleyrand was
Ambassador. The rooms of the Embassy at Hanover
Square were fitted up with all the splendour of the great
French aristocratic *salons* of the eighteenth century ;
the *cuisine* was perfection ; and the inexhaustible wit
of the host, notwithstanding his seventy-eight years,
and the amiability of the hostess, made these receptions the most brilliant and the most sought after in
London. Even the Court was so anxious to please

* When Prince Talleyrand, at that time Napoleon's Foreign Minister, sought a wife
for his nephew, ' Napoleon appropriated all the heiresses of France for his aides-de-
camp,' and the Prince accordingly arranged, through the intervention of Alexander
I, a marriage for his nephew with the youngest daughter of the widow of the last Duke
of Courland, who was the friend of King Stanislaus Augustus and many other Poles.
The marriage took place in 1808, and Talleyrand afterwards gave up to his nephew
the title of Prince Dino. The latter was, however, so addicted to riotous living
that his wife obtained a divorce from him and took up her residence with Talleyrand.

Talleyrand, that the Princess Dino, although not his wife, was admitted, in contravention of all the rules of etiquette, to the position and privileges of an Ambassadress.*

'As for the Princess Lieven, the wife of the Russian Ambassador, everyone has heard of this consummate type of a Russian political agent in petticoats.† The poet Niemcewicz, who was at that time Polish envoy in London, and who did not spare people whom he did not like, expressed surprise that this 'old and ugly woman, with a red nose, should possess such influence and make everybody submit to her decrees ;' but this is explained by her rare intellectual qualities, her dialectic skill, and her extraordinary pliancy in social intercourse. She had been in London for eighteen years, and having in this long period made many friends and acquaintances, she was not only an agreeable companion but a political force. More than once she influenced not only the decisions but the fate of Cabinets, even in England. The most distinguished English statesmen—Lords Liverpool, Castlereagh, and Aberdeen, the Duke of Wellington, Canning, Peel, and Lord Harrowby—were her confidential friends, and although by disposition and training she was an ultra-Tory, this did not prevent her from being on the best terms with Liberal

---

* One of Talleyrand's greatest admirers and pupils in the art of diplomacy was Lord Palmerston, and a comic paper published a caricature representing them walking together, with the inscription, 'the lame leading the blind ' (an allusion to the fact that one of Talleyrand's feet was deformed).

† The Princess Lieven, a descendant of the Esthonian family of von Benkendorff, was the sister of General Alexander von Benkendorff, the confidant of the Emperor Nicholas, and the creator of that mysterious and all-powerful institution, the Secret Police, known in Russia by the modest appellation of 'the third section of the Imperial Chancellery '.

Ministers, " for the advantage and glory of the policy of the Czar." The only prominent statesman with whom she could never agree was Palmerston; she used to call him " un très-petit esprit, lourd, obstiné," and she cordially detested him. He, on the other hand, used to say that he had been in a Tory Cabinet, and knew what her services cost. Of Earl Grey it was reported that every morning before he got out of bed he used to write her a note on paper scented with musk, in which he mingled gallantry with politics.

' Being a zealous servant and admirer of the Czar, Madame Lieven showed bitter hostility to the Poles and their cause. She would not allow any Polish sympathies to be expressed in her presence, and she carried her animosity so far that when one of the secretaries of the French Embassy said something in favour of the Polish revolution, she went to Talleyrand and insisted on his dismissing the culprit from his post.'

Such was the position of affairs in London when Prince Adam Czartoryski, eager as ever to serve the cause of his unhappy country, came to advocate it before the members of the Government and the continental statesmen who had assembled from all parts of Europe for the Belgian Conference. He was received in London by the poet Niemcewicz, who still remained there after the close of his functions as envoy of the Polish National Government. His venerable appearance, his perfect knowledge of the English language and English customs, and his reputation as a companion of Kosciuszko,* had made him generally liked

* He was Kosciuszko's aide-de-camp, and afterwards accompanied him to the United States, where they remained together for several years.

and respected. Niemcewicz was too plain-spoken and hot-tempered, however, for a diplomatist: 'Palmerston,' he says in his Memoirs, 'found me too hot, and I found him colder than ice.' But his unflagging industry and perseverance made up for this defect, and Prince Adam, in his life of Niemcewicz,* says that 'perhaps he never showed more boundless attachment to his country than in this last and difficult public service. . . Notwithstanding his age and growing infirmities, he thinks of everything, and I saw him day and night working solely for his country's cause.'

After narrowly escaping capture by the Russian army at Cracow, Prince Adam had travelled with a passport given him by Metternich in the name of 'George Hoffman.' This was a necessary precaution, considering the power at that time exercised by Russia throughout the German States. 'He arrived,' says Niemcewicz in his Memoirs, 'without a servant, deprived of all property, and his whole luggage represented by a small trunk. . . What a freak of fortune! I well recollect when I was his father's aide-de-camp fifty years ago, and when during an inspection of the Lithuanian army the tents of his suite were carried by 300 horses and fourteen camels. His son is now destitute; but he feels the misfortunes of his country more than his own.'

Prince Adam's first visit was to the French Embassy. The Princess Dino was an old acquaintance of his, and in 1808 the Abbé Piattoli, who was a friend both of the Prince and of the Duchess of Coburg,

* Published at Berlin and Posen in 1860.

had endeavoured to arrange a marriage between him and the Duchess's youngest daughter. Although nothing came of this project, the young Duchess, even after her marriage, remained on the most friendly terms with Prince Adam, and Talleyrand had also for many years been well acquainted with him. In 1807 the French Minister was opposed to the Poles, saying: 'avec les Polonais on ne fait que du désordre;' but he afterwards changed his opinion on this and other subjects, and showed some favour to Poland at the Vienna Congress. So much, indeed, was he regarded as hostile to Russia that when he was appointed French Ambassador in London, the Emperor Nicholas is said by M. Louis Blanc* to have considered this appointment 'as a sort of declaration of war;' and Count Walewski described him as 'one of those who were least indifferent to the Polish cause.'

Talleyrand and the Princess Dino received Prince Adam in the most friendly manner, and repeatedly urged him to take up his residence in their château of Valençay. Talleyrand added that in view of the general desire for peace, the only means of raising the Polish question would be to appeal to the Treaty of Vienna, which, he thought, all the Cabinets would insist on maintaining. Prince Czartoryski would, he said, be especially qualified to carry on the negotiations on this subject, as he had acted during the Vienna Congress as a sort of mediator between the Poles and the Emperor Alexander.

The Christmas of 1831 was a melancholy one for

* *Histoire de Dix Ans*, vol. ii, p. 101. Guizot, however, says that Talleyrand's Polish sympathies were purely historical, and that he was then entirely absorbed with the Belgian question (Hist. vol. ii, p. 229).

Poles in all parts of the world, and Prince Czartoryski and his few Polish friends in London spent it in sad reminiscences of the terrible struggle through which their country had passed. Most of the Prince's English friends and acquaintances were out of town, but on the 29th of December he obtained an interview with Lord Palmerston, then Secretary of State for Foreign Affairs, which he thus describes in a letter written by him shortly after:

'Lord Palmerston struck me as a man of very cold temperament, who, having made up his mind on the Polish question, only thought of rebutting our arguments on the other side. I began by saying that although England had not given the Poles any help, they owe her gratitude for her good wishes. To this Palmerston rejoined that if the fate of the Poles had depended on his personal wishes and those of Englishmen generally, their struggle for independence would not have had such an unfortunate result; but that circumstances and treaties often prevent States from following their most just impulses. I here remarked that if treaties prevented the Powers from interfering in behalf of Poland, they should at least see that the treaties are carried out. The Emperor Nicholas had appealed to the Treaty of Vienna during the progress of the Revolution, and he could not repudiate the Treaty now that the Revolution was over. . . . We Poles have nothing to ask for or to expect from him, and we only refer to the Treaty of Vienna as a means of diminishing our sufferings. The maintenance of the treaties which relate to Poland is a matter which specially concerns the Powers that signed those treaties.   Lord Palmerston made no reply to this remark, but said that it is a principle among States not to interfere between a Government and its subjects except in cases where a State has a direct interest in so interfering, or is distinctly authorised to do so by treaty.   The stipulations of the Treaty of Vienna with regard to Poland were not clear, and might be variously interpreted.   "It provides, for instance, that the kingdom of Poland is to be united to Russia by its Constitution, but it does not say what the Constitution is to be, or that the Emperor is not to have the power to alter it.   The Powers are not therefore bound to resist any modifications the Czar might deem fit to introduce in the Constitution; and Austria and Prussia, which are the Powers most interested in the question, concur in this view. . . ." I answered that it was not to be wondered at that the article about Poland is not clear and precise, seeing that it was hastily put together, after much opposition, at the moment when the news arrived of the return of Napoleon from the island of Elba, and those who drew it up, even on the Russian side, did not agree with the Emperor Alexander on the matter.   It was evident, however, that the word 'Constitution' was not inserted in the Treaty as an expression without any real meaning.   By that word was meant the Constitution which Alexander had designed for Poland, and in using it Alexander spoke in the name of his successors, and bound himself never to alter it. Moreover, all the members of the Congress had specially expressed a wish to maintain the Polish nationality, and any change of the Constitution tending to weaken that nationality must be opposed to the spirit of the Treaty. As to the allegation of Austria and Prussia that a separate Polish State under the Russian sceptre does not afford more security to its neighbours than a Poland annexed to Russia as part of the Empire, it was thoroughly understood by the Congress that although a contented Poland would increase the Czar's defensive forces, a Poland with a Constitution and a separate army of its own would diminish the force of Russia for purposes of aggression. Lord Palmerston seemed to admit the justice of these remarks, and after some questions as to the Poles in Austria . . . he looked at his watch, and as we took our leave he told me that whenever I should wish to see him I would find him at the office every afternoon.'

On the following day Prince Czartoryski saw Earl Grey. He said that the Ministry would be glad to interpret the Treaty of Vienna as much as possible in favour of Poland, but that in his opinion this must depend on Austria and Prussia, who were directly interested. The Treaty would be maintained, but the question was how it was to be interpreted. Prince Lieven, Earl Grey added, had communicated to him a memorandum in which Austria holds that the Treaty does not demand adherence to the Constitution, that the Powers cannot prevent Nicholas from altering it at his pleasure, and that no more can be required than that the Kingdom of Poland should have a provincial diet like Posen and Galicia. 'Prince Lieven,' Lord Grey continued, 'was not at all satisfied with my answer. I told him that we could not accept this interpretation of the Treaty of Vienna, and that in our opinion the Constitution should be maintained in the shape in which it was granted. But what can we do when Austria and Prussia are of a different opinion ? If those two Powers, the neighbours of Russia, are not convinced of the necessity of limiting Russian power by maintaining the concessions made to the Poles, how can we insist on their being maintained ?' Prince Czartoryski having here remarked that the Poles did not look to their oppressors Austria and Prussia, but to England and France, to decide their fate, Earl Grey continued : ' Ah, but things in France are so unsettled. The preservation of peace depends there upon a single man, M. Périer. If he falls, God knows what will happen. But I will do my best to maintain the Anglo-French Alliance, for I agree with you that it is necessary for the good of the two countries and of the whole of Europe.' This conversation produced a bad impression on the Prince. ' The Ministry,' he says, ' does not seem to feel strong, or to be conscious that it stands at the head of a great nation capable of exercising a powerful influence on the destinies of Europe. All this leaves a free field to our enemies in the north.' The two friends dined together next day at Earl Grey's house at East Sheen, and after dinner the latter admitted that England's policy had been ' too timid with regard to Poland ' and that ' England and France had not been sufficiently conscious of the means at their command.'*

The high social position of Prince Adam Czartoryski, the prominent part which he had taken in the

* See also a letter from Earl Grey to Brougham in Brougham's Autobiography, vol. iii., p. 164.

Polish Revolution, and the savage ukases issued against him by the Emperor Nicholas, made him a remarkable and interesting figure in London society, where he was received with an esteem almost amounting to veneration. This feeling was not confined to aristocratic circles, where he was personally known ; it also spread to the middle classes, and on the 2nd of January 1832, the 'Literary Union' club gave him a dinner, at which the poet Campbell made an enthusiastic speech. The Prince's popularity was still further increased when it became known that Prince Lieven, the Russian Ambassador, had complained to Lord Palmerston of Earl Grey's having invited 'the President of the rebel government' to his house, and that the Princess had at the same time addressed a letter full of bitter reproaches to Earl Grey.

Some days later the Prince had an interview with Brougham, who had now risen to the position of Lord Chancellor, and whose official position and advancing years had greatly calmed the fervid enthusiasm with which he had taken up the cause of the Poles eighteen years before (see Chapter XXI). 'Your Highness will understand,' he said, 'the difference between the feelings of a private individual and the duties of a Minister. The opinions of Lord Grey and myself as to Poland are well known to you ; but we were obliged to adapt our policy to the condition of England, who was absolutely incapable (*sic*) of making war.' 'But,' said the Prince, 'why did you refuse to join France in diplomatic representations at St Petersburg ?' 'Such a step,' answered Brougham, 'would have been of doubtful efficacy. . . . The fate of Poland will always interest us, but unfortunately the Polish cause is opposed to the wishes of all the other Powers. They all want peace, while to take up the cause of Poland means war.'

Though discouraged, Prince Adam did not lose heart, but prepared a memorandum, entering fully into the rights of Poland under the Treaty of Vienna. After showing it to Talleyrand, who highly approved it, he handed it to Palmerston. The latter said he would do all he could for the Poles, but that nothing could have been done by England during the Revolution, as the proclamation of the deposition of Nicholas by the Poles had deprived her of the only ground on which she could interfere in their behalf. . . 'Now that the struggle is over, however,' he added, 'we have forwarded our representations and remarks as to the maintenance of the Treaty of Vienna. We recognise that Russia has not fulfilled it, for she has done nothing in the provinces, and after granting a Constitution to the kingdom, has violated its provisions. We adhere firmly to this view, although Austria and Prussia dissent from it. We hold that the Constitution granted by the Emperor Alexander should be maintained, and can only be altered by the Diet; also that the Polish provinces of Russia should have a representative assembly and a provincial administration.'

The Russian answer to the representations referred to by Lord Palmerston came at the end of January. It was very courteous in tone, but it decisively rejected the English view of the Treaty, pointing out that Russia had a majority in her favour of three to two, as Russia, Austria, and Prussia were on one side and only England and France on the other. 'Russia is quite wrong,' said Palmerston to Prince Adam, 'but how can we force her to accept our view? We cannot send an army to Poland, and the burning of the Russian fleet would be about as effectual as the burning of Moscow.' The Ministry did not, however, even attempt to pursue the subject diplomatically. France was beginning to strive for the favour of the Emperor Nicholas, and England, wishing above all things for the settlement of the Belgian question, also found it her interest to remain on good terms with him. Under these circumstances it was not surprising that not only Russia but Prussia repudiated their obligations towards Europe. Ancillon, the Prussian Foreign Minister, cynically advocated the complete annihilation of Poland 'so as to have done with her once for all,' * and when the British Ambassador at Berlin appealed to the Treaty of Vienna, he sharply replied that 'every one can do as he likes in his own house.' † In Austria, too, Metternich, terrified at the re-appearance of the revolutionary spectre in France and Germany, although he had admitted that 'he would rather have a friendly and peaceful Poland for a neighbour than an aggressive Russia,' ‡ began to talk of a renewal of the Holy Alliance, and of the two evils—Russia and revolution —preferred the former as the least.

Although it has often been shown that the cases

* Conversation with General Flahaut, the French Ambassador, reported by Count Walewski in a letter preserved in the Polish Library in Paris.

† Letter from Prince Adam Czartoryski, dated the 24th of January, 1832.

‡ Despatch of the 25th September, 1830 (*Memoirs of Prince Metternich*, vol. v. p. 77).

of Poland and Ireland bear no resemblance to each other, it is still the constant practice of Russian writers and their sympathisers in the English press to compare them. Earl Grey, in a conversation with Prince Czartoryski on the 8th of March, 1832, told the Prince that this comparison had been used as a *tu quoque* argument by the Russian Ambassador. 'The Czar,' he said, 'will not allow anyone to interfere in the affairs of Poland.' 'Le Prince et la Princesse de Lieven ont répété plusieurs fois que l'Empereur ne permettra jamais que d'autres puissances se mêlent dans les affaires de la Pologne, de même que l'Angleterre ne permettrait pas qu'on se mêle des affaires de l'Irlande. . . .' Lord Palmerston, referring to this remark two days later, said to the Prince : 'There is not the smallest similarity between the two cases. Ireland has belonged to us for centuries ; it speaks the same language as England and is the same nation.'— ' Moreover,' observed the Prince ' the union of England and Ireland was not the result of a European Treaty.'

In the conversation above referred to Earl Grey added some interesting particulars on Continental and English politics. ' Russia,' he said, ' is backed up by Austria and Prussia, and we cannot rely on France ; her position is too unsettled. . . As for England, public opinion is certainly interested in Poland ; but it is much more interested in various internal questions, and in the maintenance of peace. Moreover, we have other questions pending with Russia, which demand mutual concessions. . . . We have financial difficulties, but if public opinion were in favour of war, means would be found of raising the necessary funds. What most troubles us is the uncertain state of Europe. Some want to maintain everything by force, others to upset everything by force. . . . Party feeling, too, runs very high here. Wellington is opposed to all liberal plans, and force is his only policy ; this pleases the other Cabinets. He thinks he will yet return to office ; he had never been beaten before, and will not believe that he is beaten now. I did not seek office ; my advanced age did not allow me to do so. The King himself called upon me to form a Cabinet, as the Duke after his declaration could not remain in office.' In reporting this conversation the Prince adds that Earl Grey asked him several times if he had seen Lord Palmerston, 'as if he feared to say anything which might not be in accordance with Palmerston's views,' and that he 'looked very anxious.'

The priceless collections of Pulawy, the relics of his fortune that had survived the confiscations of Nicholas, and his duties to his family, now urgently claimed Prince Adam's attention, but the interests of his country were in his eyes paramount over all private considerations, and he stuck manfully to his post so long as a spark of hope remained. In a letter written about this time to one of his friends he says : ' I am glad, at any rate, that I have, though in a somewhat violent and expensive way, liberated myself from the chains that bound me. I will certainly not resume them even at the price of my whole fortune. . . . Every Pole should all his life be prepared for oppression or exile. You have experienced it already. My turn has come, at too advanced an age it is true, but I feel strong enough to bear it even with good humour.'

All through his long life his proudest boast was that he was the servant of his country; while he was Foreign Minister of Russia he did not draw the salary of the appointment, and repeatedly refused the decorations and other dignities which the Emperor Alexander pressed upon him. In one of his speeches to the Polish Historical Society he said he would like to add to the family motto of the Czartoryskis—'Come what may'—that of the Black Prince, 'Ich dien.'

Although it was evident that neither England nor France would do anything for Poland, Prince Adam was anxious at least to bring into prominence the fact that international engagements had been broken, and that a wrong had been done which, if not protested against, might be given the appearance of a lawful proceeding, and be accepted as such by public opinion. The state of the Continent, too, was then so unsettled that a conflict might at any moment arise in which the Polish question, if kept alive before Europe, might play a prominent part. The Prince accordingly did his utmost to keep both the Government and the public fully informed as to the position of affairs in Poland. The whole of the London press—notably the *Times*, the *Morning Herald*, and the *Morning Chronicle*—advocated the Polish cause, and the Foreign Office readily accepted the information communicated by the Prince on the subject, especially as Lord Heytesbury, in his despatches from St Petersburg, was completely silent as to the persecutions and cruelties of the Russian

Government in Poland, the destruction of the national collections,* and the suppression of the university and schools. 'These,' said Lord Palmerston to the Prince 'are the results of animosity after a sanguinary war.' 'But,' observed the latter, 'victory should produce leniency.' 'True,' Palmerston rejoined, 'in civilised countries; in half-savage ones victory only produces increased severities.' Among the documents which reached the Foreign Office in this way were two letters from a Pole named Borowski, who was taken in his childhood to South America, fought there for the independence of the Spanish republics, and afterwards went to Arabia. Here he heard the news of the Polish Revolution, upon which he at once proceeded to Persia, where he was well received by the heir-apparent Abbas Mirza and attempted to induce him to take active steps against Russia. His last plan of helping his country was to equip two cruisers on the Black Sea for the capture of Russian ships, and he asked that letters of marque should be granted by England for this purpose.

With a view to spreading information as to Polish affairs, Prince Czartoryski, assisted by several English political writers, founded a monthly Magazine, 'Polonia,' afterwards expanded into the 'British and Foreign Review,' containing articles on Polish history and other subjects connected with that country. He also collected for the use of English writers a number of historical works about Poland, some of which had

---

* The total number of books (most of which have been destroyed) taken by the Russians from the great Polish libraries is about 700,000. Of these 17,000 belonged to the Radzivill Library, 400,000 to the famous Zaluski Library, 200,000 to the University of Warsaw, 30,000 to the Society of the Friends of Science, 20,000 to the University of Wilna, and 15,000 to the Czartoryski Library at Pulawy.

already been sent to London in 1814 by his secretary Biernacki, and he presented some of the latest works published in various countries on Polish affairs to the British Museum Library. On the 25th of November, 1832, 'The Literary Association of the Friends of Poland,' a society which has ever since continued to be the head-quarters of all English action on behalf of the Poles, was founded. A 'Polish Committee' for the relief of Polish refugees had already been formed by Messrs Bach, Hunter Gordon, Arthur White, and Kirwan, but, thanks to the influence and efforts of Prince Czartoryski, the scope and importance of this committee was considerably enlarged, and it became the association above described, which consisted entirely of Englishmen. Its first President was the poet Campbell, and among his most distinguished successors were Lord Dudley Stuart—the most devoted, zealous, and indefatigable of the English friends of Poland—and Lords Harrowby, Houghton, and Lytton. The Association took up its quarters at No. 10 Duke Street, St James's, where Oliver Cromwell and Milton once lived; and there it still remains, relieving out of its scanty funds the helpless survivors of the Polish Revolutions of the last sixty years.

Another matter to which the Prince devoted much attention was the introduction of the Polish question in Parliament. Neither the adherents of the Ministry nor the members of the Opposition were inclined to take such a course, the former because they feared it would embarrass the Government, and the latter because they looked upon the Poles as revolutionists. At length Mr Cutlar Fergusson, M.P., an independent member with a good position in the House and considerable talent as a speaker, consented, after consulting Lord Palmerston and Sir James Mackintosh, to undertake the task. As his motion would necessarily have to be based on the Treaty of Vienna, he had to be supplied with as much information as possible on the subject; unfortunately the Prince no longer had his papers relating to the Vienna Congress, including despatches from Pozzo di Borgo, Stein, and Castlereagh, as they had been taken out of his wife's carriage by the Austrian customs' authorities. Ample material, was, however, collected by the Prince and his untiring companion and friend Niemcewicz for the proposed debate, but the Belgian Question and the Reform Bill prevented its coming on so soon as was hoped, and finding that for the present there was nothing to be done, and that his slender resources were being exhausted by the expense of living in London, the Prince left in March, 1832, for Clifton, where he could live more cheaply and have more quiet for his political and literary work. He also wanted to become more closely acquainted with rural life in England, that being the country which he liked better than any other, and where he hoped ultimately to settle with his family. He returned to London at the end of March for the Polish debate in the House of Commons, which took place on the 18th of April.

In June the Prince's family* also came to London,

* The Prince married on the 25th of September 1817, the Princess Anna, daughter of Prince Alexander Sapieha-Kodenski. He had three children : Prince Witold, who died on the 14th of November 1865, Princess Isa, and Prince Ladislas, the present head of the family.

but the English climate acted so injuriously on his wife's health that he was obliged to give up his plan of settling in England, and at the end of August he took up his residence in Paris. During the interval two more interesting debates on Poland occurred in the House of Commons. The first was on the 28th of June; the subject was again introduced by Mr Cutlar Fergusson, who was seconded by Lord Sandon (afterwards the Earl of Harrowby). As on the previous occasion, the condemnation of Russia's proceedings in Poland was unanimous. Lord Morpeth spoke of 'the immortal memory of the land that first resisted the torrent of Mahommedan invasion and secured the liberties and the religion of Europe,' and O'Connell even went so far as to call the Emperor Nicholas 'a miscreant.' This elicited an expression of regret from Lord Palmerston at the use of such language in the House, upon which Mr Beaumont declared he was delighted at the appellation which had been given to the Emperor, and entirely concurred in it; and Mr Hume said he would not only call the Emperor a miscreant, but a monster in human form. But nothing was to be done by denunciation, however eloquent. Poland was in the iron grasp of three of the strongest States in Europe, and England had no power to help her.

CHAPTER XXVI

1834

THERE is a curious note in Prince Czartoryski's diary,
dated the 12th November 1834, on the relations
between Talleyrand and Lord Palmerston. 'Talleyrand,' he says, 'formerly in strict friendship with
Palmerston, has now had a little quarrel with him
because, when the latter complained that France did
not respond to the overtures of England in the Eastern
question, Talleyrand replied that France was only
following the example of England when she was asked
to act with France on behalf of Poland during the
Revolution of 1831.' In a subsequent conversation
with Lord Brougham (14th December 1834) the latter
said of Talleyrand—' I think he does not just now know
what he is talking about. Imaginez qu'il m'a parlé de
la nécessité de rassembler un Congrès Européen qui
aurait pour but de garantir les institutions existantes,
et pour calmer les esprits, et qu'à ce Congrès la France
et l'Angleterre déclareraient qu'ils mettraient des
limites à la licence de la presse. C'est de la démence.'

During the same conversation Brougham said that

the reason why the English Government had refused
to join in a demonstration in favour of Poland in 1832
together with France, and with the concurrence of
Austria, was that it would have been necessary to
arm, and the Ministry was uncertain of its existence
in consequence of the Reform bill. He called Thiers
'un petit littérateur,' and said that even Lord Durham
had not been able to say a word at St Petersburg.
Prince Czartoryski here remarked that Lord Durham
had told him he had spoken very strongly on the
subject of Poland at St Petersburg. 'Oui bien,'
answered Brougham, 'à M. de Nesselrode; mais à
l'Empereur lui-même il n'a pas osé dire un seul mot,
parcequ'il lui ferait la cour pour obtenir un cordon.
C'est l'homme le plus vain, le plus aristocrate, qui
existe. Il a tourmenté pendant dix-huit mois Lord
Grey parcequ'il ne l'a pas fait de suite comte. Il a
été contre Lord Grey pendant le Ministère Canning,
qui l'a fait entrer à la chambre des pairs. Ce qui a
été mal calculé, parceque dans la chambre des com-
munes il avait quelque influence, au lieu que dans la
chambre haute il n'en a aucune. C'est mon ami, et
cependant je ne puis m'empêcher de le dire. On a
voulu nous brouiller, je n'ai rien dit de ce que m'on a
attribué; ce sont les journaux qui ont fait ce pâté.'
He afterwards proposed to the Prince to go to Italy
with him. 'If you do,' he added, 'people will say we
are plotting for Poland, and I shall be delighted.'

CHAPTER XXVII

1839

CONVERSATION WITH LORD PALMERSTON.—CIRCASSIA.—PROPOSAL TO SEND THE BRITISH FLEET INTO THE BLACK SEA.—RUSSIAN DESIGNS ON INDIA.—PERSIA.—AFGHANISTAN.—PALMERSTON'S OPINION OF METTERNICH.—TURKEY AND RUSSIA.

On the 13th of February and the 10th of March 1839 Prince Czartoryski had conversations with Lord Palmerston on English Foreign Policy generally, and about Circassia, which had been invaded and nearly conquered, after a heroic resistance, by the Russian troops. The following is the Prince's report of these conversations:—

PRINCE CZARTORYSKI.—You have lost Persia ; you are engaged in a costly war in India ; Turkey is vacillating, and Circassia will fall if she does not obtain help. Why not send a British fleet into the Black Sea, or even only before Constantinople ? This would produce a great effect upon the entire East and restore your influence with the Porte.

LORD PALMERSTON.—The war in India is not very expensive, and Russia has been obliged to give up her plans as to Herat. Persia, it is true, is lost to us for the moment, but the movement at Candahar and Cabul, and the restoration of the old legitimate sovereign in these united Kingdoms, will secure the independence of Afghanistan and serve as a barrier against Persia and Russia. A British fleet cannot under the Treaty of 1809 enter the Dardanelles without the permission of the Sultan, and I am not at all sure he would give it. And what would the fleet do once it had got there? It would have either to blockade the coast of Circassia—which belongs to Russia, or at least was ceded to her by the Treaty of Adrianople, which has been recognised by England— or it would have to attack the Russian fleet, harbours, and arsenals. In either case this would be war. Now the English nation is able to make war, but it will only do so where its own interests are concerned. We are a simple and practical nation, a commercial nation ; we do not go in for chivalrous enterprises or fight for others as the French do. Even supposing, as you seem to think, that Russia would not make war upon us if our fleet were to appear in the Black Sea, she would bitterly complain of our conduct, and we would have to explain it to Parliament, which would certainly not be satisfied with our arguments. We have a strong majority against us in the House of Lords ; in the House of Commons we have an uncertain majority of thirty votes, which we would lose, and then we would be driven from office.

Prince Czartoryski.—You might act without compromising yourselves officially. In Russia everything is done by the Government ; in England much is left to the initiative of individuals acting in a private capacity. You might help the Circassians by private effort without open Government intervention.

Lord Palmerston.—Possibly; but we have no secret funds which we could employ for such a purpose. Besides, it would soon be known; nothing can long remain a secret in our country.

Prince Czartoryski.—But then you are not on equal terms with Russia. She does not scruple to use every possible means of injuring you.

Lord Palmerston.—That is an advantage enjoyed by despotic States. Free States have other advantages.

Prince Czartoryski.—By leaving Russia to act as she pleases you expose to the greatest dangers the independence of the Asiatic States, and your own dominions in India.

Lord Palmerston.—True; but John Bull will not go to war to save Circassia.

Prince Czartoryski.—It is not only the fate of Circassia that is in question. You are losing all your influence over the Sultan; already he has accepted the demands of Russia as to Wallachia, and if you continue your policy of non-intervention he may abandon you altogether.

Lord Palmerston.—I do not believe it. Our influence is like the tide, which, though it advances and then recedes, yet steadily gains ground. . . . Mehemet Ali is an animal that Russia is fattening before she sacrifices him. . . . Russia is unfortunately surrounded by weak neighbours like Turkey and Sweden, and by others attached to her either by an alliance of fear (Austria) or an alliance of relationship (Prussia).

Prince Czartoryski.—So long as Poland remains

divided between the three Northern Powers, you cannot rely upon Austria.

Lord Palmerston.—No doubt; but how are we to induce her to change her policy? Prince Metternich is undoubtedly a man of great talent, but he is timid and prejudiced; he fears revolution more than anything else. He is accustomed to the admiration and incense of his *coterie,* who are offended if he is only praised in ordinary language. He cannot be persuaded that anything he thinks or does is not right. Besides, if there were an independent Poland, do you think Bohemia and Hungary would not claim independence too? Poland would no doubt want a representative Government, which implies a parliament. freedom of speech, and a free press. The very idea of these institutions would make Metternich's hair stand on end, he is so accustomed to be adored without the slightest opposition in his drawing-room. He said once that he would rather be a convict than a Minister in a free country. I do not think he would ever consent to the restoration of Poland unless there were a war, in which case Austria might find the Poles useful for defence or aggression.

Prince Czartoryski.—The new French Ministry is strongly inclined to go hand-in-hand with England; and this would add weight to your representations at Vienna.

Lord Palmerston.—It would no doubt facilitate our action, but France must first reassure Austria as to Italy. She must be disabused of the idea that we are revolutionists, and she must be able to rely upon our support in the event of a war with Russia; but she does not trust us. I know that many people whose opinions I respect are in favour of sending our fleet into the Black Sea, but I have fully considered the matter and I do not see how such a course would be either desirable or practicable. . . . Besides, it would be a bad plan to try to secure the Sultan's independence by forcing his hand.

PRINCE CZARTORYSKI.—You have often done such a thing, as at Naples and Copenhagen.

LORD PALMERSTON.—At Constantinople, more than anywhere else, good can be done and evil prevented by an increase of *moral* influence. Our influence, joined to that of France and Austria, would produce an effect upon Russia which might be attained without a war. She will not be allowed to make any more victims.

PRINCE CZARTORYSKI.—Yes, but how about those she has made already? Your policy ought to satisfy Russia entirely if she is reasonable. She has taken so much that she can wish for little more. She is allowed to tear up and devour at her leisure all she has unjustly appropriated, and the sufferings of her victims are not even recognised.

LORD PALMERSTON.—I know that fresh horrors have been perpetrated in Poland of which people have no idea ; but this can only be remedied by a war. Yet who knows? If we could only [inspire Austria with full confidence in us and detach her from Russia, I am convinced that her moral influence might have a good effect on the fate of Poland.

PRINCE CZARTORYSKI.—The Opposition seems very warlike, and it would probably support you in a warlike policy.

Lord Palmerston.—Yes, they want us to augment the army and the fleet ; but when the money will have to be found they will oppose every new tax and leave us in the lurch.   These are the usual tactics of the party, and we are not going to be duped by them.

CHAPTER XXVIII

ONE of the most ardent supporters and patrons of the
Literary Association of the Friends of Poland was
H.R.H. the Duke of Sussex, who used to say that
he once wore the Polish crown, as that of the latest
Polish King, Stanislas Augustus, was put on his
head by the guardian of the crown jewels at Berlin
when he visited that city. The following letter is in
reply to one from Prince Czartoryski thanking him
for a speech he made at a meeting of the Association :—

MON CHER PRINCE,—Une multiplicité d'occupations auxquelles j'ai dû faire attention m'a empêché de
répondre plus tôt à votre aimable lettre. Aujourd'hui,
me trouvant plus en liberté, je m'empresse de vous
remercier pour toutes les expressions obligeantes que
vous avez bien voulu me marquer au sujet de notre
réunion en faveur de la cause de la Pologne, à
quelle occasion j'ai eu la satisfaction de présider.

Mes opinions en faveur d'une liberté réelle et
constitutionelle ayant pour base et guide des lois
sages, explicites, et definitives, sont trop connues pour

que j'aie besoin de vous les exposer ici, encore moins de les répéter dans cette occasion. Ce sont des principes que j'ai adoptés après une reflexion la plus sérieuse ainsi que d'après une longue expérience. C'est une matière de conscience la plus sacrée pour moi, la considérant comme formant partie de ma religion. Je n'ai donc fait que remplir mon devoir en élevant ma voix contre des actes que je crois injustes et contraires aux lois divines et humaines.

Dans un gouvernement constitutionnel comme celui de l'Angleterre, où les ministres sont responsables à la nation pour les conseils qu'ils soumettent à leur maître, *le Roi n'a jamais tort*, mais dans un gouvernement despotique le souverain ne jouit pas d'un pareil avantage ; chaque acte de l'exécutive est attribué à sa personne, comme émanant de sa volonté immédiate, sans qu'on réfléchit qu'il peut y avoir été poussé par des factions qui dirigent souvent les affaires de l'Etat en secret, ou que dans certaines occasions sa raison peut être ou avoir été surprise par la misréprésentation de quelque ministre ainsi que de quelque autre individu qui est irresponsable, puisque la loi ignore son existence, et qui n'a en vue que ses propres interêts en flattant l'ambition du Prince sans consulter aussi peu le bien être de sa patrie que le bonheur général du genre humain.

Si mes remonstrances pouvaient parvenir aux oreilles de l'Autocrate, comme les opinions désinteressées ainsi que comme les expressions d'un cosmopolite qui ne cherche que le bonheur de son voisin et qui travaille incessamment pour établir une harmonie universelle dans ce bas monde, et qu'elles puissent lui faire peur

pour quelques moments, je m'estimerai bien heureux ! ! !
Ce n'est pas seulement par des conquêtes qu'un
souverain se rend célèbre, ou qu'il gagne l'admiration
du monde, encore moins se fait-il aimer par de tels
procedés, mais c'est par des actes de justice et de
bienveillance qu'il contribue au bonheur, à la sécurité,
à la tranquillité de ses sujets. C'est en réprimant les
vues d'ambition et d'accroissement dans les autres, en
maintenant la paix, en encourageant les arts et les
sciences, ainsi qu'une bonne intelligence entre les
nations voisines et la sienne, qu'il acquiert l'estime des
hommes sages, justes, et loyaux, et qu'il laisse son nom
et sa renommée comme un héritage ainsi qu'un souvenir
précieux à la postérité. Voilà mes idées, mon cher
Prince, que je vous communique franchement, vous
priant en même temps d'être l'interprète de mes sentiments connus auprès de ces Messieurs qui avec vous
sont à la tête des différents bureaux pour conduire les
interêts des Polonais et qui se sont unis à vous pour
m'adrésser une lettre à laquelle je mets le plus haut
prix, la regardant comme un témoignage public et
précieux de leur approbation de ces principes que je
me fais, et que je me ferai toujours, une gloire de
professer et de plaider dans toutes les occasions, quand
ils pourront produire du bien.—

Agréez, mon cher Prince, les assurances de mon
sincère estime et de ma haute considération, aussi de
mon amitié, avec lesquelles j'ai le plaisir de me dire

Votre dévoué et sincère ami,

(signed) FREDERIC, DUC DE SUSSEX.

AU PALAIS DE KENSINGTON,
ce 16 *de Juillet*, 1839.

CHAPTER XXIX

1853-5

ALTHOUGH Lord Palmerston did not conceal from Prince Czartoryski his conviction that in the state of affairs which then prevailed on the Continent nothing could be done for Póland, the noble character of the Prince, his devoted patriotism, and his wide knowledge and experience of European politics, made him a welcome visitor at the Foreign Office, and Lord Palmerston repeatedly took occasion to express his admiration and sympathy for the Polish nation and its venerable chief. After the last spark of Polish independence had been extinguished by the absorption of the Republic of Cracow into the Austrian State, notwithstanding the protests of England and France—which as usual remained fruitless in presence of the alliance of the three spoilers of Poland—Lord Palmerston made some appreciative remarks in a speech at the Mansion House on the devotion of Lord Dudley Stuart to the Polish cause, and a deputation from the Polish Historical Society took the opportunity of presenting him, in recognition of his sympathy for the

Poles, with a medal of Prince Czartoryski, on which was the inscription: ' H. T. P. Vice Comiti Palmerston quia memor exstat fandi atque nefandi. Societas Historica Polona grata offert.'

In 1853, when the Prince came to London to sound the disposition of the Ministry in view of the crisis in the East, he records in his diary (June 27) that he found Lord Aberdeen ' abaissé ; il a l'air de succomber sous le poids de la responsabilité.'   A few days after he saw Lord Clarendon, Palmerston and Disraeli.   The former gave him an impression of ' indécision—désir de conserver la paix.'   His description of Palmerston is ' visage de bois, regard impassible, bouche close, pas un mot de réponse à tous mes arguments,' and of Disraeli, ' excellent pour la bonne cause ; nous causons en parfaite amitié sur la Pologne.'   Lord Malmesbury called upon him and expressed ' excellentes intentions.'

In Paris Prince Adam Czartoryski was one of Napoleon III's most trusted counsellors, and he sent numerous memoranda to the Emperor on the conduct of the Russian campaign which, though the Prince was then eighty-three years of age, entered minutely into every detail and showed an extraordinary power of remembering past events and adapting the knowledge derived from them to existing circumstances.   He was a warm advocate of an Anglo-French alliance, and in a memorandum* addressed to the French Minister of Foreign Affairs on the 10th of February 1853, he pointed out that such an alliance would be the only means of preventing the encroachments of

* The drafts of the memoranda and notes drawn up on this occasion are in the Prince's own handwriting.

Russia in the East. 'The conduct of Russia and
Austria towards Turkey,' says this document, 're-
sembles in all respects that pursued by those Powers
with regard to Poland, and undoubtedly tends to a
similar result. Turkey and the peoples forming that
country can only be saved by the simultaneous and
united action of France and England. They alone,
acting with the same object, can neutralise the
deleterious influence and the immense weight of the
two former Powers. . . . Such an alliance, though
evidently necessary for the good of Europe, yet
presents many difficulties. Under the Restoration
the French Government was alienated from England
and sympathised with Russia. The policy of Louis
Philippe, though more friendly to England, was too
vacillating and timorous to inspire British statesmen
with confidence; and the recent talk of French officers
about an invasion of England has naturally increased
the distrust towards France on the other side of the
Channel. The subordinate British agents in the East,
on the other hand, show an extreme jealousy of their
French colleagues, and instead of acting hand in hand
with them in matters where the two countries have a
common interest, they often foil them at the risk of
injuring the interests of their own country. The
struggle which has begun between the Protestant
propaganda and Roman Catholicism in the East may
add to these difficulties. Yet they must be overcome
in view of the supreme interest of justice, of the
common good, of the security of all Europe, and of
the dignity of the two Powers which are its true
guardians. A sincere, decided, and persevering line

of conduct will remove many obstacles, and if frank communications and friendly overtures do not prove sufficient, France should prove her sincerity by at once offering to act in concert with England in any warlike step she might propose to take. Russia and Austria should not be allowed any longer to pose as the protectors of the Christian subjects of the Porte. It should be pointed out to the Sultan that if in his relations with his Christian subjects he acts at the dictation of his two enemies, he will only humiliate himself in the eyes of the peoples under his rule, while if he listens to the counsels of his allies, he will gain both in security and in strength. To put a stop to the abuses of the Turks with regard to the Christians would be to render a signal service to the Ottoman Empire and furnish it with the most efficacious guarantee against its early dissolution.'

In a further note, dated the 28th of March 1854 (the date of the declaration of war against Russia), Prince Czartoryski gave some valuable hints as to the best means of carrying on a war against Russia by England and France. 'Russia,' he says, 'is defended on the west by the two German Powers, and cannot be reached from that side so long as their neutrality is maintained and respected. But her frontier may be attacked at other points with advantage. The first of these is the Crimea and the adjacent territories. The second is the Lower Danube and the Polish Ukraine on the borders of the Black Sea. The third is the coast of Lithuania on the Baltic. These three points, if attacked simultaneously, would all have the advantage of being in territories inhabited

by populations which wish to throw off the Russian
yoke.   It would first be necessary to conquer the
Crimea and Sebastopol, which would entail the
destruction of the enemy's fleet; next, and if possible
at the same time, to occupy with an expeditionary
force the country between Batoum and Anaklea. The
Russian part of the coast, being undefended on the
side of the sea, could be easily captured in a few
hours.   The country is surrounded by mountains
which cannot be crossed by an army with artillery, so
that the expeditionary corps, being master of the sea,
would be perfectly safe, and would be able, together
with the Turkish troops in Armenia, to march on
Tiflis by way of Kutais and Gori. The people of the
Caucasus, who would be supplied with arms and
ammunition, would rise *en masse* from the Caspian to
the Black Sea; while the Georgians and Imeritians,
who also are far from satisfied with the methods of
Russian Government, would ask to be allowed to constitute a separate State as formerly. As the Russian
army in these districts contains a great many Poles, it
would be desirable to attract them to the armies of
the allies by displaying the Polish flag. At the second
point of attack—the Lower Danube and the Polish
Ukraine—the allied armies would find themselves in
a country rich in grain and with a numerous and
friendly population and large towns. The Cossack
legion,* if raised to 10,000 men, with a corresponding
proportion of infantry and artillery, would here
render important services. The people would regard
them as their brothers and co-religionists, and would join

---

* Formed of Poles who had taken service with the Sultan.

them under the national (Polish) standard. Finally, while the English and French fleets would threaten Riga, Revel, and Cronstadt, thereby forcing Russia to keep a large force at those places, an expeditionary corps landed in Lithuania would produce most decisive results, for it would penetrate into the very heart, so to say, of European Russia. It will be for experienced naval officers to determine at which point of the coast of Lithuania, or the adjoining coast of Courland, the landing could most easily be effected. The corps should consist of from 30,000 to 40,000 men. It would find itself in a wooded country surrounded by marshes and lakes, well suited to a guerilla war, and lying across the chief line of communication between the capital and the western frontier. This country is inhabited by a Roman Catholic people who are thoroughly Polish in sentiment, and would at once join the national standard. The combined force, after securing its communications with the sea, could then either assist the fleet in an attack upon Riga, or march upon Wilna, supplying the people with arms, destroying the military magazines of the Russians, and cutting off the Russian forces in the north from those in the west and south.'

Prince Czartoryski's scheme, it will be seen, aimed at striking Russia where she is most vulnerable—in Poland. But the allies, fearing to raise Austria and Prussia against them, only adopted that part of it which relates to the Crimea and the Baltic. Moreover—as was said by Lord Palmerston to General Zamoyski when the latter proposed that the Polish legion, which formed part of the Turkish Contingent

during the war, and was paid by England, should be
allowed to carry the Polish flag—the allies did not
wish 'to make an enemy of Russia.'   It was not
to be a war 'à outrance,' but a mere trial of strength;
Russia was not to be crippled, but only to be forced to
abandon (for a time) her designs on Turkey and the
Black Sea.   Under these circumstances it is not surprising, though surprise has been expressed on the
subject by some English writers, that the Poles
should during the war have maintained a passive
attitude.   There were 100,000 Russian troops in
their country; the Poles were without arms or war
material of any kind; and they were not willing to
be massacred *pour les beaux yeux* of England and
France.   The following passages from a letter addressed by Prince Czartoryski to his countrymen on
the 26th of August 1854, throw an interesting light
on the views of the leading Poles at this period :—

'It has been said that you have everywhere
entered into a conspiracy of calmness and wisdom.
Let us strive to justify this charge. Receive advances and offers from whatever side they may
come, but before taking action insist upon substantial guarantees for your future. Such guarantees
would be afforded by the creation of a Polish force
under Polish leaders, to serve as a nucleus for an army
to be formed out of those whose ranks are filled by our
countrymen; by the recognition of independent Polish
authorities; and by a declaration on the part of the
Powers, or any one of them with the consent of
its allies, that Poland has a right to an independent
existence. . . . We have been too often deceived by

promises, and been made the victims of our too adventurous and trusting spirit.   My advice and that of all the sincere friends of Poland is that you should keep quiet and wait events.   This is not, as some suppose, a proof of apathy, but of wisdom and prudence ; of the strength of a nation which knows how to restrain itself, and which will only show the more energy when the time of action arrives.'

What his own course would be in such an event he had already stated in an address to the Polish Historical Society.   'When,' he said, 'the decisive moment comes, I will go with my sons where duty calls me, and will not hesitate to give up to my country, which I have served all my life, the last remnants of my strength and my abilities.'

CHAPTER XXIX

1855-61

THE following are extracts from letters sent by the
Prince to London during the Crimean War :—

> '16th *May* 1854.

'Sweden is ready for everything, and wishes to
act with considerable forces. She asks and offers to
join the allies. What folly if they refuse ! Clarendon
knows all about it, and I hear would like to accept.
The negotiation is being conducted through his
brother Charles Villiers. Here (in Paris) all is for
peace. Persigny now declares that the naval superiority of the Powers is sufficient.'

> '19th *May* 1854.

'The allies can only expect a fruitful result from
the war in the alliance of Sweden, who is ready and
willing to act at once, and of Poland, who only waits
to be called upon and armed. These are the only
real allies of the Western Powers. The Roumanians
also should not be neglected. . . . If peace is impossible, can the Powers refuse the overtures of Sweden,

who would probably be followed by Austria? I
cannot believe that the British Cabinet would neglect
such an opportunity or not use every means at its
disposal to induce France also to take advantage of it.'

'*18th December* 1854.

'If the Polish question should be raised by the
war, and Austria be unwilling to mix up Galicia in it,
Russian Poland alone would rise if it were declared
independent, and this would be a decisive force on the
side of the allies. Galicia and Posen will remain
quiet; for that I will vouch.'

'*20th December* 1854.

'On nous reprochait jadis que nous étions prompts
à nous jeter en avant de toutes les aventures; à
présent nous sommes plus réfléchis, moins audacieux,
moins imprudents, et on nous reproche aussi. Je
crois que nous avons raison d'être sages et de demander
des garanties, avant d'offrir un dévouement sans bornes.
Telle est l'opinion positive du pays, et telle est celle de
l'émigration, avec les modifications que sa position
comporte.'

'*23rd April* 1855.

'Lord Stratford est un terrible homme; son
ambassade et les grandes affaires qui lui ont passé par
les mains, et les événements, qui ne furent pas
toujours heureux, l'ont rendu je crois encore plus
nerveux, plus irascible et difficile à vivre, qu'il ne
l'était naturellement.'

Prince Adam Czartoryski's long life was now drawing to a close. The Treaty of Paris, which closed the Crimean War, was a great disappointment to him; but he did not abandon all hope. At the time, says M. de Mazade in his introduction to the French edition of the Memoirs, when the negotiations of the Paris Congress were still going on, the Prince was preparing a fresh memorandum on the Polish question, when a friend informed him that the bases of the Treaty had been agreed upon, and that Poland was not mentioned in it. An expression of pain passed across his face; he stopped writing for a moment, but soon proceeded with his manuscript, saying: 'It will do for another time.' The accession of Alexander II, notwithstanding his brusque speech to the Polish nobles—'Point de rêveries! tout ce que mon père a fait est bien fait,'—seemed to offer some prospect of a change of system in Poland,* and after the conclusion of the Treaty of Paris, Prince Adam drew up an elaborate paper, fully describing the rights and grievances of his country, for the use of M. de Morny, the French Ambassador at the Russian Court, on his proceeding to Moscow to take part in the ceremony of the coronation. During the first few years of his reign, the new Emperor seemed almost as well disposed to the Poles as his uncle, Alexander I, had been. But, like him, he admired liberty in theory and abhorred it in practice. He gave the Poles some liberal and national institutions, and persecuted them directly they made use of

* In May 1855, Prince Orloff told Lord Clarendon that the Emperor was well disposed towards the Poles, but would do nothing if any of the Powers should interfere. (M.S. Diary of Prince Czartoryski.)

their newly acquired liberties. The result was the national movement of 1861-2,* in which the Poles opposed a passive resistance to the oppressive measures of the Government, until the Wielopolski decree for drafting the youth of the country into the Russian army drove them into insurrection. Prince Czartoryski admired and praised the movement, but did not live to see its sanguinary consequence. In a letter written to Count Andrew Zamoyski in his own hand, at the age of ninety-one, a few months before his death, he says (20 March 1861) :—

' For the last fortnight we have been full of anxiety, emotion, admiration, and inexpressible joy, as if we had been present during those days with you in Warsaw. One may well say that God has manifested a great deed in you. In one day he has raised the nation to such a height of moral power as no other nation has ever reached ; it can only be compared to the inspiration of the first Christians, who conquered the world armed only with the palm of martyrdom. God forbid that you should descend from that position ; for if Poland remains there, she will attain her great object.

* It is known that after the Crimean War Austria began to show herself favourable to the Poles. This change of policy became more evident during the insurrection of 1863, and the Poles in Austria now have free institutions and a national self-government which make them the envy of their countrymen in Russia and Prussia. The following extract from a letter addressed to Prince Adam Czartoryski on the 15th of May 1860, by a personage holding a high position at Vienna, may be quoted in this connection :—

' On m'a indiqué comme candidat proposé (pour le trône de la Pologne) le second fils de la Reine d'Angleterre. On envisage ce choix comme un moyen pour calmer les inquiétudes jalouses de la Grande Bretagne. Le Cabinet d'ici ne voit pas d'un mauvais œil cette question. Il lui sera même favorable du jour ou il saura ce qui lui reviendra en échange pour la Galicie. Le besoin d'un intermédiaire entre l'Autriche et la Russie se fait sentir tous les jours davantage. L'Empereur F. J. (François Joseph) reconnaît toute l'infamie du partage de la Pologne et toutes les difficultés qu'il a amenées à l'Autriche. Il s'est exprimé plusieurs fois très-clairement à ce sujet. Ces jours-ci cette question sera portée au Conseil des Ministres afin de formuler les instructions à donner au réprésentant de la cour de Vienne à Saint-Pétersbourg.'

'So long as the news which arrived here only spoke of street disturbances and broken windows, the Emperor said this ought to stop, as the movement was an untimely one and would injure the cause instead of helping it. But now, after the important events which have occurred at Warsaw, showing how strong is the national spirit, he thinks otherwise. The Western Powers, at first not believing the news, and then astonished at them, cannot as yet understand what is going on and fear that the only result will be an exacerbation of Russian severity. No one thinks of giving us any official help; do not therefore in any way reckon upon it; but be convinced that if you adhere to your present line of conduct, public opinion in Europe will be on your side and will insist on a more moderate policy on the part of Russia. The present friendly understanding between that Power and France, has enabled Napoleon III already to make confidential representations on the subject at St Petersburg.

'In conclusion I must again urge you not to descend from the position which is your strength and moral support. Let all good citizens unite to strengthen the conviction among our countrymen that if they allow themselves to be drawn into an armed struggle, they will only bring upon their country fruitless defeats, while by an unarmed resistance to unjustifiable and wicked oppression, they will avert it and gain a moral victory.'

In the same spirit the Prince addressed his countrymen in a speech made on the 3rd of May, 1861.

'Do not descend,' he said, 'from the elevation

where nations and sovereigns must respect you. By
firmly remaining there you will be safer and more
certain in seeing your goal and continually approaching
it. Though racked by bitter suffering, though driven
to despair by treason and violence, resist the tempta-
tion to fight your oppressors by meaner weapons.
You shine above them by your virtue and goodness:
these are the indomitable forces of Poland, and in
them lie her hopes for the future.'

He died at Montfermeil, near Meaux, on the 15th
of November 1861. Like his great contemporary
Pitt—Prime Minister of England when he was
Foreign Minister of Russia—Prince Adam's last
words were of his country. Pitt, with the sudden
despair of baffled genius, lamented the misfortunes
which he thought were about to fall on England;
Czartoryski's tender and hopeful spirit pictured to
him a new Poland rising chastened and invigorated
by her long martyrdom. There was as little ground
for despondency in the one case as for hope in the
other. The disappointment of Austerlitz was soon
brilliantly retrieved by the British victories in the
Peninsula and at Waterloo; the hopes raised by the
noble self-sacrifice of the Polish nation perished in
the midst of blood and ruin.

THE END

ALPHABETICAL INDEX